ACROSS UNSTILL WATERS

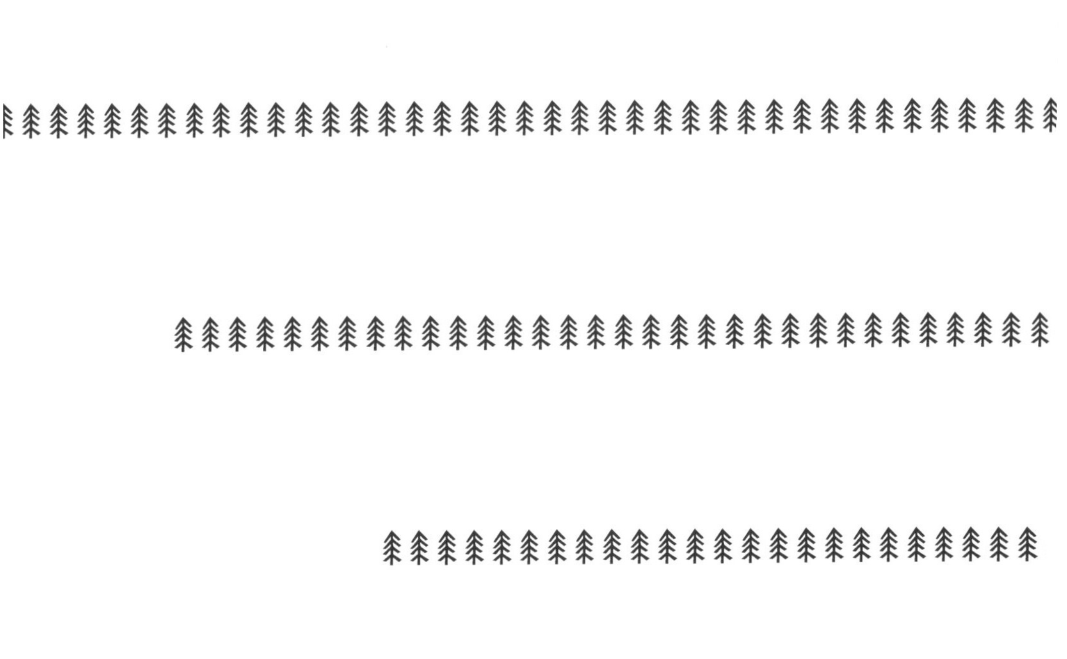

ACROSS UNSTILL WATERS

To: Joe
See you across the river
D L Andersen

D.L. ANDERSEN

THE STEPHENSON HOUSE CHRONICLES: BOOK ONE

First Edition ISBN 13: 978-1-937484-61-3

AMIKA PRESS 466 Central AVE #23 Northfield IL 60093 847 920 8084
info@amikapress.com Available for purchase on amikapress.com

Edited by John Manos and Ann Wambach. Cover and author photography by Tessa Schrader. Map illustration by D.L. Andersen. Designed and typeset by Sarah Koz. Body in Bell MT Pro, designed by Richard Austin in 1788, digitized by Monotype in 2001. Titles in Blandford Woodland NF, designed by Blandford Press in 1929, digitized by Nick Curtis in 2005. Ornaments in P22 Koch Signs, designed by Rudolph Koch in 1930, digitized by Denis Kegler in 1997. Thanks to Nathan Matteson.

For Randi

HOUSE SWEARINGEN 1799

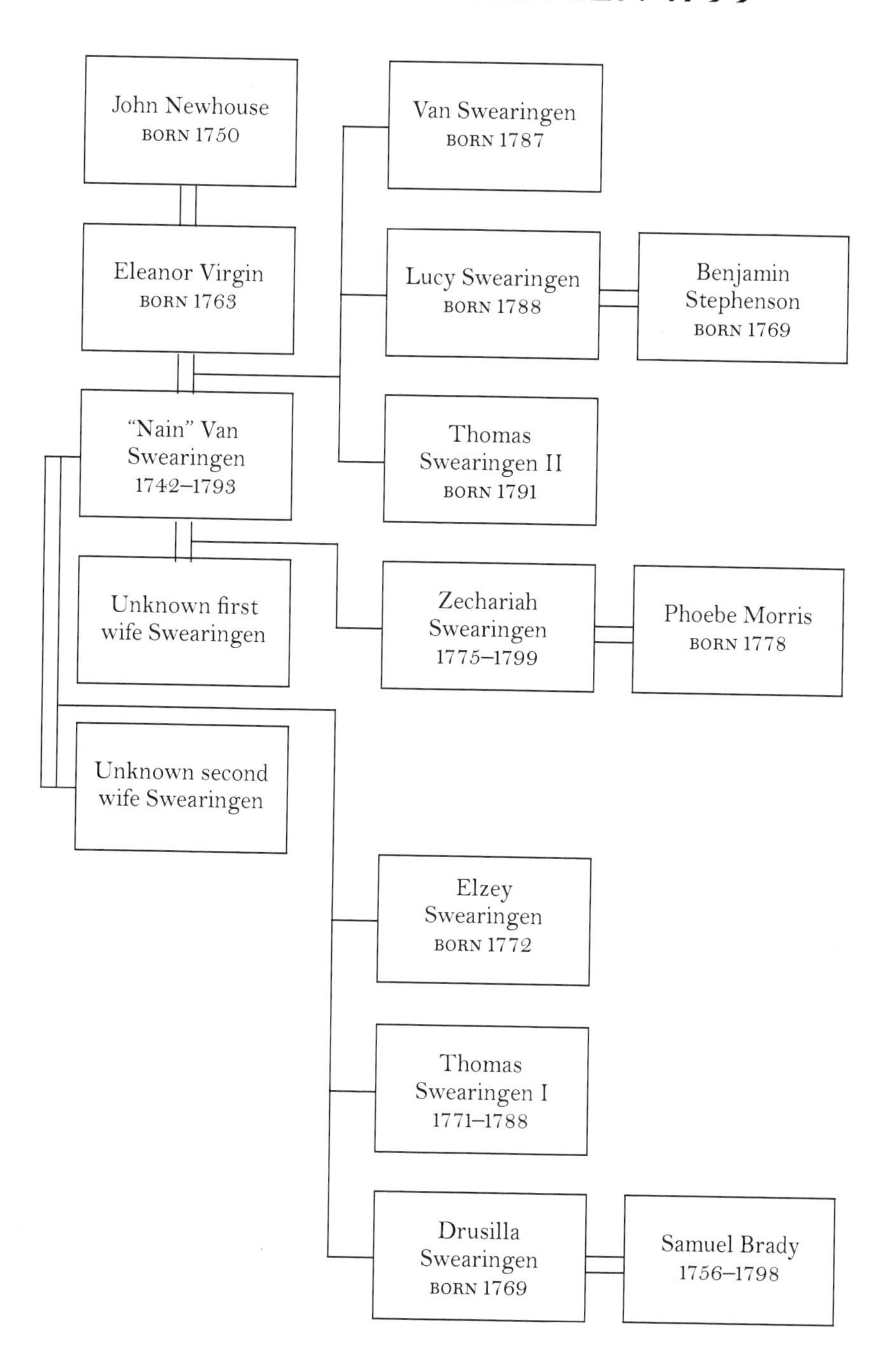

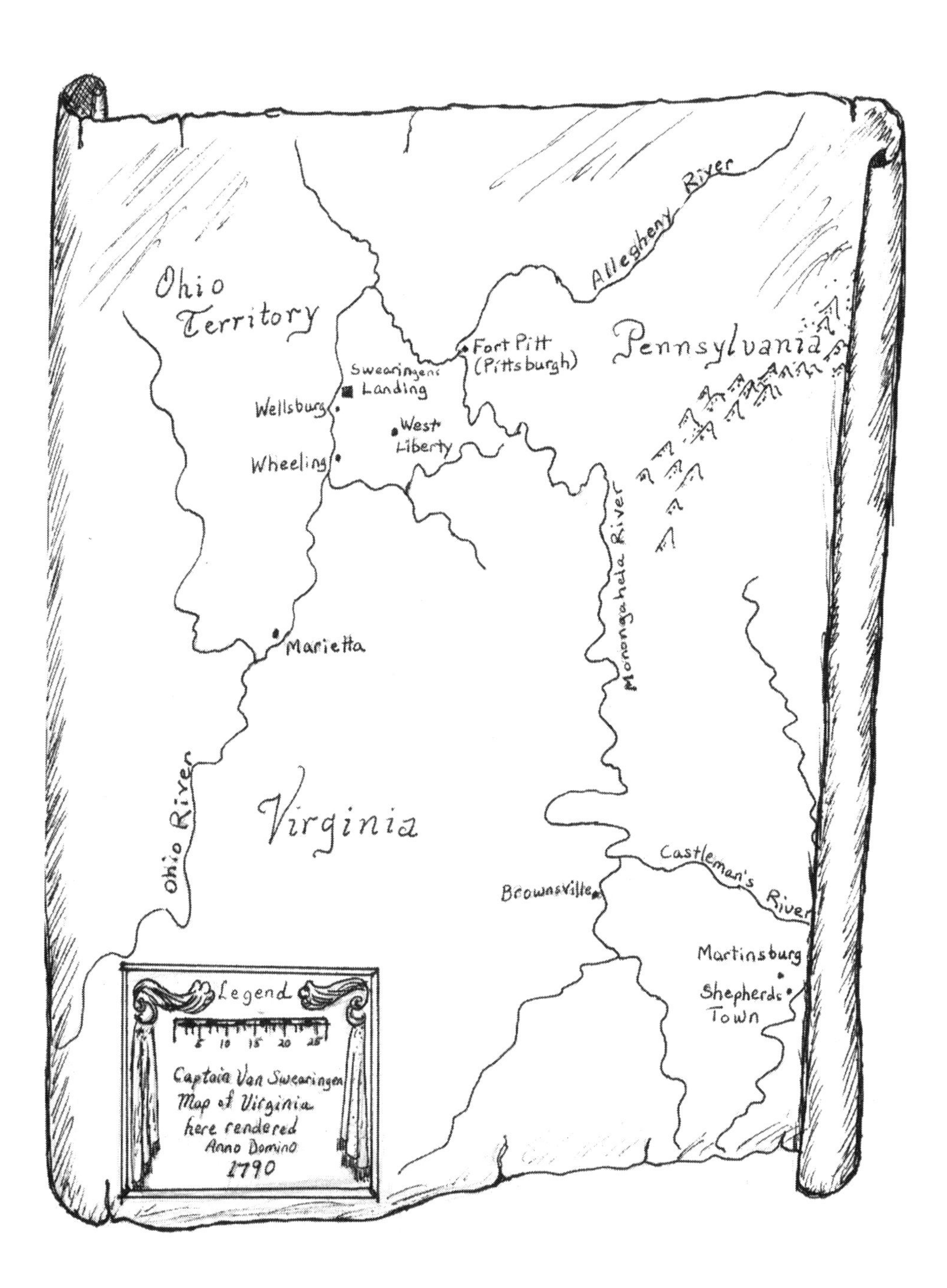

Ohio Territory
Allegheny River
Pennsylvania
Fort Pitt (Pittsburgh)
Swearingens Landing
Wellsburg
Wheeling
West Liberty
Monongahela River
Marietta
Ohio River
Virginia
Castleman's River
Brownsville
Martinsburg
Shepherds Town
Legend
5 10 15 20 25
Captain Van Swearingen
Map of Virginia
here rendered
Anno Domino
1790

Therefore tongues are for a sign, not to them
that believe, but to them that believe not.
—I Corinthians 14:22

Then if angels fight, weak men must fall:
for heaven still guards the right.
—William Shakespeare,
Richard II, Act III, scene II

Words were *her first remembrance. Words singing her to sleep. Words guttural and harsh. Lyrical as the air she breathed or the waters lapping at her toes.* Nepi. Eau. *Water. River. In every tongue it breathed the song of life, of death. A cricket chirp. A song of hovering wings. Every creature has its own tongue to speak, to soothe, to rage, to laugh, and to sing the song of life.*

The wings held her, gave her breath and song and words. She heard them all in her cradle, in her mother's arms, trembling and weak. In the arms of a stranger, torn from her home, from the safety of her warm, tiny cradle. The warrior, fierce and proud in forests primeval where fear lurks but also is banished upon a word. Wendigo. Demon. Pailissa, Hileni, Homme. *Man. Son of Man.* Spiritus. Cautantowwit. *Great Spirit. Father.*

A warrior's daughter. A child of light living in the darkness.

Rage and then fear. What was there to fear? Here in the woods, among the trees where the Life Rivers flow. The words pour from her childish lips. All is calm. All is banished upon a word. Perfect love casts out fear, for the one who fears is not made perfect in love.

Do you see? He comes! He comes to save! To protect! Do not fear! Do you understand?

But they did not understand. Feathers folding around her, comforting her. Warm. Embracing, yet menacing, to those who do not understand, to those who do not love. Tears and feathers. Light and dark. Death had come, but so had life. And then the Time was ended and the child returned to grow. And the words she once knew, the world she once knew, would be forever changed but not quite forgotten.

CHAPTER 1

Benjamin Stephenson searched the shadowy woodlands at the edge of the Ohio River waiting for Swearingen's woman to arrive. The note was the only reason he'd be enduring an idle winter's eve when there was plenty work to be done at the trading post. The scrap of paper crinkled in his hand, a worrisome matter that prickled with all the possibilities for her summoning him here. He pondered again the note's cryptic intent.

Met me Zane Ridz
effor darzwerk dun
Fee

Phoebe Swearingen. "Fee" to everyone who knew her well, including her devoted husband, but Ben preferred the elegance and formality of her Greek name, though Fee may have suited her better. The woman was never one for book learning, but that didn't seem to matter to Zechariah Swearingen who fell under her charms readily enough. Ben shook his head and chuckled into the winter stillness, broken only by the wind's whistle through barren trees and the pulsing hoot of a horned owl mournfully seeking his mate. Truth be told, there wasn't much time or need for reading or writing, beyond keeping accounts at the shop and assisting the paymaster for the militia. Few among these hills were able to match Ben's thirst for books or Swearingen's engaging wit. If only he had thought to bring one of his books to keep him from thinking of all the work he had yet to do.

A ledger awaited his accounting, among numerous other tasks at the trading post. Shipments should arrive any day now, as midwinter's thaw foretold an early spring—although the weather was a capricious mistress. Supplies were low, with some weeks of winter remaining before Farming Man's Spring, come March, ushered in the planting time. Until then, folks would be in want of staples to extend their larders until kitchen gardens yielded summer's bounty. It was his task to supply the essentials that made survival possible and the luxuries that made life livable, ultimately at a profit to the store and to him as well.

With the coming of spring, there'd be more settlers heading across the Alleghenies and down the Ohio looking to make a new start in the valley. Most would likely be pushing onward into the virgin forests and fertile bottomlands where the great rivers met and promised rich rewards for those with the mettle to hew trees into farmland and settlements. It meant a fine crop of customers would inevitably pass through to trade goods, hopefully exchanging a few silver and gold coins he could add to his meager savings hidden in a sack beneath the floorboards of his storeroom quarters.

Ben folded the note, contemplating all possible meanings once more before tucking it into his coat pocket. Swearingen must be ailing again, or he'd have sent word himself, if there were further developments in the matter at hand. He tried to brush a twinge of guilt aside; perhaps he should have sought out his friend in recent weeks. But, Phoebe could have come by the store. Perhaps Zechariah was still stewing over their last quarrel, and she wanted to save her husband's pride or avoid wagging tongues. It wasn't like him to be so pigheaded and contrary. No, that was not like him at all. Clearly, the note was not the man's hand or even his dictation…unless…

He should have called on the stubborn fool long before now, before it was too late. Another shiver of regret came and then coursed away like the river beneath the crest of the ridge. The meandering Ohio kept its steady path regardless of what befell it. The river, ever constant, ever moving, offered the kind of inward sustenance no preacher's sermon or pious hymn singing could provide. There was no use borrowing trouble. Sufficient unto the day, is the evil thereof. Those were the words he chose to live by, never looking back to misspent youth or past errors, and never counting chickens too far into the future. He preferred going forward, like the steady flowing river. Perhaps he should have swallowed his own pride and gone to see Zack, but there had been other matters to settle, promises to keep, always another promise to honor and a favor to return. He didn't mind, though. It was all good business.

Leaning his long gun against a nearby oak and setting the unlit lantern on a dead log, he impatiently scanned the silent trees towering over him. He should check on a few traps in the waning daylight, put idleness to constructive purpose in case she didn't show. *She better come soon,* he grumbled inwardly as he retrieved the long gun, left the lantern for later, and made a quick turn through the dense trees and snow-frosted creek bed where he'd placed a few beaver traps.

In the dusk, settling across the woods, the air misted and clung to barren branches and lurked at the creek disappearing into the horizon beyond the endless river flowing west. Shadows drifted through the thicket and across the ravine in a muted play of light, conjuring images of nocturnal creatures and apparitions in the distant, whispering pines. A trick of the eye. *Childish delusions,* he thought, as he tended another game-less trap. But only a fool was not on guard in the woods, or so his militia scout training had taught him, if not his youth living in the outlying woods of Western Pennsylvania during the last war. Peace treaties had settled conflicts of late, be it with natives or redcoats, still his skin prickled warily and his fingers twitched to aim his gun. Another moment scanning the hazy woods, ears pricked for the slightest snap of a twig. *A mere illusion,* he thought. Couldn't be what—or even who—he saw reflected in the icy ripples of the creek and then wafting silently into the shadows between trees. A slice of blue against gray-white wilderness. Ol' Blue was thought to be long dead by now, or at least faded into obscurity somewhere beyond the English Lakes, after Fallen Timbers settled the score. Ben was too pragmatic to believe in ghosts. Yet deep in his bones he sensed the old scores were not yet settled. His hand eased the flintlock at the ready. He could shoot the tail feather off a sparrow at a worthy distance, but this was no sparrow, nor could it be

Swearingen's woman lurking silently among the dimming woods. A glimpse of feathered flight, the soft fall of snow from a branch, and his firearm was cocked and aimed into the misty chill. The shadow moved between trees and then was no more. An owl hovered and circled from his perch, dusting snow on the trap at Ben's feet. One last hoot and flutter of hovering wing and all was still, but the hairs standing on his neck told him he was not quite alone.

"Ben." The small voice, barely a whisper at his back, wafted through the cold, winter air in the wake of the owl's departure. He turned to see her standing a few feet away, a slave girl followed a few paces behind with downcast eyes, just enough to suggest submission, though the stubborn jut of her chin spoke otherwise. Ben wondered if indeed her eyes would echo the chin if revealed in full view and how her mistress would address this silent protest? Both women staved off winter's chill swathed in woolen shawls and hooded cloaks, the squire's lady and her handmaid. Phoebe's eyes sparkled against rosy cheeks.

"I thank'ee for comin' out here like this." She bit her lip and took a step forward. "I didna keep ya waitin' long I hope?"

"No, not long." Ben measured a patient breath, stepped over a dead log, and offered a gentleman's hand to steady her footing on the uneven terrain. "What's this all about?" His voice sounded far more pleasant than he felt, though curiosity grew like a weed in his bosom.

Her gloved fingers gripped his hand, firm and true, as one narrow boot landed over a tangle of frosted roots. She looked back to the slave gazing warily around the thicket. Ben wondered if the girl had seen what he had, but then dismissed the thought when she returned her sullen look toward the toes of her boots at her mistress's command.

"Achsa, you best go on now and see if any o' them sugar maples is getting ready for tappin'."

"But Mizz Phoebe, it be too cold still, and—"

"Just do as I say, girl. Y'hear?" She turned blinking eyes at Ben. "Mr. Stephenson and I have some matters to…discuss."

"Yas'm." The girl raised a sidelong glance before trudging off, one heavy foot at a time through the snow-covered trees.

Before addressing Ben, Phoebe turned to her slave one last time. "And don't be poking back 'round here until I come fetch you. Y'hear?"

"Yas'm."

Ben kept his eyes peeled between the two women, waiting for Achsa to disappear into the packed trees and wishing somehow he could follow her rather than face whatever was behind Phoebe's eager gaze. The girl was right, too soon for maple sap to flow. She'd be back right quick enough. His attempt to speak was met with Phoebe's lifted finger and a sign to be still until they were assured of privacy.

Once the slave was no more than footprints in snow, he said, "Now, what's all this about, Phoebe? How's Zack been these days?" He affected a disinterested, light chuckle and then clamped his jaw tight at her stone-sharpened mask.

"I didna know any other way to speak to you without..." Phoebe tugged on the fringe of her shawl, scanning the glen as if for some sign of danger lurking behind every darkening tree. "Things, they ain't been good. Figured you oughta know, is all." She folded her arms, pulling woolens tight. "He's talking crazy these days. I thought you'd be comin' 'round again. I know you had words that last time, but it weren't his fault...what he said."

"Phoebe, I bear no malice toward him."

"What you mean by that?" She wrinkled a puzzled nose. "Bear him...no..."

"Malice. Ur...hard feelings...ill will." Ben tapped a finger on the gun barrel, standing upright by his feet. He hadn't come out here to teach a vocabulary lesson. "We just had a...difference of opinion. I've the shop to keep and little time of late to pay a call." The lie was plausible—perhaps not even so much a lie as a weak excuse.

She flashed a look of watery fire at him. "Oh and don't let me keep you for certain, from your 'portant dealings. Never mind about your friends and all." She was not above crying to get her way, but this seemed more than mere feminine wiles, or Zack's provocation.

"What is it, Phoebe?" He brushed snow off the log, offering a place to sit, which she at first refused.

"No one's been by, which is fine on account o' Zack...he don't want no one to know...not the way he's been. Especially not his kinfolk, not that they take much mind to stop by...haven't since we wed, least not since Christmas anyways. And that's just when the worsening come."

Ben studied the trees, taller now as he sat on the cold log, diminished near the forest floor. The setting sun fingered its soft rays through the haze, shielding his view of the river beyond the crest. "Then it's begun again? The fevers? Mayhap it be another bout that'll run its course. It's no different than last time."

"It be different. Worser now than the last bout at harvest time." Her voice broke the stillness like the crack of an ice-laden branch. "I been hopin' he'll get better. But hopin' ain't change nothin' and prayin' only seems to make it all worse."

"Bilious fever," Ben muttered. "It comes and goes. Most everyone's had the ague at one time or other."

She shook her head, her lower lip trembled and then steeled into a firm line. "This ain't no regular ague. I seen it afore when it get this bad. Once. I oughta knowed. I did know...and still I took to marry him, 'cause I thought there'd be time. It'd all work out right."

"Time," Ben whispered the word reflectively more to himself than to her. He suspected what she meant. Hadn't Zack argued about just this notion? The lawsuit. The land claim. Inheritance rights and a man's mortality. Perhaps in his friend's illness he'd lay it all to rest, put matters in order, and resolve the past once and for all. It was one small tract of land among the hundreds the Swearingens owned.

"Shepherd's back in these parts, Ben. It's up to us now to make it right. You understand? I'm all they've got and now... I can't do this all alone. Not now anyway...."

He recalled his friend's pensive agitation that day in early December, when there had been a brief respite between snowfalls. They had returned early from hunting, Zack growing uncharacteristically tired, his condition clearly deteriorated since summer, but somehow Ben refused to see it then. Perhaps he had noted it but assured himself a long winter's rest and a decoction of yellow bark he had sent for in a recent shipment from New Orleans would restore him to full health.

"Yellow bark?" Zack had said, a hint of sweat on his brow and a tremor in the hand circling his drinking mug as if his life depended on it. "A good bleeding might be all I need, Ben."

"It's said to cure fevers." He laid the bundle on the table and sat down opposite his friend. "The doctor down in Wheeling sent this receipt on how to brew it up proper. The Spanish priests have been using it for a couple centuries now, ever since the conquistadors discovered it from the Incas."

Zack lowered his head with a miserable laugh. "You are ever the one for useless information, Stephenson. Who the hell cares out here where some ancient mystics got their potions? Likely be witchcraft. Naw, might be my humors just need fixin'." He drained his mug, tea laced with whiskey, and called for Phoebe to fill it again. "Well, I got a bit of information for you too, and I need you to mind what I say."

"There's no use fretting over it now." Phoebe sat close enough on the narrow log for him to feel her thigh against his through the layers of woolens. He shouldn't be alone with her here on Zane's Ridge. With the setting sun came a deepening chill, his thoughts wandering between the past and the present and where in all this he might find his way through. He should get them both to shelter soon, somewhere away from here, out of the cold or, better yet, back to her ailing husband.

"If there's no use fretting, then why'd you call me out here like this? Now, of all days?" He hadn't meant it to sound quite so harsh.

She flinched and shuddered slightly. "You're his friend. I'd hoped you'd be mine as well. We've all had our good times together. Hain't we?"

Ben softened at the smallness of her voice and the pleading of her pretty face. "Aye, that we have. You won't be going though this all alone, Fee, no matter what comes. Neither you nor Zack, regardless of what's been said or done."

"I'd hoped you'd say as much." She sat a bit straighter with eyes shining in an air of readiness.

Softly, carefully, he spoke, their clouded words spread into the chilliness filtering into the trees, absorbing shared secrets along with those of ancient times. "I should've come by long afore this and made everything right."

"Aye, ya shouldn'a done a lot o' things different." Eyes colder than the ice creek pierced at his soul. "We all shouldn'a. But no use frettin' over milk what's been spilt on the barn floor."

"I'll take you home now. Fetch your slave girl and we'll get you both out of this cold."

He stood with hand extended to lift her up.

"No, not till I say my piece." She rose slipping free of his aid and placed a hand on a nearby sycamore, picking at the bark. "He'll be dead afore long. Likely afore winter's end." The corner of her mouth snaked into a wan smile. "There. I said it. Hain't wanted to think on it, but it's said and done. Not even married one full year and already be a widow woman." She snorted, worrying a lower lip tight against her teeth. "Best get used to wearin' bombazine."

Ben drew toward her, stunned as if she'd slapped him. "There now, Phoebe, let's not talk like this." He lifted a comforting hand toward the back of her hood, letting it drop to his side when she abruptly turned.

"I got to know what will happen to his land, his property. Will it all be mine?" She ran strips of shorn bark between nervous fingers, letting them rain onto the frozen ground. The newly bared patch on the tree lay naked and raw.

"Lass, you can't think on that now." Acid burned his stomach, paining him more than the slap of his words earlier, yet they bore the truth of it all. His argument with Zack weeks ago ate at his conscience. Land rights. Family disputes. Prior claims. None of it was his worry and yet...

Would his friend have put his wife up to this? Sent her to do his bidding in his deluded state? Was he becoming as conniving as his other kin? It wasn't like the man he knew, though mercenary greed was the more palatable option than fever, leading him to hide behind his woman's skirts leaving her to act alone in the woods on a winter's eve on his behalf.

"I got to know," she nattered on, curling her hand into a fist and pounding the tree. "They won't take it back, not all of it. His family...and now that Newhouse...takin' up with another what's come to make his claim all over again? Now that Zack's..." Her voice reduced to trembling despair. "What's left for me now?"

"No one's going to take anything away, if it's your home and things you're fretting on about. You're entitled to what's your husband's property under the law. Who's tellin' you this?" A cold wind blew down from the north, and the smoldering light tamped down beyond the distant hills. He knew what she feared, though he still found the notion as delirious as a fevered man's ravings. "Did Zack send you out here? Come now, we'll fetch you and your girl back to the house and settle this together over a cup of warm coffee and some of your fine biscuits. Night's coming on and as you say, it's high time I pay a call and eat my share of crow."

She shook her head, brooding into the distance, ignoring his urging to leave. Her pale lashes lay in a soft curve against the line of her gently rounded cheek. "He don't know I'm here. This is the best way, talk it out tween us, plain and simple and no one knowing."

"If you want my help, such as I'm able, we'd be best hashing it out with Zechariah present." He drew back, ready to gather his gun and lantern before darkness completely overtook them.

"I mean to say... It's just that... No one can know just yet." Despair tempered her tone. "Please, hear me out. He don't know much of anything lately, where I go or even who I am most days. Just keeps sayin' he's got to set all to right. Keeps reliving things what should be dead and gone. Fights Injuns in his sleep. And he...he..." She lowered her hood, causing Ben's next breath to seize at the base of his throat. His hands clenched reflexively, fighting a desire to reach for her, comfort her, embrace her. And to strike his absent friend hard and true, everything fought in a clash of wills at the sight before him—a bruise, the mark of a man's palm colored her neck. Even in this waning light, he knew that's what it must be.

"Did...did Zechariah...Zack...? No," Ben whispered, incredulously, thinking of his fevered friend's hand against this delicate throat. "No, it can't be."

"He didn't mean to. It's the way o' the fever when it gets real bad. I knowed that. 'Twas the other night. Him fightin' Injuns again like in the last war. He didn't mean none of it agin me." She removed a glove and tenderly traced the bruise.

"We'll keep him tied down. It's the only way. A dose of laudanum will..."

She breathed a weak smile. "You doctorin' now as well as lawyerin'

...and surveyin' too, I hear? Shopkeeping for Gibson not enough for ya, is it?"

"Phoebe, you called me out here. I'm offering help."

"Got all the answers, don't ya? We been tryin' to keep him tied down. Me and Hawger and the few other manservants I still got workin' for me. I just can't do it no more."

"Then I'll stay with you both and help look after him," Ben said, soothing. "Maybe fetch the barber from Wheeling for a physic... Or a good bloodletting might help."

"It'll take more than a Wheeling barber to fix this, and you know it. If it come to bleedin' I got a lancet and know the way of it. But the last time, he turned so pale...I was afeared he'd... Maybe if'n you've a mind to...and know something about doctorin' from those books you always a-readin'?"

"I'd rather we fetch a proper barber or surgeon." He never quite held to depriving a body of its lifeblood in curing fevers. But if his friend's fevered mind could be relieved somehow and the madness quelled, it would keep his family safe. As Phoebe said, he was no doctor, not even much of a lawyer, but right now all that mattered was getting this woman out of the woods before nightfall brought more trouble of its own.

She curled her hand into a fist and stamped her foot. "Hang the barber and the leeching. That's not why I come. I can take a little bruising, a few clouts. But I got to know. They won't take it back, like I was nothin'. Like I never was his lawful wife. I got to know afore it's too late." Her voice was unsettling, her gaze fixed and disquieting.

"No one will take anything away that is rightfully yours. You're entitled to everything he has by law. Where you getting this idea?"

"The land," she said, "it ain't rightfully his, not according to the law. It may even be none of it is rightfully Swearingen land. How many others gonna come claiming land what we worked years to clear? He keeps sayin' things I can't make out to be true. I know some of the dealings were worked out twixt you."

What had Zack been telling her in his fevered state? Who else might have been putting these ideas in her head? "Only thing I done was help him with a few legal matters, pointed him in the right direction of the law and land rights. You were there plying your needle whilst your husband and I talked. As I told him then, the rest is all for the courts to decide."

Her lips curved into a wistful smile. "I remember that day. I was mending an infant gown of Zechariah's that his mama made for him. I sat there thinking on how someday...there'd be another..." She turned to him, more determined, a look of fire in her ice-blue eyes. "Then you get my meaning. It's the old man's will and tester-ment, the way he worded it all clean and tidy for his kin, his blood kin. But I know what he put in there for you, if'n you be willin' that is."

"This isn't about me, Phoebe. I've no claim to anything old Nain had." He was no Swearingen descendant. Only a promise he made to an old man's desperate wish, sealed in the captain's own hand, offered him any leverage, but at a price he wasn't willing to consider at present, if ever at all.

She leveled her gaze at him. "You was like a son to him. You can't ever forget that. That's more'n I'll ever be, even with a church wedding sealing our union good'n proper."

"I'd not likely forget," he muttered the words, puffing into the chilly dusk. "It's not that simple." *Even for me,* he was going to add, but thought the better.

"I'd-a said yes," she whispered hoarsely, "if'n you'd asked me afore Zack done."

He let the words hang between them as he considered the bruised sky waning across the western hills, the shadowy trees, and whatever else was still lurking out there. The cold ground on which he stood seemed less solid, more like the meandering river rippling beyond the ridge. If only he could see the river now, get his bearings and consider his words. There was strength in the river. It cared not who came or went, who owned the land it coursed between, cutting and consuming whatever deterred its path. Yet it brought life and wealth to those who revered and minded it. Whoever passed through this land may claim it, clear it, and later sell it, but the river endured longer than any peoples ever had or would

She'd have said yes? And what good would that have done either in attaining Swearingen land, wealth, or dominance? In the lengthening shadows he considered the set of her dimpled chin, the gleam in her dewy eyes. Was it from the cold? From fear? Or, something deeper she had longed for all the while this past year to say? But why now? She was up to some ruse, no different than the schemes of any land speculator or politician, words sweet as honey dripping from the tongue of a viper—so, like another who's dewy eyes and pleasing smile beguiled him once before.

He could not think on the past now. The cold seeping through his leather soles emboldened his resolve. "Zechariah asked you first." Grazing her chin with his gloved finger in chaste, brotherly fashion, he chuckled, "You're a Swearingen now. I'll never be, no matter how the old captain might've treated me, son or otherwise. You've got that at least."

"Even without no Swearingen land or fortune or family name behind you," she pressed on, as if taking his words for encouragement rather than a rebuff, "we'd a done all right together. I see that now. You've got more than land and family name to get you where you're going. I knowed that."

Ben set his jaw, forcing back another chuckle that set his teeth on edge and emerged in a mild cough. "I don't recall askin' you nor was I of a mind to. Zack had his sights on you all along, darlin', and you on him." Prettiest maid in the county, she'd been then, but her flattery was lost on him now.

"But I might've turned my head, set my cap different, if'n I thought you'd a-wanted me."

He chewed the tip of his tongue a moment. "And this is all now just because you don't want to be a landless widow? That about right? I've no mind to do the askin' once you're a widow, if it even comes to that."

A brief glimmer, desperate and pained, marred her lovely face, almost as if he too had struck her. She lifted her chin into a look of fierce determination.

Ben regretted his retort and gentled his tone. "Now don't go on so. You were better off with Zack, you know. I've no land to speak of, no prospects here. Besides, I've got other plans that don't include settling down and no guarantee that—"

"Better off, am I?" she said, absently, "I remember how fine you looked on Public Day two year ago. All dandied out in your new roundabout and yeller waistcoat. You asked me to dance and I wondered then what it would be like to have you twirl me about, holdin' me…and not just for dancin' neither…but other times too. You ever think on that when you're a-lyin' on that straw pallet in back of Gibson's store?"

He did remember that day. He remembered her tawny hair caught up in blue ribbons, curls tumbling down the back of her neck and bouncing with every jig and turn of the reel. He remembered Zack confiding that he'd kissed her roundly before the night was through and she'd be his bride come spring. He shrugged off the memories, tamping his boots to warm frozen toes. "I got my own plans. Don't be holding on to things that make no difference now. Dancin' and dreamin' aren't real living."

"Oh, I know what plans you got. It's all in the old man's will, like I said. Ain't it? The fine and noble Captain Andrew van Swearingen, or whatever name he done called himself. Nain Swearingen. The mighty Injun Fighter of the Ohio River Valley. He bought you body and soul, just like he done the rest of us, like we's just another of his slaves. A wheeling and dealing his way into most of the land claims in this here valley ain't enough for him."

"You don't know what you're saying. I never said—"

"Don't I know? A fine lot they are, them Swearingens, ain't they? My Zechariah was the only decent one of the whole litter. Elzey is nothing more than a roustabout, who don't care a stitch for the land but sure drink and rut his way through the money reaped from it. Drusilla? She got herself all set now, even if she be a widow, too. The fine Mrs. Brady, ain't she? Got two high and mighty names behind her now and the land to boot. And her husband's reputation to back her up, along with her dead pappy's glory. And two fine sons, too."

"Phoebe, enough!" His words fell empty against the darkening wilderness as the woman fretted.

"Then there's them three young 'uns, but you're watchin' out for them now, ain't ya? Got your reasons too. Don't think I don't know it. That part of your plan?"

"Phoebe." Ben returned to the sycamore tree and laid a hand against hers, stilling her incessant tearing of tree bark. "What's any of this got to do with Zack ailing?" Softer now, he added, "Please, don't do this now. You're upset. It's understandable but this will do no good."

"So, I'm asking," she said, turning as if not hearing him, caught in her own fervent zeal, "can they truly take it all from me? If'n there be no heirs from Zack? That's all I need to know."

Ben took a step back and swiped a hand down his face. In the fading traces of sunlight, pale wisps glowed from under her bonnet. Her rosy mouth panted curls of warm breath into the chilling evening. He thought carefully what more to tell her. "When the time comes...if it does...hopefully, not for many years, mind you...you'll be entitled to something, and by then there may be young 'uns of your own to rear. Yours and Zack's. In the meantime, if the worst should happen, you won't be left destitute. There are legal provisions for widows, regardless of heirs. It's called dower rights, a one-third portion—"

"But I won't get it all, will I? Not what I'm due as his wife, his legal heir." She clenched fists firm against her side and stomped away. "The land, the slaves, and even the fine things in my house, they all go back, like they never was Zack's to begin with. I get the slave girl Achsa—she was a wedding gift—and the money we been saving and that's about all?"

"You are entitled to keep the house, a place to live and enough household goods to sustain your living for as long as you need. As I said, a one-third dower's portion as befits the law. It'll amount to a bit of money to see you through. I'm sorry, Phoebe, I don't see why we're discussing this now, and without Zack." Ben shook his head, incredulous. His friend possibly faced a dreadful end—lingering, painful, and debilitating. And here this woman stood fretting over a few acres of land and some family baubles. How much had she worried Zack with this nonsense? "I think it best we get you home and see to your husband. Who's with him now?"

Phoebe clasped hands beneath her chin, seemingly lost in her own thoughts. "Big Axel's keeping watch. He'll keep him contained till I get back. We got to settle this, here and now, afore it's too late."

"We can settle this easy enough back at your cabin."

"I tried to speak with Zechariah on all this, but it's no use. He keeps frettin' over those little ones. They's only his half-blood kin, two brothers and that little sister. Dotes on 'em like they's his own issue, especially that sweet little girl," she said as if spitting bitter water. "But nobody knows that better'n you." She searched Ben's face for solace, for answers—which...he wasn't sure and he shook his head, listening with an open-handed shrug.

"He wants her to have the Dutch Lady. Keeps asking me to give it to her, but I don't know where he hid it. He blames me for losing it one moment, and then the next he'll say he already done give it away and ain't nothing I can do to get it back. Like as if I'd try to steal it back from Nellie, who ain't no Swearingen kin neither, just his stepmaw."

Ben gaped, not certain what to say to this woman here in the middle of the forest. "Phoebe, Zack will need you to be strong in the days to come. His family will need your strength as well. You must know this. You're upset and that's to be expected. This isn't him."

"All I know," she blathered on, "it be worth a fine cod of money, they say. I only wore it once, the day we wed." Slender fingers played at the hollow of her collarbone, inches from the thumb-size bruise circling her neck like a fiendish purple ribbon. "Everyone said I looked prettier than any of them fine Eastern ladies."

He gentled a gloveless finger against her neck. "You got to know he would never, in his right mind, do such a thing. Not to you. Not to any woman."

She turned on him with the sharp look of a cornered cat, grasping his hand into the curve of her throat. Charmingly, she softened into a bewildered smile as she melted toward him, placing a slender hand over his, still nestled in the hollow of her neck. "You'll help me, won't ya? He'll write no will, if that's what you're aiming at. That's a certainty. I done asked him time and again already. But I know tween us, we'll find a way."

"I'll do what I can to help." Ben remained there with her curving into him, pulling him toward her into the twisted bole of the sycamore. He stood entirely too close without resisting, but she had been hurt, needed comfort, that was all. He wanted to help, to calm her troubled spirit. She was entitled to her husband's estate but would surely be provided for regardless. The Swearingen necklace was a family heirloom, likely of more sentimental value than pecuniary. "There would be provisions for you, if a will were properly drawn," he whispered, his finger trailed up from the bruise on her neck to the delicate bone of her jaw. "A judge might rule in your favor and you'd get at least a decent size tract to call your own, considering you've been working the land along with him this past year. There's another possibility, as you mentioned. We'll petition for a recounting of the captain's will, a survey of land tracts, to settle disputes, including the allegations by—"

"Shepherd?" she snorted and shook her head, letting it loll back against the bared trunk. "We all know 'bout that, don't we? Dead these five years now and still the old Injun Fighter's got his hold on us all, but he never figured on his old foe returning. Thought he had the cur chased off with his tail tween his legs, from what I heard." She flashed steely eyes that sent a disturbing blast through him. "I trust in you, Ben. You'll do right by me, by us. I knew you would. Next to my Zack, you're the best man this valley's ever seen. Maybe you're lawyerin' could do us all good."

Next to Zack he was the best? There it was, her means to wheedle him into her mercenary plans. Ben wasn't quite sure who she meant by "us all" but easily dismissed it as befitting a sense of family unity. A threat to any part of the family homestead was indeed a threat to all concerned. She was a Swearingen by marriage and thus entitled to something, but with no heirs, the possibility of Zack's land passing out of the family legacy had been the concern. And then there was the recent threat that had spurred their argument. As she trailed his hand down the bodice of her gown, allowing him to feel her warmth, her every curve, he recoiled, gaining his bearings and shaking off wayward thoughts. Pacing to the dead log, he retrieved flint and steel to light the lantern he set there earlier, mulling over the name she mentioned and the subject he had been avoiding for weeks.

Shepherd's back in these parts. Maybe there was a way to make this work for all, but he'd have to know more. Perhaps he should have taken Zack's last plan more to heart.

"Phoebe, has Zack said anything more about Abraham Shepherd?"

He studied her for any sign since she had brought the man's name up first, but she only leaned against the tree, gazing at some indistinct point. Could she be seeing what he sensed earlier, hidden there among the shadowy branches? There was something out there, he could sense it. His musket was still within easy reach.

"Shepherd? Yes, I know about that man. It's all he's been talking about. How he's got to protect them little ones—Van, Lucy, Tommy. That's all that matters. And likely it be John Newhouse behind it all. Nelly shoulda never wed him. Can't say I blame her, though." She angled her head toward him and moved closer to the log. "Five years is long enough for any widow to mourn, even for a Swearingen. Old Injun Van sure be rolling in his grave knowing a man like that is taking his bed. Zack 'ud a took in them three young 'uns to live with us when Eleanor wed last fall, but they's better off with their mama, even with the likes of a step-pappy like him."

She blinked, pressing her mouth into a thin line. "Ben, you could write Zack's will for him. You know the legal way. All he'd need do is make his mark on it. You could help him with that as well. The way he's been lately, he won't know no different. And no one else'd be the wiser." She leaned over him, her eyes gleaming with a wild hopefulness that disquieted him further.

"I won't do that. I'm not a proper lawyer at the bar. It damn sure wouldn't be legal, nor ethical, especially not in Zack's present state of mind." *Unless...he recovers from another bout of fever.* But something in her words and desperate look sent a dread under Ben's skin he couldn't shake. His friend wasn't dying. No. There was too much to settle, far more hunting trips to make, wagers to levy across a card table, and, most of all, deep philosophical discussions that had no resolve. He glanced again at her worrying the fringe of her shawl between trembling bare fingers. Her gloves lay discarded on the log. A man didn't need to pass the bar to write a will. Anyone with an ability to write and a rudimentary understanding of the process could draw up one, even for his own self, so long as there was a witness or two to verify it. And that would be the knotty business. Would she be resolved enough to find someone else who would not be so ethical and find false witnesses or forge the signatures?

"Then I know of only one other way." She dug a toe into a snowy patch. "A way out for us…all of us, that is…including the young 'uns that be Zack's kin." She sipped the air, determined desperation in her piercing eyes. "If'n the only way to get the entire fortune and keep my land is by blood, then…Ben…" A swallow of air drew the steamy breath back behind teeth pearled over a soft mouth. "I got to have a babe, for Zack. But I fear there ain't time afore…he can't…I mean he shouldn't. Any child he beget now mightn't be right." She poked a finger at her temple and crossed her eyes.

"Phoebe what's your meaning?" Ben paused to consider her words. "It's nonsense…ignorant superstition. You can't possibly mean…" A flicker of movement deep in the darkening woods caught his eye again. Another trick, a phantom playing on his mind along with her devious words. "Let's get you back home now. Call your girl back. Achsa is it? I'll go fetch her or we can together. No one should be left alone in these woods after nightfall."

"'Tis so. I heard such as this. I seen the hydrophoby when I was young, back in Pinkney Creek. I know what it can do, turning a man to raving madness and tainting his seed. This fever ain't no different." She pressed her lips together and a crease formed between her eyes, sapphire orbs darkening to the color of a midnight sky as her hand played at the tender discoloration at her throat. "But if'n someone else was to get a baby for Zack, someone close 'nuff to be a Swearingen, so's he wouldn't mind…not that he need know…nor anyone else neither. It'd be our secret, we'd take it to our graves."

"After you put your husband in his grave? Is that the way of it?" Ben locked his knees as a spark caught on the char cloth. He kept his breath in even strokes, concentrating his efforts to ignite sparks to wick. "Or have you…? You can't possibly mean…? What have you done, Fee? Who you been with?" The wick caught flame, illuminating the glen with a flash before settling into a soft glow that outlined the stock of his gun still set against the tree trunk near the log. He pondered the purple trace around her neck. Was that indeed Zack's doing? Had it been in a jealous rage over an incontinent wife? Is that what she was here to tell him? Seduce him along with how many other lovers before? He shook his head. "What are you trying to say,

Fee? You'd so easily cuckold your ailing husband and cully me into the sordid mess?" She'd likely have her pick of bucks, given how other men looked at her and envied Zack, who seemed to take delight in the knowledge that he alone possessed his lovely prize.

"I done nothing…wrong. Only wanted to help matters along…for the good of all." She withdrew into the shadow of the tree and ran a finger along the steel barrel of his long gun. "I know you'd help me… You'd want to help Zack, being his friend and all, being how he and all his kin have done for you…for us… And we'd….we'd do right by him, in honoring him…and his birthright. Keeping the land in his name."

"*His* birthright? In his name?" Ben blinked wryly at her. "By presenting him an heir not of his blood? A changeling of sorts?"

She shrugged, still threading trembling fingers through her shawl's fringe. "If it can't be Zack's…it should be someone he'd allow. Someone like…you."

Realization flooded over Ben with sickening weight. She wasn't touched in the head. This was no idle, totty-headed lark. She must have thought long and hard on how to calculate her every move and trap him into her scheme. "You're upset, that's clear enough. And you don't know what you're saying. Let's get you home, Mrs. Swearingen. Your husband has need of you, of both of us. His good wife and his good friend, and that's the way of it."

Phoebe eased closer and moved the lantern aside to sit beside him on the log. For a moment, she cast a desperate, wild look into the forest and swayed. Ben steadied her with a hand at her elbow, fearing she'd faint. He tried to aim her toward the path out of the woods.

She resisted and leaned into him, close enough for him to feel the warm vapor of her breath that could cloud his judgment if he weren't mindful. "You'll help me, then? I know full well what I'm saying and what needs to be done. We'll make a babe for Zack and everything will be all right, won't it?" Whether she spoke more to herself in reassurance of a dastardly plan or to convince him, he didn't care at any rate.

Ben stroked her cheek with the back of his bare fingers and clenched his teeth. A hint of lilac and wisteria feathered across his face, into his nose. It curled deliciously into the ridges and cavities between his cheekbones. Five-and-a-half pence per ounce for French eau de toilette. A full, four-ounce bottle at the store could set a man back just under two bits, same price as a small ax. Either, well applied, could tear a man asunder. She must mean business to wash herself in fine cologne just to come traipsing in the winter woods to ply her trade.

"No." He collected his thoughts and casually replied, "I don't intend to stay here in these parts long, you know that. I don't need anything tying me here, least not you and some kid you'll pass off as some other man's. Not to mention, siring a bastard, should your scheme be uncovered." He spoke evenly, lightly, hoping to appease her and show the utter foolishness of her thinking. It took every fiber of control not to grab and shake such an insidious notion from her devilish mind, but he tried to understand. She was confused, frightened, like a cornered panther ready to scratch and claw its way out of danger. No. He was the cornered one and if he didn't see his way out of this, what might she be capable of to keep what wasn't rightfully hers?

In the silence, she maintained a penetrating gaze. "I know about old Swearingen's will. He done his part by you, didn't he? Set you up right fine, he did." She laid a trembling hand on his arm. "But I also know what you got to do to get that share of Swearingen holdings. That's why this could work."

"It'd never work. And it wouldn't be right, no matter how you try and make it so." He backed away and retrieved her cloak, still lying on the frozen ground where she had left it. "Now with or without you, I'm heading over to see Zack." He placed the cloak around her shoulders; she flinched at first before accepting its warmth.

"She ain't even bleedin' age yet." Phoebe spun around, her face skewed in anger. "Won't be for nigh on three maybe four year or more."

"That's none of your concern."

"Hear me out." She held up a hand. "You don't have to wait that long. Once I've got a babe for Zack, the land will be mine. You can still come 'round whenever you like, and then when the proper time come, you can still have…all the rest." She spread her hands wide as if to indicate what was left unsaid.

"All the rest?"

"You know what I mean." She gazed up under hooded eyes. "It be in the old man's will. The land that's to go to you when the little one comes of age. You'll have everything. We'll have everything."

"That's about enough. I've got no claims on anyone's land here or intentions of being tied down to anyone. Not you and certainly not some arranged…" His shout reverberated off the trees as his anger and patience reached their limits. A pair of cardinals fluttered to a higher limb of a nearby elm—or, had something else startled them? An odd, yet too-familiar shape, one he was sure he'd seen recently in the woods, melded into the trees, shadowy and silent. He couldn't be sure and he didn't want to cause alarm, but his protective instincts took over. Gently, he drew her down behind the log, his rifle drawn low. "Be still," he hissed. "Stay here. It's probably just your girl, but I'll make sure."

She crouched behind the log as he walked a few paces out, alert to every crack of twig and rustle of nocturnal life emerging from its den. *Probably just a possum or owl winging its way through the trees.* In his present mind, he could easily have been looking for any distraction to induce her out of the woods.

He returned to her hiding spot, "It's nothing." But he knew otherwise. He knew as certain as he had the last time he felt this sort of presence. But for now, it had slipped silently back into the darkness of the forest and perhaps would be no more trouble. "Let's get you home now. It's getting dark." He bent to offer his hand. "There's more to consider here. Just give me some time on this and I'll see what can be done legally." His voice caught with the dread of his next words, "While there's still time."

She took his hand but remained on the ground, beckoning him down toward her. "But…you'll give a mind to what I said? You're a good man, Benjamin Stephenson. I know how you feel about Zack, and it pains me to think how awful I must sound to you."

In the shadows, her watery eyes shimmered up at him, melting his anger. "I know you're scared, and I promise I'll do all I can, but legally and without any deception."

"But…my idea ain't so bad, is it? We got to do something, while there's still time on our side?"

With one firm pull of his hand, she stood, teeth rattling, a shivering sob escaping into steamy breath. "First is seeing to Zack's needs, then worrying about the claim Shepherd has. After that..." He wasn't sure what to say to this woman's worries. "Your right to land and property will work itself out in good time. You won't be left destitute. Shouldn't that be enough?"

She took his hand and straightened to her full height, staring at the frozen ground, shivering, sobbing. "And now that Zack is...he can't pursue the legal way no more. It's all just...despairing and hopeless?"

"No, not despairing... Maybe...," he spread his hands in helpless exasperation, "I don't know just yet." His head throbbed and his chest pounded with notions entering his mind that had no place there. She remained far too close, sheltered there between the trees as darkness poured over them. They were alone. The thoughts he had kept at bay washed over the dam of his resolve. She had told her slave girl not to return until called. The shadow in the woods hadn't been her and couldn't have been what he thought. He tried to convince himself of that, even as his reason told him otherwise.

Lilac and wisteria. A diseased friend and the certainly of what would transpire in the weeks to come. The quarrel of a few weeks ago was only a prelude to this final madness. It wasn't her fault...none of this. There were others to consider here as well. But he couldn't think on all that just yet. They were alone. She was hurting, saddened, dreading what the future held, and the realization of losing his friend settled over him like the dark clouds of night snuffing out the light of day. She was already mourning, but so was he. Lilac and wisteria.

"There now. Who is telling you all this? Giving you such notions?" Ben had an idea, but wanted to hear it from her. He remained too near, sheltered there between the trees, the cold not so chilling anymore. She wasn't really a bad sort.

"It's what the old man's will say. I know how they feel about me, how they've always felt. Them Swearingens think they's so high and mighty. The old man always did say they come from Dutch noblemen stock." Her voice broke as she turned to lean against the sycamore again, clenching fists at her side.

"He'd never have allowed Zack to marry someone like me, someone who come from…" A baleful laugh filled the unspoken gap. "He give his own bastards a claim, but not his lawful son's wife. The high and mighty Injun Fighter. No heir, no land claim. That be what they will say."

"I'm heading back to see Zechariah now, Mrs. Swearingen." Ben reached for her arm to lead her out, hoping she'd not try any more tricks. He didn't want to leave her here but would if she refused to follow.

She clutched the tree, as if drawing one last ounce of strength, a mad, cold resolve lighting her face in the soft glow of eventide. "I'll get me a babe for Zack, one way or another, and breed their next Swearingen kin to keep what's mine, right and proper, I will. Whether it be you or someone else. I will, I tell you. And I'll not leave my land."

It was the scream of a panther in the distance that drove her to him. Or, had it been her own cry, angered and desperate? In the end he wasn't sure, only that she was cold and shivering and safe in his arms. He only meant a momentary embrace—reassuring, shielding, and warm. In the dusk, she was so soft and warm in his arms. The cover of darkness surrounded them, holding them and their plans together as one. Shadows and wilderness sheltered them from sight and sound, in a place where no one need know. Here between the trees he kissed her, full and deep. Or she kissed him. Did it matter? He should cease, push her away. But rivers can't be stopped on their course—winding, searching, beyond the reaches of any man's reckoning. He had plans of his own. He couldn't possibly want her, not like…

"Miss Phoebe?" Achsa stood trembling on the path. "I know ya'll said to wait, but it be getting mighty late now. I thought I heard a panther over yonder. Beggin' your pardon, ma'am, Mr. Stephenson, sir, but shouldn't we be getting home now?"

CHAPTER 2

The fire did little to keep her warm. Even with the hearth's glow swathing the log kitchen, Lucy still shivered worse than she had earlier when fetching in firewood. She had not minded the cold then, tending chores with her little brother and the family slaves. Being outdoors on a winter's morning was still better than sitting inside sewing or listening to Mr. Newhouse bluster about, finding fault with everything she did, his usual morning diversion after breakfast on these long winter days.

Even in the midst of chores, they were permitted a bit of freedom in the fresh air, the snow-coated land in soft curves like a down-filled counterpane. There was comfort in the open air, the wide expanse of sky and hills, even with winter's chill, made tolerable when there was mischief to distract them. Van, being the irksome older brother he was, took them all by surprise and started a snowball fight. Of course being mischievous, he assaulted his little sister first, avoiding Tommy altogether.

The cold wet sting that exploded across the side of her face left an armload of kindling scattered like ninepins across the lawn. A wicked laugh and then another icy assault met the back of her head. Lucy fell in a heap over the discarded wood and lay there a second gaining her composure. Shocked and angered, she knew this meant war.

"Lu! Are ye hurt?" Van said running up behind her.

"Mister Van, what has you done? Miss Lucy!" Winn said.

Lucy could hear all but lay still, thinking, scheming. Then when her older brother bent to help, up she shot with a handful of snow to shove into her attacker's face.

"Aha, dear brother, you got a bit of your own, I'll be bound!" Lucy scrambled to her feet and moved a safe distance away.

"Wretched fiend!" sputtered Van brushing wet snow from his own face. Snow clung to his eyelashes and cheeks in glistening patches giving the impression of a winter sprite.

"Look, children 'tis St. Nicholas! You've come a bit late this winter, good sir. 'Tis more than two months past your holy day," Lucy gave a mocking bow.

"And...here I was trying to help...and see what thanks I get!" Van continued to sputter as he gained his composure shaking off the snow and arming himself for another round.

"Help?! By Jove! You were starting a bit of sport of your own while we toiled!" Lucy said, standing arms akimbo.

Before Van could respond a ball of snow rounded upon his shoulder. Brother and sister looked beyond to see Winn laughing while Tobe shrugged wide-eyed with feigned innocence.

"Ho! Ho! A worthy opponent it is!" Van took this opportunity to pack the snow between his hands and volley back a well-rounded icy ball of ammunition. Upon release, Tobe conveniently ducked causing the shot to miss its intended target and land on Winn's neck splattering down the front of her cloak soaking her neckerchief. She gasped and dropped her own load of wood. The game was afoot. All armed with frosty weapons abandoned thoughts of chores or winter doldrums. The battle continued with each on his own, including young Tommy.

Why had it been just then that Ben Stephenson arrived to find them in such a folly? A snowball fight, of all things, so childish. Now it all seemed a part of that other time, the slice that came before and would never be again. Lucy had reckoned the events of her life in just such a way, in little slips and slices, each kept neatly in its own particular box. If she had a journal to keep, as Zack, her dearest brother did, what would she record on this day? A time to laugh and a time to weep, a time to rend and a time to sew. But what about the time to wait? That was the hardest of all.

This morning had been the time to laugh, playing in the snow, Winn squealing with delight as Tobe pelted snowballs at her. Tommy's curiosity over finding a possum behind the woodpile and thinking it a hedgehog to foretell the coming of spring by its shadow. All seemed foolishness now with the news Ben Stephenson brought.

Zechariah was missing and ill with fever and ague. The hushed whispers drifting in from the front main room earlier were not for her hearing, but Lucy caught enough to know the truth of it from her perch at the top of the stairs.

"No, he isn't here," Mother explained to Ben, who refused the seat she had offered. He stood fingering the brim of his felt hat, his brown hair neatly drawn back in a pigtail, after the manner of a gentleman soldier. She noted every detail about him as he spoke to Mother, from his ink-smudged fingers to the stately way he held himself. Though not a tall man, he carried himself with an imposing authority that intrigued Lucy.

"We've not seen Zechariah in about a fortnight. How is Phoebe?" Mother insisted, when Ben pressed her, agitated but patient and respectful.

"She's concerned, frantic, as is expected," Ben said. "I wanted to rule out, that is...I had hoped he might have come here."

"He's delirious?" Mother whispered the word, but Lucy knew well what it meant. The fever was affecting his mind. They must find him soon. She clenched her hands and fought the urge to run downstairs and begin her own desperate search. But instead Mother had called for Van.

"My eldest son, Van, might help with your search party, Mr. Stephenson," Mother suggested. "If it's agreeable with you."

Of course Ben had agreed, leaving Lucy and Tommy behind to wait in the kitchen and wonder. Tommy serenely dangled a Bilbo stick at Shadrach, who pawed at the swinging ball suspended from the cord only to have the little boy jerk it just beyond the cat's reach. "Enough, Tommy-kins. Leave kitty alone now." Lucy scooped up Shadrach, in spite of her little brother's pout. "I don't see why I can't go along to help find him."

Ester kept her station at the fire, calmly stirring the steaming kettle as if she hadn't heard. At last she shook her head, wiping long, callused fingers on her apron. "It ain't for womenfolk to go searchin' the woods for lost menfolk, child." The cook slave could not mask the concern in her tone even while she resumed her task of preparing a noon meal of savory stew. Lucy had no appetite for any of it.

Tommy, still pouting, plopped down on a stool. "Van got to go. I don't see why we couldn't."

"Because you're still just a little boy," Lucy said, her attention drawn to the swirling snow outside. "And Van only went to alert a few neighboring settlements who mightn't hear the signal bell from our fort."

"Is he gonna join up with the militia now, too?" her little brother asked. "Van is nigh on a grown man. Ain't he? That's what he keeps saying."

"He sure didn't act like a man earlier throwing snowballs at us while we did our chores," Lucy grumbled, nestling the purring cat against her chest.

Ester gave a smirk and a barbed glance. "I dinna see you mindin' none, Miss Lucy." She shook her head, clicking her tongue sternly. "Tossing snowballs like a passel of bumpkins whilst I'm in here a-cooking dinner and your poor mother is at her mending. And none of us a-knowing what's befell poor Mr. Zechariah."

"I'm gonna join up with Brady's rangers someday, too." Tommy shot bolt upright on his perch, ignoring Ester's chiding. "I'd help search for lost folks and fight Injuns too, just like Pa done."

"Maybe you will Tommy-kins." Lucy didn't care if her voice was tinged with bitterness, ladylike or not. "But I'm always going to be a girl," her voice trailing off as she considered a future of staying at home with nothing to do but sew and mend and serve guests while waiting for men to come home. Van would not be militia ready for another few years. Yet at age twelve, the day would come soon enough for him to join their elder brothers, Zack and Elzey, in the local militia corps. She would be left behind to watch and cheer them on as they drilled in military reviews during Public Day and Independence celebrations and then marched off to their soldiering duties. She would never have adventures of her own, tell tales of triumphs and defeats. There would be no exploring the wilderness, unless she married a soldier and became a camp follower, which didn't quite appeal to her either. She longed for a home of her own more than anything else—a place completely hers where she could set the rules and order for daily living.

Ester tapped the wooden spoon against the kettle, continuing to chide her. "Now don't be that way, missy. There be a lot o' ways we women folk can help. Once they find Mr. Zechariah, he gonna need a lot of tendin' just like before, and that's where your ma and I could use your help getting the possets and such ready."

"As if they'd even let me help." Lucy set Shadrach down on the floor, to Tommy's great delight. She slumped onto the bench under the window. Cold seeped between glass and wood frame. Winter air tinged with the mustiness of seasoned wood masked the smell of Ester's potions. From the cooking arm a small pail sizzled and popped over the fire. Drawing the wool shawl around her, Lucy wished she had held onto the cat for added warmth, but the tabby had resumed his play batting Tommy's Bilbo tether.

"Oh, you be getting on in age, yourself, Miss Lucy. Not so young no more." Ester winked as she ground a pinch of herbal mixture with the mortar and pestle. "Might be your brother could use another nursemaid. You know he always fond of you."

"He's got his wife now." With forehead pressed to the glass, her breath steamed the crystal patterns into rivulets, trickling into the wooden frame. "You think he'll be all right out there? What if they don't find him?" She tried not to think about how cold it would be, alone in the woods, chilled with a fever. She willed the men to return with news. "Supposin' he…?" She drew in a breath and gentled fingers over the melted trails left on the window.

The slave did not answer, but the crease in her chin coupled with the soft hum of her voice indicated she heard, in spite of her preoccupation on posset-making. Zack may not be easily found, and Lucy knew the consequences when a body was wracked with fever. She knew this, even if grown folks tried to pretend she was too young to understand. She knew and heard more than her mother realized, though Ester always seemed to understand her better than she did herself at times. Eleven winters was surely old enough, even if by the calendar she had yet to pass her eleventh natal day. Some girls by her age tended the birthing of another child in the family, be they bonded or free, or cooked meals when there were no slaves to serve the farms, and yet here she sat, helpless to do much of anything.

"Phoebe should have minded him better," she muttered to the fogged glass, not meaning to be heard. But Ester's sharp ears did not let this pass.

"Now don't be that way, child. Miss Phoebe got enough on her mind these days. It ain't easy being a young bride taking on all she done tending Mr. Zechariah these past few months."

"I would never have left his side. I'd be out there searching now, if they let me." Was Phoebe out searching too? Perhaps had her brother not married last summer, he would still be here and not lost somewhere. He mightn't even have gotten so ill. She never cared much for the girl Zechariah had taken to wife. It was wicked of her, she knew that, but no denying the unease and mistrust she felt whenever the woman was around. It was more than petty jealousy. She tried to push those childish feelings aside. Mother's marriage later that year, with the coming winds of autumn, made it harder still. She read the Good Book's command at Mother's insistence. She penned it dutifully into her copybook along with other adages of selfless devotion, duty to one's neighbors and kin:

"Charity suffereth long, and is kind; envieth not; charity vaunteth not itself, is not puffed up."

"Here now." Ester flipped open the receipt book. "I needs you to read me this here ingredient list for the 'coction. You can do that for Ester, now can't ya?"

Lucy pulled herself away from the window, knowing the woman had every receipt in that book committed to heart and more likely had adapted them to better use than what was listed. She suspected the woman might also know how to read or else how would she know which page to turn to? This was just another ploy to lift her from doldrums to a useful task.

"There," Ester pointed a floured finger to the list, "what that say?"

"Take an ounce of sweet basil. Grind three ounces of yellow bark,"

Lucy muttered, setting the book down. "Ester, you know this receipt and can put it together faster than I can read it."

"Maybe so, but...do you want to help your brother get well once they find him or not?" The woman drew a few gnarled pieces of dried root from a jar and laid it on the table. "Would you mind grinding this whilst I set to making a tincture? 'Bout time I learnt you how to make possets and tinctures, for when you runs your own household someday."

Lucy drew in a breath, glancing at the kitchen door. Thinking about that far-off day running her very own household, seemed a pointless exercise now. But the thought of her own home, her own kitchen to putter in, helping her servants as she pleased, perhaps treat them far better than some now did—namely, her stepfather—it did have a certain appeal. Zechariah had treated the slaves with respect, had encouraged the family to work with them, not order them about and threaten them at every turn, as Mr. Newhouse now did. But then, he ordered her and Tommy and Van, and even Mother, in ways that seemed untoward.

"We have an obligation to care for those in our charge," Zack would often say, "those of lesser rank that we are in command of. 'Tis our duty and obligation. Slaves must obey their masters, but masters have a duty to them as well. Kindness, gentleness, and long-suffering are the fruits of the Spirit. That's what the Good Book says."

More was the pity that Mr. Newhouse had no such fruits of the Spirit.

There had been that one afternoon she sat behind the corn shed sketching with charcoal on a piece of smooth bark, when she overheard her older brother argue with Mr. Newhouse about the slaves. It had all stemmed from Zack merely helping Millie carry a bucket of water, only trying to assist, as the woman was great with child. But Mr. Newhouse felt otherwise.

"The slaves of this household are no longer your concern, sir," Mr. Newhouse had said to Zack. "You may have insinuated yourself into this family, sir," Zack replied, "but I will still see that those in this household are treated with kindness, decency, and Christian charity."

Lucy had never heard Zack raise his voice in anger to anyone before. She had cowered in the shadows of the shed, hoping they did not see her, though part of her had wanted to run out and defend Zack, particularly when what she heard next was far more disturbing.

"The slaves in this household are no longer your concern. You have your portion to mind and a charming wife to boot. Those in this household, be they slave or my wife's progeny, will be left to my care and keeping."

Her stepfather had stormed off with one final dismissive statement: "I'll thank you to mind your own affairs, sir, and your own household or it shall be the last thing you ever do."

It was those last words that haunted her. They vexed her thoughts and fueled her fears, especially now. Though, Mr. Newhouse was indeed known for his idle threats—that much she had learned in the months since he wed Mother. Still she preferred to stay as far from him as possible.

Her stepfather would certainly not have approved of them helping with chores earlier in the day, let alone a snowball fight with slaves. It had been the only bright spot in an otherwise dreary week. The look of sheer joy on Tobe's face as he lobbed a well-aimed snowball at her was beyond words. If only she could capture that in a sketch with charcoal or pencil. She closed her eyes, wishing away the hours in between.

"Why are the good times so brief?" she whispered into the dish of ground roots. "And the bad times, like now, waiting, so unending?"

"What's that, sweetie?" Ester paused, wooden spoon midair from stirring the stew.

"N-nothing." Lucy resumed grinding the yellow bark with increased fervor. "I...just want to know that Zack is all right. And... things could be as they were."

Ester nodded. "We's all praying for your brother's safe return and good health. It be the best thing we can do. But things is always changing. Can't stop the world being what it be, with all its good and evil."

Lucy drew her mouth into a tight bow. The crackling of the fire, the simmering of the kettle, and Tommy's mewling to the cat played on her nerves as she ground the bark into pulverized bits. Later she would think on these things and other matters—things she ought to have asked Zechariah long before now, thing she should have told him. But there would still be time; she kept bidding away all other thoughts than this.

She hadn't heard the kitchen door swing open, so deep in thought was she.

"Ester?" Mother peeked inside the kitchen door, donned in her second-best bonnet and woolen cloak, ready for travel. "How are the remedies coming along?" The worry lines on her mother's face nearly made Lucy drop the dish of ground bark.

"Almost ready, ma'am," Ester replied, pouring the decoction into a small jug and corking it. "It keep a while, but..."

Mother's fretful brow relaxed and then buckled again. "I know. We'll just have to hope it will be in time. I'll take it over to Miss Phoebe and wait with her there. Noah is saddling up a horse for me."

"May I come too?" Lucy stood tall and steadied her voice, suitably respectful, but with a grown-up air. "I could help keep Phoebe company. I won't get in the way. I promise. I've learned how to make decoctions and..."

The barest of nods and beckoning fingers lifted Lucy's hopes. "Yes, I do suppose you could be of use."

"Me too?" Tommy clapped his hands, bouncing on his toes.

"No, Tommy. I need you to remain here and be the man of the house until Father gets home."

Hearing her mother refer to Mr. Newhouse so casually as "father" still rankled like the shock of slipping on an icy trace. It wasn't only that she felt it a betrayal to her own father, whom she barely remembered. She had still been tied to Mother's leading strings when he died that cold December day, a week before her birthday. Father had been strict and harsh, or so many folks said, but she only remembered his laughter and the way he held her high upon his shoulders as she bounced across the hillocks and valleys of their land. Perhaps it was the freedom she knew in the absence of a "firm hand" to run the household. Or at least that's what Mr. Newhouse kept saying was lacking in them all from the field hands to the house servants to even her brothers and herself. At first Mr. Newhouse had been kind, perhaps too kind, during the all-too-brief time he courted Mother, but once they were wed, everything changed. She bit her tongue and prayed forgiveness for the wicked things she wished to say every time Mother insisted on calling him their father. She tried her best to be the properly bred lady everyone said she should be. But right now all that mattered was seeing her brother safely home again. Being included among the other grown women while they waited was better than waiting here with her baby brother.

Around the bend emerging from the craggy tangle of trees was the square-cut-log, dogtrot cabin that was Zack and Phoebe's homestead since their marriage last June. How happy they had been that warm summer day celebrating with all the kin and neighbor folk right here on Swearingen land. Uncle Joseph and Cousin Thomas had arrived just in time from Shepherds Town and stayed long enough for Independence Day celebrations a few weeks later. The day was fair, filled with delicious food, celebratory toasts, stumping speeches, and, of course, the inevitable reading of Mr. Jefferson's Declaration. The best part was dancing with Ben Stephenson later. He had asked her like a proper gentleman, though it may have only been at Zack's insistence and more to keep her from having to dance with that Horace Madsen. Still, it was the first time she felt like a full-grown lady and it pleased her.

Now, all she could see was the cabin through the twisted, lifeless branches swaying like keening sentinels. The wind kicked up and whistled a mournful tune around her as she sat atop Natty Blue who shuddered beneath the sidesaddle. Cold settled into her bones.

Ben Stephenson stood beside his horse, hitched to the post just outside the cabin door. He smoothed a hand across the stallion's withers and leaned his head against the thick, black coat. For a moment he remained before turning a hard, weary face toward her and Mother, as if they were intruders. Lucy locked eyes with his vacant stare and began to dismount. He held a hand up signaling them to remain still and motioned to a nearby servant to tend Lucy's horse and help her dismount.

Mother smiled with a nod to Ben's tipped-hat greeting and lop-sided smile. "You found him?"

"Aye, we did." His tone, unreadable.

"And?" Mother lifted a stalwart chin and squared shoulders.

"I'd have a private word with you, Mrs. Newhouse, if you please."

Another furtive glance from Ben. Another slice of time, glimpsed and then gone. Another season between joy and weeping. The wind rushed in Lucy's ears and sucked the breath from her body. They had found Zack and he was dead.

CHAPTER 3

"For as much as it has pleased Almighty God in his wise providence..."

Lucy could hear the parson droning words at the graveside, surrounded by kith and kin from the surrounding settlements and forts. The news had traveled fast, along the rivers and creeks bringing so many to bid farewell to her dear brother, now lying cold and lifeless in the pine box. Both her sisters were widows now within the same year. Drusilla and Phoebe resembled two old crows in their black bombazine gowns and gossamer veils floating over bonnets tied with equally dismal black ribbons. She should shed a tear for them, garnering sympathy for their plight in losing husbands so soon and in such a short time. But neither were true sisters to her, mayhap for being so much older and grown up. Dusy, as the family affectionately dubbed her eldest half sister, was more than twice her age and a scant five years younger than Mother. That fact had been made quite plain, especially by Mother, who adopted a reserved sisterly affection with her husband's eldest daughter. Phoebe, though closer in age, was solely responsible for her husband's death, or so Lucy reckoned after seeing the events unfold at Windy Hollow. Somehow she knew it the moment she and Mother rode upon her brother's land. Ben Stephenson hadn't wanted to tell her, wouldn't even let her see her brother, dead or not. Only Phoebe was allowed to sit vigil with him all that long day into night. Mother said it was her right and everyone understood, even to letting only Phoebe and her slave girl,

Achsa, wash and prepare Zack for burial. There was no one to blame for any of this. That's what they kept telling her. Blame was all she had at the moment—anger at things she could not change, anger at those that could have prevented this. Though it may be wrong, sinful even, it fueled her rage. And that was better than sorrow and tears, which solved nothing, only leaving her weak, drained, and helpless. Anger gave her strength and purpose and a means to see this through.

How could it have pleased the Almighty to take her brother, who had so much yet to do—a new wife and a farm to tend, children to rear, and years to serve as a captain in Brady's rangers? Thinking of her second-eldest brother becoming a father someday had both delighted and perplexed her. He had been like a father to her as well as a doting brother since their father died. Sam Brady, too, had been kind to her, even if Dusy found her a troublesome child, always in the way of everything. Even while Sam lingered with the fever in his lungs, after falling from his horse into an icy creek nearly a year ago, he never grew cross. She had helped Mother and Ester tend him through the summer and fall, making the same balms and physics that so recently were made in vain for Zack. A ruddy lot of good they did either man in the long run.

Lucy clutched the black wool cloak around her white muslin gown tied with a black silk sash she rolled between her fingers. Only little girls wore white bedecked with black ribbons for mourning. Grown ladies wore full black, though to be draped like a crow and forced to wear such things for nigh on a year into widowhood made her glad to still be yet a girl of only twelve winters. She preferred to think of her age span as how many winters she'd seen rather than her actual birthday crossings which to date, only amounted to. December was an eternity away. Not quite a woman grown, forever caught in the nib between childhood and womanhood.

Van stood nearby, staid and resolute in his dark frockcoat and black armband. Little Tommy fidgeted next to Mother, one hand clinging to her skirts and the other, thumb wedged between two front teeth. A strange lot they must seem to the birds calling from the trees and woodlands hedged back to make room for this small family plot atop the hill overlooking Waddle's Run. High on the snow-dusted hill with a stream coursing down the hollow, settlement folk and militiamen formed a dismal assemblage.

The events of the past week were like an eddy of the nightmares from her infant years returning to haunt her sleep. It was always the same. She was lost in a forest, chased by some fearsome creature. The dreams sent her searching for Zack, calling for him and almost finding him, but not quite. Last night she awoke, startled at the sight of her brother standing at the foot of her bed, smiling with a beckoning finger. Only for an instant she was certain he was there, and then he faded into the shadows of the glowing embers of the hearth. But he had been there, hadn't he? She wanted to believe it was him, disturbing though it was to think his spirit still lurked about, even with all the shiny surfaces and mirrors covered. He had said something else as he stood by her bed, hadn't he? If only she could recall the words. Her thoughts kept teasing a phrase he had uttered, or thought he uttered, just before he faded away. Something about a coat, a roundabout...a jacket? But what did that matter now?

"...To call out of this world the soul of our brother, Zechariah..."

Reverend Godbey's words lay as heavy and miserable as the surrounding winter air. Zack was no more. She wanted to be done with all this and harness the tears welling against the back of her lids, unbidden and severe. Clenching her fists and biting her lower lip, she willed the tide of sobs to cease. *Be strong. You are the daughter of Captain Van Swearingen, commander of the local militia, officer in Washington's army, and founder of Swearingen's Fort.* Silently she recited the litany her brothers had drummed into her head as she marched and drilled at their heels. "A good soldier does not cry. A good soldier is stalwart, brave, loyal, and never shows the chink in his armor." Later in the dark stillness of her bedchamber, when all was quiet and no one would hear, she might release every ounce of courage into her pillow. Perhaps she was not the sturdy soldier her father wanted her to be and would never serve as her brothers had or someday would. Later she might steal away to the place where she would feel closer to her lost brother, at his favorite fishing spot on Catfish Creek, her father's favorite too, or so he always told her.

"...We therefore commit his body to the ground. Dust thou art, to dust thou shalt return."

The minister reached out his hand and crumbled cold earth over the rough-hewn coffin, raining dry tears in the frosty stillness over her brother's remains. She mustn't sweep them away, much as she wanted to, as if that would sweep away the pain, sorrow, and memory of this terrible week.

Reverend Godbey raised his hands heavenward, his voice full and strong as he led the concluding prayers. Four men took hold of the ropes twining beneath the coffin and lowered it gently into the hole. Zack would rest here twixt their pa and another brother Lucy never knew—Thomas, the elder, as she had come to know him, only by name. He had died a bare four months before her birth, a young man of seventeen attacked by a roaming band of Wyandot while he was hunting for ginseng root. She might have been the next Thomas, bearing the name to honor this lost son and be a comfort to her father. Instead, she was born a girl and earned her Grandmother Swearingen's name instead. It would take another three years before her father held another son who would carry on the dead son's legacy. Little Thomas Swearingen still clung to Mother's petticoats; someday mayhap he'd be a great soldier too, though now he was still her baby brother. The thought of something dreadful happening to him made her want to rush him into her arms and never let go.

But who would be there to carry on Zechariah's name and legacy?

As the reverend concluded his service, several men from the local militia led off a musket round to honor this soldier who had served with Captain Brady's rangers since his sixteenth year. In the ranks stood Elzey, her other half brother by her father's first wife, who had also birthed Drusilla. Zechariah's mother had been the second wife who died shortly after her only son's birth. Both women lay buried in graves alongside Father's and now two of his sons. Sam Brady was buried farther down the hill in a family plot of his own, someday to be joined by Drusilla and perhaps their two sons and future family. *But that seems far too morbid to think on now,* Lucy shuddered.

The deafening din of musket fire sent a shiver down to Lucy's toes. Six men primed and reloaded before she could count ten Monongahelas, her way of reckoning time by seconds as the schoolmaster had taught. They shot and reloaded one more time. Her eye lingered on one particular soldier, a tad shorter and leaner than the other soldiers flanking him. She hadn't wanted to take note of him or think on how he must be grieving. There would be no more contests of shooting skills between him and her brother in the clearing behind the fort. No more hunting or fishing on a summer's morn. She would miss that too and most of all their stories of daring and glory and the amusing tall tales. There'd be no reason for him to come calling now, and that was as it should be. She resolved to expect nothing more, 'twas no matter to her now. The ribbon sash wrenched around her finger till it pinched and turned the flesh red.

As soon as the echo of the report cleared, leaving only the odor of burnt sulfur and wafts of powder smoke lingering in the wake, a low hum reverberated across the field. Noah stepped out from the group of slaves, huddled on the edge of the small cemetery, and lifted his rich bass above the haunting drone of singers.

I am a poor wayfarin' stranger,
A travelin' through this world of woe...

On the next phrase Ester's clear vibrant voice stirred the air:

But there's no sickness, toil or danger
To that bright land, to which I go.

Harmonies swirled with the chilling breeze as more slaves joined in, swaying with the rich, languorous melody. Layer upon layer of tones intermingled, harmonious and dark, yet somehow airy and full of hope. Adding her own voice would be easy enough. She knew the words after one verse—simple, repetitious. It spoke of a place, a home. Heaven perhaps. But also somewhere "no more to roam" a place "over yonder." It could be no more distant than a trip to town and back or a journey to New Liberty or what folks moving west talked of and were calling the Promised Land. Was death really so different as that?

She closed her eyes and swayed, thinking of a lovely country, a home of her very own, a place where she would never have to part from those she loved. Her voice was silent as the grave, but she mouthed the words just the same until another thought struck her like a cold wind to her cheeks. *He's watching you, sweet one. He knows.* The next verse of the song choked behind her tongue. Her eyes flew open with a start to see Ben Stephenson's steady gaze and bemused smile leveled toward her from across the gravestones.

Had anyone else noticed her swaying to the singing? It hardly mattered, since his gaze felt like a thousand bearing down on her in full scrutiny. She lowered her head dutifully with the surrounding mourners, none who seemed to not have noticed her either. The other militiamen stood stalwart as tin soldiers with fixed, unseeing eyes. Returning an idle glance back to Ben sent a quiver down to her knees. Was that a wink he gave her? She jerked on the edge of her black sash, still entwined around her forefinger, and untied it in a most unladylike display. It drooped, loosening the fit of her bodice waistband. Lucy clenched her arms to her side in an attempt to pin the ribbon in place at the gown's high waistline. Later she would find a moment to retie it discreetly or enlist Winn's or another maidservant's help.

Of all people, why had it been him that saw her and mocked her silent singing? Thinking of her as a fanciful child, no less. She wanted to hate him, to place all her anger and blame on him, wishing him ill luck at everything he did. He brought the news of Zack's disappearance. He found Zack freezing and near dead in the woods and fetched him home. He could have saved him, could have found him sooner, or kept Phoebe from letting him run off like she did. She wasn't so young she didn't overhear the whispers grown folks made in their secret, cloaked words she wasn't supposed to understand. He could have saved her brother, but didn't. And to add further insult, it was from him, she had to learn the horrid truth, as he stood outside Zack's house greeting them as if it were his place to do so.

As the crowd dispersed, Uncle Joseph strolled up behind Lucy and Van and placed a comforting hand on each child's shoulder. "We Swearingens have had more than our share of grief, but be ye mindful, true strength is garnered not in the pleasures of life but in its sorrow." His kind eyes crinkled beneath graying brows, more gray than she remembered from his last visit a year ago.

Beyond him, there stood a young man nearly the height of his father. Lucy barely recognized the gawky boy from last summer as this much taller young man. "Cousin Thomas," she cried, dashing toward him with Van trailing behind.

Cousin Thomas met them with a warm smile and was ready to embrace but stopped and stiffened to attention. One stern glance and a sharp clearing of the throat from the old colonel and the boy heeded his father's gentle reprimand. "Dear cousins," he said dutifully, "you have our deepest sympathy at the loss of your brother and my esteemed cousin Zechariah, who was like a brother to me as well."

Lucy suppressed a giggle at the relieved look of her cousin and satisfied nod of his father. Likely the boy had been sufficiently schooled in funeral manners on the long journey from Shepherds Town. Her momentary amusement fought with the flooding reminders of why they were there. How truly irreverent of her to be so cheerful in greeting her cousin when only moments ago she had fought back tears, and the dirt not yet settled on Zechariah's grave.

"Thank you, cousin," she intoned, casting her gaze to the tips of her best leather shoes. She searched for something else to say in the uncomfortable silence, when Mother, of all people, salvaged the moment.

"You needn't be so formal, Thomas. My goodness, Colonel Swearingen, is this your handiwork? Such a fine and proper young gentleman he's become." She exchanged a weighty gleam between her own two children and their cousin. Lucy pondered this a moment, sheepishly wondering at Mother's meaning. Yes, her cousin had grown a head taller than she, who was already tall for her age, and he seemed mannerly enough, but neither grown-up had seen the cross-eyed smirk he shot to his young cousins while the parents conversed. The three exchanged the familiar sign—crossed fingers brushing the nose—that was their secret code for all was well and there'd be more to share later when they were alone, away from adults and proper behavior and all manner of politeness and protocol. That moment came sooner than expected as Uncle and Mother continued to talk, oblivious to their children's whisperings among themselves. It was really the two boys who struck up a conversation about horses and racing and such, while Lucy's attention drifted toward the various folk scattered around the graveyard or heading for the path leading home.

"Ah, indeed, Nelly," Uncle Joseph remarked as Mother daubed a handkerchief to a teary eye, "I would have it no other way. We received your summons and made haste to leave at once. I do wish we could have gotten here sooner and helped with the search."

"You are here now," she said, "and that is all that matters."

Lucy could hear the startling words, even as she caught an even more disturbing view—Mr. Newhouse standing over her brother's fresh grave with none other than...Benjamin Stephenson. And neither appeared the least bit grief-stricken. How could Uncle Joseph have known of Zack's disappearance and gotten here in time to help? Perhaps he was only being kind, or had everyone somehow known of Zack's illness far longer than they'd said?

"To think," Uncle continued, "'twas not even a half year spent since we gathered for Zechariah's wedding. Such a different time." His sympathetic eye veered across the way to where Phoebe stood a few feet from the grave, comforted by a few other women. "His widow? Phoebe, as I recall?"

Mother nodded sadly. "Yes, another Swearingen widow, I fear. They say these matters do come in three. First the captain, then Sam just after Christmas, and now our dear Zechariah."

"Ah, yes," Uncle sighed through his teeth. "But three is all in how you count these matters, Nelly. Five years since my dear brother's passing and lest we forget, five years before that our first Thomas, namesake to my father, was taken from us."

"I must think of it this way," Mother said, dull and soft, "in threes, so that we are done with all this burying for a time."

"Sam held up valiantly through his illness, as I understand, and so did my nephew through his fevers. I was glad to see them both last summer and that is the day I will think on best and most."

Mother daubed a lace-edged handkerchief to her nose. In her other hand she held the black ribbon sash from Lucy's gown. In her haste to see Cousin Thomas, she had forgotten to keep it pinned to her side, and it must have slid to the ground. Mother's discretion would no doubt later be a lesson on keeping fidgety fingers in their place. One last look over her shoulder at Zack's grave, and there stood Ben with Phoebe supported on his arm. A shared exchange, both disquieting and incomprehensible, united them.

CHAPTER 4

The Swearingen home was the largest in Brooke County, a double cabin that boasted an impressive four rooms, two upstairs and two down, besides a kitchen in the back attached with a dogtrot to the main house. When Captain Swearingen first arrived and claimed his bounty land, he had built a modest, one-room log cabin. That original cabin became the front common room, the one Mother like to think of as her "parlor." The small nook to the east of the parlor had been added on before Lucy learned to walk. It was her favorite place to read, curled up on her father's cot from his military campaigns. On the wall above was a small shelf of books including several well-read volumes ranging from Shakespeare's plays to treatises on government and philosophy. There were also books on navigation, mapmaking, and assorted histories of ancient countries. It had been her father's place to work and read and later Zack's, when he served as man of the house until he married Phoebe, and later that same year, Mother wed Mr. Newhouse. Since then, the house that had once felt spacious, warm, and comforting had since become cold and all too crowded.

On this day, of all days, her home felt even smaller and more congested with all the guests pouring in from the grave site. It was not the season to be outdoors or else the funeral supper would have been served out on the gentle sloping lawn or under the grove of ash trees. But this was not a warm spring day or breezy summer afternoon. It was the dead of winter, and so the common room had to accommodate the entire lot of company. Perhaps being so congested would mean folks would not be staying long. If it wasn't for the signs of mourning, black armbands for the men and somber-hued gowns and bonnets for the ladies, it almost felt like a Sunday meeting picnic. Josiah Gibson from the trading post meandered along in the train of people along with other familiar faces. Mr. and Mrs. Greathouse rode double on their Morgan, she sitting primly on a pillion behind her square-shouldered, portly husband. Daniel Poe hobbled along next to Uncle Joseph, nodding greetings to old friends as they passed. Cousin Thomas paced along with Van, still talking about whatever it was boys felt worthy to discuss and didn't want girls to hear. Rebecca Girty strode arm in arm with Drusilla, whose two boys trudged along behind, fussing at having to walk so far and bidding their mother to carry them.

Lucy searched the crowd for Mr. Gibson's partner from the trading post, hoping to find him walking alone, then just as quickly scolded herself for such folly. Why should she care where he was? 'Twas no matter to her. Perhaps he wouldn't even come to the luncheon, and she would be spared his worrisome inspection as she had endured in the graveyard earlier. He most likely would return to the store, anyway. Yet what customers would there be today, of all days? Surely everyone from New Liberty to Wheeling and beyond was gathered here and would have no need of a shopkeeper's wares. It amused her to think of Ben sitting idly in the shop awaiting customers that would not come. Perhaps he'd be wishing he had stayed for some meat and drink at their cabin.

Mother bustled about between kitchen and dining table, giving gentle instructions to the slaves. The bounty of the Swearingen farm along with the kindness of neighbors assured full bellies for all, even as winter stores waned. Savory roasted chicken, smoked ham, cornbread and fresh-baked Sally Lunn, Queen's cakes, and apple pasties filled the log house. Yet even with such delicacies, Lucy's plate remained untouched on the bench near her seat. She had no stomach for food, and she felt weary of the women's gossip. From the hearth the men talked louder, intriguing her with something worth digesting with the study of their spirited debate. Men were such curious ones. Always finding more interesting things to discuss than the ladies and their dull discussions on the finer points of stitchery and meddlesome gossip.

"But, sir, the very idea of Mr. Adams's acts to limit our speech and presume a suspicion of guilt undermines the core of our Constitutional Freedom. 'Tis no better than when we were under King George," Mr. McBride boomed across the circle of men near the hearth, as if he were stumping for election. "We fought a revolution, did we not? To rid ourselves of tyrants? And here we have done nothing short of elect another."

Lucy's ears perked when the discussion turned toward impending war. It seemed all that men ever wanted to talk about. With treaties now settled among the Shawnee and Cherokee nations, surely there would be no more trouble. "Adams was to blame," as one man asserted. "Another tyrant," as another agreed with Mr. McBride. Talk spread of the recent troubles with the French, which both alarmed and perplexed Lucy all the more. Would the French really attack them? Zack had always said they were friends—allies, he called them—during the War for Independence.

"Mr. Adams is no President Washington," William Engel said, picking his teeth with an index fingernail, "I'll grant you that. Pity the old general didn't remain in office for at least one more term."

A few men laughed and murmured their views amongst themselves. One man Lucy couldn't see sitting behind the rather massive Mr. Zehnder, posed a question, "Engel, who're you aiming to vote for then? Will it be Mr. Jefferson?"

He contemplated a moment and replied, "I can't say I'll tip my hat toward the Democratic-Republican either. The man may have framed our Declaration, but he has shown indiscretion in governing the state, as well as intemperance in other matters."

A rousing banter of men's voices filled the cabin air now suffused with tobacco and the odor of dampened wool from so many walking through snow-packed fields then sitting too near a glowing fire. Most of the men sided with Mr. Engel's view, while a few defended the stately Virginia governor.

"Enough of these infernal Federalists, I say," Mr. Tidwell shouted above the din. "'Tis Jefferson who's for the yeoman farmers like us.

What more reason do ye need than that? He'll bring strength to our new territories, usher them into statehood. Less government is what he stands for. Lower taxes and improved trade. It's what will preserve and secure our new nation."

"True, but I still don't trust him…"

Toward the other end of the room, near the dining area, a coterie of young women consoled Phoebe.

"And my Horace is growing taller than his pappy and strong as an ox…."

Lucy had no interest in hearing about that horrible Madsen boy from school so she pitched an ear closer to the men. It was the shrieks and gasps from the women that further broke her concentration.

"Phoebe, dear! Are you certain?"

"Oh, 'tis a pity poor Zechariah won't… Oh, but what a comfort for you!"

Lucy tried to ignore the women's silly words and focus more on the men. Yet without Zechariah to explain the men's words and arguments to her, what difference did it make now?

The election was to be in another year, and she secretly hoped Mr. Jefferson would win. She had tried memorizing the Declaration last year, after hearing it again in July. She had it almost learned by heart and had hoped to show Zack…. But now there was no use, was there?

"Indeed war with France must be avoided at all cost…," the Reverend Godbey managed a gentle reprove, dewy eyes peering over his spectacles as he sopped up the last bit of gravy on his plate with a biscuit.

Lucy leaned in closer to block out the women as the men talked politics amidst quaffs of drink. Boisterous statements and toasts were fired like rounds of powder and shot above the din of polite discourse and clink of Mother's fine china mingled with the saltware and china guests brought with them. Lucy feigned contemplating her next bite of food, forcing back any reaction that might reveal her curiosity to join the political talk. For a moment she forgot herself and turned to seek out Zack's reaction, wondering why he hadn't spoken up. She would ask him later when—No. She could not. The realization seized in her chest like the cold sting of Van's snowball the day they learned of their elder brother's disappearance. How could she have so easily forgotten? Would there be a day she no longer expected to see him? Even with the jolt of realization hitting her, for that brief instant it was sweet surrender to have him there, in her mind, as if the events of this past week had not occurred. But they had, and she could never will that away, much as she would have liked. No more would Zack read to her the writings of Mr. Franklin, Mr. Jefferson, or Publius, the odd name for a few other men who wrote ideas about government in some collected essays Zack was always reading and quoting from. Some of the words were beyond her, but Zack was a patient teacher and a lively reader. He explained what it meant to have a separation of powers, and how the consent of the governed factored into it all. Perhaps Phoebe would allow her to borrow some of his books and tracts, though they might be difficult to read without Zack there explaining it all to her. Even still, she would try her best to keep learning, just as Zack said their father wished for them all—even his daughters. What would Phoebe want with his books now? She never seemed interested in reading or thinking on much beyond herself and her pretty face.

No, that was an unkind thought for her newly widowed sister.

There was only one thing Phoebe could want—the one thing Zack had asked her to keep safe. Lucy held a secret she had yet to decide when to reveal and to whom. It was no sin to keep a lie to honor her brother's last wish, was it? And since no one had yet asked her directly, she had not told any lie at all. The package Zack had given her last Christmas and told her not to open until later still remained in its hiding place. She suspected what it was, but preferred to keep it unopened and hidden, lest she be asked and forced to tell a lie. Christmas was the time for secrets and so she had kept it safe just as Zack had wished. Perhaps it was time to find out what he had given her.

For now, she tried her best to ignore the women, especially Phoebe who beamed every time one of the older ladies mentioned her "condition" as if it were some ailment. Could her brother's widow have caught the ague too? She did look rather wan and sallow of face, but grief was hard to bear. She must miss Zack desperately, after watching him die in her arms. That is what everyone whispered around the coffin's viewing three days ago and all through the ordeal of the funeral. He had been alive when Ben found him, though no one else beyond Ben or Phoebe had seen for sure. She had born it all bravely, is what everyone was saying. Lucy studied her sister's pallid face and considered some widows succumbed to grief and followed their husbands to the grave. Such wicked thoughts again. Mother had not died of grief when Papa died, and where would they all be if she had? But Phoebe had no children to leave behind, no one to keep her husband's legacy alive.

She should feel sorrow for this woman, whose eyes shone with tears as a warm smile washed her face in sweetness. Lucy caught her gaze and smiled back with a nod to indicate she, too, understood their shared grief and remembrance. But Phoebe wasn't smiling at her. Someone else across the room must be the recipient, someone she prized more than a mere little sister. A slight shift of her view caused Lucy's breath to freeze and sink to the core beneath her stays. Unnoticed until now, Ben Stephenson leaned against the wall on the other side of a crowded room, his face sending a tender smile toward his friend's widow—a surreptitious gaze with a slight nod, as if assuring her of something. But what? The icy breath turned into a flaming poker down her gullet pinching beneath her ribs. Why should she care if Ben had slipped into the house without her knowing? Why should she give a fig that he seemed to be looking at Phoebe in a way most unseemly for the occasion or that Phoebe laid a delicate hand at her throat and let it trail around the ruffle at her collar?

Turning her attention to something less distressing, she caught Van behind the circle of men around the hearth. His dull eyes and curling lip gave her something new to ponder. Why should he be so sullen? He at least could hear the men's invigorating discussion and should be grateful for their company. But instead, he stifled a yawn and focused his attention out the window toward the barn. That's where he wished to be, out riding Lancer, his beloved sorrel. She clenched her mouth tight to smother a spontaneous titter.

When Van turned abruptly and plastered his hands to his sides, dignified and poised, Lucy nearly bit her tongue, sensing something was not right, as if they'd both been caught in some mischief. Unease laced her chest in a binding hold, harder than the wooden busk keeping her mindful of a lady's posture. Mr. Newhouse stared cold and stony at her from a clear vantage point at the edge of the sideboard. The room narrowed into a pinprick as the buzz of murmured voices filled her ears. His eye bored into her as if he could read her throughts. The untouched plate of food teetered precariously on her lap. Boiled potatoes and roast ham smeared against the delicate painted roses into one mass of pink and brown. If only she had remained with the ladies, unseen and demure, instead of taking such obvious note of the men's conversation.

He turned his attention easily enough back to the company, and Lucy breathed a sigh of relief. With glass in hand, Mr. Newhouse pointedly rose and addressed the guests. Lucy picked at her plate of ham again, expecting yet another pompous ceremonial toast, as if there hadn't been quite enough of those already. Whiskey flowed freely along with toasts that seemed to turn more ribald with each drain of the glass. She desperately wanted to be done with all of it and be alone to sort out all of this.

"Enough talk, gentlemen," her stepfather ordered. "Enough of politics, tyrants, legislation, and so forth. Leave that for the next stumping, if you please. Lest we be remiss, we are here to pay homage to our lost son of House Swearingen. Raise with me your glass to his honor." His affected sympathy and sweetness infuriated Lucy all the more, although at least his attention was diverted from her or Van for whatever grievance he chose to levy. He could indeed be charming. She recalled the same smug curve to his lips and the gracious tip of his drooping chin when he came to court Mother, just shy of a year ago now. That same look had been shared between him and Ben Stephenson earlier, who now was nowhere to be seen, though Phoebe was still present in her corner. Newhouse's voice was like an ace splitting timber, cracking out the words he surely couldn't mean. "To House Swearingen," Ed Zane offered in full voice, echoing Newhouse's toast with the addition, "and to our own Zechariah, may he rest in peace."

Another round of toasts, each more spirited than the last, each more audacious than the last, lauded Lucy's brother. Some were lofty and eloquent, some full of rowdy tales and exploits that sent a few of the women blushing or hiding their faces in hands while the men stamped and cheered A few more pious sorts, like the Reverend Godbey, extolled sentiments of the dead man's virtue and bravery until Mr. Newhouse once more gained command of the room.

"To *our own* Zechariah," Newhouse said, regaining control of the room, "may he be in Heaven an hour before the Devil knows he's dead." With the final toast, men raised tankards and mugs in grand Virginia voice with more whoops and hearty "Huzzahs!" A few from the militia stamped their feet, nudged one another jovially, or clinked cups together.

Devil indeed. Lucy glared at her stepfather, who smirked and slapped his knee at his final toast as if it were the most clever of statements instead of a tired old one nearly every man in the county had said at one time or another. Still, it sent an alarming chill through her bones.

Lucy tried to block out the noise, the din of voices, to no avail. It simply wasn't ladylike to plunge fingers into her ears and draw undo attention. Even that would not cease the images of late flooding her mind. For the three days before the funeral, they had received nearly every man, woman, and child from the county in an endless parade through the house. Whiskey and ale flowed freely while her brother's body lay cold and unnatural in the hastily crafted pine box. She closed her eyes to will away the image. The scent of dried sage and rosemary, mixed with rose water and lavender, still hung in the air with the fetid odor of tallow tapers. Now it competed with the rough, earthy scent of male sweat, liquored breath, and tobacco. It made her head swim with its sickening pall.

"Little sister, mind what you are doing," Drusilla said as she hovered above. Taking the plate from her drooping hand before adding, "Here, let me have that." Turning, she called to the servant, "Millie, do clean up this mess."

The heavy plate had tipped and bits of cornbread, ham, and potatoes littered the floor.

"I wondered where you got off to." Drusilla meant to lead her toward the women again. "Your mother wishes you to be closer to us now. My boys have been asking after you as well. You won't mind looking after your two nephews now, will you? Be a good girl for us."

Lucy nodded, absently allowing her sister to lead her away. In the background she still heard Mr. Newhouse, his glass replenished and raised once more. "I give you, on this momentous day, a lad of great renown, our own departed Zechariah Swearingen. A fine credit to our militia, a devoted husband and son, and...," here he paused to raise a drink and a shrewd eye toward Phoebe, "to his dear widow, let us also raise a glass to her constant faithfulness in this last, most trying year. Too brief a union, but nevertheless, she is still a beautiful bride."

"Here! Here! To Phoebe. To Zechariah. Huzzah! He was the best of us all."

Shouts, stamps, and more toasts escalated until Newhouse raised his hand to still the din. "Let us now pay our respects with the singing of an anthem, one I'm told, our dear son knew and loved well. I would offer my own voice, but...," he rubbed his chin and chuckled self-deprecatingly, "I am no great singer. But we have one amongst us who is a budding songstress, a veritable tunesmith whom I dare say, we may persuade to lift us from our depths of despair and lead us all in a song."

At this Lucy turned on her heels from her prior direction toward Mother, but now to her dismay, saw Mr. Newhouse making a great pretense of searching the cabin room for her. He well knew where she was, given the close quarters and that she had not moved more than a few paces from the bench where he surely had seen her last. Their home may indeed be the largest in Brooke County, but it was still not hard to find her even among such a packed house of guests.

Drusilla's hand pinned her shoulder, preventing an avenue of escape, though there was little hope of that given the limited access to any doorway or even a means to flee upstairs to the safety of her bedchamber. "Lucy, he wants you to sing for us, for our departed brother. You will be a dear and do as he bids?"

Her cheeks burned, and the few stinging bites of potato oozed up her throat. She turned to see the entire company staring at her.

"Ah! There she is." Newhouse beckoned with his long, spidery finger. "Come, dear Lucy. You must favor us with a song."

Through a mouth dry as cotton she managed a crackle. "I am not inclined to sing today." She offered a quick curtsey in spite of shaky legs. "Pray, do forgive my lack of...of...voice." Perhaps that last squeak on the final word would convince them. Instead, all it did was elicit a rousing guffaw from the men and a birdlike twitter from the ladies.

"Such modesty." Newhouse rolled his hand into a gallant bow. "Here, darling. Come take a draft of our tonic to clear your lovely throat. Show these gentlemen what heavenly gifts you possess." Turning to the guests he added, "And I assure you, those are not the only qualities she will someday favor upon one lucky gentleman."

She stood her ground, fists clenched at her sides. No one, especially not him, would bid her sing today.

Newhouse's eyes widened before narrowing as if trying to burn a hole through her, forcing her to comply. "One song, surely nothing you haven't done before," he said through gritted teeth forced into a smile. "And here you have just the ready audience." Nodding to some unseen person behind her, he added, "And our fiddler is here to accompany you. What more could induce you?"

The manner he said this flooded her head along with the times he'd threatened her, scolded her, and called her "wicked child" and "incorrigible brat" before threatening to sell her to the savages for further insolence. Had he too noted her silently singing along with the slaves in the graveyard? She was not ashamed of it, though she did not wish for him to make an issue of it here before everyone.

"Now, that's our good girl," Newhouse inveigled, "Perhaps favor us with one of those Frenchie songs your schoolmaster has taught you. Gentlemen, our dear daughter speaks French the like of any who've toured the continent. We've spared no expense on her education."

I'm not your daughter and never will be. What did he know of her schooling? He, who complained at every charge and expense for the simplest of household spending, from their schoolbooks to repairs of a fence line on Van's tract of land bequeathed to them by their own father. Yet he never lacked for money to spend at the tavern nearly every night. Fury boiled within her, stoked by grief and disquiet of the day. She would sing. Oh, she would sing a song such as he'd never heard before. The opening chords of Sam's fiddle hummed silky warm, abruptly pausing when she didn't follow his cue. The room shifted in odd shapes. Mother's face blurred, leaving only piteously pleading eyes for Lucy. She couldn't sing the awful song she had in mind. The one she had heard the militiamen singing would distress Mother with words no proper lady should ever say—words she'd heard among the soldiers when they thought she wasn't listening. Sparkling points colored the walls and ceiling. Blood roared in her ears along with other words that came only in the darkness when all was still and abed.

No. Not here, before everyone, especially not...him. Not now. The words to the song turned to babble in her head, and other words, the dream words, replaced them.

She turned and dashed past the women's skirts, past the table littered with dirty plates and ravaged trays of food. Toward the kitchen she ran before such words she could never explain escaped her lips. Just as she was about to reach for the iron latch, the door opened and she faced Millie carrying a tray laden with pots of coffee and tea.

"Lord a mercy!" The woman's voice swirled with the shower of brown liquid, tumbling china, and silver spoons clattering all around. The strong, plump arms flew in all directions to avert the disaster. Lucy felt hot, wet droplets spray over her as she ran past the kneeling slave collecting her wits and sopping up the steaming brew seeping into the cracks of the floorboards.

She sought escape through the open back door leading out toward the kitchen garden and fields, past the other startled slaves preparing food around the hearth. The brisk open air stung her face. The cold wind seared her damp gown, chilling her instantly to the bone. Her good white muslin was now besmirched with brown stains, as if further proof of her disobedience.

Up the hill she spied the fort, a place of refuge. She kept running, running, her feet barely skimming the frozen ground. The fort stood empty now. No one would be there since all rangers, scouts, and militiamen were likely either nestled in the cabin for the funeral dinner or gone home by now. She at last had the fort to herself, the place her father had built when he first came to this valley. No one would dare come look for her here, and, if they did, she knew places to hide.

Inside the stone perimeter were two blockhouses, each at opposite corners, stationed at the perfect vantage point overlooking the Ohio River to the northwest and the rolling hills to the southeast. Several small shelters served as an armory and a storehouse for supplies, should they seek refuge during times of danger, and other outbuildings were designed for quartering soldiers during campaigns, musters, and general guard duty when called upon. It was one of a dozen or so her father had built along the river between Wheeling, New Liberty, and Charles Town to serve any and all settlers in the surrounding communities. But this one was the largest and finest, in her opinion, and it was all hers for now. She needed a place of refuge, though not from the Blackfoot, Shawnee, or Cherokee as this fort was intended, and, for now at least, not even the British or French, if the gentlemen's words on rumors of war be true. She had heard all the terrifying tales of adventure and daring told around fires on still winter evenings. Those war years were over now, or so the men had said. The treaties settled it all. General Wayne proved victorious at a place called Fallen Timbers and everyone lauded the treaty he helped negotiate. It meant there was little fear of Indians attacking settler homes, scalping innocent women and children, or taking them captive. She sometimes wondered what that might be like, to be taken away with the savages or even sold to them, as Newhouse threatened.

It must have been the stories that incited her dreams ever since she could remember. The same recurring image of a terrible blue beast with an angry face like a bear and wings like an eagle, swooping into her room to carry her off. Always it was the same, she tried to scream but only silence came forth. Sometimes strange words formed that she couldn't comprehend. She would awaken babbling incoherently, sometimes to the befuddled, bleary-eyed looks of her two brothers or one of the servants.

She stood alone in the middle of the vast fort, surrounded on all sides by stone walls and reveling in the delicious freedom of space, solitude, and protection. It encased her like a warm, woolen shawl. She headed toward the blockhouse facing west and climbed the ladder to the lookout platform. Sunrays filtered through chinking between the logs, scattering patches of light across the rough floor. Lucy stood at the top of the ladder, taking it all in. The musty, acrid smell of seasoned logs and dried mud tingled her nose, causing her to cough. Her warm breath hit the air in a heaving mist as she stepped toward the gunport slits facing the western sky.

The river, with its surrounding bluffs and jagged ridges, invoked a sense of another place and time, a slice of eternity where all was possible and problems evaporated into the mist. The majestic Ohio carved a watery path through the ridges and hollows, pulsing its way from the Monongahela to other rivers beyond. She had only heard of these and knew them as crooked lines on maps her brothers studied. Traders and trappers who came up river told tales of such places as well, an endless comingling of land and river where trees still grew tall and thick in forests full of natives and fierce creatures known only in legend. She tried to imagine all the places the river might take her if she were to set a course by flatboat or sailing ship.

It felt as though the world was literally at her feet as she surveyed the land in all directions. Nearly every tract of it, as far as the eye could see, belonged to her family. All was still as she gazed across the rolling, snow-covered hills with valleys nestled in between like the folds of lace on a lady's gown. She could now think on all that had happened here in this peaceful place. This was where she had concealed it, the secret package given to her last Christmas She had kept it hidden just as she promised and told no one, just as he bid her, but perhaps now it didn't matter anymore. And what person could she tell that she might trust in any case?

Her fingers moved along the lower edge of one wall to a little crack in the log edifice, just under a protrusion that served as a small shelf for soldiers to set a pouch of tobacco or mug of coffee while enduring the tedious task of sentry duty. Underneath was her own secret hiding place, just out of view where the chinking had eroded away, in the hollowed-out niche where no one thought to look. She couldn't imagine why Zack charged her with such secrecy, but there had to be a reason. Of her two eldest brothers, Zack was the reliable caretaker of them all, not like Elzey, who was given to frivolity and carelessness. Yet her dearest brother had acted so strangely since Christmas. He seemed troubled, agitated, and abrasive the few times she had seen him last. But he had entrusted her with this one secret, the only thing she had left of him now.

The small wooden box fit neatly in her lap, cold against her trembling fingers. Zack was no longer here to bid her to silence and secrecy. Impatiently she flicked aside a tear and poised her hand to remove the lid.

The sound of footsteps and men's voices halted her hand. She recognized the one man but couldn't place the other at first.

"It needs to be dealt with, Ben. There's no doubt about that," one man said. "Damn shame it's got to be you caught in the middle. What d'you plan to do?"

"I won't be caught in the middle, for one thing." Ben Stephenson—without a doubt it was Ben. "Don't know yet what I will do. The man only left a few ramblings there at the end that I can't believe..."

The first man to speak must be Mr. Gibson, Lucy reckoned. He let out a snort. "Everyone knows you found him that way. Not much else you could've done. At least he was still alive when you found him. That's at least something. No court o' law would convict you."

The crunch of boots against stone sounded as if one man had kicked the side of the fort in frustration. "I shouldn't a told you. What I said...we'll keep it between us."

"Nothin' to worry about, Ben." A slight chuckle and something muttered she couldn't make out. "And it was me what figured it out. You couldn't a kept this from me, no matter how hard-headed or learned you think you is."

A long heave from Ben before he spoke. "I suppose it's a relief someone else knows, but this is where we let it lie."

"It ain't like you kilt him in cold blood. No one would ever have reason to place blame what you done."

"I done?"

A pause lingered in the air before Gibson spoke, almost in a low whisper. "'Twas the fevers done it, pure and simple. He died in his dear wife's arms. That's all anyone need know."

"Fool should have planned ahead." Ben's retort sent Lucy into disbelief, thinking it must be the other man still talking or did a third join them? Her brother's friend would not be so unkind and disparaging, not on this of all days. And then the words that followed shivered her to the bone. "Leaving a young widow to fend for herself without legal recourse and then expecting me to..." He trailed off his thoughts, uttering a word, unfamiliar and crude, likely one Mother or Ester would not want her repeating or recording in a copybook.

"Aye." This time it was Mr. Gibson. "And knowing how land hungry and wily them Swearingens be. They's the ones what should'a been tendin' him better in his last days, 'stead of frettin' over who gets what tract o' land. And then Nelly goes and weds to that—"

"Eleanor's marriage has nothing to do with this," Ben muttered in return, "least not that I have reason to suspect yet, and none of that concerns the rest of the county folk either."

"There's a few might see it different."

"Her reasons are still her own just as Zechariah's were his to make."

"You coulda had either o' them gals. Nelly's not so bad to look at and still young enough for you. You'd a made a good pa to them young 'uns, same as Zack done. He'd just been their big brother and got on with makin' his own family then."

Lucy bit her lip to stifle a gasp, wondering if they could hear her breathing or her heart thumping like a jackrabbit in her chest. This was her family they spoke of. Ben, her brother's dearest friend, married to Mother? How could he say such things?

"The old man cottoned to you like a son, he did." Gibson carried on, past Ben's guttural retorts, giving Lucy to wonder just how their faces read. She could always read the manner of folks better in their eyes and creases of their smiles or frowns than in the words they said.

Pressing her ear to the window ledge, she strained to hear while willing her breath and pounding heart not to betray her position.

"The captain's dead and gone too, these five years now." Ben raised his tone a pitch amid heavy footfalls beneath the blockhouse. "I still got the man's sworn statement and his gentleman's agreement. He names me, but I never intended to make good on it. Not even sure why I kept it all these years. Just so you mind my meaning here, best not be getting any ideas on counting chickens just yet."

"Whoa! I meant nothing by what I said, the other day, Ben." A light chuckle. "I know you got your reasons and if you choose not to take what's been offered free and clear—"

"There's nothing free nor clear in this situation." Ben lowered his voice and spoke again but too softly to be understood.

"Damnation and tribulation! I figured as much." Gibson laughed with a baleful drip to his tone. "And then there's this business with Shepherd. Mighty fine o' him to show up on today of all days, showin' his respects by comin' uninvited to a Swearingen burying."

"If he doesn't make trouble, neither should we."

"Who says we're making trouble?" Gibson retorted. "It ain't my fight nor yours. Swearingens got themselves into this mess and that's where it all should lie. So long as they keep their accounts paid at the trading post, what we care who owns this or that tract of land?"

"Precisely," Ben said, "there's no other course for us except to fund our next venture west. That's my only aim now."

Another lull enticed Lucy to peer over the edge, thinking they must have moved on. Mr. Gibson punched Ben on the arm and tittered through his teeth. "Aye, my friend, I mind your meaning. Reckon you done got it all figured out then. Just make sure you get this settled free and clear whilst getting something outa this for yourself, ya hear?"

"I get your meaning, Gibson," Ben replied. A sly toss to his head made Lucy shrink back behind her barrier. "I'll make out with this all right. Always do."

He clapped Gibson on the shoulder and both headed away as Ben continued talking. "I got a good deal invested in this already, and I sure won't let either of us down."

Lucy strained to hear more as they faded away around the corner to the other side of the fort. She plunked down on the hard, cold floor, not certain just what to make of all this. Ben had never been anything but kind to her, in a playful sort of way, even if he sometimes exasperated her like he did earlier in the graveyard with his teasing winks. He was always loyal to her family and served well and true in the militia under her father and brothers. He had taken supper with them and shared tales with her brothers around the hearth on cold winter evenings. Married to Mother? Preposterous! Perhaps he'd have made a better choice than Mr. Newhouse, yet the idea turned her stomach in ways that made her grateful, however grudgingly, for her mother's ultimate choice last harvest. Instead, Ben had stood up at Zack's wedding last summer and danced with her afterward. Nothing she heard just now made sense in light of all that came before.

On the floor lay the wooden box, forgotten during the men's strange talk. What if they knew she had it? Something of value from her family might be just what they were after. She had heard the words "investment" and "funds," having listened to Zack worry over the family ledger until Mr. Newhouse took on the task. The box contained something of value, or so Zack said. Something he wanted only her to keep safe. Impatiently, she scooped it up. A simple wooden box was all it was. She remembered her brother, one winter, carving each piece and joining them together before etching in the black lines across each flat side with a burning tool. On the surface, it didn't even look like a box, just a fancy carved block with no purpose at all except as a paperweight or doorstop. In actuality, it was a puzzle, a trick box with a secret opening. Both she and Van had competed to be the first to open it and find the hidden compartment. The one to open it first received what Zack had hidden inside—a lump of sugar maple. No one expected Lucy to solve it so easily, no one except Zack, who smiled knowingly at her as she maneuvered the pieces to spring open the top and discover the sweet treat inside.

Carefully she turned the box, running a finger along every mitered joint and polished edge. From the outside, it was a solid square, but if she put her finger along the corner and pushed it just so, a piece moved and displaced the entire side, allowing the top to slide over a tiny bit. By carefully working each piece back and forth, the top continued to open to reveal a compartment. She took her time moving the wooden pieces carefully, all the while something heavy thudded around inside.

Once the box lid slid out of place, she held her breath, blinking in anticipation of what was in the linen pouch. A tangle of blue and white beads tumbled out of the loosened drawstring and clattered onto the rough floorboards. She covered her mouth, praying the two men were nowhere near. A quick peek out the gunport proved she was quite alone. Lucy delicately grazed a finger across the strands leading to the center oval pendant, about the size of a small skipping stone. She had seen the necklace only once before, last summer at Zack's wedding when Phoebe had worn it. With frozen trembling fingers, she lifted the coil, draping it around her wrist and allowing the late afternoon sun to catch the shimmering jewels. The Dutch Lady, a carved piece of stone with the image of a beautiful woman in side view, her hair curling delicately over her shoulder, white as snow against a background blue as a summer sky. Such carvings had a special name. What had Mother called it? A cameo! Yes, that's what this was, but she knew it best as the Dutch Lady, a gift given to some Swearingen ancestor by a member of the Royal household, possibly even a queen. It was worth a king's ransom, or so Zack had often said, but she always thought he was teasing her with another of his tall tales. There were no kings or queens in this country, so why should that matter. She dangled the necklace, delighting in the shimmer of tiny crystals surrounding the cameo and interspersed between blue and white pearls. What would it be like to wear it? No one could stop her, though she didn't have any sort of looking glass to see her reflection. Had Zack truly meant for her to keep this for her own? But why?

She briefly held it up to her throat, feeling the cool weight against her collarbone. To be a fine lady at a royal court must be a grand thing. She only knew of such places through stories and one book of plays in Father's library. The plays were a collection of tragedies by an Englishman from long ago that told of courtly dances, castles, and lords and ladies. Perhaps they wore such finery as this. One told of a young lady standing at a balcony window secretly meeting her young suitor. Gazing out the window, she tried to imagine being a princess in a castle tower overlooking her kingdom. Or perhaps she was that young nobleman's daughter, like the one in the play, gazing from her balcony and calling to her lover.

"Where art thou?" She whispered into the breeze, then cleared her throat and tried a little louder. "Wherefore art thou, Romeo?" Yes, that was more what she recalled from the story. Mother had said she needed to be older to read such an "indelicate" tale, but she found ways to sneak it from the bookshelf and read it when no one was around, though she had yet to finish the tale. She had found the two lovers a bit foolish and reckless and hoped all would turn out well, especially for Paris, whom she felt rather sorry for. Perhaps Juliet would finally realize what a silly and foolish boy Romeo was and give her heart to a man who truly loved her and was willing to wait for her. Nevertheless, she did like the name Juliet or rather Julia. Wouldn't that have been a finer name than her own, even if she had been named for her dear grandmother?

The muffled sounds of footsteps and men's voices wafted from across the field. She dropped the necklace into her pocket beneath her gown, planning to mull this over and decide what to do later. After the incident in the house earlier, she would be in enough trouble for one day. Carefully, she replaced the box in its hiding place. The wind whipped around her skirts as she bounded down the ladder toward the main entrance gate of the fort. Just as she was rounding the tall log gateposts, she slammed into the buttons of a man's roundabout jacket.

"Whoa there, little filly." Strong arms reached out to steady her. "Just where do you think you're going in such an all-fired hurry?"

Lucy looked up into the smiling eyes of Ben Stephenson.

CHAPTER 5

A gudgeon, according to the local anglers, was any of a variety of small fish easily taken and used for bait. The term was also sometimes applied to those folks easily imposed on or ensnared in diverse schemes. Standing on the path leading out of Fort Swearingen between the blockhouse hiding place and this man standing before her, she was indeed gudgeoned, foolishly trapped and easily reeled in by none other than the one person she wished to avoid most this day, aside from her stepfather.

"Cat got your tongue? Is it now?" He remained in her path, taller and more imposing than she recalled when he stood in the firing line between two taller soldiers at the graves.

"I...uh...was..." Her mouth was dry as dust and scorched like a hot iron.

"Ah!" Ben stroked his chin, warily surveying the wall of the fort. "Are those brothers of yours in a game of cat and mouse again?"

"Uh...no..." Lucy searched for a reason to explain her unseemly behavior or a means to easily slip away from him without having to explain anything at all.

Surely he had seen her unladylike display in the house, possibly knew she was hiding in the fort all along and now teased her as if nothing were amiss at all. Perhaps he had slipped away unnoticed, except by her, before all the toasts. That must have been when he left to go walking about with Mr. Gibson. Could he have seen her fleeing the house toward the fort?

"Some fresh air?" Ben nodded, eyebrows receding above a merry gleam, as if considering the possibility. "Yes, I quite had the same notion myself. Things were getting a bit too close in the cabin. Not much for crowds, myself."

Lucy gazed down the hill toward the inevitable scolding she was certain to receive later and considered the lesser of two evils. Brushing her hands over the coffee-stained gown, she muttered, "I don't want to go back just yet." Not what she meant him to hear.

"Neither do I." Ben gestured toward the path. "It seems we are of one mind, then. Perhaps you'll accompany me on a little walk?"

A walk down the path with Ben in the waning, winter afternoon. A shudder convulsed through her, not so much from the cold, though the wind whipped around the fort and plastered her thin gown to her ankles. This chill was something quite different, both diverting and discomforting all at once. An adventure beckoned, and what would come later was inevitable. But for now, there was freedom and a choice.

"You're shivering." Ben removed his roundabout jacket, placing it gently around her shoulders. Only then did Lucy realize how very cold she was, as the soft wool warmed her. She inhaled the heady mixture of whiskey and wood smoke tinged with the earthy smell of sandalwood and lemon.

"Perhaps you'd best get inside by the fire. A walk can wait for—"

"No," she said, impulsively, "please, I'd rather not go back. I mean... I'm not so cold."

Ben nodded toward the gate. "The old fort's a rather quiet place these days."

If he meant to scold or threaten her, what was he playing at now? Being so easy and genial made no sense, unless that too was a trap. But something in the way he gazed at the fort spoke of sadness, longing, and grieving. Could he have wanted to run to the fort to find more than a misbehaving child? Perhaps he didn't suspect what she'd heard, what she now knew, even if she didn't fully understand. She swallowed her thumping heart and kept an eye toward the trail winding into the woods.

"I suppose the militia will muster soon." It was the best response she could conjure. "But then things will be different now that..."

Eyes stinging, blinking. Lips pressed tightly together. His jacket. The warmth. A scent of something that reminded her of something she'd sooner not think of, or rather—*someone*. Brother. Father. Friend. Who was this man to her now? To anyone, for that matter, now that their one true friend was taken away.

"Aye, that it will," he responded to her spoken thought, now forgotten in the snap of time she let her mind muse on other things. He had barely uttered the words, flat and almost too casual, while he led her away on the walk, her feet obeying as her mind still weighed against stubborn will and reason. But it was as if he read her mind and...*understood*...as if he welcomed this time to share a walk with her or to be far from the nattering crowd in the cabin. Perhaps they wouldn't miss her quite yet, one less body to take up space, especially a silly, stupid girl. All that mattered now was being wrapped in the warmth of this man's jacket, his kind smile and pleasantries filling her head with notions of what it would be like to be a grown lady out walking with a gentleman on any ordinary afternoon.

They walked on together down the trail and up the next hillock in silence. Near the top of the next crest, Lucy paused at a tall poplar with three deep gashes hacked into its trunk. Ben too came to an abrupt halt, wonderment in his serene gaze.

"A marker of Swearingen land, I suppose?"

She registered his words but was somewhere else now, lost in a memory, a happier springtime. Sunday after they had all returned from meeting, not like today.

"'Tis Van's marker," she said, not really to him or anyone in particular. Perhaps it was directed more to the tree itself, the river winding its icy rills through the countryside beyond the fort, or to something else unseen that might be listening.

"The southeast corner of my brother's tract." Closing her eyes a moment, she was there on that warm Sunday morning.

"You walked the land together, did you?" He was far away now, speaking as if calling down a deep well and she was fallen and lost in its depths. Other voices blurred her thoughts, speaking to her in words she must not repeat. Not here before him. She must think on other things so this time out together would not end too soon.

"Each spring on a Sunday, we always...walked the land." Strange words blurring her thoughts. Another time, another place in the woods where gashes marked a tree of remembrance, of things no one need remember. "It's a custom of ours once or twice yearly. We all walk the length of our own tracts that would come to us in turn. By walking the land we'd be certain to know it was ours and no one else's." She took in the valley between the barren trees, remembering that last year her father toted her on his shoulders before he, too, was no more than a pine box beside an open grave on a cold winter's morning and ever after, toasts and takes round the fire lauding great deeds.

"The best part was watching Van get bumped." Talking helped, to keep talking helped stem the tide of tears that might dissolve all reason and fortitude. "When we would come to a marker, like this one, either Elzey or...any elder brother..." She paused, the weight of his name, his memory, prickled on her tongue like iron.

"Bumping." Ben smiled, merry, but cautious. "'Tis a fine custom, indeed. Walking the boundaries of one's land and knowing it's every rock and tree like the back of one's hand—that is no small thing. On Rogation Sunday, was it?"

"I suppose. Sometime after Eastertide, I reckon," Lucy shrugged.

"Rogation, or Rogate, comes about mid-April or May," Ben said. "The ancient custom of blessing the fields."

"Just our way of knowing the boundaries of the land so's we'd ne'er forget." She brushed a stray droplet trickling down her cheek. Turning away, she tucked a lock of hair under her cap. "Last year was Tommy's first walkabout, he being breeched just the winter before."

"A young man's first set of breeches," Ben said, thoughtfully, "yes, quite a momentous occasion to be sure. And how did he do?"

"Oh, he didn't like the bumping so much, but Van sure enjoyed it. At least he was no more the youngest of us to be bumped."

Ben stood behind her listening. She could sense this though she dared not look back, lest she dissolve into sorrow and the strange words teetering on her lips gush forth unfettered. Instead, she rambled on, trying to sound somewhat dignified, the memories bringing calm and order.

"I have my own tract of land too, just over yonder beyond that crag." The words tumbled out, reassuring and solid as the land on which she stood. "Most of the hollow and the river valley are mine. The creek makes one border along to the western hills. From there it runs all the way to Catfish Camp."

"A fine bit of land, indeed. We shall walk it now so that you may show me." Ben moved to her side, leaning against the tree. They surveyed the ridge together in quiet contemplation, the soft evening light casting shades of peach and blue across the snow-patched hills. Lucy followed his line of sight, wondering if he though it as lovely as she did. He might think her a foolish girl, so she kept quiet, barely breathing as she worked out what to say next.

With a slight lift of her chin, she pointed across to the rolling bluffs below. "It's a fair piece of land, don't you think so?"

"Indeed it is," Ben said, impressed.

"Though I do wish it included the fort." She looked back over her shoulder, the blockhouse and walls peeking above the bare-branched woods. "My brother, Elzey, gets that tract now, I suppose. Or shall it go to Phoebe?"

The muscle tensing in his jaw and the hard line of his mouth made her wish back those words. Their walk had gone so well until now. She was always saying the wrong things. Would Ben berate her for being a willful child as her stepfather often did these days? Taking a step back, she eyed the frosted ground, waiting for what would come. He would know now that she had been hiding in the blockhouse and might even suspect the things she had overheard.

"I'm sorry. I shouldn't have said anything about the fort." She poked a toe into the snow. "Coveting is a sin and its right and proper that Phoebe get Zack's tract, isn't it?"

"Now what would a pretty lass, like yourself, do with an old fort?" He relaxed against the tree again, arms crossed, as if this was something worthy to consider. A mischievous grin played at the edges of his mouth. "Would you be keeping it for a place to hide from those bothersome brothers of yours?"

"I...I wasn't hiding." Blood flushed her face, pulsing at her temple and prickling her cheeks. He had seen her run into the fort after all.

Perhaps he had even come around to the gate to find her, trap her, and winnow the truth from her, but first he might toy with her, as an angler with his line or a cat with a mouse. "I only meant to…to be alone. I never…" She clamped her mouth tight. She would say no more. Let him ask. Let him prove she was there. "Methinks the woman doth protest too much." That's what Zack would say, when she tried to defend herself in arguments or when she had done something wrong. It was another line from the book of plays, but not the one about Juliet she had quoted earlier in the fort. It was another darker play about witches and wicked deeds. There were also the words Zack used to tell her about knowing one's rights. Something about wise prudence in giving witness. It had been written into the United States Constitution at its drafting, the year before she was born. "No person shall be held to answer for a crime, nor shall be compelled to be a witness against himself." There were more words to it than that, which her brother had made her learn, but this was the crux of the law that outlined her rights under the Constitution as an American. Would it help her here though, being only a child and a girl?

"At ease, Private Mouse." He grazed a finger to the tip of her nose with a conspiratorial nod toward the house. "Your secrets are safe with me. We shan't let the enemy ranks know of our vantage point lest they learn of our operation."

He was playing the soldier's game with her, the one that often amused her and her brothers wherein they each took on an animal name from the song about the Courting Frog. Van was always Colonel Frog with his sword and pistol by his side. Little Tommy was Private Bumbley Bee. While it actually told the tale of a strange wedding between a frog who first courted Miss Mousey, they had all decided it made a much finer tale for playacting when re-spun as "A Frog Went A-Warring." Lucy became Private Mousey parrying her sword rather than meekly sitting at the spinning wheel, awaiting her suitor, Mr. Froggie, like the song said.

"I no longer play such childish games." She contemplated the coldness of her toes in shoes unsuited for walking.

"Many pardons, dear lady," he said, bowing graciously. "I suppose I misunderstood your haste in leaving the fort." His reference to the fort, even with his gallant apology, clearly begged an explanation that she was determined not to give. "And I haven't seen either of your puckish brothers about."

With a smart salute she played along hoping to divert him back to the game. "Aye, Captain Rat, sir. We have fulfilled our mission as ordered." Better he thought her a silly child playacting rather than admit to overhearing his conversation and have him discover her secret gift hidden in the blockhouse.

"Excellent!" He said, playing along before being taken aback. "Captain…Rat? Is that what you think of me, Private?"

"No, sir." She saluted again, standing at full attention, shoulders arched back as far as her stays would allow. "'Tis only a name, sir. Would you prefer another? Big Black Snake? Old Gray Cat?" As she took in his discomfited, steely gaze, she swallowed and added, "When my brothers and I play at soldiering, we are animals from the song about the—"

"Frog that went a-courting? Ah! Yes. He weds Miss Mousey, as I recall? And a grand wedding affair it was at that, with every critter and varmint in attendance." He scratched his chin again, humming the verses lightly. "Without my Uncle Rat's consent I would not marry the…," he paused as if considering the verse's meaning.

"So…I am Uncle Rat, am I? And who pray shall I give consent to marry you, my sweet Miss Mousey."

"No one! I shall marry no one, sir," she said, with great zeal. "I am no one's sweet Miss Mousey. I am a soldier, brave and true, and live to serve." She softened her stance and laughed. "Perhaps…another name would suit the good captain? What shall you be?"

He frowned, running the list of various vermin and bugs from the song verses as he sang before reckoning on his choice. "Shall we say… Captain Muskrat then?"

"Muskrat!" she mused. "There is no such varmint in the song."

"Well, I shall add a verse of mine own then. Ah! You think the muskrat not a fitting captain? I shall have you know, soldier, we muskrats have a long history to our credit, most vital and propitious."

"How so?" She wrinkled her nose, not wishing to admit she had no idea what his lofty words meant.

"'Tis said it was the muskrat that dove under the primordial seas and returned with the mud that created the Earth, after the other animals had tried and failed." He paused, changing his mysterious tone to one more matter-of-fact. "That is, according to many a native legend in these woods and yonder."

She nodded, solemnly taking in his wondrous tale. "Then Captain Muskrat you shall be."

"Very good," he said, resuming his commanding stance and play-acting. "I trust you have obtained the battle plans from across enemy lines? You are prepared to implement them, Private Mouse?"

"Aye, sir," she responded, standing at full attention. "The mission is certain to be a success and victory shall be ours." She liked this Ben Stephenson much better. How he could turn so easily from the coldhearted man she heard earlier to playacting like a schoolboy was hard to fathom. But at least this Ben was easier to talk with and she liked that. He wasn't asking about her whereabouts in the fort or taking her back to the house.

He stroked his chin. "Very good, Private. Carry on." Together they laughed and walked on a bit farther down the winding path, talking of battle plans and singing a familiar marching song. Occasionally they paused as if scouting the woods for phantom enemies lurking among the trees or behind a rock or log.

"So, what are you going to do with all this land?" He returned to the serious, grown Ben once again when they reached the cove at Catfish Creek.

"I suppose I'll live on it and farm it, just like my father and brothers," she shrugged. "And I'll build a house of my own someday."

"A house, is it?" Ben skewed his face in thought. "Where to place such a house, ah, 'tis the rub. It should have to be a fine one indeed. Perhaps made of fieldstone? Or brick? Yes! Red brick fired from the clay along the rivers and streams."

She simply stared at him. He veritably read her thoughts, which was both intriguing and disconcerting. "I…don't really know. I hadn't given it much thought. Probably just another log home. Round logs. Not the square-cut ones like we have now."

He balanced a nod, side to side. "I'd say you've some time to consider it, that is, before you reach an age to marry. Or do you plan to live in such a house all alone?"

She lifted her chin. "Perhaps. If I found a husband willing to build me a red brick house, or even one of fieldstone, I'd not mind. But then, why should I have to marry?"

Ben frowned at her as if she had said something completely wrong again. She didn't want him to be cross with her, not after their game of playing at soldiers. "You think it wicked of me to say such things."

"Wicked?" he replied, eyes widened with surprise. "No, lass. There's nothing wicked in wanting fine things for yourself, and a piece of land to call your own. No one could fault you for being proud of what is yours by right."

"Some people certainly do," she sighed, breathing out the remaining tension held in since leaving. "I suppose they'll call me a spinster, but I don't care. Is it really so awful?"

"Is being a spinster truly what you'd want? All alone? No family? No children of your own?"

"I have my brothers," she proclaimed, "perhaps one or two will come live with me, or my nephews, Dusy's boys, could live nearby, too."

"Ah, Drusilla's boys," Ben cocked his head in consideration. "They are quite the handful, from what I've seen."

"I'll adopt an orphan, mayhap, or start a school," she countered. "I'll have my garden and my servants to take care of and keep me company. Maybe I'll free them and they'll want to stay and..." She was rambling about dreams she never spoke of to anyone before, and he would certainly consider silly girlish whims.

"But...besides..." She turned and bent to lift a stone to toss across the creek, something, anything to distract her from saying more. "Lots of people never marry. You haven't. Widow Tucker is yet single and lives alone. Maybe Phoebe won't remarry either. She shouldn't."

"'Tis not a bad thing to marry, nor is it to remain single, if that is one's lot." He shook his head sadly. "Don't compare my situation, or any young widow's to yours." When he turned to her again, the merriment had returned but not as merry as it had been before. "It's a bit early to be marrying off your sister-in-law, though. A proper mourning period must be observed." He muttered this more to himself than to her, with a dour look clouding his face, leaving her a bit uneasy.

"They say the American continent stretches for thousands of miles," he said, changing the subject, "clear to another ocean due west of here. In between are rivers interconnecting all across like a spider's web emptying into the sea. Did you know that, Lucy?"

It was the first time he had actually uttered her name since they collided at the fort. The word wrapped a layer of warmth around her heart like a down quilt.

He stood behind her now, turning to gaze across the river valley. One hand pointed toward the western horizon, now hazy with the glow of day's end. "If you sail down the Ohio, it is said, you'll eventually meet an even greater river that flows south to the Port of New Orleans. Farther north, there is another great river that some believe flows all the way to the other ocean."

Lucy looked askance over her shoulder, feeling his warm breath against the back of her neck, where the Dutch Lady had so recently been clasped. Her fingers gentled over the pocket hidden beneath her gown. It was still there. "You've been this far? What is this great ocean named? I only know of the Atlantic Ocean, the Indian Ocean, and the Mediterranean Sea."

"Indeed! Good to know your geography." He stretched his arms out before her, fluttering and then lacing his fingers as if to form the interconnected rivers. "But these rivers all connect…," he splayed his fingers out wide, "and empty into the Pacific Ocean."

"The Pacific Ocean?" She wrinkled her nose at the peculiar name. "I've never heard of it. And you're certain of this? You've been there?"

He laughed and pulled his arms back to his sides. "No, lass. I've not traveled that far, but someday. No one is certain of the Northwest Passage, as it's called, but someday we may find out." Ben shrugged, and a tender smile warmed his face. "You aren't the only one who reads. Oh, I do know your penchant for books. Can't get enough of them, can you?"

"Where did you read about this Pacific Ocean? I want to know more about this place out west." Now it was her turn to cross her arms in challenge.

"Where shall I begin?" He tapped a finger to his chin, thinking. "Captain Cooke, a great sea captain and explorer, wrote quite a bit on the subject. He sailed the South Seas, as did Ferdinand Magellan who gave the ocean its name. Then there are the maps and journals of the French and Spanish explorers."

"Oh, I do know about some of them," Lucy said, excitedly. "Pere Marquette and Pere Joliet." She rolled the French names as best she could, from the bits of French learned in school and from Mother. "Sir Walter Raleigh and Sir Francis Drake. They came to America and founded settlements."

"Indeed, you are well-read."

"My brothers told me. And I do listen when the soldiers are telling their tales, making maps, and such things."

Ben nodded, either impressed or in polite weariness at her musings. "Someday, maybe we shall see such places," he said, "and learn if the Northwest Passage is true. Some say it is only a myth, but who knows?"

"*We* shall see such places?" She wondered what he meant by this.

"Well, perhaps not me, nor you. But, some American. Someday." He bid her walk with him again as they headed along the winding creek.

"But isn't there a law? Something called an 'ordinary' that forbids traveling west?"

"A what?" Ben looked at her with a bemused smile. "I don't...understand. Oh! You mean the Northwest Ordinance."

"Ordinance." Lucy played the word on her tongue. "Yes, I suppose so. Means we can't go west, ever? Those lands are forbidden?"

Ben tossed back his head in a hearty laugh. "Yes, I suppose it is a law, but it does not forbid moving west, nor exploring such river routes. It only means..." He cleared his throat. "Perhaps we best return you home."

"No, please tell me. What does it mean?" She stood in his path, stubbornly refusing so move. She was beginning to enjoy his company, and she did not relish returning home quite yet.

"Must I haul you over me shoulder and carry ye back, lassie?" He affected a Scottish brogue that some still clung to in the settlements from their ways across the Eastern Sea.

"Tell me," she said, eyeing him over her shoulder, "or I'll…I'll jump in the river."

"You wouldn't dare. Now don't make me drag you back and haul you home."

He was speaking but the words rippled like water in her ears when she sunk down in a tub full of bathwater and all the world disappeared beneath the surface into the warm, soapy calm. She couldn't fight the words any longer, the ones from the distant memory, from the "Time Forgotten," but not so forgotten.

"No!" She headed toward a dead log transecting the stream as a natural bridge. She would show him what she was made of. Something there in the woods, just beyond the gnarled birch tree in the northwest corner of Tommy's tract, a flash of blue, a bird's feather. Had she truly seen it? A voice calling to her deep inside her head, wafting through the air and then flitting from whispering sumacs to stately elms. It summoned her toward the creek.

"Lucy, get back here this instant."

"Tell me or I'll cross this bridge, and if I should fall…" *If I should fall.* There the words dissolved like snow melting into the river. Ice to water, one substance to another, that's what her words were now. *Eau. Water. Nepi.*

"You expect me to save you?" He crossed his arms, seemingly indifferent, though his eyes widened with concern. "Enough of this play, child. Come back here now."

"Child?" Something took hold of her, a chill, a voice, a whisper. Was it hers? "I am no child. I am old as the river and strong as the current flowing over the rocks, smoothing, washing. *Nepi.*"

"W-what did you say? Lucy?" He stared incredulous, pale as the snow at his feet. But it wasn't only at her. His gaze shot between her and something else, something she saw, too. Shadows in the trees, midnight blue against the ashen hills. Had he seen it too?

She inched a bit farther onto the precarious log, creaking under her, yet she felt light as air, as if she floated with each footfall.

"Lucy," he said, strangely calm though with an ever so slight waver, "look at me. Do you hear me? There is nothing there. I will tell you all you need to know if you will please come back before you hurt yourself." He uttered the words as if he had the power to beckon her back, back from some dark place that circled in her mind. What did he know, this pale man living in land bought by blood?

"Listen to me. Easy now. I'm coming to fetch you," he said. "Nothing can hurt you, hear? Do you understand me?"

She blinked. He wasn't so pasty white as before, but he seemed to call to her from some faraway place, across the valley or deep in the woods where no one could ever find her. Words jumbled in her head along with strange images and the sound of rushing water pounding in her ears. Had she fallen into the river? No. Her feet still remained dry. The woolen jacket encompassed her like fire prickling her skin.

Ben took another tentative step forward. "Come now, it's time to get on home. This is no place for you to be. Please…come back, Lucy. I'll tell you everything. Only listen to me." He stood beside her now on the log. How had he gotten there when he was far away across the valley?

"A piece of legislation called the Northwest Ordinance, written to prevent the continuance of…," he took hold of her hand in a firm grasp, "slavery, into new territories. Mind your step and follow me. You're safe now."

When they were back on the hard, frozen ground again, her mind cleared. "Why are you telling me these things?"

"You asked me to tell you." He peered at her as if she were about to faint. "Do you remember?"

Remember? Yes, there was remembrance here in the woods, among the trees. Wings, strong and terrifying, but not to me. Only to those who do not understand, those who do others harm.

"Lucy?" He held her hands firm in his, perhaps too firm. Their noses nearly touched and she could see the tiny gold flecks like wagon spokes swirling in his amber eyes with dark centers boring deep into her soul. *He cannot know. He mustn't see what I see. The words. The knowing. The remembering.*

"Yes. I remember now." She tried to laugh but it came out a garbled cough, not light. She must have said something strange for him to look as he did. "I…didn't mean…anything. Just…a game."

"Do you know what you were saying?" He still held her hands but wasn't looking quite so deeply at her. He gave a faint smile. *"Nepi..."* He spoke clearly, carefully in words she understood but shouldn't. And then she remembered why.

"I am a warrior's daughter. *Pawajissa. Nepi."* She glimpsed back at the water behind her, the *nepi.* Shaking her head, she tried to pull her hands from his grip. "Stop it. Stop saying those things."

In English he said, "It's Shawnee. You...were speaking..." He cleared his throat. "It's no matter now. All's well."

"I was...we were speaking Shawnee?"

"A few words here and there." Ben shrugged, as if that were something everyone did. "You learn words very easily, don't you? 'Tis a gift. A rare gift indeed."

"For a girl, you mean?" Her wits were coming back. She recalled what they said together, but what did it mean?

"For anyone, I'd say."

"You...won't tell. I...was only...playacting." She wasn't quite sure if he could be trusted. Was he merely aiming to trick her? Or could he really be concerned for her welfare? Swallowing, she decided on another tack. "The Northwest Ordinance. Of course! I asked you to tell me, and you wouldn't. You were trying to trick me. So...I played a trick myself."

"Yes," he chuckled, "very clever and it nearly worked." But the intensity of his eyes told her he wasn't playing games anymore. He was trying to cajole her, as if she were some infant child or wild creature.

She shook her head, swishing her day cap strings against her throat. "Tell me more about it. The ordinance. It has something to do with...slavery?"

Ben studied her intently as he replied evenly in English, the other words melting back from whence they came, into the river of darkness. "Maybe we best go home now and you can rest."

"I don't need rest," she insisted. "It will end slavery?"

"For the most part," he said, still holding her in a wary gaze though somewhat easier. "At least in the new territories and any others to come west of the Ohio."

"My father promised our servants they'd never be sold and a few are to be freed by a certain age." She bit her lip, considering. "That's as it should be, is it not?"

"Some would say so." He eased back now, his hands at his side as he motioned toward the path. They walked on in silence, as if they hadn't stopped at the creek at all.

"You don't own slaves? And would never?" It was more statement than question. She recalled a conversation between Ben and her brother that involved a discussion about one of their slaves, or was it slavery in general?

"I don't own slaves," he replied, "As to never owning? Likely not." His tone more despairing than resolved.

She was, still trying to shake the shadowy voices lurking in her befuddled head and avoid glimpsing the presence hiding beyond the creek. *He can't see it, can he?*

"Lucy? Listen to me." Ben stared into the same copse of trees she did. Together they stood and didn't move.

"He...he is there?" She let the words slip and then hoped he didn't hear.

"Let's be on our way, shall we? It's getting too dark and chilly to be out this winter's eve." It was as if they had been on a pleasant walk on any ordinary Sunday, and hot tea awaited by the fire.

She nodded, meekly following and turning the topic back to slavery and ordinances. "So, you are against slavery? You would not move into a free territory if you owned slaves? Or would you free them and ask them to stay?"

Ben laughed, as if he were relieved, as if some spell were broken and all was righted. "I cannot afford to keep slaves, nor do I need any at present. 'Tis not a matter for us to discuss, at least not now." He stood tall, making her regret her question. "I've answered your questions and kept my bargain. It's time we returned home. It'll be dark soon." He paused and scanned the trees. "You'll catch your death of cold if we stay much longer."

His grip was strong and warm against her small hand as if he would never let her go. Though it was nearly as lean and slight as her own, his hand held a strength she could not match as he coaxed her along. They walked back toward the house now, with the day waning and shadows falling in muted patches along the woodlands and valley beyond the hills.

"Slavery is not a fit subject for a young lady, and we shouldn't be discussing the politics concerning it." He paced a bit farther before speaking. "Truth is, I haven't the answers and don't know what to make of it all." He wasn't only talking about slavery, but something else. She knew this but kept focusing on the path ahead, one heavy foot before another. His words kept her moving onward, distracting and comforting. Was that his intent?

"A man's property is his own, be it a horse, a house, or land."

"Or a person? *Kweewa? Hileni?*" His grip tightened as she spoke. "Is it right for one person to own another? To steal them away?"

"You ask too many hard questions. These are matters grown men wrestle with, and you but a lass of what? Not yet...what? Twelve?"

He reckoned her near twelve, did he? She started to correct him, but then the words didn't come.

"I will be...that is...I was twelve, come my last birthday, the sixth day of December."

"You've had a hard spell this week. The strain of it all is what it is. We'll get you home and speak no more of it." He muttered to himself —or for her hearing—she wasn't sure. It was only a little lie she told. Everyone lied to her, even him. Likely, he wasn't truly paying attention like most grown folks when asking simple questions of young ones. Somehow since crossing the unstill waters of the creek, she felt far older than her mere ten years. Even twelve seemed far too young. She was as old as the river and strong as the current. She belonged to them. Isn't that what the voice had told her?

"Indeed!" Ben surmised, as they reached the bend that led up the hill toward the Swearingen house. He held her hand high over her head, twirling her around as if in a dance. "A fine young lady. Never forget who you are. You'll be fending off the bloods and bucks from three counties in no time at all, if they can match your strong wit and ornery stubbornness, that is."

"Tell me more of this place out west." Her former mood returned, hearkening the sadness of the day. The funeral. She had run from a room full of people for some reason. In her pocket was the necklace. She must find a better hiding place. "Are there really such fierce beasts larger than a bear or creatures larger than ships and some that feast on human flesh?"

"You've been listening to the tall tales of those rivermen, have you now?"

"I read Robinson Crusoe and we've begun reading the *Iliad* in school. 'Tis part of learning Latin." She recalled other stories too, legends and tales told by the fire, ones that Mother would not allow, but Zack whispered to her when no one was around. He knew and understood what she felt. Didn't he? But she dare not tell Ben what she now realized had happened back there on the log. The words she said were not for anyone's hearing and certainly not his. She hadn't understood what she said.

Ben seemed to take her new discourse in stride. "Indeed, Daniel Defoe and Virgil are excellent reading for a roving mind. But what is beyond the Ohio none of us can say. I would not take all those tales from rivermen as truth, nor fanciful tales in novels or literature."

"But what if I know they are true?" she wanted to ask. But instead she settled on, "What do you recommend reading then? Books on mapmaking and exploring? I saw the one you and…the other men have been working on."

"I happen to be rather adept at mapmaking, or some have said. It comes with surveying, I suppose."

"I'd like to be a surveyor someday and make maps, but if I am not to go exploring on my own, I shall settle for reading about it in stories."

"A mapmaker? And a wanderer? I thought you had your heart set on being a landowning spinster."

"I don't really know, I suppose. I just like to read all I can."

"Well, then I may have just the story for you to sample next. It's about a youngster much like yourself and like another young one I once knew, perhaps."

"Not a ladies' novel. Those don't interest me at all."

"I would not be one to recommend ladies' novels," he laughed. "But I just might have a book you'll find worthy. When we reach the house I'll fetch it from my saddlebag."

The road forked, one way toward home and the other leading down to Catfish Camp.

"There's my marker up ahead." Lucy pointed toward a low ridge, recalling their discussion earlier, almost as if nothing had happened in between. An oddly shaped boulder nestled at another bend in the road winding down through the woods toward the creek. "It has the mark of some fierce creature from an ancient time."

"Yes, Fossil Rock. I had no idea that was your marker." He led her toward it and with one strong lift she was set atop the ridge facing the ledge with the boulder jutting from its face. Gently she traced the partial skeletal outline of what could have been the tail of some fearsome creature long before the first man set foot on this land. Lucy always fancied it might have been some ancient serpent or the long neck bones of a dragon.

"Is this where you had your bumping to mark your land boundary?"

Lucy squinted at the river shimmering in the setting sun, remembering another time. "I was not bumped like the boys were. Being a girl, they thought it not seemly. Van did try once a couple years ago. He said I needed some way to remember which boundary was mine. As if Dragon Rock wasn't enough for me to remember."

"Dragon Rock?" Ben gave her a puzzled look.

"That's what I decided to call it, not Fossil Rock like others call it. I like to think a terrible dragon lived here once long ago. And a brave knight slew it, leaving only this tail blazoned in this here rock."

"And that was your bumping? Telling a tale like that?"

Lucy giggled and shook her head at him; the intent scrutiny in his eyes was gone now. "No, that'd not made for a good enough bumping according to Van. I showed I was brave by walking across the creek on that log yonder. Like I did before."

Ben's face was awash in alarm. "That's what you were aiming to do? And you've done it before have you?"

Lucy nodded eagerly, amused at his shock. "Yes, indeed. A few more times since then as well. Would you like to see again?"

"No." He held out a hand to stop her. "We're almost home now and it's getting on in the day. We best be getting back now."

As she gained her footing down from the rock, a glimpse of a familiar shade caught her eye. She nearly slipped to the bottom had Ben not caught her. She stifled a screech, her heart pounding, more from what she saw, or thought she saw, than the actual fall.

"Easy there. Are you all right?"

"Y-yes." Her tongue felt thick again. Her eyes were playing tricks like they had before. It wasn't Zack she saw there in the woods, as he had been on a day not so long ago. That summer day they had come fishing. A flood of memories. The scent of Ben close to her. His arms bearing her up, encompassing her for just that instant. She felt safe, and yet something in her mind drew her far away. It was more than she could bear and the tears flowed.

"You're all right now. I've got you," Ben soothed, easing her down to the path. "Shall I carry you back if you feel faint? You've been through so much. That's all it is. There, there."

She shook her head not wanting to trust her voice.

"What is it?" He glanced over his shoulder at the spot where she stared. "You are not well."

"I...thought I saw..." Shivering with cold, she blinked. "It's just the cold."

"You're pale as a ghost."

Had she seen a ghost? No. But for just that one second she wasn't sure.

"You saw something didn't you? Or someone?" Ben turned to look over his shoulder again. "Was it...Zechariah?"

"It couldn't be. I don't believe in..."

"I don't either. But, sometimes, there are things we just can't explain." Ben leaned down to look her straight in the eye. "Lucy, it's no disgrace to think you've seen someone you've loved who's now departed. Nor is it wrong to give in to your heart's grief." His voice was comforting, washing over her like warm milk.

"I have heard that the Seneca believe you should not say the name of the departed." They journeyed down the path now. Lucy kept a corner of her eye peeled at the spot until they were past the point.

"Yes," Ben said, "not only the Seneca. Many tribes follow this custom. It is an ancient belief, as old as these hills, perhaps. Yet I've never understood the reasoning. There is no dishonor in remembering and keeping our friends close and recalling their names. It's as though they are never truly gone then."

"I did think I saw…something." She swallowed a croak trying to keep her tongue fluid. "And the other night. Before the viewing. He was there in my room. But it couldn't be. Could it?" She had seen other things in the woods earlier. Would he believe her if she told him that also?

"I don't have the answers to that either, though I have to admit, there were times this week…" He cleared his throat. "We've all been through a dreadful ordeal. Most likely we can chalk it up to that. It's all part of letting go."

Ben pulled a linen handkerchief from his pocket and held it out to her. "Go ahead and have yourself a good cry. Sometimes that's all there is to it."

Lucy could contain the floodgates no more. Gingerly she lifted the folded square and held it to her face as it fell into a soft, white veil over her nose. She was grateful of the dusk enveloping them along the pathway home. The sun set low dipping behind the ridge of hills as they neared the clearing where the Swearingen log cabin sat. She drew in a long, slow breath. For a moment she had even forgotten the episode earlier and the dread of the punishment to come.

Many of the guests had left by now, and only Uncle Joseph and Cousin Thomas would remain for the night. Ben would be returning to his room at the trading post. Or would he be escorting Phoebe home first? She would have to face whatever came alone now. Perhaps Mr. Newhouse had left for town already, but that would only put off her punishment for another day.

Around the back of the cabin, Noah led one of the horses into the stable. He paused when he spotted Lucy and her companion. "Why Miss Lucy, we was wondering where you were off to." He offered a slight bow to Ben and added, "Evening, Mr. Stephenson. I 'speck Mr. Newhouse and Miss Nelly be mighty grateful you brought our girl home. Miss Eleanor been asking after her and I's about to come fetch her back."

"Where is Mr. Newhouse, Noah? I would like a word with him." Ben affected a casual tone as if he merely wanted to discuss the weather or a matter of trade. But Lucy feared otherwise. The scolding she'd avoided in the woods would come now, and her wanton antics revealed. Her pleading glance was useless at best, yet he did smile at her with a conspiratorial wink. "Never to worry, lass. I have a matter to discuss with your stepfather and all will be well." To Noah he added, "If you see Mr. Newhouse, ask him if he is game for a hand of whist. But first I've something to return to Miss Lucy."

"I'll fetch him now, sir." Noah led the horse around toward the stable and disappeared behind the cabin.

Ben motioned for her to follow around to where his horse was still hitched to the post. From his saddlebag he pulled a small brown volume and handed it to her. "For your reading pleasure. Telemachus."

"A story?" She brushed a finger greedily over the tooled letters of the title. "Is it Greek? Or Latin?"

"You've read Virgil's *Iliad*, have you now? You know of Odysseus?"

"Yes, I already told you we're reading it in school." She squinted, recalling a recent lesson. "Telemachus is his son?"

"Correct." He winked his approval. "'Tis one of my favorite stories, a modern retelling of the son's journey to find his father. With his friend,Mentor, as a guide, he learns the ways of the world a bit better."

"You think I need to learn such things, too, because I'm so young?" He was neither her schoolmaster nor her older brother to be assigning lessons. He was...what? She really had no idea what she wanted him to be and that was most disconcerting of all. She wouldn't take the offered book, even if it might be a story worth reading, an adventure and a quest for knowledge, just the sort she preferred.

He pressed the book into her hand again, letting her question hang in the cold evening air. "I imagine we all are on our own journeys, searching for answers each needing a Mentor of our very own to guide us. And this book is certainly no child's play." He added, "At the very least, it's a story worth the reading of as an adventure."

It was as if he read her own deep thoughts. Or had she betrayed her feelings in some show of interest in his offering? She tried to affect indifference. "Perhaps it's unseemly for ladies to read."

"If you think so." He pulled the book away and tucked it at his side. "Your brother and I had many a fine discussion over its meaning, as well as the feats of daring and adventures in distant lands. I will miss those talks." He was lost briefly in some faraway memory. "But it is late and I do thank you for a fine walk today and your pleasant company. I do believe it has done me some good, and I had hoped to repay the favor."

"I...well...I do love a good story, and I suppose there are things I could learn. It has feats of daring and adventures? Truly?" She pressed her lips together, trying to take a good swallow to soothe a dry throat and think of something better to say.

"I would be honored to have you read it, Miss Swearingen. And I do hope you will always regard me as a friend."

A muttered "thank you kindly" was all she could manage as he handed her the book once more. She turned and ran toward the kitchen door. Reaching the cabin she realized she still held his handkerchief in her other hand. Uncrumpling the wad of linen, she noted delicate embroidered letters, BS, in one corner. Lucy wondered if this had been the handkerchief Ben offered to her sister-in-law, Phoebe, just before the funeral when she had cried on his shoulder. Stuffing it into her pocket along with the book, she no longer cared. It was hers now.

CHAPTER 6

"Hold still whilst I scrub you clean." Ester held Tommy over the washstand, aiming a dripping sponge over the boy's pale neck. Lucy smiled from the opposite side of the bedchamber, pulling a linen bedgown over her head, her own skin rubbed to a ruddy glow from the woman's vigorous effort.

"Cleanliness is next to godliness," Ester primly versed the children nearly every night as they endured the bedtime ritual since leaving the cradle. Lucy smoothed the soft linen fabric down around the angles of her yet girlish frame, just beginning to show the buds and curves of womanhood, but not nearly soon enough. Sharing a room and a bed with her two brothers was all she had ever known. When they were small, Ester dressed them all together but lately insisted Lucy undress behind a makeshift screen consisting of a quilt suspended over a rope draped at one corner of the room.

As if she didn't know the differences between male and female, nor was this a secret to her brothers either. After all, they lived on a wilderness farm among cattle, horses, hogs, and barnyard cats. And then there were the wildlings in the woods—beaver, muskrat, fox, and possums. The birds were quite entertaining, too, when mating season began in spring. They didn't need barriers to preserve modesty, but then they had their own coverings of feathers to keep them clothed at all times. The privacy was rather nice, but it still felt odd to be set apart from her brothers, to know that they were no longer equals in dress or manner of behavior.

Was it so long ago she and Van toddled about in their long gowns?

Boys were breeched, but girls had to wear gowns all their life long. What was it Ben had said earlier at the bumping tree?

"A young man's first set of breeches. Yes, quite a momentous occasion."

She had no such momentous event separating infancy from girlhood. Rather she continued in her long gowns with grow stripes to be let out as her gangly legs peeked out too far beneath the hem. Legs were to be covered if one was a girl, but could be easily encased in trouser legs allowing for more ease of motion in running, hunting, and especially riding.

The limp mourning dress lay on the floor after Winn had helped her undress. No one had said much about her excursion into the woods with Ben. To be safe, she had lingered in the kitchen until bedtime. Thankfully, everyone was too preoccupied with the events of the day to pay much mind.

In the opposite corner, Van and Cousin Thomas snickered and teased. "Ho, there Tommy-kins. You best get that neck scrubbed clean or you'll be growing rows of corn behind those big ears of yours."

Tommy turned a petulant pout at them. "Make them stop, Ester. I'll tell Mama on you or..."

"Aw, is widdle baby boy going to cry now?" Van rubbed balled fists at his eyes, a mock attempt at babyish crying. "Widdle Tommy Tinker sat on a clinker...."

"Stop it! Right. Now." Tommy stamped his foot and scooped a handful of water toward Van, splattering soapy droplets across the bed coverings and Ester's lavender-sprigged gown and good petticoat.

"Now look-a what you done! And after I just got you all cleaned up." Ester dropped the sponge and reached for a towel. "I works hard 'nuff tending you boys and if'n I want a bath, I sure 'nuff can tend to it without your help."

Van and his cousin snickered in the corner while Ester dabbed the towel at her dampened gown before rustling the towel over Tommy's head and shoulders. "You young 'uns mind your manners. And just look at you two, being nigh on to young men. Should be ashamed of yourselves and far beyond these childish ways." She dropped the towel on the washstand and wagged a finger at the offending older boys who sobered and began collecting their discarded clothing.

"Here, Ester," Van said, "We'll help by picking up after ourselves. Right, Thomas?"

"Yes, sir!" Cousin Thomas whisked up a discarded neck cloth and began wrapping it into a neat coil around his palm.

As Van gathered up his breeches and shirt, a slim object fell to the floor from one pocket, hitting the boards with a dull thunk of leather to wood. Both boys dove for the item, but Cousin Thomas was quicker, snatching up the slim, well-tooled sheath, laced with sinew.

"I say! What's this?" Thomas ran his fingers across the flap, releasing the rosewood-handled knife. "How'd you get such a fine blade? I've never seen its equal."

Van made another attempt to grab it away. "No! And you won't either. Give it here! It ain't yours."

Little Tommy pulled away from Ester just as she readied his nightshirt over his head. "That belongs to our brother Zack," Lucy's little brother ran naked as a jaybird across the room. "He give it to Van, not you."

A scuffle ensued as the older boys vied for possession of the knife with Tommy in the midst joining in the fight.

Ester dropped the towel in the bowl of water and threw her hands to the top of her turban-covered head. "One of you is gonna get hurt with that blade. Mister Thomas, Mister Van. Stop! Now!" She desperately grabbed at Tommy's bare arm, his spindly legs flailing as the two older boys tangled on the floor. The elder Thomas still held sway with the knife in hand, slashing steel gleaming in the dim candlelight.

Lucy rushed forward in an attempt to help Ester keep little Tommy from harm's way. "Van, please! Just let it go." She shushed under her breath, as forcefully as she dared, trying to keep the noise from penetrating to the floor beneath where the murmur of adults, still gathered, filtered up the log stairs.

If anyone, especially Mr. Newhouse, should find them in such a state, especially after her indecorous behavior earlier, it would be a worse fate than she had anticipated earlier. The strange episode she had while on the creek bridge with Ben still haunted her thoughts and wrestled with her tongue. She couldn't risk anymore of their stepfather's ire. What if Ben had told him all that had happened and the things she'd said? The flood of events returned to her now, as if from some recurring dream.

Somewhere in the midst of the scuffle, her mind registered the fact that Van had Zechariah's prized knife, the one he had custom-made by the blacksmith in Wheeling. How had Van gotten it?

Mr. Newhouse's voice boomed up the narrow stairs. "What's going on up there?"

Van and Cousin Thomas immediately froze, one still atop the other. Thomas still held the knife poised inches from Van's eye as he lay pinned beneath. He and Lucy exchanged a look of dread.

Lucy let go of Tommy's other arm and sank to her knees beside brother and cousin. She grabbed hold of Thomas's knife-wielding arm. "Please, give it up, Cousin." Her voice shook with the excitement of the moment and terror for the future—for the mortal danger that could befall either boy. It all combined in a flash of the day's events.

Thomas released his hold, and the knife transferred easily into Lucy's hand.

"What the devil are you all doing up there?" their stepfather bellowed again. "Ester? Are you minding the children?"

"Why...y-yessir." She swallowed, her throat bobbed and chest heaved. "They just being young 'uns is all."

"Merry well not in my house," he growled, this time closer to the bottom of the stairs. "Mrs. Stephenson has gone to bed and I'll not have you disturbing her. She is not well, and I am in need of quiet and peace."

"Yessir," Ester cooed, "it be a weary day for all us."

"Humph!" Newhouse growled, as if he could little be bothered with the day's events. "You just get them urchins bedded down or I'll come up there and show you all who is master of this house."

"No, sir!" she retorted, obsequiously. "They's all good children. Just had a misunderstanding as children do when they's worn out from too much visiting and reveling." Though her tone was obedient and conciliatory, her glare spoke otherwise to Lucy and the wide-eyed boys standing like soldiers on guard.

"Very well then," Newhouse grumbled, after an agonizing pause.

"I'm too tired myself to deal with you all. See that we hear no more of them till morning." His voice faded into a more pleasant tone as he bid farewell to the last few remaining guests.

Van took the knife from Lucy and resheathed it. Lucy closed her eyes in a sigh of relief, unaware until then how long she had been holding it.

"What the deuce is the matter with that new father of yours?"

"Stepfather...Mr. Newhouse," both Lucy and Van corrected in unison.

"Very well then, stepfather Mr. Newhouse," Thomas parroted back "He is quite the boorish sort I'd say, putting Lucy through such a trial as if she were just another one of his trained Negroes, too."

Here Lucy looked over and saw Ester stiffen and turn away to tidy up the room. She briskly picked up Lucy's discarded shift and busied herself shaking it out and brushing off traces of dirt. Lucy felt uncomfortable when references to the slaves were made in their presence as if they were not there or couldn't hear or comprehend what was being said.

"He's not so boorish all the time," Van said.

Lucy glared at her brother. "That's only because he's helping you train your precious racehorse." She turned away to study her oval face framed with brown curls in the mirror. She combed her fingers through the tangles, then reached for the brush.

Thomas shrugged. "How you stand him is beyond me. Here! Fancy this! How about you three coming to stay with Father and me in Shepherds Town this summer? We have more than enough room, and we'd have loads of fun together. With just Father and me it's rather dreary." He shrugged and tossed his head back with a glint in his eye. "But that all will change soon enough."

Lucy turned to look at her cousin. She curled a wisp around one finger and worked a stubborn knot.

"I'll be starting my apprenticeship with Mr. Stephenson soon." He motioned a hand toward Van, "Perhaps Father can arrange an apprenticeship for you as well."

Lucy paused mid-stroke of brushing her hair, "Mr. Stephenson? You mean our Ben Stephenson? He's the clerk at the mercantile, how do you know him?"

"Who?" Cousin Thomas gave her a puzzled look. "No, I'll be working for Mr. James Stephenson. He's a fine lawyer and serves in the Virginia legislature. I think the Mr. Stephenson you're thinking of is his brother. Father's been friends with the family for years. I believe he fought in the war with Mr. Stephenson's father. He plans to take me to Williamsburg this summer. Wouldn't it be grand if you all could come along too?"

"I doubt that would happen." Van pulled back the covers as Ester approached with the copper bed warmer. "We'll be needed here on the farm, to tend the land."

Ester held the long, wooden handle and ran the gleaming copper pan across the sheets, while Lucy held up the top covers. When the sheets were properly warmed, she climbed in bed next to Tommy, snuggling under the sheets of the trundle.

"But aren't your slaves able enough workers? Surely your mother and stepfather could spare you a few weeks," Thomas said.

Ester finished with the last bed and plunked the copper pan down on the hearth. "I'd say it be high time you children get to sleeping and stop this silly nonsense about traveling." The slave woman's voice cut through the children's chatter like a wick-trimmer snuffing out a lit candle.

Lucy relished the idea of a trip to a city by the sea. "Ester, what do you suppose Williamsburg is like now? Didn't you say you were born there?"

"That be a long time ago, now child." Ester fluffed up the pillows on the trundle bed. "I's not much bigger than you when I left."

A wistful smile played across the woman's warm, bronzed face. "Now, don't be forgetting to say your prayers." The children knelt by the bed, with folded hands and bowed heads for this nightly ritual before settling down to slumber—Lucy beside little Tommy at the trundle, with Van and Cousin Thomas on the other. Ester recited a lengthy litany, the evening suffrages she called them. Van often said they had to "suffer" through it each night, but Lucy loved the lyrical words.

"I will lift up mine eyes unto the hills…" Ester intoned the familiar words of the psalm with the children's dutiful responses. Lucy tried to keep her thoughts on the prayers, but kept recalling Ben's voice and the feel of his touch on her shoulder as they gazed at the hills bathed in sunset. Why hadn't she asked him about Zack? Maybe he knew about the gifts he had given them, and why he wanted them hidden. Her mind had been all befuddled this afternoon. He had sought her out in the woods. She knew it certain as she knew she would never see Zack again this side of heaven, but she puzzled over what could have prompted him to follow her.

She studied Van's face across the bed. He had reacted in panic when Cousin Thomas took the knife. She thought she'd seen a small, folded piece of paper fall out of the sheath that Van quickly snatched up, terror registering in his eyes.

"The Lord preserve thy going out and coming in forevermore."

Lucy heard a sigh of relief from both older boys at this final verse. She smiled at their vigorous "amen" reply.

The prayers done, the children crawled under quilts; Van and Cousin Thomas were in the big bed, while Lucy curled around Tommy on the trundle.

Tommy's wide eyes gazed into the woman's dark, careworn face as she knelt to tuck him in. "Ester, will you tell us a story, please? A story about Papa."

Lucy stroked her little brother's hair, thinking how Thomas always lured Ester into telling him a story just to forestall bedtime. It most always worked.

"Not tonight, Mr. Tom, you just be getting to sleep now," the slave woman said. "You children done had quite a day."

Tommy's chubby hands reached up to the slave woman. "Ester, d'you think Zack is telling Papa about us now? Up in heaven I mean?"

The slave's eyes misted and squeezed shut a moment before answering. "Yes, sir, I suppose he is now."

The day's work finally put to rest, Tobe's mother bent over the flickering candle aiming the delicate linen thread through the tiny needle. Her soft humming wound a benediction as Tobe scratched the dust of the cabin floor with a stick. Benediction had been his new word for the week from the Good Book and spoken at Mr. Zechariah's burying. Quite an eventful day, but work was never done in the meager solace of the slave quarters.

Sprawled across Mama's lap, a pair of Master Van's castoff breeches awaited mending before they became Tobe's newest work togs. Her skill with the needle would make them almost as fine as the first day Mr. Van had worn them.

Tobe peered at the scratchings from the stick onto the dirt floor. From the glow of the firelight, the letters took shape forming his name. Miss Lucy was teaching him how to read and write and he diligently practiced each evening when the day's work was done or whenever he could catch a chance throughout the day. Although that was trickier now that Mr. Newhouse took charge of things around the farm. Yet no matter how tired he was after all the work, he made sure he practiced before going to bed each night. With winter, there was less work and more time for reading and practice, just less daylight to do so, but that would be changing as the days melted toward spring. As he wrote he mulled over the events of the day. Something just didn't sit right with the goings on between the white folks.

"Mama, why do you suppose Master was being like that with Miss Lucy today?" Tobe scrutinized his work before wiping it clean for another try.

Without looking up, his mother sighed; the question hung in the balance. "What way you meaning, child?"

"Well, I mean telling poor Miss Lucy to sing like that when she be powerful sad on account of her departed brother."

"What made you think of that now?" Ester laid down her work a moment rubbing her eyes. "That what you been stewing on since we got back?" She shook her head and resumed sewing. "Child, it ain't for me to guess the ways of white folks. You know that as well as me."

"It just seems strange the way he treats his own kin," Tobe said. "Sometimes it's like he thinks he owns us all, even Mister Van and Miss Lucy, like we's all his slaves."

"According to the law, I 'spect he be in charge now. Owns us all, you might say." Ester slipped the needle under the seam and drew it through the worn fabric. Tobe knew this trick as a means to avoid tying a knot. He had learned a few sewing tricks from Mama. "It best all boys know how to sew too," she often told him. "Don't be countin' on the women folk to do it all for you, now. May come a day you need know how to sew a button or mend a seam."

"Mister Van, Miss Lucy, and Mister Tommy? They's all his young 'uns now, him being master of the house."

Tobe put a finishing flourish under the letters of his name, drawn to his satisfaction. Leaning back to admire his handiwork, he considered his mother's words. "That just ain't right. Something just ain't right about none of this. They's Swearingens, not Newhouse kin. The captain's name mean something around here. Mister Van, he not too fond of the new massa. Miss Lucy not liking him neither. Some folks at the bury grounds—"

"Now don't you be getting yourself mixed up in any of this, ya hear? This ain't nothin' to do with us. What I tell you about sticking your nose in white folks business? You just keep clean of it all and do your work proper like the rest of us."

"But Mama, they be my friends and I don't want to see nothing bad happen to them. Sometimes, I think it better living out here. I sure wouldn't want to be Mister Van living under the same roof with a man like that."

"Ain't nothing bad gonna happen to them young 'uns." Mama shook out the breeches to examine her work. "Both them kids stand to own a whole passel of land and be richer than most folks in this county one fine day, 'count of their pa. Ain't nobody gonna mess with the ol' Injun Fighter's kin."

"But if Massa Newhouse be head of house now..." Tobe skewed a quizzical brow at the woman. "Mama, that just don't add up."

"Do I look like a white lawyer man? How do I know any of this? Just you remember they ain't no friends of your'n. They be white folks same as the ones that own us. You just mind your manners so Massa Newhouse don't take a notion to..." Ester's voice broke as she turned the breeches to darn another fray.

"No reason to what, mama?" Tobe looked up in puzzlement. He studied his mother's face but figured what she might say. "Mister Van say I belongs to him so there ain't no way Mr. Newhouse can sell me or any of us, so long as it say so in the captain's will."

"Mister Van got no business telling you such things. He just a boy hisself. Got no legal training, either. But one day he gonna be your master same as the captain was mine and Noah's. He may be your playmate now, sharing secrets, but one day he gonna be a fine gentleman and Miss Lucy a fine lady wanting fine things and folks like us doin' for them."

"But my friends are different. Miss Lucy learnt me to read, and Mister Van say that before I turns thirty I can be free. The 'denture laws say so."

"Do they say that now?" Ester pitched her voice with her cocked eyebrow. Tobe knew the meaning of that tone well. "You ain't no 'denture servant like some in these parts be." She unwound another length of thread from the wooden winder and deftly threaded the needle. "Well, according to Captain Swearingen's will, I 'spect that be so. It what Miss Nelly say when the massa taken to his reward. But you can't count on nothin' in this life. He done write one thing in the will, but it up to the living to see it through now. Ain't no telling what the future hold. Don't go counting no chickens..."

"Before they hatched," Tobe parroted back the old saw he'd heard his mother repeat a thousand times. "But don't you think Mister Van would set me free one day? It do happen to some folks what's been slaves."

Ester laid down her mending and leaned toward her son, "Hard tellin', son. I won't say it can't happen, and it make me right proud you learning your letters and taking to reading like you do.

"Things could be a lot worse for us, even if they was a tad better when the cap'n were here." Mama bit her lip and looked past Tobe in that weak-eyed mist she got sometimes.

"He is a bad 'un, ain't he, Mama?" Tobe shook his head as he wiped away his lesson practice from the dirt floor. "If'n our new massa is up to no good, why do Noah keep spendin' time with him? Maybe he not so bad."

Footsteps on the cabin doorstep ceased the discussion. Ester laid aside her workbasket as the moonlight streamed through the entryway revealing the tall, lanky outline of her man, home at last. He staggered into the small, one-room cabin shutting the door behind him.

"Well it about time you got here," Ester squared off, hands on hips. "I s'pose I can thank you for getting home just a mite sooner than ya'll did last night." Ester's scolding facade barely masked the undertone of relief at having her man home safe and sound. Tobe too responded with resounding glee.

"Howdy there, Ester, honey," Noah slurred. "How's my sweet persimmon?" He sidled up to his woman with a nuzzle of chin whiskers against her smooth neck.

"Don't be giving me none of that sweet nonsense. I s'pose I should be grateful ya got home 'fore morning this time?" She spun around to the hearth reaching for a rusty pie pan covered in a tea towel. She lifted the cloth and placed a piece of johnnycake in a wooden bowl in front of Noah, now sitting at the table. The glow of the hearth cast her elongated shadow with a ripple across the cabin wall. "Here, get yourself a bite 'fore bed at least."

"Naw, Ester, I had my fill down at the tavern. Massa Newhouse had one lucky night tonight both at the card table and the cock fightin'. Bought me a fine dinner with his winnings. Even sent it out piping hot to the wagon whilst he stayed for one more round of cards inside." A sly grin spread across his face. "That ain't all." He reached fluttering fingers into his pocket as if he were a magician conjuring a trick. "Pick one, boy." Two strong dark fists were presented to Tobe. He knew this trick. He'd seen which hand went into the pocket, but Tobe also was wary of Noah's devices.

He thumped a finger against his chin as if thinking it through carefully. "That one!" he proclaimed slapping the left hand, not the one he'd seen slip into the pocket. He was wise to that trick.

Noah grinned, "You sure, boy?" Tobe nodded, knowing he had him this time. "Let's just see."

Opening his left hand slowly, Noah revealed nothing more than his worn, bare palm in the glowing candlelight. "Nope, son. Fooled you again." His fingers spread to drop several assorted coins clinking onto the table.

"Whoa! Pa! Where'd you get all that money?" Tobe ran the coins through his fingers, feeling the cool weight of them.

"I done told you. The massa had a good night at the gaming tables."

"You've been gambling as well as drinking," Ester chided. "What I tell you about getting mixed up with the massa's evil ways?"

"Aw, Ester, honey, ain't no use fretting over this. Massa he give me some of his winnings for helping him with his newest cock. Ol' Blue-Eyed Wonder. The feisty bird done right well tonight agin George Ferris's prized fighter. Ya should a seen how them two went at each other, a scratchin' and a peckin'. But Ol' Blue, he the cock of the walk now. Massa had no less than five offers for him, but I tells him it be best to keep it for more fights or breedin' later." He scooped up the coins and handed them to Ester. "You done countin' them, son?"

Tobe nodded slowly, thinking through the figures in his head. "One dollar and forty-two and one-half cent."

Noah winked his approval. "'Bout what I figured as well. Not bad for a night's earnings."

Ester counted the coins herself before depositing them into a stone jar on top of the rough-hewn mantle.

"Ya don't like how I gets the money," Noah said through bites of the johnnycake gulped down with cold chickory, "But ya shore don't mind how it spends." He dobbed another slab of johnnycake with butter and molasses.

"It ain't the spending concerns me, it's the savin' for our future."

"Pa, can I go with ya'll next time?" Tobe sat down on the stool opposite the man waiting for tales of the evening's events.

"Well, son, that be up to your ma, now wouldn't it?" Noah dropped his head and looked askance at the woman placing the jar of coins ceremoniously back on the shelf.

"Ya'll do no such thing, young man. Not while I still got breath in my body. No son of mine will mix his self up with none of that gambling business. It be the tool of the Devil for sure. Only leads to misery for one and all."

"It don't look like no misery nor Devil's tool went into that money jar o' your'n," Tobe grumbled back.

"Ya'll mind your tongue there, boy," Noah reprimanded. "Mind you show some respect speaking to your ma." Then looking over at his wife he continued, "If your ma say it ain't fittin' for you to go to the tavern then that's the way of it. I only goes 'cause Massa Newhouse needs me to go and I helps him with training and feeding the cocks. I'm a darn sight good at it, if I do say so myself."

"Pride goeth before the fall," Ester teased.

"And it also means I gets to earn a few coppers for myself and us too. Lord knows there ain't much to be gained by slaving all your life, but this be one thing I can do and I does do it well." He punctuated the final phrase and winked at Ester who slapped a wooden spoon at him playfully. "And your ma know it, even if she like her primrose pathways."

"Does Mister Van ever get to go with ya'll?" Tobe tried to sound disinterested while hiding his disappointment. He hoped that Van too was left behind to wonder at the ways of grown men. But he feared, as his mother foretold, the world of his privileged white friend would soon diverge from his own. Perhaps he could learn the ways of cock fighting and training from Noah, and one day it would be him and Van working together, sharing winnings, a few men's drinks and fine eats at the tavern. It wasn't so bad, not for some grown folks at least. "Did he come, Pa?" Tobe asked again.

"Tavern ain't no place for young 'uns. Why you be thinkin' Mister Van be there?" Noah chided and then softened with a tussle of the boy's hair. "Naw, he ain't come with us. Someday maybe you get your chance."

Tired satisfaction lined the man's face after a momentary frown. He cleared his throat and spat a yellowish glob into his mug. "I 'spect you best be getting along to bed now, young man. Tomorrow's another day with trouble of its own."

Tobe crawled under the covers of his straw pallet in the corner. Nestling into the cool, prickly softness, breathing in the tang of packed earthen floor, the sweet hickory scent of the hearth mingled with dinner residue from the iron kettle, he waited, willing his eyes to remain open, his mind alert. There was something in Noah's tone and a gleam he gave Ma that meant there'd be something whispered later. He had nearly drifted off when his efforts to remain awake proved not to be in vain.

"I done heard from Achsa," Ester whispered. "She say Miss Phoebe and that ol' Ben Stephenson from the trading post is up to no good."

"Naw, woman," Noah countered. "What you doin' getting in white folks gossip?"

"Somethin' just not right. Achsa always say Mister Zechariah a fine man, the way he be lookin' after his kin, especially the little sister. She say there's been talk of Blue Jacket comin' round again. She sure she saw something out in the woods, just a day afore Mister Zechariah gone missing. You know what that mean? And that man Shepherd back startin' up his old tack again. Now with the cap'n dead and gone, ain't no telling..."

"Blue Jacket?" Noah mused sleepily. "Now there's a name I don't relish hearin' ever again. White folks done made their treaty now. He ain't gonna challenge that. Not to worry. Injuns got more to worry about than we do, even if they be free to roam this land however they like."

"Roamin' free? Like heathen savages?" She rolled and adjusted the covers, rustling the bedding. "Ain't nothin' free 'bout that. No, sir! They's lost in bondage in another way."

"Now don't go preachin' to me, woman." Another rustle of bedding and a groan. "I got me a full day's work tomorrow and I's tired from a long hard day today."

"Huh! Cock fightin' and drinkin' is work?"

"I done brought home real money, didn't I? And hard-earned coin at that! Specie, woman, not worthless paper, neither. That be the best kind o' work." He lay still. Tobe figured it was all he'd hear when Noah's sleepy voice broke the silence. "Still, I do remember. Don't gotta tell me what that savage done to them innocent babes. Caused folks white and black a heap of hardship and trouble."

"No matter what color they be, he didn't care," Mama interjected, encouragement brightening her tone. "He just after ridding the world of the captain's kin. That's what he say. You know what he done vowed and he not likely be forgetting. Treaty or not. And now with Newhouse taking up with—"

"Shush, woman. I gotta be up early tomorrow groomin' the horses and such."

"I don't trust that man," Mama's voice softened to a low murmur, but Tobe still heard. A rustle of straw ticking and exasperated "humph" told of Noah's end to the talk.

"I raised that baby girl, I did." Mama again. "Her momma don't care squat for her now she's got a new man. I tried to warn her it wouldn't fair well, but she say we need to give him a chance. Well, he done had his chance."

"You done jabbering yet?" Noah rolled back. The rustle of straw and cotton with the heave of his weight crackled in the darkness.

"She helping my Isaac to read, and that's enough for me and I ain't gonna forget it. That all I'm gonna say."

"Good! Night, already!" Silence, then Noah replied groggily, "Tobe. His name be Tobe now. But since you're fixing to keep me up, woman…" The sound of a peevish hand slapping the frayed woven quilt punctuated Mama's next words.

"'Nuff of that! To bed, now. Hush!"

Tobe drew in a breath, fearing they may be talking to him, knowing he was listening.

"I done named my boy Isaac, and that be his name. 'Laughing boy,' like the patriarch in the Good Book. The one to lead a nation."

"Laughing boy," Noah snorted lazily, the rustle of straw continuing. "Like we got time to do much laughin' let alone worryin' about Injuns the like of Blue Jacket, land speculators like Shepherd, and such."

No more words were said as their breathing settled into rustles and moans Tobe knew well enough he should not be hearing. Soon enough a steady comforting rhythm accented with occasional snores assured him they were lost in blissful slumber, and so should he. Tobe stared into the darkness thinking on all he had heard and seen that day. Misty shapes formed like sugar snow. White into black bled crimson gray into blue.

CHAPTER 7

"Threes've got nothing to do with this, Martin." William Engle clapped another checker across two jumps, collecting his opponent's pieces. "Mere superstition, I will not abide. The man's dead, nothing anyone coulda done about it."

Ben Stephenson leaned over the smooth, oak counter of the trading post on another not-so-ordinary Monday, the usual company gathered to chew the fat and wile away a winter's morning.

George Martin contemplated the remaining pieces on the board, scratching his chin whiskers. "First Sam Brady. Now this'n." Satisfied with his next move he glinted at his opponent. Or was that intended for Ben? "I tell ya, it always come in threes."

"Brady died a full year ago after catching a cold from falling off his horse in a creek. Still took six months to finally do him in. Fought God knows how many Injuns and then done in by a cold in his lungs. But he still put up a good fight to the bitter end. Coulda happened to any of us."

The older man scratched his jaw, considering the notion. "Maybe so, but I say it's the Blue Jacket curse. The ol' Shawnee chief said he'd get every last one ol' Injun Van's kin."

"Them fevers nothing to fool 'round with. Comes o' living near swamps and bogs and sleepin' in the night air." Engle sat back, shaking his head. "I told him once if I told him a dozen times, the best cure for the fever is to take a witch-hazel stick and burn it by the light of the full moon. Then mix the ashes with boiled wine and take a spoonful every day. It worked for my grandfather who lived to see eighty-two winters."

Ben offered another round of grog and noted the chiming wall clock before burying his nose in the account book. A lull allowed him diligent attention to his bookkeeping while the old men studied the checkerboard at the barrel game table. Ferris Tidwell had been quiet all morning as he pondered the *Wheeling Gazette*, catching the morning light from the front window. Working his jaw on a bit of chew, he flipped the pages, shaking his head while lips moved in silent reading.

Ben's attention still on his books, he didn't have to see this scene to know each man's position and occupation. Life moved forward as if nothing had happened, or so he hoped. The routine of work and the men's usual gathering offered a level of stability and assurance. Once the talk died down, as it surely would, he could put it all into perspective—leave the dead to bury their dead and move past this maddening place. Not yet twenty minutes into their arrival and after a starter round of whiskey and ale, the obligatory pleasantries and banter turned to the events of last week.

"Superstitious fiddle-faddle," Engle peevishly responded, taking up the talk along with his next move across the board. "All my eye and Betty Martin."

"Leave my wife out of this, Engle."

"Just a saying." He shrugged and drained his mug. "But it seems such thinkin' must come with the name Martin, eh?"

"It was bound to happen," George nodded thoughtfully. "No witch hazel woulda cured this fever, if'n it be the fever what done him in."

"What you meaning now?" Engle's question alerted Ben, causing ink to splotch on the edge of the page. He daubed the pen onto a rag and wiped his stained fingers on his apron.

"I'm sayin', something just weren't right about all this." Satisfaction beamed across his face as if a clear win was in sight on the game board. He glanced at his opponent with a decided nod toward the shopkeeper. Ben aimed his pen toward the inkwell again in spite of the slight tremor in his hand and the increased pounding of his heart.

"Like I said before, Martin, threes've got nothing to do with it. Happenings come in the way they come, often when we least expect 'em. Just like this. One. Two. Three." Engle clapped another checker across the board, collecting his opponent's pieces. "Brady couldn't stop a cold turned putrid in his lungs. But he still put up a good fight to the bitter end. Just like you're a-doing here, Martin, but I'm still gonna win."

The older man adjusted his spectacles, rubbed his chin whiskers, and firmly restated, "Maybe so, but I say it's the Blue Jacket curse. No other way about it."

William Engle puffed a few draws on his clay pipe, nodding. "Hadn't thought of it that way. I s'pose you're lumping ol' Injun Van's death there, too? Five year afore?"

"Possibly." Martin brightened with the offering to his case. "Don't it seem odd, all three now dead and gone after a treaty done settled it all? Right on the heels of that savage levying his heathen curse?"

"I do remember if it weren't for Brady's rangers and the ol' Injun Fighter's brigade we'd probably still be having uprisings and trouble with them savages." George pronounced as he made another move across the checkerboard. "Stephenson? What you make of all this?"

Ben gripped the pen over another row of figures and was considering his reply when the door swung open and Emil Zehnder tromped into the shop. "Mornin', gentlemen. Ben, I'm here to pay my account." He plopped a small sack of coins on the counter. Grateful for the distraction as well as the cash to add to the store's coffers, Ben set about reckoning the account.

William tamped another measure of tobacco into his pipe and lit it from a nearby candle. He studied the shopkeeper at work as he took a few leisurely puffs. "Ben, glad to see you do your part with the militia at the burying on Saturday. You planning to stay with the rangers, ain't ya?"

Without glancing from his work Ben responded evenly, hoping his voice did not betray him. "Of course. Why wouldn't I?"

Engle drummed his fingers atop his chair arm. "Dunno. Just heard you may be leavin' us soon. But if there be trouble again, as some are saying, we'll need every able-bodied man. Good to be prepared and all."

Ben ran a smudged finger down the next column of numbers, oblivious to the sums and giving more value to Engle's words than he cared to admit. "More reason to remain with the rangers, I'd say. But I don't anticipate any trouble." A charmingly smile settled the matter, or so he hoped.

George leaned on one elbow across the table toward his opponent. "Aye, Engle. What sort of trouble you anticipating? Mad Anthony's treaty settled all that. Remember?"

Ignoring the jeer he shrugged and nodded toward the shop counter. "Glad to hear we can count on you, Stephenson. I'd join up myself, were it not for..." He patted his knee and frowned at the cane hooked around the other chair arm. "Yorktown took care of that for me. 'Sides, who'd want an old geezer like me shootin' Injuns?"

"What makes you think it be Injun trouble again, Engle?" Tidwell rustled his newspaper, looking up from his post at the window. "Treaty's still holding like Martin says. Injuns don't want no more trouble if we don't go looking for it neither."

William sucked his one remaining front tooth. "I heard some talk there's been sightings of Blue Jacket in the region again. You know anything about that, Ben?"

A drop of ink spotted the last row of accounts. "Not that I've heard." He tried to keep his voice even, forgetting the image he had seen, or thought he'd seen, flitting through the trees the week before Zack's death. Then that last day, the search, finding his friend and seeing...what? The image drifted and then submerged again into pain, guilt, death. Ben cleared his throat. "Times are different now. I doubt there's much concern, even if..." He let his words dissolve into a disinterested shrug to settle the matter. "Brady's rangers are equipped either way. Always are. You know that."

"Ben's right," George concurred. "Why look for trouble? With as many folks we got settling the valley these days, no Shawnee tribe, Blue Jacket or not, would dare raise their hands against us now."

Tidwell rustled the *Gazette*, jabbing a finger toward some pertinent headline and speaking the first time that morning. "It's official. Says right here. We're now a settlement on the way to being a full-fledged town. Name's to be Wellsburg, not Charlestown no more."

"Well dang it, if I didn't know that." George sarcastically slapped a hand on the arm of his chair. "We've only been callin' it Wellsburg for the past two years. Nice of the county magistrates to finally make it official now, ain't it?"

"Aye, that it is," William replied, "we keep growing like this, we'll be near as big as Wheeling soon." With another puff on his pipe he added. "There's those thought Zack Swearingen would fill his brother-in-law's boots as captain of the rangers, till this happened."

"It could fall to Elzey, the next boy in line, but I'm afraid he's all spitfire and no fire in the belly for taking his pa's place." Tidwell folded the paper and laid it on the windowsill. "Or maybe Ben here would take it up. He's next thing to a son, from what I've heard." The man leered at Ben in way that warranted a good cuff to the jaw, but prudence and calm were the better paths.

Engle surveyed the situation with narrowed eyes, puffing on his pipe. Small curls of smoke wormed through the heavy storeroom air. "Ben's his own man, now. Leave him be. He done his best finding Swearingen like he did, making all the arrangement for the burying, and contacting the family. Don't make him any more obligated to them. Seems to me, they oughta be grateful and owe him something."

Ben wiped an ink-stained finger on his apron. "No one owes me anything except what this account book says. As for me and the rangers, I do have some business prospects with Gibson and may be leaving for my first keelboat run down to Port Orleans come spring. I can't guarantee anything right now."

William leveled his gaze at Ben with a determined incline of his head. "But you'd consider a captain's position if it were offered? I think you would now."

Ben returned the look. "I don't recall it being offered."

The older man's chuckle dissipated into a raspy cough. "Fair enough, my good man. Say what you want but you got the makings for something more than a river-settlement trading post can offer."

"Keelboat run?" Emil Zehnder had been studying a crudely drawn map on the wall while Ben settled his account. Drawn into the conversation he added, "What Gibson got you into now? Those new keelboats are reckless crafts, and boatmen are a cursed and ungodly lot."

"There ya go, Ben," George Martin chortled, clapping a hand on his knee. "Zehnder's got you turnin' to piracy. A nice shopkeeper like you, if that don't beat all."

Emil continued as if not interrupted. "More than Injun troubles, or river pirates, we got to be wary of land speculators looming about and the government selling off tracts faster than a whore can lift her petticoats. Aiming to make us a full-fledged town may sound good to some, but I'll be heading west where a man can make his own way without federal law making a nuisance of themselves."

"Maybe so, Zehnder," George uttered, scratching the red-gray stubble on his jowl. "Gibson's Trading Post is going to need more fixins and finery with more folks, 'specially them lady folk, settling in the valley. You ain't been married so it's different for you heading west." He addressed Ben. "Means better business for you and Gibson, I reckon."

Emil scowled back at George. "That means more government officials sticking their nose where it don't belong." He smacked a hand down on the wood counter. "A ready militia will always be needed. Keep everyone at bay and ready to defend ourselves, just like we done back in '91 when Washington tried taxing us like another King George."

"Zehnder?" George said, "you bucking for another whiskey insurrection, are ya?" The prodding infected the room with chuckles and jeers.

Ferris Tidwell lifted the rolled-up *Gazette* and waved it in the air. "World's in a sorry state these days no matter where ya look. Why just hear what the paper says. England's making trouble with France after their bloody revolution. Now them Frenchies are making trouble with pert near everyone else, it say. Some new king they got named Bonaparte is aiming to set up an empire. Another kind of United States all across Europe they're saying. A Republic. But mark my words, more heads aiming to roll for certain. Wars and rumors of wars. Headed for destruction is the way of it..."

Tidwell's rant faded into Ben's thoughts of walking in the woods with Lucy. Ben had pondered that conversation a few times in the intervening days. Quite the little deuce, Zack's young sister was turning out to be. Where did she come up with her notions on world af-fairs? He probably shouldn't have encouraged her to wander off and hoped she didn't catch too much ire once she returned home. He wasn't exactly sure why he suggested a walk that day. Perhaps it was something about her, the way she looked so uneasy and vulnerable. He sensed she needed someone to talk with, to trust, but so did he. Had he taken advantage of a child's innocent nature and gullibility? Molested her sweet gentle thoughts by prying into matters that weren't his concern or cost her even more grief and comeuppance? If only he hadn't made that promise to Zack, though it was the earlier promise made to the old captain that bound him irrevocably to the situation.

"Adams not doing a lick a good either." Old William tapped the pipe bowl on the edge of the barrel. "Ben, what's your take on it."

Ben blinked, realizing he had been staring at William but not hearing a word he said. He cleared his throat, not wishing to delve into the political discussion. "I haven't formed an opinion yet. Only landowners vote in the state of Virginia. Therefore..." A shrug concluded his remark.

"If it ain't the French then it'll be them redcoats again," Tidwell persisted. "I guarantee it. That scandal with Hamilton a few years back should tell us all what we don't want in the next election and how close we all are to fallin' back into the hands of a tyrant again."

"Aye, you aiming to back Jefferson, are ya?" Engle led the new tack and the conversation turned to state sovereignty verses a strong federal government.

Ben was at least relieved the conversation drifted into Engle and Tidwell's court. Government politics was the least of his concerns at the moment. He closed the account book and turned his attention to refilling whiskey mugs. "You gentlemen ready for another round?"

"'Bout time! We've been waiting long enough, I'd say," George chided with a sly grin. "What you know about that business with Newhouse?"

Ben offered a puzzled look and a headshake. "What business?"

"Nelly's a sweet lady to be taking up with his lord-high-and-mighty. She could've had any buck in the county after old Nain died."

"Now hold on there," Ferris Tidwell countered. "What brought that up?"

"He's a damn Federalist for certain. High and mighty as they come. Said he supported Adams to boot." George raised his voice with each statement, punctuating it with a slap to his knee. "You heard what he said at Swearingen's funerary supper?"

"No, George," Tidwell said, in a disinterested tone, "what did the man say?"

With the full command of the room, Martin stood as if ready to preach a sermon. "He's looking to buy more land, even asked me if I'd consider selling the tract of land that borders Catfish Creek. Old Nain Swearingen and I used to fish there in Catfish Cove of a summer's afternoon."

"What's wrong with that?" Tidwell echoed.

Ben's thoughts again drifted to Lucy. Why on earth was the child wandering around the fort in the dead of winter without a proper outer garment?

"Nothing wrong with asking to buy land," George replied. "Just the price he offered and the way he offered. Just set me wrong, is all. And, he didn't take too kindly to me asking for the winnings he owes me from the last cock fight."

"He owes you too?" Zehnder joined the conversation again, setting a copy of the *Farmers' Almanac* back on the shelf near the map. "I been waiting a good month since he lost to my Cornish rooster."

George raised a calloused gnarled finger and added, "Well I was at the tavern last Saturday night and thought it mighty odd for a man who just buried his kin not six hours earlier to be out gambling in a tavern."

"Life goes on, Martin." Zehnder paced to the other side of the storeroom and studied the checkerboard neglected by the two other men. "The kid wasn't the man's blood kin anyway."

"Still, I don't like it." Martin returned to the game and plopped another checker across one of his opponent's. "He owed it to Nelly."

"The boy wasn't her blood kin either."

"He was Lucy's brother, though," Ben muttered the words before he realized.

"What's that, Stephenson?" Martin perked. "Lucy? Oh, the little 'un. Those three babes of Nelly's were everything to Zechariah, weren't they?"

"Any of you notice that stranger at the burying with Newhouse and Nelly?" Tidwell squinted and chewed his cheek as if considering a deep thought. "Someone said it was one, Abraham Shepherd."

"What?" Martin said. "My eyesight might be getting dim in my old age, but I'd have smelled that son of a bitch a mile away."

"He was there all right." Zehnder motioned a suggested checker move for Engle, but it was quickly waved off. "Showed up to lurk in the back with Newhouse. If'n I didn't know better, I'd say the man was there to gloat."

"It's been a long time since the captain died." Another checker move made. "Maybe things is put to rest betwixt the Swearingens and Shepherd now. Maybe he was there to show good faith and all."

Zehnder shook his head, slow and with meaning. "I doubt it after what happened the last time he was here. That business about the land grabbing, false deeds..."

"Weren't nothing false about it," George thundered back. "Old Nain done everything right under the law. He run Shepherd off pure and simple. Seems to me he's back looking for trouble, if'n he hasn't already done started it." In a conspiratorial whisper he added, "There's those sayin' Swearingen didn't die of no fever."

"No, George," Engle added, "it was the savage's curse. We know."

"Or maybe, something altogether different." Martin leaned in for another move on the board. "Maybe it was someone else wanting to do him in."

Ben frowned, the pulse in his temple throbbed. He began to speak, then clenched his jaw, reconsidering. "Perhaps we should leave Newhouse to manage his own affairs as he sees fit. Nelly has been widowed long enough taking care of the younger ones."

"Ben's right," William pressed on. "Don't be getting between a man and his wife. I trust Nelly knows what she's doing. She had them three sweet young ones to consider, especially once the older boy wed that Morris girl."

Tidwell cleaned the grit from under his fingernails with a penknife.

"A fine one, that Morris girl. And Nelly too." He cocked a raised eyebrow at Ben. "A shame Zechariah met his reward as he did. But maybe Newhouse will be man enough to keep the homestead going and watch out for the young 'uns."

A lull cloaked the room as the winter's sun slid behind a cloud cover, darkening the room a shade. William peered closer at the checkerboard. "Can't quite discern which way to move in this light," he muttered. "Stephenson? Trim another candle, will ya?"

Ben lit a taper from the stove and set it near the board and then turned to stoke the fire with another small log. Of all days, he wished the men would leave soon and he could mull over what he needed to do in peace. Ordinarily he enjoyed the banter, but today was different. Perhaps if he could turn the conversation around.

"Appears to be another storm brewing." He tried to keep his tone casual and even as he nodded toward the gloomy sky outside. "Winter's not quite done with us yet."

"With the likes of Shepherd in the valley, I'd say we're looking at quite a storm," George blustered.

Ben winced. "I meant we could be looking at more snow or ice."

"Could be a long winter to come yet before spring." Tidwell glanced up having finished one set of fingernails and moving on to the other hand. "Bad time for a young widow to be alone." The pointed look he gave Ben was clear, but he would not be reeled in so easily.

"I'm sure Mrs. Swearingen will be fine." Ben clapped the stove door shut and brushed his hands free of trace amounts of wood ash and soot.

"So formal, Ben?" William sneered. "You spent quite a bit of time out there. Always thought you and Zack were rivals in courting Miss Phoebe. Just figured now considering the circumstances..."

"Well you figured wrong," Ben snapped, perhaps a bit too abruptly. He walked back casually to the counter, picking up an empty whiskey mug as he passed by a cask.

"Meant no harm, Stephenson," William offered as consolation, though something in his tone belied his words. "There's still Sam's widow, not yet spoken for. Not certain what she's waiting for."

Ben ignored the comment.

"Well, I was just trying to help, is all, my good man." George leaned toward the checkerboard, an eager hand fluttering over his opponent's vulnerable piece. "I do think it high time you found yourself a wife. There ain't too many eligible ladies 'round these parts, let alone those what come with a fine dowry of land and property to set a man in shape."

"George has got a point there, Ben." Zehnder had been listening the whole time, even with his nose stuck in the latest copy of essays published in Philadelphia. He held his place with his forefinger, and a wizened look creased his brow. "Nothing wrong with a man getting his fortune the old-fashioned way. But we shouldn't be talking on such things just now. I know you and the Swearingen lad were closer than brothers. Better brother to him than Elzey. That's for certain."

"It was a terrible tragedy." George crowned another game piece and nodded smugly. "Terrible indeed, and speaking of which, don't it bother anyone else how hasty all them arrangements were made?"

"What you mean, Martin?" Emil Zehnder crossed his arms, the book still hanging from one hand, finger holding his place. "It's the dead of winter. The man was found wandering around near dead of fever. Nothing anyone coulda be done."

"Still. No doctor to tend to him? No sheriff to make an official report of death?" George shook his head. "Just seems to me, considering Shepherd turning up at the funeral and all, nobody allowed near him, not even the band of men that went looking for him." He shot another look at Ben, compelling an answer from him.

"We did what we could," Ben responded in a low voice, "There's nothing more to say. Phoebe…," he cleared his throat, "that is, Mrs. Swearingen wished to tend to her husband's last moments unaided. It was her right. By then it was beyond anyone's control."

"Aye, George," Zehnder argued. "Why would we need nosy folks like sheriffs and doctors poking around? It's private family business."

George let the matter drop with the final checker he moved to secure his win. "Land grabbers like Shepherd and possibly this Newhouse blood—if that's what they be. As I say, they are the least of our worries. Some are saying there's been reports of Shawnee warriors in the region again and another possible uprising by Blue Jacket."

"Now don't go spreading more rumors and getting people scared for no good reason." William collected the checker pieces and reset the board. "Mad Anthony's treaty settled all that, and after the last battle, I don't think those savages will be trying anything else for some time, if ever."

"Still, we can't forget what happened at Wabash with St. Clair."

Wabash. One word that brought a firestorm of memories and sensations Ben kept carefully at bay. Too many lives were lost. Innocent camp followers, women and children amidst the soldiers who fought desperately to protect them. He had come west to Wellsburg determined to make a difference, a new way for himself, to forget and begin again. Yet no matter where he went, death, guilt, and responsibility were never far behind.

"It's the curse, I tell you." It was George ranting again, somewhere in the distance of the log storehouse while Ben mused elsewhere, staring at ink blotches on his account book. Curses. Screams. Blood. Wabash. George's words underscored it all here in the storeroom.

"That savage isn't about to forget. He levied that curse over one of their heathen fires. And just look what's done? The captain shot hisself." He started ticking off the usual list.

"That was deemed an accident, Martin," Zehnder growled his words as he returned the book and pinched a bite of chew from his pouch.

"Aye, mayhap it was, but still mighty strange, happening within a year of the curse. Then there was Sam Brady."

"Who caught a cold from a fall in icy waters, yes, we know," Zehnder dismissed with a shrug. "Coulda happened to any of us."

"And," George resumed, a pointed emphasis to his tone, "now the oldest boy is found near dead in the woods and it's not clear exactly when and how the boy died."

Zehnder took three long strides to the counter and clapped down a few coins, which Ben absently slid off the counter into the cashbox. "Time to head out, gentlemen." Turning to George he offered one last remark. "I say leave it be. If Ben ain't worried about it and the Swearingens aren't making a fuss over it, then why should we? No one had cause to hurt a kind soul like Zechariah, and any notion of

Blue Jacket or any other Shawnee, Pawnee, Cherokee, or any other 'kee' out there stirring up trouble is just a bunch of hogwash."

The men all concurred, chuckling and murmuring, save for George Martin who stood and ambled toward his cane. Ben returned to his next task of sorting mail. The clock chimed the hour, signaling the end of the morning.

Martin headed toward the door with one last gloat to Engle over having bested him again at checkers. Agreeing on another match for another day, the two men filed out of the door behind Zehnder and Tidwell, anticipating the noon meals waiting on the hearths at their homes.

The welcomed silence and solitude was brief, broken by the tinkling of the bell and a blast of cold air through the opened door. A pair of snow-crusted, leather boots was the first thing Ben saw as he glanced over the letters he had been sorting. He might have thought he'd seen a ghost, given the familiar gait, stately height, and broad, strong features of this latest customer, so alike the captain and his brother were.

Ben remembered his manners, dropping the letters as he moved around the wood-slab counter to greet Joseph Swearingen with a firm handshake. "Colonel, sir, 'tis good to see you again. What brings you here this fine morning?"

The older man removed his tall beaver hat and placed it under his arm, before warmly taking the proffered hand.

"Good day, Benjamin. Thought I'd stop by and see this fine shop of yours." Joseph surveyed the store. "It appears you've made out well for yourself, I see."

"Oh, I can't take all the credit." Ben gestured toward a stool and then sat across from him. "The trading post is actually owned by Josiah Gibson. I'm working as his clerk right now, but in due time, a shop of my own."

Joseph nodded approvingly. "Yes, Ben, I'd say you have a good shot at it."

Ben's face tightened along with the spot just under his ribs. "I'd hoped to speak with you before you returned east. The events of the other day were..."

"Yes, funerals are not the best place to discuss business. Too many emotions at play. Too many people. Though it was a comfort to the family to see a fair show of mourners."

"Zechariah was well thought of, to be sure."

The colonel cocked a shrewd eye. "The Swearingen name commands a great deal of respect and...dare I say? Tragedy often brings out the curiosity seekers."

Ben remained silent, considering the words and letting them linger in the smoky air that held a remnant of the men's pipes mingled with the smell of stale whiskey.

"I'll come right to the point," the colonel said, seeming to sense Ben's reticence to talk. "I know my departed nephew was filing a suit to settle my brother's estate. I came to see what, if anything, you know of this?"

Ben bit a fingernail into his thumb. There was no avoiding this question and certainly not from Colonel Swearingen. "You're aware of Abraham Shepherd's claim I gather?"

The elder man nodded, prompting Ben to continue.

"Zack told me very little. Only that he was planning to square things away once and for all. I believe he was gathering evidence, building a case. And then...," Ben released a long, slow breath, choosing his words carefully, "he never expected things to turn out as they did."

"Yes, I'm sure he assumed there would be time." Joseph cast a faraway look beyond Ben's shoulder. "A young man, so recently wed to a lovely young bride. I gather he had far more on his mind this past year than the legal matters to wrangle out family land claims."

"I want you to know, sir...," Ben began and paused to clear a choke from his voice, "I did all I could. I only wish..."

A raised palm and a slight, weary smile prefaced his soft words. "We are ever grateful for all you did for our brother's heirs. Each of our lives hangs by such a narrow thread." He gazed, unfocused at the floorboards before closing his eyes. "As for man, his days are as the grass. My brother never expected to leave a young widow with three small children either. Truth be told, I did advise him not to marry such a young thing half his age. After losing two other wives, who left him sons and one daughter, I saw little need for it. But my brother was a stubborn one."

Ben swiped a hand across his chin. "The captain was fond of the ladies."

"That he was," Joseph slapped his knee. "I couldn't fault him for that, I suppose, though he could have been a tad more discriminating."

The unspoken words were enough. Ben thought of the two bastard children the old man had claimed in his will and several others he left neglected, perhaps never even knew of. Phoebe's desperate scheme laid out days before her husband's death still festered.

"My Hannah and I offered to take the wee ones after Van's death, but Nelly would have none of it." A spark lit the man's eyes, even though sadness was carved into every crevice in his age-worn face. "That incident with Blue Jacket," he added after a brief pause accented by the crackle of wood in the iron stove, "might've been far too recent, I suppose. I can't blame a mother for wanting to keep her child near, but given the circumstances, Eleanor's sensibilities..." He recrossed one leg over the other with a middling wave of his hand. "Well, I shouldn't say."

"They've done all right," Ben offered, weighing how much to tell of what he knew and what he saw there in the woods with Lucy. "All of them, your niece and your nephews."

"And I imagine our Zechariah was a large part of that." He narrowed his eyes as if deducing answers Ben was not able to give.

"He did his best, sir. I can assure you of that."

"You were both there that night, weren't you?" The question came at Ben like a knife slicing into a boil, though in truth it had been lingering in the air since the colonel's arrival. "You saw?"

"I...don't really know what I saw." He looked away. "We saved her. Isn't that enough? Perhaps we should have been there sooner...for the others."

Joseph leaned back in his chair, hand on the top of his cane. "I regret bringing all this up again. We are all ever in your debt. Not a night has gone by I haven't prayed that sweet baby girl grows up safe and strong, unmolested by such memories." He shuddered.

Another sight came to Ben that he preferred not to revisit—not the one this man mentioned, but another. Both visions now swarmed the room in the silence as he searched for something to say, a change in discourse, to resolve it politely and send the colonel on his way. He would need to deal with matters but on his terms and without revealing more than was necessary. Ben considered the colonel raising the captain's three youngest and that brought another lad to mind.

"I had a chance to speak with your son at the gravesite. He's grown to be near a man from last I saw."

Joseph's face spread with a proud smile. "Thomas. Yes, my only child. Raising him alongside my brother's three would have been good for him as well, I don't deny it." He sighed and spread his fingers flat against the table. "As it turned out, I lost my Hannah just a year later, so perhaps 'tis God's providence that my niece and nephews remained with their mother. Lucy, especially." He extended a dismissive hand. "What would I know of raising a young lady?"

"I was sorry to hear of your wife, sir." Ben explained further when the man looked puzzled, "My mother wrote me about her passing."

"I do thank you," he said, sorrow in his winsome eyes, "'twas good of you to do so, Ben.

And may I say it pleases me to hear you are in correspondence with your family."

"Mother writes," was all Ben would admit to, then added, "Mrs. Swearingen was a most kind woman," hoping to turn the conversation to cordial matters.

"Yes that she was. I never could bring myself to marry another." He punctuated his words as if for a double meaning. "Though, perhaps it would have been best for young Thomas. Bachelorhood has its merits, though I certainly wouldn't advise that course for every man."

"And there are many widowers who would agree," Ben said, lightheartedly. "Your brother, for example."

Joseph conceded the point, punctuated with a hearty, if sardonic, smile. "My brother. Yes. Two wives he buried and grieved over before wedding a third and final time. I was witness to each." He looked away, wistfully remembering, before turning with intent. "Ben, when are you going to come home? Stop all this nonsense about making your way west. Put the past behind you and make peace with your father."

There it was. The reason he had come and the topic looming in the air since his arrival. His face hardened, though he kept his words leveled. "Is that what you came to discuss, sir? Did my father send you all this way to convey that message and retrieve his prodigal son home?"

"Now you know better than that," Joseph countered. "He's a stubborn Scotsman and you are your father's son, more so than your brothers ever were."

"Am I to presume Jamie or Will sent you then?" Ben brushed an imperceptible speck from the table. He had the floor still to sweep, the whiskey mugs to wash, and firewood to stack, gotten in trade this morning. "Some things don't change. Besides, I'm doing right well out here. Maybe not as well as Jamie with his political aspirations. You'd think my Father would be content I'm building my fortune one shilling at a time."

"I'm not here at either of your brother's bidding either, though I do know James is concerned for your welfare." The colonel studied him hard and long. "When you came and asked my help, I told you then, I'd needed no explanation and I stand by that now. You were a young man dealt a bad hand. No one could have foreseen—"

"I truly don't think on it much." Ben stood and tucked a barstool snug under the counter. "I've a life here now, and it's a good life." With all there was to do this morning his patience was wearing thinner than the hair on this old man's pate. "I'm the third son of a small yeoman farmer. A division of a small farm is not enough to prosper on. Jamie has his political ambitions and William can have the farm. And I—"

"A deputy sheriff!" Joseph interjected, brightening. "Would that entice you home? You'd have a good salary and prospects."

Ben made no reply, his back toward the colonel as he collected mugs and tankards and arranged them on the bar. "You came to discuss the younger Swearingens' welfare? The concerns about their inheritance? Land rights? That is the more pressing matter, isn't it?"

Joseph relaxed into a conciliatory smile. "Aye, that I did, among other matters. First, what do you know of my sister-in-law's new husband? How is he in regards to the children's welfare?"

All the drained whiskey mugs stood in a row at one end of the bar.

He rubbed a thumb along the handle contemplating a subject no less troublesome than the colonel's intriguing offer. Deputy Sheriff? He could not let such matters distract him now, or could he? Absently, he picked up a cloth, wiping it across the smooth wood.

"John Newhouse arrived in the valley just before midsummer. Took a room at the tavern for a while and soon after began courting Mrs. Swearingen."

"A New Englander, I understand? Boston?"

"So they say." Where was he headed with this line of tack? It could only have one purpose and he would not take the bait. "There's no crime in that."

"I never said there was," Joseph leveled his tone. "I spoke with the gentleman at the funeral repast, not nearly as long as I should have, but far longer than I cared to. I can't say for sure, but something does not set rightly with all this."

He sat back, drumming fingers on the table, a pensive expression setting his rounded chin and slack jowl. "I by no means intend to draw you into our family affairs unduly. God knows you've had enough trouble of your own. I only hoped—"

"You're calling up a favor." Ben crumpled the dampened rag in his hand with one more swipe across the counter. "And I do owe you that." Among a growing list of Swearingens he was now in debt to, it would seem.

Leaning back, shoulders squared, the colonel replied, "I'm not here to hold you to any obligation. I'm an old man who's seen far and away enough troubles. I'm here for my own reasons. I'd hoped we were of one mind in our concern for certain innocents who as yet are unable to defend themselves. You're oath as a militiaman, which from what I've seen has the makings of a most excellent deputy sheriff...but we'll return to that later."

"I am well aware of my sworn oath." Though, what would this man think if he knew the truth of the deceptions he had perpetrated under the guise of keeping the peace and protecting the people he served? "Your nephew had his concerns and possibly for good reason." Ashes littered the floor from the men's pipes earlier, their words still lingered in the air: *"Earning a fortune by old-fashioned means."* Phoebe's desperation still taunted his thoughts. "He took ample care of his younger brothers and sister, even after his marriage. He did what he could, even with the malaria taking its toll."

"Can I trust this new husband of Nelly's to do as well for them? To be entrusted with their care and welfare?"

"I don't see that you have much choice, sir."

"You were absent from the cabin for a time the other day? As was my niece, I gather?"

Ben was taken aback, uncertain whether he was being accused of incivility or commended for gallantry. "I took a walk to get some fresh air. On the way back I did happen upon Lucy. She apparently left the house to play in the fort. Probably just needed to be alone, considering the occasion and overflowing company in the house. Perfectly understandable."

"And you comforted her?" The tone was smooth, matter of fact, though Ben couldn't help but feel an accusation lay hidden.

"I spoke with her, yes. She was very fond of Zack, and he set a lot of store by that young lass." He finished wiping the bar with a cloth and tossed it into a bucket. "I felt she needed a friend, someone to talk with." Her odd behavior that day, the incident crossing the creek, he should tell Joseph, but would he understand? Would he even believe him? "She's a child, a very bright and…singular child, but still…I…"

Joseph gestured his understanding. "I'm accusing you of nothing. Certainly no impropriety. No one who knows you well could think the worse of you." He walked to the window where the soft winter haze washed over his venerable face. "She is a willful, impetuous creature. She'll need a strong hand, though I don't know that this Newhouse is the sort."

"Your concern is more for your brother's land interest, I take it?" Ben hoped to steer the direction of the conversation and find the purpose to his visit. "The girl's interest is her mother's affair from here." He suspected Eleanor had little use for the child, or else Lucy would not have been out wandering in such a state as he found her. But who was he to question a mother's care for her child?

Joseph closed his eyes, nodding, "You think me so mercenary? I care so little for my nephews and niece? I know of Nelly's fits of melancholia since my brother's death. I admit I should have been more attentive, but..."

"I am not here to judge you anymore than you are my...misbegotten past." Ben trailed off his words and quickly resumed the matter at hand. "I can say, Zechariah had plans for a lawsuit. We were in the midst of making plans, securing deeds, evidence."

"He had reason for concern then? Just as I suspected." A pound of his fist jostled the table. "You were with him when he...when they found him?"

"Y-yes." Ben glanced over his shoulder and turned toward the shelves behind the counter. Jars of nails, skeins of thread, and yards of rope. Papers of pins all in line. Though turned away, he knew Joseph's eye was unrelenting, questioning. He would not revisit those last moments again. Not just yet.

"He was yet alive?" Joseph persisted. "When you found him? Please, I must know. There at the end, did he say anything important or... lucid?" His voice nearly cracked on the final word.

"His last words to me were to look after the younger children." Ben measured his words at Swearingen's beseeching eyes. "I wish there was more I could have done, but there wasn't. I respected Phoebe's wishes to tend her husband's last moments alone." A small lie, did it matter now?

Joseph smiled in reassurance. "You're a good man, Ben. I'm proud of what you've done here. And I know you'll be watching over the matter and keep me informed. That is all I ask. Do right by my brother's family and land. I shall make it worth your while in due course. You can be assured of that."

The old colonel rose painfully to his feet and leaned on his cane to shake Ben's hand. "But I now must bid you adieu and take no more of your time."

"I foresee only a matter of filing a few legal documents to ensure claims and all will be well." Ben said nothing of Phoebe's concerns, but there was no need. The old man was more focused on a little girl's fortune than his nephew's widow. Gibson's words had echoed Phoebe's earlier about the Swearingens' elitist notion of family.

"We'll be in touch, to be sure." He took his beaver hat and hesitated at the door. "The offer still stands, Ben. As county magistrate, I'm seeking men I can count on to keep the peace. Perhaps you'll pay a visit home soon. No one blames you, Ben. It's all in the past."

Ben winced; his tongue clung dry and heavy behind his teeth. "Yes, sir, I'll make it home again one day. All in good time, and perhaps I shall take up your offer, but not today."

"Don't wait too long," he said turning the knob of the sturdy shop door. "One day you, too, may have a son. Then you'll understand your father a mite better." The gentleman walked out the door, the tinkle of the bell underscoring his exit.

Alone at last, Ben swept the smoker's ashes into a small pile and gathered the clay pipes into a crock. In the silence, he was still not quite alone. Words haunted him, drifted in the hazy air. *"Look after them, Ben. Don't let my father's land fall into no greedy land speculator's hands. Keep her safe."*

The demented ravings of a madman. Was it only the fevers? How could he be sure which desperate pleas to heed? If he had only remained that last night instead of heading back to his room at the store... Damn Phoebe for allowing Zack to wander off. She should have kept him tied down, in spite of his ravings. He couldn't be responsible for what happened. Yet he would never divulge the truth, even to himself. Phoebe had her secrets and so did he.

Ben swept the dustpan out the door and returned inside, absently arranging and rearranging jars on the shelves, bins of notions, seeds, pencils. He dusted shelves already in pristine order. The two Swearingen boys would be easily dispensed with. The little girl, now she was another matter altogether. Zack spoke of provisions in his father's will. The old captain had indicated as much all those years ago when he had first arrived and joined the militia. Lucy was a dear one, all right, though stubborn and strong willed just as the colonel said. Already she showed signs of blossoming into a beauty. She'd be tall and lovely as her sister Drusilla. Perhaps lovelier. More like her mother, Eleanor, who turned every man's eye in the settlement and could have had any of them, just as the men had surmised earlier. And yet she waited some five years and then succumbed to the likes of John Newhouse. Could the man be the sort to take advantage of a naive widow and her three young children's legacy? Especially the young girl's welfare, if what he witnessed in the woods was indeed not some childish trick. But how could he explain...? *"He'll stop at nothing to gain the land and power he wants, he's always craved. Don't let that happen."*

Who had Zack meant? Presumably it might be Shepherd, once the rake appeared back in the valley. Though perhaps his friend had another in mind. Either way, he would be sure to profit by this and see all put to rights.

He had learned the ways of prudence and legal stratagem. It was the only means to outsmart this sort of gentleman. He sneered at the thought of even equating Shepherd with this term of respect. Newhouse, he wasn't yet sure of, but he would be on the watch to find out. However at the moment he had a more pressing matter to consider.

The river beckoned beyond the shop window, and a keelboat slid into view. His eye traced it's course until it passed a copse of trees and disappeared around a bend on its journey west. He and Gibson had planned their venture for more than a year now. With this foray into the riverboat trade, he might arrange his own business deals at ports like Lexington, St. Louis, Natchez, perhaps even New Orleans. His pulse quickened at the thought, his fingers twitching to feel the smooth, coolness of the coins. Prime cigars, silks, sugar and spices in exchange for the corn, flour, cotton, and whiskey produced here in Virginia and coveted elsewhere in the world. It was the stuff of men's fortunes. Settlers were moving west at an alarming rate, increasing the need for such goods and the stores to carry them. If the prices of corn and cotton remained stable, he could do well.

When he first arrived here, this view of the river had been blocked by trees. Only the tavern and sawmill staked a claim as a settlement alongside the pulsing, winding river. Now a blacksmith shop, gristmill, and a cluster of cabins formed a community on its way to being a town. The river was unobstructed now from his vantage point on the shop's front porch. Up the hill, Swearingen's Fort stood sentinel as an ominous reminder of his obligations.

Ben sighed, pushing aside the memories and voices. He breathed in the clean, fresh air from the open doorway and picked up the *Wheel-*

ing Gazette discarded on the windowsill. A notice caught his eye—"Officials Declare County Seat Wellsburg."

He put thoughts of children's inheritance, family squabbles, and parental obligations aside for now. His hand groped under the counter for the *Ohio Navigator*. Published barely a year before, it was the definitive source on river travel for all who dared its winding, treacherous circuit. Ben thumbed through the pamphlet, then settled into a chair, propping his feet on one of the barrels. Soon he'd be drifting down the Ohio on a keelboat to uncharted places. Places where a man could disappear into the wilderness with nothing more than his ax, his long gun, and a bag of seed corn and carve out a home for himself.

CHAPTER 8

"'Tis a most obstinate girl we have before us this day." Mr. Newhouse sat at the head of the breakfast table, the same one that had groaned with food for mourners a few days before. His voice commanded with a cold steeliness. "All I asked was for a simple song to gladden the hearts of our guests, to show them some measure of gratitude for their solicitous attendance at our family's grieving."

Lucy stood silent behind her chair, eyes lowered to her empty plate, trying not to flinch or react in any manner to his presumption of being her "family." To her left, Van spread butter on his toasted bread. Tommy swirled a spoon through his porridge creating canals for the milk to flow. They must indeed be glad to be spared from the usual morning lecture on manners and protocol. Mr. Newhouse had saved this moment just for her, waiting three days till after Uncle Joseph and Cousin Thomas were well on their way back to Shepherds Town.

He reached for a sausage from the steaming tray Winn brought around to his left. "A mere request was all it was, in an effort to bring culture and refinement to these woodsmen."

Before Mother married this man, he had been deferential toward all aspects of household management and insisted nothing would change. But that was when Zack had served as head of the house until he married that summer before Mother wed. Even when Newhouse had given them gifts upon his marriage to Mother—a packet of ribbons for Lucy and clay marbles for the boys—it seemed something lurked beneath his stiff smile and maple-syrupy words, a duplicitous nature.

"In my day children stood for the entire mealtime." Newhouse jabbed a sausage with his pewter fork. Even with eyes lowered, Lucy noted every detail, including Mother rubbing a thumb and forefinger across her temple while fidgeting with her spoon in the other hand.

"John, dearest, I'm certain Lucy meant no harm. Did you, my darling?" A wan smile reinforced her words as if to settle the matter. "Consider the day, her own dear brother, after all."

"Nelly, she needs discipline." He pounded a fist to the table rattling the dishes and startling Tommy from his industry in channeling milk through his porridge. "They all need a firm hand. You are far too soft on your children, if not the entire running of the household. I thought we agreed that would change, and now that I am here, we shall see it does." The man sitting at the head of the table surveyed them all, including a stern eye aimed at Winn, busy arranging dishes on the table.

"The children are far too free with their own fancies, especially this girl." He gestured his fork toward her. "You think yourself above reproach, do you? A rebellious and defiant child."

"No, sir," Lucy muttered in what she hoped would be in an appeasing tone, though it came out in a hoarse whisper. Incomprehensible words swirled in her mind, things she had said standing on that log across Catfish Creek. Had she truly said them? What must Ben Stephenson think of her? He had said nothing, treated her as if it were a game. Perhaps that's all it was. Perhaps he had tricked her somehow.

Eleanor lifted her teacup for a sip, averting her gaze under the delicate gold rim. "Lucy, dear, you do understand, it wouldn't have hurt to sing just a little song."

Yes it would have, Mother. Those words in my head, no one needed to hear them. How could she explain that to them what didn't make sense to herself? She had to leave and go to the fort, she knew she had to. There was no other way to explain it. She was no lady and never would be. She was something more, something less.

Ester entered from the kitchen with a fresh pot of coffee. The tantalizing aroma tickled her nose, but children shouldn't have such stimulants, even Mother forbade that and all her older siblings had abided by it. The scent of coffee stirred her appetite more than watching her stepfather shovel bites of eggs and sausage from his heaping plate. She would not give any of them the satisfaction of thinking she was the least bit bothered by his scolding. She would stand there all day and not eat a bite just to spite them.

"Well, no matter now," Newhouse said with a smug grin. "I'm sure it won't happen again. Considering the day and all, you may sit." He motioned to the chair she still gripped with knuckles white from digging fingernails into the painted wooden back.

"The evening wasn't a complete loss," his voice brightening as he sliced another sausage. "That Stephenson is quite the card player. You were right about him, Nelly. He surely isn't the wagering kind."

Lucy's ears pricked at the sound of Ben's name. His last words to her had been something about a card game. Could this be what he meant? If he wasn't the "wagering kind," why would he have bothered? She held her breath and ghosted her fingers across the chair back, steadying herself to sink noiselessly into the seat. As hungry as she felt, she still was not going to eat at his bidding.

"Yes, indeed, I didn't mind in the least relieving him of a few shillings." Mr. Newhouse swallowed another bite and sipped his coffee. "Says he's not much of a gambling man, so I went easy on him and let him win back a bit of his wager, given he's a friend of the family and all."

Ben had said he would be her friend as well. He was supposed to have been her brother's friend, too. She still had the handkerchief stained with her own tears along with those of her dead brother's wife. Could this man be trusted at all?

The linen cloth blurred beneath Lucy's weary eyes, still smarting from fighting the tears at breakfast. Sewing was hard enough but especially on cloudy days, and her stepfather had refused to allow any more work candles than absolutely required for the task. What he might consider sufficient light for sewing and what she preferred were as wide apart as the Ohio River. She struggled to keep her row of stitches even with exasperating effort and an aching back and shoulders. Outside the wind pelted cold rivulets against the window panes. No use bemoaning the chance to walk the creek today. Endless stitching stretched before her, and it was only the third hour of the morning.

Mother sat serenely embroidering fine white work over a small piece of muslin. A fleeting look from her confirmed her keen eye for proper conduct was on guard. How the woman sat so erect, maintained such perfect stitches, and worked so quickly even while keeping Lucy on task was astonishing especially with Mother looking particularly pale and tired since breakfast. It was the third day this week she had refused everything but a few bites of toasted bread and chamomile tea.

"Lucy, do sit up straight and stop fidgeting," Eleanor said. "Proper carriage is always important."

Dutifully she pulled her shoulders back into a line square with her spine as if a rod were impaling her from her seat. "But it's hard to work this way, and no one else is here," Lucy said. "My shoulders are stiff from sitting so long, and my leg is cramped. These new stays are pinching me."

Eleanor's weary smile was tinged with sadness. "At least you can be thankful for these new styles that offer a woman more freedom of movement. In my day we were fitted into stays for the proper silhouette that truly flattered a lady's form." She lowered her stitching to her lap and placed a gentle hand on her abdomen. "The gowns accented a woman's slender waist then." She winced and bit her lip, pressing her hand to her middle. "My first ball gown was a confection of ruched ribbons along a wide skirt held out by panniers and a velvet stomacher that matched the quilted petticoat," she sighed. "When it comes time for your first ball gown, I certainly hope the styles are equally as elegant and well appointed."

Lucy had heard Mother recall before the voluminous gowns of her youth, the tight-bodiced waists.

"My waist was the narrowest of all my coterie of friends" was a frequent refrain. Lucy waited for this to be her next remark. Or would she yet be complaining of a sour stomach as she had of late?

"It's because of the French and their ideas of liberty for all, isn't it?" Lucy interjected, hoping to distract Mother from more lessons on etiquette. "They fought a revolution just like we did. That's why the gowns are like this." Something more interesting might lift Mama's spirits today, at least it would hers.

Eleanor looked at her, startled. "Lucy, where do you get such strange notions?"

She lowered her eyes back to her stitching. "I heard it somewhere, I suppose."

"You must stop dawdling about the men, especially the militia. Is that where you heard such unseemly notions?"

"I cannot say," Lucy mumbled. It was indeed where she had heard it. The men had passed around a newspaper with etchings of Eastern ladies dressed in the Paris fashion, according to the words beneath the pictures.

Eleanor resumed her stitching. "I know you love their stories, but it's unseemly. It was fine when you were small but..." Her voice broke and she drew in a sharp breath. "Some of their talk is simply not for young ladies, certainly not their views on a lady's wardrobe."

"But I like hearing their talk," Lucy said. "I don't see why things have to change. They never mind when I watch them march and drill. And I learn things too."

"And that is precisely what I'm afraid of." Eleanor lowered the needlework to her lap. Her face softened. "I know 'tis different now with Zechariah gone. I should never have allowed him to drag you off traipsing through the woods with Van. But he did love you so. He was just like..."Lucy shot a curious look at her mother, "Just like Papa?"

Eleanor's brow puckered and her eyes flitted toward the front door as if expecting someone to walk in at that very moment. " 'Tis no matter now. She picked up the linen cloth and pulled the needle through another careful stitch. "Your stepfather is right. I have indulged all of you far too long. Now that we have a man in the household, all will be right again."

Lucy bit her lip to keep from saying something she knew would distress her mother even more. Mother was always so tired lately. She was right about one matter, though. Everything on the farm had been run with little restraint since her father's death. No one thought she remembered the former time, when Papa was here. The vague memories that came to her dreamlike and wooly were all she had of a time when her family prospered in contentment and Captain Van Swearingen roamed his land. Sometimes she wasn't even sure how real these memories were or if she only wished them so. As she drew the needle through the soft cloth, she tried to imagine another place and time.

She was a small child again, riding upon Father's strong shoulders as he crossed the fields and valleys along the river. With the endless blue sky above her, the tree-covered bluffs beneath her feet, and the rolling winding river slipping its way through the valley and pulsing as the lifeblood of this new and vital country, Lucy believed she could fly and that nothing could possibly go wrong in her world so wide and free. Had it been real or merely the stuff of dreams and childhood fancy? Either way, it was where her father, and now Zack, lived and remained ever with her. She saw Zack again last night, standing at the foot of the bed, and the night before, hearing his familiar gait across the downstairs floor.

There were other dreams too, she hoped were not real. They were always the same. Terrible images of being chased, of being torn from her cradle and carried away by a large bird with blue feathers and the face of a wolf and a long tail like that of a snake. Since the funeral the dreams had returned. Sometimes it wasn't a bird but a man who wore a soldier's roundabout coat—a blue coat. She had never told anyone, not even Van or Zack about her terrible dreams. They always ended with someone calling for her.

"Lucy! Did you hear what I said?" Mother's voice jolted her back to the present moment. "The subscription school will be resuming again now that Reverend Godbey has returned."

Lucy nodded but kept her eyes focused on her stitching. "Yes, ma'am."

"You will be starting etiquette and dance lessons soon."

Lucy looked up sharply. "With the Reverend?"

Mother's voice remained soft and even. "No. You'll only attend school three days a week. The other two you'll be home with me. You want to be a fine lady, don't you?"

Lucy wasn't quite sure how to respond. "I suppose. When will I begin?"

Eleanor pulled a length of thread from the winder made of carved bone. "Well, for the moment, you'll learn the proper things such as serving tea, deportment, dancing, et cetera. We'll begin next week, at least for now. As long as I'm still..."

"Still what?" Lucy peered at her mother's benign visage.

Mother flicked her hand aside as if dismissing a servant from the room. "No matter. The Reverend Godbey will instruct you and Van at school in your other lessons."

Lucy didn't like the sound of this. "But I already know how to dance. I danced at Zack's wedding last summer," Lucy said, recalling the jig she danced with Ben, swirling and weaving among the other couples. "And learning to drink tea can't be all that hard."

Mother sighed and ran a hand across her temple. "Lucy, these dances are different, not the common country dances of folk out here in the settlement. I may not be the best at *le ballet*, but I do remember a few minuet steps, a gavotte, and other courtly dances I learned as a girl and so should you. It's best for a young lady to know these things before being introduced into society."

"Why?" Lucy studied her mother's face. "Wouldn't it be better to know how to load and shoot a musket? Learn sums to keep an account book? And know which seeds to plant in the garden?"

"Those pursuits are all well and good," Mother said, "for some folks, but not for fine ladies who have servants and a husband to tend these matters. You won't need to worry about keeping an account book. Planting gardens are matters for field hands and overseers. And as for shooting a musket?" Her lips pinched together in the way she held sewing pins before piercing them into cloth. "I should hope you'd never have need of such dreadful skills."

"Zack showed me how." Lucy drew her thread through the linen with a decided tug. "It's easier than sewing. You merely put a pinch of powder in the pan and then—"

"Dearest, I don't need a discourse in firing flintlocks," Mother interrupted with a rise in her tone that startled Lucy, putting the matter to rest. It seemed any time she mentioned Zack's name these days she was shushed. The pursed lips relaxed into a wan smile, and Mother's hand wafted gently over a stray curl. "I know your brothers have been quite useful in that regard, but hopefully you'll have no need of such endeavors…ever."

"But, I want to be like my brothers." Lucy thought of someone else, not quite a brother, who she hoped to impress now. "Like Telemachus." She muttered the last phrase, not for her mother's hearing.

"What did you say, dear?" Mother held the needle mid-stitch with the threads dangling beneath the taut cloth. "Telemachus! Whatever made you think of that?"

"It's a story…," Lucy scrambled to explain, fearing Mother would take away the book if she knew Ben had given it to her.

Mother's eyes misted with sympathy. "I miss him too, dearest. We all do. Zechariah was full of such wonderful stories, and it's good you remember them."

"I didn't say it was…my brother," Lucy fought brimming tears to think of another excuse. "Mayhap it was…schoolmaster…during Latin studies." She jabbed her needle into the linen and tugged the thread through. *A soldier does not cry.*

"Sounds like a lot of bother to me." *All those lessons on tea and courtly dancing.* She wrestled with another knot in the thread, muttering, "Why would I need to learn such fancy things around these parts? Who would I dance with?" Her thoughts drifted to the wedding dance and then what a fine ballroom dance looked like, and she stifled a giggle.

"Oh, certainly no one around here, of course." Mother lifted her shoulders and gazed wistfully toward the ceiling beams. "But someday, perhaps in a place where gentlemen twirl a lady across a lovely marble dance floor with fine music playing. You'd like that, wouldn't you?"

"I suppose." It sounded nice enough, but it depended on who she'd be dancing with. The image returned of Zack's wedding. But there were no marble dance floors around here, even if she could conjure such a notion of what one was like. The only image she could see was dancing in a meadow with a certain shopkeeper donned in a fancy uniform and powdered wig like some of the regular officers who paraded past town.

Mother dropped the embroidered linen in her lap and rubbed her temples with slender fingertips. "You are nigh on to reaching the end of your eleventh year come next winter, and no longer a babe on leading strings. A young woman, you'll be before long, and you must be ready. I only wish we could secure adequate instruction in drawing, French, and perhaps music." She gave Lucy a wistful, fond gaze. "All in good time, I suppose."

"I can speak French. A beaver is called *le castor.* I can count too. *Un, deux, trios...* "

"What did you say?" Mother's face was whiter than the linen cloth that lay idle in her lap. "Lucy? *Ma petite?"*

"N-nothing. I didn't say...anything."

"You were speaking French." Mother's tone held a mingling of admiration and disturbed awe. She blinked twice in an instant that suspended them both in timelessness before cradling her daughter's chin. "You have been working at your studies with the good reverend. I shall have to extend our appreciation to him at next Sunday's meeting."

It wasn't Reverend Godbey Mother should thank, but how could Lucy explain the words she'd heard from the passing trappers and Canadians down at the riverside? That had to be where she'd learned these words that seemed to spring to her mind like weeds in a garden, unwelcome and yet taking root with such tenacious strength.

She continued counting in French with every stitch resumed as Mother chattered on about the merits of her schooling. *"Quatre, cinq..., nànan, ningodwàswi, nìjwàswi, nishwàswi..."*

"Lucy!" Mother's shriek called her back. "Stop that. Do you hear me?"

The room had gone dark, her hand jabbing the needle into the cloth in rote rhythm to her counting. Those last words were not French. What were they? How did she know them?

"I'm...sorry, Mother." Her work was a mess of tangled threads crisscrossing the linen with no semblance of order or reason. "I am listening. I didn't mean to..."

"It's no matter, *ma chère."* Mother took the handiwork from Lucy's trembling fingers. "Nothing that can't be fixed." She picked up her scissors and started snipping the threads and deftly removing them.

No more was spoken for a few moments. Lucy searched for a means to prove she had been listening to Mother all along.

"What about Van and Tommy? Will they take lessons in dancing too?"

"Of course," Mother said, handing back the mended stitchery. "Every young lady needs a suitable gentleman partner." She studied Lucy as if she were not to be trusted with a needle ever again. "Your stepfather will guide them on matters of business and running a plantation while you learn deportment, etiquette, and...," she sighed, reaching over to run a pale finger along Lucy's cheek. "Dearest, don't be so sour. I wish you would accept your new father. He so wants us to be a family."

He is not my father. Only the Great One, the Mighty Spirit is our Father, she wanted to shout, but instead, bit her lip and shook the errant words away. Lucy squared her shoulders and took a breath.

"You don't help matters when you are so disagreeable, Lucy. Mr. Newhouse is trying to elevate our status. He only wants to help you and your brothers to make a place for yourselves in society. He has lived out east and knows the ways of proper English society. You'll have a chance beyond this place. It's important to begin thinking of suitable matches for you, dear. That's why you must always behave appropriately in social settings, even in Wellsburg."

Here it was. She was to be scolded again for her behaving deplorable after the funeral, for ruining her gown, and for running away after causing a scene. She lowered her head concentrating on her stitching. "I'm sorry if I displeased you, Mother, last week, I mean."

Mother was silent a moment and then said, "I know you meant no harm. You need to understand the new role you must lead. We want so much more for you."

"But I don't like to sing for others. And I didn't like the way he just expected me to," Lucy said. "As if I were nothing more than..."

It wasn't so much singing for others, though she had felt flustered and tongue-tied when asked. It was more to sing at Mr. Newhouse's bidding. She thought of Cousin Thomas's words but couldn't bring herself to say them aloud.

"He meant no harm in showing you off a little. He is just so proud of his new family, of all of us." Eleanor's voice was soft. "Still, it was no reason to run off as you did. You must have a care at all times now."

"Why now?" Lucy looked curiously at her mother.

"I mean, you mustn't run off into the woods by yourself anymore. It was very kind of Mr. Stephenson to bring you back, but it was not appropriate for you to be wandering in the woods unchaperoned. It's a dangerous place to be."

"But why?" she searched her mother's face but it was unreadable, except for the drawn lines at her brow. "There are no more Indians to harm us, no bears or wild animals on the paths we traced." She winced, knowing she should have said "I" and not "we."

A ghost of a smile taunted the corners of Eleanor's mouth. "We? Yes. As to the matter of wandering off alone with a gentleman, this is another matter to consider. For a young lady of breeding and of your burgeoning womanhood, it is best you have a care in this as well."

"Burgeoning?" This was a new word, one she had not heard any grown folk, let alone Mother, say. She craved learning new words and waited for her mother to explain. "Is that like burden? Like bairns?" Bairns are a burden. She had heard Newhouse utter this at least half a dozen times a week, when he thought she or her brothers weren't listening.

"No, not burden." Mother's color rose slightly. "Burgeoning..." Her rosy lower lip caught between two lovely rows of teeth as she blinked feathery lashes searching for just the right words. "It means, dearest, that you'll be a woman full grown soon and...men...that is...a gentleman may start to take notice. We must be prepared."

"But it's just Benjamin. He's no gentleman." Lucy giggled at the thought. "He's just...Ben. He's a good friend. He was...Zach's—" Her voice caught and Mother's eyes misted. "I mean...he's our family's friend. Papa's friend, too. Wasn't he? I was in no harm with him there to watch out for me. He is quite kind." She swallowed trying to hold back the tears from flowing yet again. "We were just talking."

"Yes, of course he is. We are all fond of Mr. Stephenson. But things are going to be different from now on. You are growing up, and we must give a proper impression at all times," Mother punctuated her words with a tap of her needle in the air as if brandishing a sword.

Things were changing all right, and Lucy did not like it one bit, perhaps that was why her thoughts were so contrary and strange. Is this what it meant to grow up? She wanted to ask, but what if there were something wrong with her only? What would they think if she told about the strange words she heard in her sleep calling to her? What was that odd thing she saw in the woods that beckoned her to cross the raging creek? Ben had not noticed or was he being too much the gentleman to tell her? Or was he waiting for the right moment to tell everyone else?

She looked around the room and noticed things missing. Mother's silver tea set and punch bowl were not in the cupboard, and the Delft blue china urns that always graced the mantle and had been there just last week were now absent. Mother idly dismissed her questions before, but maybe now she might tell her. She mustered courage to ask, but then held her tongue when her mother gave yet another piece of instruction.

"I also want you to spend less time with the slaves, especially Tobe. You are not to conduct reading lessons anymore."

"But why?" Lucy yanked her sewing needle through the next stitch causing the thread to knot. "I like teaching Tobe. And he is doing so well now."

"Your stepfather thinks it's wrong. He has new ideas on keeping slaves. There are laws now in some states, and he means to follow a more proper order for running the household. A better way for us all, especially as our settlement becomes a place of refinement and elegance." Mother looked away, out the window, shaking her head. "I've been far too lax in tending to them the past few years."

"I can't stop now." Lucy sat up, shoulders squared. "Tobe is like family. He will be hurt and maybe mad at me."

"There are things that you won't understand until you are older, Lucy dear." Eleanor's words were gentle. "I've let our slaves have free rein in ways that are unseemly for their station. I see that now. They need to know their place and we ours."

"But they've worked hard for us. Ester cooks and cleans, and we help, too. Noah is helping Van with the horses, and Van is learning so much. And the others tend the fields and such. Haven't things gone well so far?"

"Yes, in some ways. But things will go even better now." Eleanor patted her daughter's arm. "Lucy, just do as we say. I just can't have this now that...just not now."

Lucy's tongue swelled in her mouth, fearing her Mother meant her daughter's strange behavior.

Eleanor pressed the narrow thread end between her lips before slipping it into the needle. "I will need your help more than ever now."

"What do you mean, Mother? Is something wrong?"

"I suppose you might as well know. " She secured the threaded needle into the linen and set her needlework down on the sewing stand. Her once pale cheeks were now tinged with the barest hint of blush. "You see, Lucy, my dear, you're going to have a new little brother or sister come next fall."

Lucy had barely time to absorb her mother's words, which landed between them like a swinging wood ax into a stump, when another question was put to her.

"And by the by, my dear one," Mother fed the silvery needle through the cloth, drawing it into another perfect knot, "perchance did Zechariah give you the Dutch Lady? It seems Phoebe has misplaced it and knows nothing of its whereabouts. It is imperative it returns to Swearingen blood kin."

Lucy formed her answer as her eye fixed on the spot where the silver tea service once sat but now, like the Swearingen Dutch Lady, appeared to be missing.

The strange words whirred again like a spinning wheel as she resumed her careful stitching counting each circuit of the needle. *Nishwàswi. Shàngaswi. Mitàaswi.* The Dutch Lady was missing, but so were other family treasures. What did any of them matter anymore?

CHAPTER 9

Sunlight streamed through the glass windows of the one-room school. Lucy studied the dancing particles of dust that shimmered in the beams. "Fairy dust," Zack used to call it. *"If you catch it and hold it to your heart, all your wishes will come true."*

When she was small, Lucy believed this and everything her older brother told her, and she spent hours trying to catch the shimmering particles in her hand, only to have them disappear into nothingness.

"Miss Swearingen," Reverend Godbey's voice called her back to the lesson, "'tis your turn to recite."

"Hmm?" Lucy looked up to see the matching, covered buttons of a plain brown waistcoat. Above it the bewigged schoolmaster towered over her, his Franklin spectacles tipping to the end of his broad nose. "I, uh…"

The man pinched the bridge of his nose with an exasperated sigh. "Miss Swearingen was a two month respite from your lessons too long?" He reached a long fingered hand to grasp the book she had let droop, forgotten to her lap. With a firm thrust he lifted the tome to place before her gaze.

"No sir, 'twasn't at all, sir." Lucy fumbled with the book, searching the page for the missed place.

Van suppressed a snicker behind his own book and exchanged a mischievous glance with Jacob Keble. They were the only three at this level of Latin, Reverend Godbey's prized students, and here she was at idle reverie. Lucy's heart was beating fast as she swallowed and tried to think of a response, but she had no idea where Jacob had left off in the text. They were reading portions of the *Aeneid*, and today the Latin words seemed irrelevant to everything else happening around her.

"Miss Swearingen, Virgil's Aeneid, liber the second, at the fourth stanza on page six and twenty, if you please." Reverend Godbey punctuated his words as he tapped the toe of his buckled shoe against the wooden planks in counterpoint to the ticking clock on the wall. His bushy eyebrows arched, creating deep furrows across his forehead.

Lucy's mind was on anything but the craftiness of the Greeks in defeating the Trojans, as told by Aeneas at a banquet at Carthage. She tried to ignore the titters of the other students as she scanned the page for the place to begin, but the Latin words swirled in her head like fairy dust along with other words nonsensical and foreign. *Latin.* She must remember how to pronounce the Latin only.

Slowly she began to decipher the words before her.

"O patria, O diuum domus Ilium et incluta bello moenia Dardanidum!" She began hesitantly and gained momentum as she read, the words coming to her lips with full clarity. *"...Instamus tamen immemores caecique furore et monstrum infelix sacrata sistimus arce..."* When she came to the end of the page, she waited for the schoolmaster's verdict, the dead pause filling the room more agonizing than his earlier scolding. "Shall I continue reading, good Reverend?"

"No." He cleared his throat and pulled out a handkerchief to blow his nose. "Excellent diction and elocution, Miss Swearingen," Reverend Godbey said, slowly. "I see you have not let your mind dawdle too far from your lessons. Now translate, if you will."

Translate? She knew what that meant, but the words seemed to need no translation. Didn't he understand them clearly? Another thought struck her as to what language she should translate them to. It all made perfect sense in the reading itself. Many, many languages cluttered her head. Which one did he mean?

"Miss Swearingen?" The Reverend lowered his head to peer at her, before turning on his heels to reprimand a few snickering students. "A translation is in order? What, in your words is happening within the text? How would you convey those words in our own native tongue?"

Native tongue? She blinked at the pages, blurry with letters and words. "Reverend, sir? Which native tongue shall I translate it to?"

The giggling erupted again between the two boys sitting beside her and echoed through the younger children who took the opportunity to pause their own lessons. With one stern glance from the schoolmaster, the first- and second-level students resumed chalking their sums on slates but continued to exchange mischievous looks.

"Are you being impertinent?" With hands on hips, whipping the tails of his frockcoat behind him, he scrutinized her over his spectacles. "'Tis not like you, Miss Swearingen."

"*Pardon*, I...only meant..." She wasn't sure what she meant but what she said didn't come out as she intended.

"*Je voulais dire?*" The schoolmaster stood straight as an arrow, eyes wide, repeating back her words but not as she had meant to say them. "French? Is that it? You prefer to think your native tongue is French?"

"I...did not speak French." She caught a look of guarded sympathy from Van. Or was that an unspoken warning as he shook his head ever so slightly at her.

The reverend chuckled. "As I understand French, child, that is indeed what you were speaking. 'Tis not like you to be so obstinate."

"I did not mean to be obstinate or impertinent, sir."

"Perhaps not, but we shall see." He ran a finger across his chin. "I shall expect a perfect translation...of lines 32 through 37, in French! And for your impertinence, if you are unable to do so to perfection, you'll spend the rest of the day standing on the stool wearing a sign to note your stubbornness and impudence. Do I make myself clear?"

She nodded and studied the assigned lines in her book. French wasn't all that different from Latin, closer than English. Yes! *Anglais*. That's what he wanted her to translate from the Latin. Why had she uttered French? She barely knew a smattering of phrases from rangers, trappers, and various other travelers that wandered through. But it was too late to fix her gaff now. She hadn't really meant to be impertinent. It would mean the stool, something that had never happened to her before. There would be worse at home, once they learned of her shame. She had to at least try, and so with a deep breath she began. What came next was beyond anything she could have hoped for, let alone expect. Did she ask for this? Some thought inside her told her,

Yes! You can make these words. In perfect French she uttered the lines retelling the tale of the Trojan horse's triumphal entry into the city and the merrymaking of those duped into accepting it as a gift only to succumb to its cruel treachery.

When she came to the end of the assignment, she looked up to see a classroom full of students looking aghast at her, the silence of the room a deafening blow against the hollow echo of words still dancing around her like fairy dust.

"Sh-should I take my place on the stool now, sir?" She had spoken perfectly, she hoped, but still the reverend had every reason to punish her for her defiance.

"No," he said, softly. "That was...quite...astonishing." He cleared his throat. "Adequately accomplished. Class, back to your lessons." He rapped his teacher's rod against the desk. "That will be all for today's lesson. You all may spend the remainder of the hour in silent reading and...contemplation."

"If you please, good Reverend, sir," Lucy said, prompting the man to turn on his heels again, his countenance filled with peeved exasperation mingled with a touch of alarm, almost as if he feared what would come from her mouth next. Lucy swallowed again, her throat dry and raspy. "I don't understand why the Trojans allowed the horse to enter their city. I mean, shouldn't they have known it was a trick? Why didn't they listen to Cassandra?"

"So you do understand the reading beyond any translation?" The reverend gave her a look of curious scrutiny, near admiration. "I have only one thing more to say to that: Beware of Greeks bearing gifts." He continued to stare at her with raised eyebrows as if that should settle it.

"I suppose the horse was merely a ploy, or a trap to entice the Trojans to think the Greeks were friendly. And they believed them because...they were hoping for friendship...and peace?" Lucy said. "But in the end the Trojans lost everything."

"Indeed, you have answered your own question," the reverend said, nodding his head. "Perhaps you had better attend to your reading rather than...daydreaming out the window. At least you have become adept at your French during the respite. My compliments to your mother's tuition, I may say." He seemed to mutter the last part more to himself than her.

Lucy returned to reading the next verse of the *Aeneid* after one last glance around the small room that served as both school and Sunday meeting house. She was glad to be back at her studies and away from home for at least a few hours each day and must ward against ever letting such impertinence happen again. What if Mother or Mr. Newhouse should find out? What if she was expelled from school, if those other words that came to her at times—unbidden, strange, and ancient—would spew forth? It wasn't possible that she could speak perfect French when she barely understood the Latin let alone her own native English.

She was fortunate to be able to attend school and must not risk losing this opportunity and shaming her family. Only a few students from the valley settlement could afford to attend the subscription school and even fewer could afford to bring their own books. In spite of Reverend Godbey's strict and exacting standards, she knew he cared about his students' education, even for the few girls who attended. He willingly shared the books from his own meager library with them, like the one she held in her hands for this lesson. Lucy enjoyed learning about history and literature, but her favorite time was at the end of the day when she received music lessons after everyone had gone. Now she dreaded being alone with him and what he may ask or even demand to know about her errant behavior.

At half past eleven the reverend rang the bell for the midday break. The students scrambled to retrieve their baskets and leather pouches and headed outdoors. It was a warmish day for the end of February. Perhaps Tommy's prediction of an early spring based on a woodland creature's shadow would come to fruition. Lucy took her favorite spot under the sycamore tree and unwrapped a brown, checkered cloth. A slice of thick bread smeared with butter, a hard-boiled egg, and a few dried apple slices. She hadn't eaten much since that morning's distasteful breakfast. A peaceful dinner alone would be welcome, especially after the morning's lesson. She did not want to explain herself to the other students. Hopefully they'd be too busy with their own dinners and visiting to care. Besides, she had been looking forward to another quiet moment to read the book Ben loaned her, tucked safely away in her pocket. One last glance around the schoolyard to ensure she was safely alone as she took note of the other students' usual places. Van joined in the usual coterie of boys behind the schoolhouse, and Tommy sat on the bench beside the door with a few of the other younger students. The other three girls chattered together over by the well. Usually Lucy ate with them, but today, time with her reading was all she wanted.

Gibson's Trading Post stood a ways down the trace, connecting the few buildings that made up the settlement. Some were calling it a town now that it was officially the county seat, even though it was little more than a few random buildings comprising the river landing to the west and edged by woods and surrounding homesteads on the other sides. The largest building was the courthouse, the only other building she had never been inside except for the tavern, where Mr. Newhouse spent most nights. Beyond that was Curry's gristmill with the rippling pond partially visible from behind the cabin millhouse. The next building over was Zehnder's blacksmith forge. But today it was the trading post that occupied her thoughts while eating lunch. She nibbled on her bread and wondered if there'd be a glimpse of him arranging a display in the window or sweeping the porch. Perhaps he'd be out soon to help a customer load a sack of grain or other goods in their wagon. But midday on a winter Wednesday meant few customers in town, and he'd likely be holed up in the shop tending to whatever tasks a shopkeeper did when not busy with customers. Perhaps he too was reading. She liked that thought and pulled out the slim leather book from her pocket beneath the slit in her gown.

For the past week she had been content merely to carry it in her pocket since reading only the first few pages. It was concealed beneath her gown where the necklace had been the day she walked with Ben. She had since found a more suitable hiding place for the Dutch Lady, one she felt sure no one would find until she figured out what she should do or who she could trust to tell.

As she opened the book she flipped to the inside the cover where an inscription was scrawled in ink:

Benjamin Stephenson, 1787.

He had written this one year before she was born, barely twelve years ago. She wondered if he had read this book in school as she was now and what school he might have attended all those years ago. Below his name, another was penned in a finer hand: Mary Reed Stephenson. Who this woman was or how Ben was related to her perplexed Lucy for a moment, forcing her attention to the next leaf.

She ran a thumb absently along the inked names and read the title page which was both in French and English: *Les Aventures de Télémaque* or *The Adventures of Telemachus, Son of Ulysses* by Fenelon, Archbishop of Cambrai. She had glanced at the French translations opposite each English page. Some of the words did make sense to her after a bit of study, but surely that couldn't account for her understanding French well enough to translate an entire verse of Virgil's Latin poem.

The frontispiece displayed an etching of a very staid priest in a strange long, curling wig, or what she assumed to be a wig—the papist priest who wrote the book some time ago. Why would Ben have such a book? She'd heard stories about the evils of the papacy and how so many were driven to American shores because of their horrors and heresies. Below the portrait was the year 1699. The book was nearly one hundred years old. She had not held anything in her hands quite so old before, except for the Dutch Lady, which supposedly dated to the earliest Swearingen woman who came to America from the Niederlander, as her brothers sometimes still called it. The tiny date printed at the bottom of the opposite page read 1760, making this a much more recent copy. Still, it had belonged to Ben since he was perhaps her age, and if he recommended it, there must be something worth reading. Books were hard enough to come by, so for him to offer it meant a great deal to her. To talk with him about something of importance sent a shiver of glee.

She already knew the story of Ulysses from Latin studies with Reverend Godbey. There had been no mention of Ulysses having a son, only his adventures and the war with the Trojans. There had also been another story she recalled, a wife he left behind who waited for him to return and rejected every advance from suitors who came her way. What was the woman's name? Persephone? No, that was the woman who had been captured by Hades and taken to the underworld. Parsimmon? Persnickety? She couldn't just recall it, only the details of how the clever woman promised to marry one of the men once she finished her weaving, but then undid all her work from each day's efforts and thus would never finish and never have to make a choice. She rather liked the idea of this woman making choices for herself and putting off marrying. It seemed the only thing Lucy had heard since birth was a recommendation on who she should and shouldn't marry someday. Now Mother was hinting all the more with her weekly lessons in etiquette and dancing. Perhaps if Lucy never perfected her own sewing skills—a must, Mother said, if she was to hope to attract a suitable gentleman—then, like the woman in the story she could hold the men off as well. Yet there was something rather charming about the notion that Penelope—yes! Penelope, that was her name—something charming indeed about her waiting for her one true love, Ulysses, to return to her, and only her.

After one more furtive glance at the trading post door she settled back to begin reading when a shadow crossed her book. "What are you doing, there, Miss Swearingen?" a nasally voice sneered at her.

She gripped the book and held her breath. Without looking up she addressed the intruder. "I'm reading if you don't mind, Horace Madsen."

He reached for the book, but she was quicker and snapped it shut to hold behind her back. "We're setting up a game of fox and geese and you're needed on the girl's team."

"I'd rather not, if you please," she settled back down with her book. "Pray, make my excuses."

"Well, well," Horace mimicked back in a haughty tone. "Think you're better than us now that you know how to speak Frenchie and Latin? How'd you do that anyway?"

Beyond Horace, the girls at the well had finished their own meals and were headed her way as well. "C'mon, Lucy, are you going to play with us? The bell will ring soon," Sarah Parker said.

"It's far too cold to be sitting here reading," Matilda Zehnder added, pulling her red woolen shawl tight about her shoulders.

"I'm not cold," Lucy insisted. Before she could stop him, Horace had jerked the book from her hands.

"What're you reading anyway? You think you're smarter than the rest of us? Huh?" He held the book high over her head. Though she was taller than the other girls, she still could not match the height of Horace, who was three years older than she.

Her pleas to give it back were to no avail and only signaled the other children to rally around them ready for a new game to pursue.

Horace took a few paces back while thumbing through the pages with dirt-smudged fingers. Lucy held her breath, aware of every heartbeat flooding heat from her neck to her temples.

"No, give it back, Horace," she seethed through gritted teeth. "It's not yours."

"Tel-ee-ma-kiss," Horace pronounced. He scrutinized her and poked the inside cover. "Ain't your'n neither. Benjamin Stephenson? The shopkeeper?"

Sarah and Matilda exchanged a glint coupled with a giggle.

"What you doing with his book?" Horace squinted. "You steal it?"

"No, it's borrowed.... I'm reading it."

"I done saw that. Still don't explain how you got it."

"What're you doing with my sister's book, Horace?" Van wove his way through to Lucy's side followed close by Tommy on his heels. "Lucy, what's this about?"

"I...nothing, Van. I'm fine." Lucy wished she could disappear somewhere. Perhaps the ground could open up or she could run into the woods. But first she must get the book back in hand.

"Your sister's got the shopkeeper's book. Tel-ee-mah-kah-mus, or some such fool thing. Sounds Injun to me."

"Tel-LEH-mah-kus," Lucy corrected through clenched teeth, swishing a fruitless hand toward the book held a hair beyond her reach. "And it's Greek and nothing to do with Indians."

"Mary Reed Stephenson," Horace shrugged, skewing his face deviously. "Who she?"

"I don't know, Horace," Lucy said, her ire rising with the heat on her face. "Now give it back."

Looking back over her shoulder Horace nodded toward a point

behind her, leaving Lucy with a heightened sense of doom. "Hey, there be the shopkeeper now. Maybe orta see if'n he be needin' his book back. He's a deputy sheriff and might just want to know about a theft. Maybe I orta ask him who this Maaaary, be." He affected a simpering pose. "Maybe he'll put you in jail for thieving."

"No!" Lucy screamed.

"You can't leave the schoolyard past that fence post," Sarah primly chimed. "I'll tell schoolmaster. Now give her book back."

Horace seemed to consider this and tapped the closed book to his hat brim. He raised a hand and with a mock friendly smile, amiably waved. "How-dee-do, there, Mr. Stephenson."

Lucy turned, and to her dismay Ben stood on the store's porch sweeping off the steps. He seemed to not be looking in their direction but then glanced up at the sound of Horace's call. He absently waved and with a shrug went back into the shop. Lucy blew a sigh of relief. She stood tall and held out her hand with an air of refined challenge. "My book, if you please?"

"Here's what I'll do, Lucy," Horace leered at her. "I'll return this here book, if'n you give me a kiss, and I won't tell the good schoolmaster, nor your Mr. Shopkeeper neither." He paused, tapping one booted toe against the schoolyard gravel. "Tell-ah-mee-a kiss or I'll tell-ah-mee 'cause I can. What'a ya say?" He pursed his lips into a smack and grinned at his own cleverness of playing on the title character's Greek name, infuriating Lucy all the more.

"My sister don't need to kiss anyone she's not of a mind to. Not you, Horace, nor anyone else." Van wedged himself between her and this challenger. "Enough already. Give my sister back her book."

"Or what?" Horace countered. "You gonna make me give it back?"

"Give. It. Back. Now." Van stood a few inches shorter than Horace, fists balled at his side. The children all backed away egging on a fight.

"I tell ya what, Swearingen," Horace held the book behind his back, "make you a deal. You let me ride that horse of your'n, the one you claim is so fast, and I'll return your sister's book and not tell nobody, Mr. Stephenson included, about this. We square?"

Van made like he was mulling things over when Lucy noted the conspiracy at hand. Matilda inched her way silently behind Horace and easily snatched the book he held lightly behind his back.

"Got it!" she enthused and handed it back to Lucy's eager hands. Lucy pressed the book to her chest a moment and then quickly turned to place it back in her pocket. The entire class cheered, though a few offered groans lamenting the lost chance to watch two of their own tussle in the schoolyard.

Horace still was not done with it all. As he sauntered off to set up the teams for fox and geese he mused more to himself, though loud enough for those near enough to hear, "Odd one, that shopkeeper. But then so're you, Lucy. Speaking Frenchie like that."

"What you mean? The shopkeeper's a good egg," Isaiah Mueller responded with a knowing look. "He is the deputy sheriff, sworn in and everything."

"Oh ain't that so?" Horace shrugged. "Where's he from? Nobody really knows, do they?"

"He knows my uncle from over in Shepherds Town," Lucy offered. "Nothing odd about that." She took her place with the girls' team waiting for the game to ensue. Van watched with a scowl toward Horace's words, then a quick glance toward the trading post before taking his place as fox while the others took positions as geese.

"Some say that," Horace smirked. "But I heared different. Some say he come from Martinsburg, but Pa say he won't talk much about his past'n all. Mighty strange."

The game ensued with children running in all directions fleeing Van, as fox.

At another lull while Van pursued one of the younger geese, Horace sidled by her and Sarah. Whispering close to her ear he said, "Some say he done murdered someone and is hidin' out from the law, here."

"Not so, Horace," Sarah managed to get a word in before running to the other side of the well to avoid Van. From her new vantage point she yelled back, "What makes you say that? He wouldn't be in the militia if'n that were so."

Another game formation brought Jacob near enough to add his own bit. "I heard he kilt his wife," he uttered in sing-song fashion. "Maybe that's who that Mary woman be written in the book."

"Aye, he kilt her and her lover, too, when he caught them together," Sarah chattered. "How romantic."

"Did not!" Lucy protested, running behind Jacob as Van tagged him and the boy went defeated to the school wall to wait the next round.

"I say he done it," Jacob replied. "Shot the lover, slit her throat, and threw 'em both in the river. Down by the banks of the Ohio." He sang the last line in the familiar haunting melody.

"If he lived in Martinsburg, how could he," Lucy taunted back. "The Ohio don't run that far east."

"Maybe he come here just to do the deed," Matilda said cryptically. "Or maybe he lived somewhere downriver and just say he come from Martinsburg. Some say he come from Pennsylvain-ee."

"That's what I'm sayin'. Do we really know anything about him?"

"It's a sin to gossip, Horace." Little Dinah Evans, who till now had been silent and focused on avoiding Van, now threw in her pious words. "I'll tell the Reverend you been bearin' false witness agin thy neighbor."

"If'n it be true," Horace shrugged, jumping a pile of dinner baskets left in a heap as he dodged Van's reach, "then it ain't gossip, is it? Ain't no false witness nor a sin, then."

The reverend rang the bell, ceasing the game though on the way inside the children hummed a last chorus of "On the Banks of the Ohio." Lucy took one last look at the shop and saw a man's shadow move across the window from inside. Children's talk was all it was. It was all just a pack of lies, just like the Trojan horse.

CHAPTER 10

Ben's arms ached with every heave of the riverboat pole. The initial thrill of leaving Wellsburg and traveling the creeks toward the headwaters of the Ohio had long since faded with every passing mile upstream. Tree stump after tree stump and endless fields cleared for planting drifted by almost as if it were the land moving and he stationary on the water. His "sea legs" were now well adjusted after passing the first of many tributaries feeding into the Ohio from the Allegheny and Monongahela.

"Almost there." One boatman pointed ahead with his pole and spoke through labored pants. "The shipyards'll be the first sight of the town, such as it is."

They had passed several new settlements already, where they stopped to change passengers or unload cargo. Most Ben had not seen before, but the only one that concerned him was the shipyard at Fort Pitt. Pittsburgh, some were now calling it, though the old name was still more familiar and rolled off the tongue easier. Every passing river mile seemed an eternity at the moment. A surge pulsed through Ben's arms as the sight of old Fort Pitt with the American flag flying over the blockhouse came into view around the bend. *Just a little ways to go.* He jammed the pole deeper into the shallow muddy bottom and heaved it back.

"Whoa, there, landlubber," the captain of the boat shouted. "Keep in rhythm with the rest of the men or you'll likely crash us into that levee comin' up. There be yet a few twists and sharp turns to make against the tide."

A chuckle mingled with a few grumbles murmured through the eight-man crew. It was a small flatboat of about forty feet, loaded with only a few goods and passengers headed toward its destination. Ben now had his first taste of working on a barge rather than merely being a ferried passenger. Working his way up the river allowed him firsthand experience along with avoiding the expense of fare and shipping the small cargo to trade from the Wellsburg Trading Post. Gibson had said river boating was the way of the future and the best way a man could make his fortune in the West as expansion continued and commerce with the native tribes and the French and Spanish governments remained favorable. A fortune and a prosperous business of his own was precisely what Ben aimed to make and possibly to acquire a fine piece of land to build a home and a plantation someday. But first there was this quest for adventure to fulfill, a chance to see where the headwaters of the Allegheny and Monongahela became the great rivers and emptied into the open sea. The idea of building seaworthy ships in a port so far inland and sailing them down the creeks and river systems seemed utter madness, but shipyards were springing up along the Ohio and somehow the impossible seemed the way of the future. In the years ahead, who knew how many would dot the river's edge? Just two more in Marietta, or so he had heard, and another one soon to come in Wheeling. The talk around Wellsburg was that perhaps their own small settlement, now on its way to becoming a village, would be a full-fledged town in no time at all, one to rival Boston or Philadelphia, all based around the shipbuilding industry.

"We'll be among the first." Gibson had been talking of nothing else for the past month. He poked at the map laid out on the storeroom counter a week ago. "There's a bit o' land I got my eye on. Wetzel says he'll sell his lower thirty down by Cross Creek. It'd make a fine place to start a yard of our own one day. From there it be just a matter of plotting out the streets and places for folks to build."

It was agreed between the two men that Ben should make the trip and scout out the potential market for ships and negotiate a price to suit potential investors. He felt a pang of regret thinking of Zack's interest as an investor, but Elzey had agreed to pick up part of his dead brother's portion in the enterprise. There was still the matter of land. Wetzel's tract was a start, but they'd need a much larger place with better access to the Ohio River and a lumberyard. Wetzel's tract shared a border with Swearingen land, a prime piece near the widest part of Catfish Creek where it fed into the Ohio. He could find his way to getting that land, but at the price of his own honor. Phoebe's desperate offer to keep her land continued to haunt him. Zack was dead and gone so what did it matter now? She'd keep her land and he'd have a stake in it too, possibly a means for them both to profit and…

No! He shooed away the thought as idly as it came. It would be living a lie. Sooner or later the guilt of what happened in the woods that day and afterward at the cabin would destroy them all, even as pragmatic and hard-hearted as Phoebe pretended to be, he knew better.

Despite the ache of muscles and back-breaking strain, this last leg of the journey kept his blood pumping as he worked the pole with all these possibilities. There was more to consider here beyond the shipyards and a desperate widow's dower rights. The odd manner of a little girl forging a dangerous current across a natural bridge the day of Zack's funeral—what had she been trying to say? A childish game perhaps? But she had spoken words no child would know and he himself barely understood from trading with local tribes. He had told no one, not even her uncle to whom he'd made a promise a month ago and before that her brother and, originally, her father. The Swearingens certainly had a way of holding him in their stead. He'd keep his promise and then, as Gibson had indicated, have something for his efforts in the end.

"Oh, Boatman Ben thinks he can row," one well-seasoned pole man, known as Hash, called out from the line of men. "All his way up the O-Hi-OH." He broke into song on the last phrase, sparking another round of jabs in verse. "He's naught but a lubber, a milksop so soft. He'll be wishin' he stayed safe t'home in his loft."

It was the way the men kept their rhythm of poling along, spurring each other on in challenges to keep up. The insults became more raucous with every passing boat headed the opposite way. Working down the line of men, it was now Ben's turn to be the brunt of their jeers.

"Ah, so 'tis a landlubber you say I be," Ben sang, floundering his way through how he'd end the line. "But as a woodsman, poling river water's nothing to chopping down trees."

The chant continued down the line after a hearty guffaw to Ben's contribution. The "blackguarding" as the boatmen called it, continued until one man was declared the winner for having silenced the rest of the crew with his celerity of wit and novel turn of speech in besting the other men. Unfortunately, it meant the last man became the brunt of all jokes for the next length of the voyage. Ben made damn sure that would not be him and used every ounce of reasoning and dry humor to best his way through the verbal sparring. In between bouts and lulls in conversation, he drank in every facet of the river, from sandbars to coves and rock formation until finally someone called out, "Yo ho! Fort Pitt up ahead on the right. Starboard poles steady. Portside keep pace."

The settlement wasn't much to speak of, beyond the shipyard consisting of a two-story, square-log office attached to a long brick building partially open on one side revealing a construction site. Smaller boats in various stages of construction littered the area inside and around the dock. Stretching back from the river beyond the log office, an array of partially built ships and apparatus filled the clearing along the embankment. Stacks of lumber and large thick masts—some still barely-roughed-out tree trunks, a hundred feet long or more—lay in piles or leaned against walls along the vast construction yard. Some workmen milled about, while others were hard at work carving a ship's wheel. Other men struggled with furling a sail onto a mast. A couple of blacksmith shops sat farther up river with forges hissing and pinging ironwork into bolts, rings, anchors, and other needed items to hold plank and beam together for a seaworthy vessel. Every stage of a ship's production could be viewed, studied, and carefully crafted from the vantage point of the levee as the flatboat eased into dock. The pungent odor of burning coal from the forge mingled with fresh-milled lumber and tar, overpowering the sour smells of the river and muddy embankment. Here something wondrous was being made, a new creature molded from the earth to navigate the river systems to the seas on a course for adventure. Ben's fingers itched to hold the wheel of such a massive vessel in his hands and perhaps steady the keel or adjust sails on her maiden voyage. Such thoughts urged him onward with every lap of the water against the flatboat, imagining the hull of his first ship heading out to open waters at the Gulf.

The riverside, just below the shipyard, teemed with flatboats, a few keels, and some trapper pirogues. A few birchbark canoes manned by native traders, brimmed with stacks of furs, presumably from the English Lakes. After settling his fare with the captain and bidding adieu to his fellow boatmen, he headed toward his destination: The Eliphalet Beebe Co. A painted sign bearing the shipbuilder's name and below it the year, est. 1792, welcomed Ben as he passed through the main entrance. A young clerk led him to the plant owner and overseer, the very man whose name appeared over the door.

"Beebe, Captain Eliphalet Beebe at your service, sir." He was a sturdy-built man, not much taller than Ben, but older and with a hard-bitten look and a face lined with a life of working out on the open sea.

"You're the young shopkeeper from Wheeling as I understand?"

"Ur...Wellsburg. Yes, Benjamin Stephenson. Most glad to meet you, Captain." Ben offered a slight bow and held out his hand to which the foreman returned a firm but brief grip of a handshake.

"Aw, hell. We don't stand on ceremony here, m'good man. Stephenson, is it? Call me Beebe, or Cap, if you prefer, as the other men 'round here do. It's the ships you're wantin' to see, is it now?"

"Yes, very much, sir." Ben followed his lead as they ventured further into the shop where the pings and smart thuds of hammer against steel and wood sang out in harmony with the hiss of forge and rhythm of cross saws.

"Ever see one of these?" Beebe stopped at the skeletal framework of a half-finished hull. "It's one of our latest designs. A bit experimental at present, but someday..." With a gleam in his eye he motioned toward a roughed-out hull. "When it's all rigged out, it'll be a schooner. Forty-five feet, one-hundred tons with four six-pounder swivels on each side."

"Impressive!" Ben croaked a feeble response as he imagined the ship in full sail headed out to open waters.

Beebe nodded his approval. "Right ye are, lad. Gibson said ye'd be a good'n for this job. Ye've got the sea in ye're blood a-callin' to ya, is it now?"

Clearing his throat he replied, "I'm merely investigating the possibilities at the moment, Captain." Heat crept up Ben's neck at being so easily assessed.

"Ye're a prudent one," Beebe nodded. "That's good. As I say, for now, shipbuilding this far inland is still in experimental stages, a bit of a gamble, but so far been a growing and profitable industry. If conditions fare well..." He left the rest to a shrug.

"Conditions?" Ben looked askance at Beebe, still trying to take in everything around him. "In light of recent events, you mean?"

"Aye, all that ruckus with Spain, them damn Froggies, and what have you," Beebe replied, scratching the back of his head. "'Tis put a bit o' a damper on commissions for the merchant line. But as of last year we landed our first lucrative government contract. It seems Congress is bent on building up the navy, in the event of war. They've gone and authorized Adams to build up to ten galleys with a budget of eighty-thousand American dollars."

Ben released a low whistle at the staggering amount. "Ships like this galley?"

Beebe nodded. "Galleys...schooners and mayhap a few brigs appear to be where our best venture lies at present. Where Congress comes up with the funds ain't my concern. Paying me on time and getting the ships launched is."

The two men shared a mirthless chuckle over the ludicrous figure allotted for such an impressive navy, given the struggling, newly built nation. Wars with Spain and France. England's continued derisive treatment of Americans through impressments to sea on both merchant and navy ships comprised their discussion as Beebe continued his tour. More ships were the answer, and it could mean a fortune for any man investing at this groundbreaking stage. He listened, learned, and took in everything from the planing of hulls and gunwales to the forging of ironwork for bolts, chains, and cannons to the intricate hand-carving of bowsprits and figureheads. When Beebe pointed toward another galley nearing completion, Ben recalled the day when the first galley passed by Wellsburg.

"Yes, I'm quite familiar with the launch last spring." The memory of that time, the waving crowds and fanfare had stirred many hearts, including his. Little did he know he'd be standing here in Beebe's shop where it all began.

"Aye, the *President Adams,"* Beebe murmured. "She was one of ours. Last May it was. Hard to believe it's been near a year since she left us." He sighed, shaking his head. "Quite a lot of folderol and fiddledeedee, but that's the general for ya."

"General Wilkinson made quite the impression among our villagers." The man, famed for his exploits during the Fight for Independence and now commander all military forces, had stood regally at the helm amid a flutter of flags, gaily dressed ladies, and a fanfare of ship horns sounding the arrival.

"Wilkinson," Beebe chortled derisively. "Aye, that be him. Likes his pomp and circumstance much like that Adams and Hamilton and other fops in Washington City, don't ya know. A lot of government waste went into the launch what could'a gone to better use, but too much of the Quaker in me talkin', I suppose."

Preferring not to delve into political views, Ben tactfully added, "Nonetheless, the *President Adams* made quite the impression to folks downriver." A fleet of Kentucky flatboats and skiffs as escorts with a crowd of well-dressed passengers on deck had provided Ben's first inkling of the potential for river trade and shipbuilding. "Wasn't there to be a second galley to accompany the *President Adams*?"

Beebe turned to him with a sly grin. "Indeed there was. The *Senator Ross* is still here waiting her turn. We had a delay in putting on the finishing touches and what with the early onset of winter, ice, and low water from fall onward, her launch has been placed on hold. Now that the river's up again, we're looking to launch her any day now. Would you like to see her?"

Ben wanted nothing more and eagerly followed the Captain to the other side of the shop.

"These here galleys are less expensive to build and easier to assemble and send down the Ohio than the larger gunners and brigs, though likely not as effective in the open sea," he said. "But General Wilkinson and Congress insist otherwise. They order it and fund it, and we build it."

Ben stepped closer, inspecting the fine craftsmanship and wondrous tools, some he knew from having helped raise a barn or two and others were specific to the art of shipbuilding. "So much to learn and I'm here to do nothing less."

Beebe turned away momentarily distracted by a worker's question.

"Especially the one I'm to navigate downriver one day, perhaps one such as this." He had been muttering more to himself during the lapse, though Beebe was quick to pick it up.

"What's that? Oh, aye," Beebe said, returning his attention. "The ship we discussed. You've got all your investors together I gather?"

"Yes," Ben replied, "we're hoping to purchase one or two keels for starters."

"Would you be interested in a position on the *Senator Ross*? They're putting the crew together now, under the command of Major Isaac Craig, and could use a few more men. It would further your experience before taking on your own boating ventures. Test the waters, so to speak." He guffawed at his own joke.

"It would be a great honor, although...you say she launches any day?" There were many things to consider—where to begin? But how could he pass up such an opportunity? "I'd have to talk with my partner and the other investors. We had our sights set on the keels."

"There's good money in this kind of venture that could aid your own," Beebe confided. "Take this here galley. You sail her downriver all the way to open waters at the Gulf, deliver her safe and sound, and head back this way on a keel loaded with trade goods to sell along the way back north."

Ben tried to imagine himself navigating such an immense craft downriver and meeting the bustling port of New Orleans. It both thrilled and alarmed him with the responsibility and all that could happen.

"You'd get your feet wet, as they say." Beebe clapped him on the shoulder, laughing at another of his puns. "In more ways than one.

Learn both kinds of craft and the ways of navigating the falls. Once you're past that, it's smooth sailing, as they say."

Ben nodded appreciatively, thinking of the dreaded Falls of the Ohio where boats crashed or, at best, were forded across at great peril to the boatmen. "There are risks to consider, certainly," Ben mumbled this to himself, though Beebe heard him.

"Risks are in everything, me lad." He turned away, levying a scowl toward a couple of men sitting astride the scaffolding and idly blabbering to each other rather than shaving the planks before them. Seeing the foreman's scowl and jabbing finger directed toward them, they reluctantly resumed work. "Got to stay on top o' them every second, I do," he said upon returning. "If this government contract with the galleys continues, we'll be looking to hire on more workers. Maybe you'd consider a position here, once you finish a tour downriver, of course."

Elation mingled with trepidation. Perhaps working at a shipyard would be more prudent. In time he might one day open his own shipyard down in Wellsburg or even farther west. "You've certainly given me much to think on, and I do appreciate all you've done today."

"Aw, 'tain't nothin' much," Beebe waved off the compliment. "Don't mind what I said about the falls, now. I know it's got you buggered up over it."

"I've seen the falls at low tide enough to…," Ben started but was quickly interrupted.

"Aw, hell! Low tide only lasts a matter of weeks out of the year. 'Tis high tide that ye pay mind to. Boatin' is seasonal work, leaving you time to spend at the shipyards buildin' the beauties you'll sail downriver come spring or fall."

Ben hadn't considered that prospect, the best of both worlds beckoned to him. Adventure during part of the year and a steady paying position the rest, where he'd learn all that was needed to run his own operation someday.

"Gotcha thinking now, don't I?" Beebe added merrily. "How long will you be in town? We've got to get this gal downriver toward New Orleans by month's end, like I said. General Wilkinson's been itchin' to get her underway since last June. But even United States generals, grand as Lord Mayor himself, have to abide by God's whims o' nature." This time Ben joined in the laughter even as another proposal flickered in his mind. *Deputy Sheriff of Berkley County.* Colonel Swearingen's offer lingered, too. Though less tempting, it would fulfill certain obligations and perhaps leave him time for seasonal boating. His eye rested upon one singular figurehead suspended from a beam. It portrayed a young girl, her hand shading her eyes as if looking into the distance. Intricately carved curls trailed behind her as if blown in the wind and salt spray. How like another young girl this was, resolved to chart her own course, crossing unstill waters via a natural bridge, and yet where would that lead? What had she seen that day and who had she been speaking to?

"Come! I'll show you where we make the sails." Beebe recalled Ben's attention to the rest of the tour. Each stage of shipbuilding was carefully and methodically orchestrated in the various buildings and open yards of the site. Ben marveled again and again at how so much could be handled and overseen in such short order by one operation. As they walked the grounds the topic turned to politics once again and the effects it would have on the river trade.

"Hamilton's doing, from the size of it," Beebe scoffed. "The secretary of the treasury has been sending his share of letters asking about the *Ross*, too. Government contracts are a tricky business as I said. Good for trade, so long as the funding is there. But it always feels more like dealing with the Devil himself, if ya mind my meaning."

"And times being what they are," Ben added, "it will take a strong, ready navy along with an army on land, to build the United States into a strong nation."

"Aye, that be the way of it." Beebe looked him over again with a keen eye. "A military man, are you as well?"

"I have served in the militia since manhood, signed on just after Washington's decree," Ben said.

"Aye," Beebe affirmed. "The Whiskey Rebellion got Mr. Washington's breeches in a twist, that it did. But I believe it does a young man good to serve and we're needing fine young men like you whatever the future holds. You'd be about the right age to have quelled the insurrection, I reckon? What regiment?"

"I was in the 11th Pennsylvania from York County. I served first there, where I was born. More recently under Captain Brady's rangers in Virginia."

Beebe arched one brow warily. "A Pennsylvanian, are ye? I've heard of Brady's rangers and their exploits. Captain Swearingen? The Injun Fighter? I reckon you remember Wabash too?" He cleared his throat and hacked as if choking back his next thought.

"Yes." He hoped the discussion would end there. If Beebe pressed for more and heard the truth, perhaps the shipbuilder would reconsider him sailing the *Senator Ross.* But what of it? He had no such aspirations before arriving here. Best to keep his eye on the business at hand and seek a more amiable subject. "Is black oak your wood of choice for shipbuilding?"

Beebe nodded. "Black oak and white oak make for crafting the finest ships. Cherry, walnut, and locust serve well also. Not much for yellow pine, though it is suitable for flats and keels."

"And all of those grow right here along the river," Ben surmised. "Quite handy."

"Yes, sir! Our best-kept secret," Beebe winked. "Along with the ease of river access to the open waters. Pity it's all being compromised at the moment, but that's the way of it."

"Surely, in time we'll see our way through." Ben winced at speaking with such brave optimism at the risk of sounding foolhardy.

"Either way, it has its points," Beebe considered. "In this venture, a good businessman will find his way through. I do like how you're thinking." He gauged Ben with a thoughtful nod. "I knew ye had the gumption and a keen mind. I'll show you the keels you're after in a moment. Got something else I think you'll find to your liking."

Ben followed the foreman to another ship in finishing stages but still strapped inside the scaffolding.

"Government contracts, Spanish embargoes or not, I'm a realist too and an old seaman," Beebe said. "Always keep aloft looking for storms brewing on the horizon and set your sails for whatever lies ahead." He paused at another ship under construction where a crew of painters detailed the bowsprit and gunwales. "By late spring we hope to get this beauty put to water, right after the *Senator* weighs anchor, if all goes well. She's a fine specimen for a gunner." He patted the bow as if stroking a beloved horse's velvety nose.

The sight of the ship, with six guns lining each side, polished to a fine sheen elicited another low whistle of admiration from Ben.

"Like her, do ye?" Beebe gleamed with the pride of a new father holding his firstborn. "Imagine what she'll be fully rigged and turned out in full sail."

"It's my understanding you send them down half-rigged?" Ben swallowed, hoping he would not sound too naive. "The winds and tides of the rivers can be a wicked business. In full sail…I mean, considering the effort to pole a flatboat upriver."

"Seems next to impossible, don't it?" Beebe slapped the boat's hull and smiled. "You wouldn't be the first one to balk at what these inland rivers can take. It's the bain of the whole industry as of now, but one we're working to overcome. That's just the thing no one realizes. We only send the maidens partially rigged, like a child bride waitin' to blossom. Float 'em downriver lookin' not much different than those flatboats or keels over yonder and let the current do the work."

Ben nodded in understanding. "So, with the tide going downriver that makes sense, but can the depth of the river support the tonnage and water draw, even beyond the falls?"

"Aye, I get that question asked a lot, before nearly every commission, actually." He chuckled and led Ben over to a shed where a framed charcoal sketch portrayed a ship in full sail on a winding river with a crowd gathered on shore. "Here's one you may recognize."

"The *President Adams,*" Ben read the title on a brass plate at the bottom edge of the frame. "May 19, 1798."

"Sure 'nuff was." Beebe ran a finger along the dusty frame. "The *President Adams*, ah! Her sister will outshine her for certain, one of these fine days. Major Craig supervised the whole operation, along with meself, and had the sketch commissioned as a Christmas gift later last year to commemorate our success."

"Aye! Quite the celebration it was." Ben rubbed his cheek gazing into the picture reliving it all again. "How was she outfitted?"

"I've got the original blueprint and specs in my office, to show you later, if you'd like," Beebe offered. "Fifty feet, six inches with a fourteen-foot beam." He recited it proudly. "Rigged with two masts and lateen sails. Sleek and sound as they come with a single eighteen-pounder mounted in the bow complimented by four brass three-pounder swivels on the quarterdeck rail."

"You mentioned the blueprints?" Ben asked. "I'd very much like to see them."

"Then, sir, to my office it is." He turned on his heels and headed down the steps from the sail loft, continuing their discussion along the way. "The good Lord provided for the perfect set up just for us shipbuilders, he did. Rivers run from north to south, all connecting like the bloodlines of the House of Lords and emptying into the Gulf basin with just as much wealth. Bottomland's rich for farming and settlers pushing west, towns like Pittsburgh will be booming in no time a'tall."

Beebe continued his tour of the plant showing off every nuance of shipbuilding as they proceeded to his office. Ben couldn't get enough of it and crammed his head with all the useful knowledge he would recount back to Gibson. They headed up a long flight of stairs to a landing that led to Beebe's office in order to talk away from the melee.

"Ah, that's better." Beebe closed the door, muffling the cacophony of construction below. He motioned to a chair in the overcrowded space and took a seat behind his desk, a plain table littered with piles of paperwork, maps, contracts, and random notes. Discarded balls of ink-smudged paper dotted the floor under the desk. On the walls were tacked prototypes and blueprints of ships, diagramming and labeling every part.

Ben took his seat, glad to be settled in at last, while Beebe continued to outline the terms for finding a crew and transporting ships. As he listened and offered his own suggestions, he became aware of something warm and wet slobbering against his hand. The scent of fur and feral breath drew his attention to the large black animal at his feet, especially after she insinuated one massive paw to his leg.

"Ah, I see you've met Lady." Beebe leaned over the desk and gave a hand signal toward the hound. "Best damn dog you'd hope to have on a sea voyage. C'mere, old girl. Leave our guest alone now."

"She's no trouble," Ben laughed and ran a hand down the dog's massive furry head. Clearly the dog did not wish to leave his side as she nuzzled her nose further into his lap. "Quite the friendly sort."

Beebe eyed him appreciatively. "Got a way with the ladies have ye? My girl doesn't cotton to just anyone. Her approval is the most important around here, or so she likes to think. I do take her opinion into consideration, but not on everything." He gave a mock scowl to the dog, who whimpered and wagged her tail in remorse.

"What sort of breed is she? I've never seen the like." Ben stroked her long, thick back.

"A Newfoundland, she's called," Beebe shrugged. "Newfie to some."

"Lady? That's her name?" Ben held out a hand to summon the dog back.

"Aye, Lady. And she lives up to it, thinking herself Miss High and Mighty. Don't ya, me pretty gal." He affected a simpering tone and smacked a kiss in her direction, eliciting a hearty bark from the dog. "Got her in a trade from a French Canadian and now she thinks she runs the place. Loves the water, can't get enough, and loyal as they come. Definitely got more than I bargained for with this one." He shook his head, "The damn Froggie didn't happen to mention she'd been bred and was due to whelp about a month back. But like it or not, she's added six pups to our production line." He snapped his fingers and the dog dutifully drew to his side. "Now that be enough tending our guest. Go see to yer brood now and leave us men to our business." He rose from his seat to scoot the dog into a small closet where Ben heard the muffled yips and yaps of a litter calling for dinner.

Turning his attention back to the work at hand, the foreman riffled through some papers on his desk. "I'll draw up the contracts for the transport and have them ready by early spring. Waters will still be high enough to sail downriver. The Falls of the Ohio will be your trickiest spot, as we said. Once past that it's smooth sailing, so long as you can avoid river pirates and Spanish outposts along the lower Mississippi."

"Sounds like you've had some experience with that." Ben rubbed a sweaty hand along his breeches. He hadn't really thought through all the dangers, but still the thrill of promised adventures beckoned.

"Went to sea at the age of nine as a ship's boy and spent the next fifteen years before the mast in service to his majesty, then rebellion started and I served under the Continentals." He spread his hands wide surveying his domain. "Took my bounty land and started this shipyard. Sometimes I do still miss the sea." He gazed wistfully at a small painting of a ship in full mast sailing across the lapping waves.

Ben's gaze moved from the painting to a calendar hanging next to it. The month of March was four days gone already. March fourth. *March forth.* Yes, that's what he needed to do next. It brought to mind the militia drilling—orders given and received. Duty and responsibilities. He had much to accomplish before taking one of these rigs to New Orleans. Before this, there were promises to keep, one to the colonel to secure his niece's fortune and future. Always another promise to keep, and then there was freedom, prosperity, and the lure of unstill waters calling him onward.

CHAPTER 11

She could *never see its face, only shadow lurking at the windows or hovering over her trundle bed shared with Tommy. Its footfalls padded across the room, soft it seemed for how large and fierce it was. Sometimes it seized her in its talons and swept her away into the night to some dark place where she waited for the thing to tear away her flesh until there was nothing left.*

She awoke with a start. The creature was still lurking in the shadowy corners of the upstairs room before it disappeared up the chimney, its long sinuous tail stirring the embers of the hearth before trailing away. For a moment she didn't breathe, trying to separate nightmare from reality. Or was there any difference? The footsteps had awaken her, not the barefooted tiptoe of her brothers but the clunk of heavy hunting boots coming up the narrow stairs and into the room. The sound echoed in her head, even as she registered wakefulness and the room took on the form of more familiar things with nothing but her two sleeping brothers beside her, Van in the bed above and Tommy nestled by her in the trundle. But the creature had been there, she knew it as certain as she had heard something that awakened her.

She sat up to reassure herself all was right; little Tommy's fingers curled around the edge of the coverlet, but Van was not in his bed. If his footsteps were the ones she heard, why had they not awakened Tommy or anyone else in the house? Perhaps it was a trick of the imagination. She certainly had her fair share of those of late. Lying awake waiting for him to return only served to pique her curiosity.

Lucy slipped from the warm covers without waking her little brother. Padding across the cold floor, she winced with every creak of the floorboards and steps leading down to the cabin's main level. The kitchen was dark except for the soft glow of coals through ash, banked sufficiently 'til morning. A small cup of milk from the cold box might settle her stomach and soothe her back to sleep. Before she reached the kitchen she caught sight of a soft glow eerily seeping through the slightly parted door of her father's study. Someone either was working late or had left an errant candle burning. For a moment she stood in the kitchen doorway taking in the peaceful recollection. How often she had found Zack reading late into the night in this small alcove off the main parlor? She would crawl upon his lap to listen to his stories, alone together where all was right, before he shooed her back to bed "lest your mother catch you, sleepwalking again," he would often say—though Mother's scolding was never much to fret over and concerns over sleepwalking had long since passed. That was until Mr. Newhouse came along. A rustle from the study set her on edge, thinking it might be her stepfather about to emerge and find her wandering out of her bed.

Perhaps it was the strange visions and footsteps earlier playing on her mind; for a moment she wanted to believe he was still there among them in the house. Spirits sometimes remained to linger among the living. She should not fear his ghost. No, she welcomed the chance to speak with him once more. Yet she couldn't help feeling a slight shiver of trepidation. As curiosity danced with hope, she crossed the room. Indeed, there was an older brother there, not reading but bent over the desk. It was no ghost but Van, very much alive with quill in hand furiously scratching away at the leaf of a book.

She stepped into the doorway and whispered, "Van, what is this?" Her brother jumped from his seat, dropping the pen with a splatter of ink across his hand and nightgown sleeve.

"What are you doing up this time of night?" Van said.

"I asked you first." She crossed her arms and awaited his answer.

"Just go back to bed and leave me be. 'Tis none of your concern, and, besides, we can't have everyone in the house disturbed." Van tried in vain to shield his work as Lucy stepped closer.

"Van, what are you doing with the family account book? And why are you copying it?" Lucy stood her ground, demanding an answer with a glare of narrowed eyes. "What if you are caught?"

"Well, it would seem I already am, but if you'd go back to bed and leave me to work in peace neither of us will be in trouble. I'll be finished soon and will return before anyone awakens."

"What if Mr. Newhouse finds out?" She glanced over her shoulder, half expecting to see him coming down the stairs. And, the image of the strange creature in her nightmares, thumping about her room, still made her shiver.

Van studied his hand as he rubbed away the ink stains with a soft cloth. "Our stepfather is gone every night until quite late. I know his manner and have been watching him closely since..." He shot her a weary look before lowering his gaze and rubbing one eye. "Very well, I'll tell you, if it will mean you'll get back to bed. But you must promise not to say a word to anyone, especially not Tommy nor any of the slaves."

Lucy nodded, eagerly waiting to hear what secrets he held. "This has something to do with Zack and what you said the other day, doesn't it? What is truly happening?"

Van nodded then put a finger to his lips, as if she had spoken too loud or perhaps too much. The house was never completely still. Some slight rustle of a sleeping family member upstairs, the creak of cabin logs against the wind, or even the scurry of a mouse nibbling at kitchen crumbs were usual sounds, but just then, it startled them both to silence, breath held until they were certain it was nothing more than the house's usual nighttime murmurings.

Assured that's all it was, Van pulled Lucy close in a whispered confidence. "'Tis true I've been copying the family ledger and account books. Our stepfather has not been doing right by us or our father's property. Zack knew it all and was watching him closely, but then..."

"He got sick and...now he's gone," Lucy added hastily, before he could say it. To think of him merely as "gone" seemed less permanent, less sorrowful than knowing he was dead, a word she didn't want to think, let alone hear her brother say here in the stillness of night.

"Our mother's new husband is mishandling the farm and pilfering our inheritance."

Lucy thought about the various things she had noticed missing and that Mother so easily dismissed. "Like the silver punch bowl? Mother's tea set and china urns?"

"Partly, but there's more. He's kept track of every bit of the money he's gained, selling off such things and, worst of all, he's—"

Outside the sound of hooves clattering up the road drew their attention. Lucy peeked out the narrow window to see the silhouette of a man riding his horse toward the stable. It was Mr. Newhouse and they only had a few moments before he would return to the house and they'd be found out. The thought of that froze Lucy momentarily until her brother spurred her to action.

"It's Newhouse, isn't it? Quick! We must get back to our beds." Van blew out the candle and replaced the ledger in the desk drawer before grabbing Lucy by the arm and pulling her toward the doorway. Just as they passed the front door, the latch popped. How had Mr. Newhouse come from the stable so soon? Lucy figured he must have had one of the servants waiting at the stable door to put his horse away. Van let go of her arm and dove behind the tall settle by the hearth. Lucy remained frozen in her spot, realizing it was too late to run.

The door clicked open and Mr. Newhouse entered and hung his hat on the wall peg. "Well, well, what have we here? What are you doing out of bed this time of night?"

Lucy floated past him as if oblivious to his words. She muttered unintelligible words and stared straight through him with her best glassy-eyed impression. Turning around she headed toward the stairs, her heart beating a furious rhythm. Hopefully, her plan would work and he'd not find Van, so long as her brother kept in his hiding place. She willed it to be so.

Mr. Newhouse stomped toward her. "Sleepwalking again? I've heard of your strange ways. Aye, that I do know well, your noddy little fits and spells. I'll be locking you in your room or the cellar, or better yet, tie ye down to your bed like your daft loon of a brother, more recently."

It took everything she could muster not to respond to this retort.

How dare he speak of Zack this way! He mustn't know she was aware of him or anything in the room as she feigned her trancelike state. For Van's sake most of all, she had to maintain this ruse. At the bottom of the stairs she pointed up toward the darkness. "There you are! I've been waiting for you. I knew you would come."

"What the...?" Newhouse's voice wavered and he recoiled back. "Stuff and nonsense. There ain't nothing there, girl. It's all in your addled head. More reason to see you put away for good'n all."

Slowly, Lucy ascended the stairs and then stopped midway.

"John! Hush!" Mother's voice called from above, causing Lucy to bite her tongue, the sharp tang of metal mingling with liquid pain and infusing her mouth. "She's sleepwalking. We mustn't awaken her. It could be dangerous."

"I know she's sleepwalking, Nelly. She's your concern, not mine. Get the tib back to her bed and see that she doesn't do this anymore."

"Yes, of course, dearest." Mother padded cautiously down the steps and gently took hold of Lucy's hand. "Come, now. Follow me, sweetling." Her hand was gentle, but her voice took on a tone of quivering desperation.

"Give her a dose of laudanum," Newhouse growled back. "That'll keep her stoppered up till morning."

"Yes, excellent suggestion, dearest." Mother pulled her along and Lucy responded as if in a daze, all the while fearing she'd be discovered. How would Van manage to get back? Would they find him hiding behind the settle?

In her room, Lucy slipped back into bed and settled down easily at her Mother's soothing, as if nothing had happened. She even added a "g'night, Mother. G'night, Tommy-kins" in her dreamiest voice, just to ensure her ruse held.

"You see?" Mother said, standing at the doorway with Mr. Newhouse behind her. "All better. She won't even remember this happened, none of it. 'Tis only the turmoil of the past weeks, but it shall pass."

"Huh!" Newhouse huffed. "I still say we'd be better off getting her somewhere secure and safe. It's what you've been wanting, Nelly. You know it's for the best."

"Perhaps you are right. But with so much happening, it's understandable she'd have a relapse. I only hope...well, no matter. She's all snug and safe for now."

Lucy huddled under the covers pretending to be asleep. They had put her in Van's bed, lest she awaken Tommy. So there she lay wide awake pondering the things her mother and stepfather had spoken all the while wondering when Van would return.

CHAPTER 12

As the day of the Wellsburg Spring Fair drew near, Van took every opportunity to ride Keeper up and down hills and across the greens in preparation for the upcoming race. Lucy watched each day through the cabin window as her brother sped along the front lane and across the barnyard, all the while wishing she could be out riding with him. At last, on a day far too lovely to waste indoors darning an old shift, she convinced Mother to let her go. Reluctant at first, Mother relented when Mr. Newhouse happened through the room and overheard her pleading. "Fie, Nelly. Let the girl have a try at it and give her brother a run for his money. The horse needs a good sparring against another to see his worth. And 'twill be good for them all to get some fresh air."

For once, to her chagrin, she found something on which to agree with her stepfather. Whatever the cause of her good fortune, she gave it little thought other than a muttered "thank'ee" as she dashed out the door on her brother's heels before either parent's mind could change. To be free and feel the wind on her face and hear the beat of the pony's hooves beneath her was all that mattered.

A short time later, Van kicked his chestnut gelding into a frenzied gallop as he raced ahead of Lucy's dun mare. He glanced back once with devilish glee, to which she stuck out her tongue and caught up on his coattails. The scent of dust mingled with oiled leather, tickling her nose.

Aha, dear brother, she thought. *Your precious Keeper is not so fast today, nor is my Natty just a mere pony even if she be under fifteen hands to your horse's sixteen and five.*

In her mind she argued again with him over the worth of her small horse to his lanky gelding. Her mount might not be the swift, agile ride Keeper was, but Natty Blue had power and determination, much like herself. Urging her pony onward with a kick and a tap of the crop, she maneuvered her way to close in on Van's left side. Only a little farther to the end, where the twisted oak, gashed by lightening some years ago, marked their designated finish line.

"I can certainly ride aside as well as any boy's aside," she muttered, glad that Noah had taught her the finer points to appease Mother's insistence of how a proper lady's seat should be. "I shall show you." Squaring her seat, she gave the pony a gentle nudge with her heel and leaned in heading toward victory. Around another bend, Van's horse faltered slightly on the turn, allowing just enough room for his opponent to pass. "Such a gentleman," Lucy smirked. "More so than his rider."

Now running neck and neck, Lucy pressed Natty Blue, "Come on, girl, we can win this one. Don't give in now."

Van shot a scowl in her direction and called to his own mount, "Yah! Keeper, keep a going. Yah!"

The oak in sight, over the next rise, just a few lengths more and the race would be won. Lucy kept her eyes only on the goal, driving ever onward. One, two three…*un, deux, trois…* A blur of numbers ran through her head. *No. I must win. Please let me win.* She was light as air, a cloud floating above the hills. She was air and feathers and breath as the wind called her name, beckoning to her while tangled vines reached from the ground and pulled her down, down into the depths of the earth where water flowed and met the sea. The earth shook and a sharp pain met her arm as the great black beast with teeth sharp as knives and talons like a great eagle that feasts on human flesh rose before her.

"Lucy! Are you hurt?"

Her ribs closed like a vice around her lungs and then someone loomed above her. She tried to speak but nothing came out. Or were those words in her head coming from her or from someone else deep within?

"Easy, there. You've had quite a fall." Another voice, not like the one before, the one within—no—this one was older, familiar, and warm. "Don't try to stand." Strong arms lifted her up and held her close in one swift movement and then set her gently against a tree.

"Leave her be. We'll be all right." Her brother's voice. This one she knew as her head cleared, her breath returning in a deep gasp. She knew where she was as she looked into the eyes of Ben Stephenson.

"Tell me what hurts. Don't try to move. You may have broken something." Ben rubbed her hands in his own. Beyond his shoulder, she saw his black stallion standing on the road. The black beast she saw, had that been nothing but this great horse? Where had it come from? She tried to put the pieces together. They had been racing. She had taken a fall.

"What's that you were saying, little Mouse?" Ben seemed alarmed now, beyond just concern for her fall.

"She's...just had a slight bump," Van said, from her other side. He knelt next to her now and seemed to be insinuating himself between her and Ben. "She meant nothing more than remembering the game we were playing before you came along." It was the way he said that last part—accusing, bitter.

"I'm...I'm fine, please! Where is my horse? Natty?" She spoke clearly now, not like before.

"Your horse is still here, but it's you we must tend to. What the devil were you children doing racing down a country road? You should've known another rider or cart might've come along."

Lucy's face flamed at being scolded by someone who had so recently claimed to be her friend. The image of him sitting at a gaming table collecting bets emerged—a sight she had tried to quell for the past three days, but now it angered her. She straightened her back against the tree and wrenched her hands free. "I'm quite well. Just a slip. I... actually intended to fall, when I saw you...you were coming at us."

A blink and a quizzical look told her Ben did not accept this excuse. "And that makes this no better. If you have no better horse sense than that, you definitely have no reason to be out racing on dangerous roads. Does your mother know you were out here?"

Van stood squarely looking down at Ben. "I should think it's none of your concern what our mother thinks. Perhaps you should have been more careful in watching the road."

Lucy scrambled to her feet, a burst of energy washing over her. "Van, please, don't be so impertinent. He only means well I'm sure."

"Both of you could have been seriously injured or killed." Ben rose and studied Lucy a moment. A flash of worry crossed his face, but Lucy had a sense it meant more than concern for her fall. "'Tis most fortunate that Lucy's fall was not worse. Are you sure you are unharmed? Here, I'll escort you both home."

"That won't be necessary," Van said. "We'll manage just fine." He moved over and stood close to Lucy.

"Please don't tell Mother." Lucy tried to smile as she limped one step closer to her pony, but Ben still stood partially in the way. "She knew we were out racing, and I wouldn't want to worry her just now, when I'm really quite well."

Van lifted a defiant chin at Ben. "Our stepfather knows we are training for this race. We had his permission to be here."

"Did you now?" Ben rubbed the back of his neck as if thinking it through. "Well, it seems to me, breaking your neck or your horse's leg won't win any race, now or ever, Van."

"My horse! Natty? Is she all right?" Lucy darted off to check on her, though she seemed well and good munching a bit of new grass peeking through a bunch of decaying leaves. Over her shoulder she heard Ben speaking in lowered tones to Van.

"She's not well, Van. Anyone can see that."

"It's not your concern. We play at games all the time. It's nothing more than that. Child's play."

Lucy took hold of Natty's reins and ran a shaky hand down the horse's velvety, speckled nose. "We promise not to do such things again," she said. "And we'll go home straight away. Just...don't tell Mother or anyone. Please?"

Ben gave her a wary look and glanced back at Van before breathing a disgruntled sigh. "Very well, then. Just have a care from now on and mind where you are racing. Don't give me, or anyone else you may find along these roads, reason to have you both turned in to the authorities or given a good whipping."

"That won't be necessary, I'm sure, unless you are threatening to arrest us, Deputy Stephenson?" Van said, sarcasm dripping in every word. "But we do thank you just the same. If you'd been minding your shop...or tending to our sister Phoebe, there'd not been any problem here and no one to run into, now would there?"

Lucy's jaw dropped, incredulous at her brother's rudeness. "Van!"

"Oh, didn't you know?" Van added. "Our Mr. Stephenson seems to have his hands in everything these days, including our business. Is that why you just happened by? Were you all done comforting our brother's widow?"

"Van! You must apologize to Mr. Stephenson." To Ben she added hastily, "He didn't mean that. We were just playing a game, as he said. We won't be racing on roads again."

Ben smiled politely, though with a keen wariness that spoke of disbelief and a measured sorting of information, truth from lies, and what could be useful later. It left her head dizzy again and her chest tight.

In the end he merely tipped his hat and said, "Well, I best be going along now. I'll leave you both to your endeavors, though I could turn you over to your parents or the sheriff for this. Just use some common sense when it comes to riding and find some other course than a public road." He helped Lucy back up on her pony; then he mounted his horse and turned off down the road. Before leaving he turned to Van one last time and started to say something before pausing to consider his words. "I wouldn't be spreading rumors, lad. You have no idea of what you're saying."

Van returned a cold stare. "I'll be getting my sister home now. I do thank you for your help, sir. But all's well now."

Ben tipped his hat once more before trotting his horse toward town.

Lucy and Van rode the stretch of road home. "Van, why on earth were you so rude to Ben?"

"He's not our family but seems to think he is," Van said. "Haven't you noticed how he seems to always be everywhere we are these days?"

"He's just trying to help," Lucy said. "I'm sure he feels bad about Zack and misses him too."

"Well, it's his fault Zack died, the way I see it." Van clicked at his horse who tried to veer off toward a clump of fresh, sweet grass he had been munching on during the recent ordeal.

"What do you mean?" Lucy said. "What happened was an accident, a terrible fever. It's God's will. No one could have stopped it."

"I think they could've. And I ain't so sure it's God's will." Van shrugged and slapped the reins, more in agitation than to move his horse's sluggish hooves. "Near as I figure, our brother was still alive when Ben found him and brought him home. No one else saw him but Phoebe and Stephenson."

"And what's so unusual about that?" Lucy's eyes were wet and smarted, and some residual voice haunted her thoughts. "He...," she swallowed a croak, "he didn't last long thereafter."

Van shrugged. "No one'll ever know, now will they? And how in tarnation did he get lost in the first place?" He said the words as if in a trance, as if quoting something he'd heard.

"Van! If Mother knew you spoke like that!" She leaned in across the breadth between their mounts to slap at his arm.

"As if you don't have your own particular way of talking that would shock Mother?"

"What do you mean?" Fear crawled up her throat and tingled across her chest.

"Pay me no mind." He shrugged and let the reins fall slack as he stared down the road. "None of the other men saw him either. We got there just after Stephenson returned. His horse was still panting and sweaty." Jerking up on the reins, he slammed a fist into his horse's withers, causing the animal to stumble and wicker.

Lucy shook her head incredulously. "There wasn't nothing anyone could do. He went fast, I suppose."

Van fixed on some distant point and shook his head. "We could have said goodbye. At least been given the chance."

"Phoebe wanted to be with him." Lucy had enough, the sting of tears, the taste of salt. "It was her right, not ours."

"Perhaps." Van looked annoyed at his sister. "You can like him all you want, that Ben Stephenson. But I don't have to cotton to him. He's just like all the rest..." He took up the reins and pulled Keeper's head back causing the horse to snort and shake his head, jangling the steel bit against leathers and mane.

"All the rest of what?" Lucy leaned in closer to hear her brother's mutterings.

"I coulda swore I saw..."

"What?"

"Never mind," Van said in renewed zeal. "Look, I'll race you home. Last one past the gate is a beetle-head."

Without giving it another thought, Lucy kicked Natty Blue into a full gallop as if her very life depended upon it.

CHAPTER 13

Lucy stepped out of the wagon and smoothed the lines of her best gown, mussed from the five-mile ride to town. She felt exquisitely grown-up in the blue cotton printed with alternating pinstripes and swirling vines. Ester had let down another tuck sewn in the band near the hemline to lengthen the petticoat, making it less of a child's gown and more for a young lady. She had arranged Lucy's hair in a cascade of curls held with a yellow ribbon that complimented her gown and brown hair.

"You is growing like a weed, Miss Lucy." Ester's words stayed with her all the way down the hill. *"Either we gonna have to put a brick on your head or Miss Nelly be needin' to buy more cotton for a new gown before spring planting."*

Only one grow stripe remained turned neatly at the bottom. Already she was taller than the other girls at the school and had nearly caught up to Van. Growing up had its privileges, and today would hopefully be just the beginning. She hoped that today she appeared older, elegant, and stylish as she surveyed the town of Wellsburg teeming with excitement over the day's festivities. All the way down the hill, Van had kept up a light banter as he rode beside the wagon on his prized horse.

"What makes you so sure you'll even win this race?" She resumed her teasing with a mischievous gleam while Van trotted Keeper to a halt and dismounted.

"He outran your pony by more than a yard the last few times we raced. And Noah says he's ready. I just got a feeling he wants this win as much as I do."

"Perhaps you should have raced with more than just my pony." She knew he'd understand her meaning and his blush told her he did. They hadn't spoken again of the incident on the road with Ben, nor had it come to the attention of either their mother or Mr. Newhouse in the past fortnight. No punishment or even a scolding was forthcoming. Still, Lucy puzzled over what Van had meant about "blood" on Ben's saddle. It could mean anything. A remnant from hunting, a scratch from some task with a knife. What was so unusual for a hunter or militiaman to have a bit of bloodstain on his saddle? It hardly seemed worth mentioning. And if Zack had still been alive, what difference would it have made? He died in Phoebe's arms. Though this did make her bristle with envy at not having a chance to speak one last word to her brother, perhaps it was best to remember him as he was, as he had always been for her, someone strong, dependable, and brave. He had trusted her and her alone with a secret, one she was determined to keep until she knew what it meant.

Mr. Newhouse disembarked from the wagon and patted Keeper's neck. "He sure better win, son. I got a lot riding on this wager and I don't mean to lose. Now you keep that horse rested till the race. I'll be around if you need me but don't be bothering me unnecessarily. I got business of my own to tend to."

She shared a desperate though fleeting glance with Van before he turned away. Since the night of the cockfight, Lucy preferred to forget all she had seen and heard, including the strange voices that returned and the things Van had feared, but wouldn't tell her. Van seemed to think this had something to do with her land, bequeathed by their father, but Mr. Newhouse had said nothing about any Mr. Shepherd visiting their home, despite what they heard out behind the tavern that night. Ever since then the words she had overheard the day of Zack's funeral kept playing in her head.

"Them Swearingens. The land is the only thing that matters to them. Wouldn't put it past them to be wrestling this all out in court, or worse."

She hadn't told anyone what she'd heard between Ben and Mr. Gibson that day at the fort, but then hadn't Van been just as tight-lipped about things he knew or heard? He refused to tell her any more about things he had seen the day Zack died or why he had been so truculent to Ben that day they raced down Brady's Ridge Road. At the viewing before the funeral, there had been an odd look to Zack's hair, smoothed over the side of one temple. He had never worn it that way before, so why bury him that way? Some at the showing whispered about a bump to the head from a fall while he walked delirious through the woods. That explained the kerchief bound tight around his chin and head to cover the bruise and keep his mouth properly closed in the sleep of death, or so she had been told. Everyone had accepted that Ben brought him home still alive, though barely, to spend his last moments with Phoebe. Why should that seem so strange to Van? A wound to the head from falling on a rock would easily explain the blood.

Today was not a day to think on such things. Van would win the race, maybe that's all Mr. Newhouse needed to pay his debts to the man at the tavern and stop stealing their family's fortune. Could it truly be that easy? On a day such as this, she had to hope for nothing less.

Lucy turned away and let the dusty streets of the village, arrayed for the fair, be her present purpose. The troubles of yesterday would still be there tomorrow. Downy clouds puffed across a bright blue sky. The early spring air, cool but with a hint of the coming summer, offered endless possibilities.

The town of Wellsburg was transformed. It seemed every settler the county over had come for the fair. The village, containing only a tavern, a few shops, and some cabins, tingled with the chatter of people and a flurry of activity. A peddler with his wares displayed on a cart caught the fancy of several women. A baker in a red stocking cap balanced a board of meat pies and ginger cakes over his head. An old woman Lucy recognized as Mrs. Jarvis from New Liberty sat with a basket of knitted woolens and spun threads in an assortment of colors Lucy had never seen all in one place before. Some farmers had chickens, goats, and prized pigs to sell along with baskets of dried apples and dried corn from the previous year's harvest. All gathered on the dirt road running alongside the river to buy, sell, and trade their wares and enjoy a day of frivolous merriment before returning to the daily grind of spring planting, working the land, and fighting for survival on the edge of the wilderness. Relieved for once that her mother still suffered the early effects of her confinement and would not be out and about, Lucy anticipated a day of pure delight. It meant she could wander alone with only Winn and Tobe to accompany her, offering them all freedom to explore the fair.

The riverfront teamed with flatboats and keels docked and loaded with barrels of goods ready for trade. Canoes and rafts laden with furs rimmed the landing. Their occupants, mostly French traders, milled about, some in buckskin trousers fringed with strange-colored beads and feathers. A few were accompanied by Indian scouts and squaws. Lucy studied them, trying to recall the difference between the tribes by their appearance. Zack always knew, and he would point out the subtle differences between paint markings, ritual scarring, or the patterns of beadwork along the buckskin leggings and tunics. As she gazed over one family of trappers, a native woman caught her eye, offering a wizened gaze and a slight nod, as if she should somehow recognize her. It left Lucy confused and light-headed, and she quickly turned away, breathing in the spring air in steady, even sips.

A tug on her sleeve diverted her attention to Winn, hand clasped to her mouth, her eyes as big and shiny as copper kettles. "Land sakes, Miss Lucy. What d'ya suppose that be?" She pointed toward the river.

Beyond the canoes and flatboats moored along the shoreline, a large vessel bobbed in the rippling water. Lucy had only seen such ships in the etchings of a volume on navigation from her father's bookshelf—and at last year's fair. That was when a ship such as this had also passed through on a day much like today. It brought another bittersweet memory of Zack lifting her high above the crowd to wave at the ship. Like that other craft, this was no mere riverboat, flatboat, or pirogue. It was much larger by far, perhaps even larger than the previous boat, though not as grand and not nearly as decked out in full rigging. This was indeed another sailing ship but one with only three spindly masts sticking up like trees in a winter without snow.

"It's another ship passing through, Winn. Same as last year. Let's go take a closer look."

"I don't know." Winn sheepishly looked back toward the empty wagon. "What about your brothers."

Van stood combing his horse's mane with his fingers while he talked with a group of other boys, including Tobe. Tommy was playing with some small critter in a clump of grass over by the privy not far from Van. They wouldn't miss her for a while and likely be glad the girls had gone. Linking arms with Winn, Lucy mischievously said, "I doubt we'll be missed. The boys are quite busy. Let's go see it."

Together the girls half skipped, half ran down toward the landing. They ignored all the greetings and sellers' cries from the tents and tables where traders displayed their wares. Some folks were already gathering along the riverbank to marvel at the ship. Lucy and Winn wove their way through the crowd to gain a better vantage point.

"Lord a-mercy, Miss Lucy! It do look like that *President Adams* coming down river same as last year. And just look who be standin' at the helm? Mr. Stephenson?"

Lucy peripherally heard the girl, having turned away to keep an eye peeled one last time for Tommy. "What do you mean, Winn? Mr. Stephenson would never..." She turned, expecting to find the slave girl in another of her tricks, only to see a much grander ship than she first thought. Three-masted and lined with shiny brass guns and right there in front of the mast flying an American flag, standing at the ship's wheel, was none other than... "Land o Goshen!" She let the words slip before she realized, thankful at least that only Winn had heard.

"You certainly got that right, li'l sissy." The familiar voice registered in her tingling ears. Lucy turned to see Elzey's broad features and square shoulders. He was clean-shaven and decked out in his brown linen jacket and mustard breeches, looking much finer than his usual unkempt appearance. "Quite the ship, ain't she? Land o Goshen?" He looked askew at his errant sister. "Might be a good name for her, indeed."

Lucy swallowed, trying to still her thumping heart. "I didn't say—"

"It were me what said those words, Mister Elzey," Winn spoke up bravely. "I shouldn'a said them, not in front of Miss Lucy, no sir."

He stood sternly taking in both girls. Lucy braced herself for his next reaction. "No, Winn, it was me. You won't tell Mother, please?" She flashed her brother wide, innocent eyes and bit her lower lip for added effect.

"I oughta tell your ma. Such shocking words from a fine young lady!" He scratched his smooth chin considering, then gave a little wink. "But she's got enough to fret over, and given your honesty and your handmaid's willingness to take the fault... I'll let it go. This time. Only if you promise to mind your tongue and..."

"We will!" Both girls chimed together. Lucy breathed a sigh and exchanged a relieved smile with Winn. "At least as much as you do, dear brother."

He gave her a churlish nod, and she regretted having pressed him this far. A change of subject was most needed. "Van is riding in the race later, so of course its best I stay to watch out for Tommy."

Elzey looked over, peering into the morning sunlight. "Yep, so I heard. Got a bit of money riding on our little brother, so I hope he's in rare form today."

Lucy felt her shoulders tense but tried to keep a pleasant smile. "I expect he'll do well. He's been running Keeper against Natty Blue every chance he got these past few weeks. I'd say he's ready."

"Do you now, little sister?" Elzey studied Lucy with a curious, amused grin. "Well, knowing how well you ride, I'm surprised you aren't racing that dun pony of yours. I hear you gave our brother Van quite a run of late."

"Oh, no," Winn shook her head and clasped her hands together near her chest. "Miss Nelly would never allow Miss Lucy to race, Mister Elzey."

Elzey looked at the slave girl and chuckled. "You just make sure our baby sister don't get into much trouble and mind your place."

Lucy stood tall and primped the lace on her sleeve. "I am not a baby. I don't need to be looked after. Winn and I will do just fine on our own."

Elzey looked up to the sky and sighed. "I s'pose I keep forgetting my sister is quite the young lady these days. Let's see, you must be?"

"Not yet eleven," Lucy crossed her arms, a twinge of guilt over her earlier lie to Ben irking her.

"Do tell." Elzey pulled off his hat and scratched his head. "Ah, well, what say we all go down and take a closer look at the fair *Senator Ross* as she takes her maiden voyage."

"The what?" Lucy and Winn both chimed in together. "Is it another like the *President Adams* from last year?"

Elzey laughed and put an arm around both girls steering them toward the water's edge. "Naw, it's her sister. Come see the latest from the Pittsburgh shipyards, m'dears. 'Tis ocean-bound on its way to the port of New Orleans."

Lucy tried to imagine all the miles this ship would travel on its way to the wide-open seas. She couldn't fathom the places this boat would go. "We can go aboard?" she asked, incredulous.

Elzey steered them toward a pirogue at the river's edge. "Just step this way." He helped first Lucy then Winn into the wobbly dugout canoe, then set himself down in the middle and began to row toward the ship.

Lucy reached over the side of the boat to skim her fingers across the rippling water. It felt cool and smooth to the touch. The ice was nearly thawed with only an occasional chunk floating down from up north. The trees flanking the far bank wafted their tiny buds in the cool breeze. The river hummed with the tune of early cicadas and frogs. She shivered with excitement thinking of standing aboard such a fine ship and imagined all the places it would travel on the open seas.

"Will we need permission from the captain to go aboard like this?" Lucy looked over her shoulder as they neared the ship.

"Yes, but that's easily gotten," Elzey grinned and raised an eyebrow, "seeing as how I'm part owner."

"It's *your* boat?" Lucy twisted half around, jostling the pirogue. The curved edge tipped dangerously close to taking in water. Winn grasped the sides of the boat and screamed.

"Whoa, there. Steady." Elzey maneuvered the paddle deftly from side to side. The pirogue leveled and spun slightly. "Now, stay still till we reach the starboard side. See that ladder? When I bring the pirogue up alongside, you gals stand up nice and slow-like and climb the ladder. Lucy, you think you can manage first?"

The pirogue inched closer to the side of the ship where a rope ladder draped down to the water. At the top a sailor stood waiting to meet them. Lucy swallowed and took a deep breath before rising slowly to her feet.

"You're doing fine," Elzey said. "I've got hold of the ladder. Just move on up to the top, one rung at a time and don't look down."

Lucy nodded and tried to smile bravely at her big brother, then looked up the ladder to the man standing far away at the top.

"Do be careful, Miss Lucy," Winn said, her voice a shrill gasp.

"Ahoy! Welcome aboard." The sailor at the top held the ladder firm and saluted as she made a steady climb to the top. "Easy goes it, little lady."

Lucy did not breathe until she stood on deck. This was still no assurance as the boards beneath her feet waffled with each step she took. She leaned over the side calling words of encouragement as Winn made the journey upward. Elzey followed close behind the trembling slave girl until both were safe aboard.

"Here it is, the mighty *Senator Ross.*" Elzey spread his hands out. "Behold the way of the future. Soon you'll be seeing the river lined with schooners, galleys, and clippers bound for the West Indies, New England, and, perhaps, even Europe and Africa."

Lucy surveyed the ship taking it all in. The deck held large barrels and crates. Clean ropes still smelling of freshly milled hemp were coiled in neat piles in open boxes. Sailors in smart, crisp-blue jackets and tan breeches climbed the two masts and worked at securing lines to hold future sails which for now, remained tightly furled around masts set to the far side of the ship that Lucy thought might be the bow, or perhaps it was the stern. Ladies and gentlemen in fine dress mingled with common settlers roaming the deck pointing, murmuring, and chatting casually with one another. Her eyes traveled upward to the colorful flags slapping against the blue sky. "All the way from Fort Pitt and down our Ohio River? Just like the *President Adams* last year?" She blinked thinking back at the fanfare and celebrations as the grand ship, escorted by a fleet of smaller boats, had sailed by, and now here she was to experience it all firsthand.

"Aye, missy. That was indeed a grand celebration. General Wilkinson gave us quite a show." Elzey smiled and winked, slyly. "All the way from the shipyards of Pittsburgh to the wide-open sea, 'tis ships like these that'll bring goods back to the ports of New Orleans, Boston, and New York, from all over the world, so my little sister can stay pretty in her fine India silks while sipping China tea." He studied her a moment with a roguish look. "Or perhaps read the latest ladies' novels from the pen of an English author?"

"Mother reads the ladies' novels," she said, dismissively. "You know she won't let me read them yet and I've no mind to." She averted her attention to some more interesting part of the ship, lest he surmise she had been sneaking a few peaks at her mother's stories, though she found little to interest her with all the swooning ladies and dastardly villains mucking about. The tale of Telemachus had been far more engaging, if somewhat baffling in places, much like the sort of man who had lent her the book.

"Lawd, Miss Lucy." Winn strode unsteadily across the deck, her eyes taking in everything as if she had just landed on the moon. "West Indies, Europe, and Africa, them's the places you pointed out in that book of maps we look at."

"Uh huh," Lucy nodded and grabbed Winn's hand to steady her. "I hardly know where those places are either. They're thousands of miles away across the Atlantic Ocean." *Like Telemachus, set for a journey,* she thought as she considered all the places this ship would go.

Winn's mouth formed a small circle and her eyes darted from one end of the ship to the other as if calculating the amount of miles the ship would travel.

Elzey looked between the two girls and frowned. "Still playing at school are you?"

Lucy offered a terse nod and then looked around the deck. Some townsfolk milled about the ship talking with the men who must be the sailors, she reckoned. A few sailors carried buckets across the deck or wiped the rails. Around the deck, barrels, sacks, and a few trunks stood ready to meet destination at ports ahead. Some were marked with words indicating their contents. Lucy watched as Winn worked out the spellings in her mind.

"F-L-O-U-R. That say flour, don't it miss?" Winn smiled, a look of accomplishment in her eyes.

"Yes, well done, Winn." Lucy pointed to another barrel. "What does this say?"

Winn frowned and bit her lip. "N-A-I-L-S. Nye...? Nel...?"

"No, try a long 'A' sound, like in 'pale'."

Winn took a deep breath and closed her eyes. "Nay-ahls. That barrel has a bunch o' iron nails in there, don't it?"

"Still teaching slaves to read?" Elzey laughed and muttered, "Waste of time if ya ask me."

"I didn't ask you," Lucy replied pertly. "Did you say this was your ship?" Lucy cocked her head and peered at her brother from under her poke bonnet. "Will you be sailing with it?"

"No, I'll not sail. And I was only teasing. It ain't really my ship, but someday, I'll have one." Elzey started to say something else but was cut off by the loud blast of a horn.

Lucy and Winn both jumped and clutched each other's hands. "What was that?"

Elzey threw back his head and laughed. "Ah, the music of the river." He motioned to the upper deck over the cabin at the stern.

A sailor stood aloft belting out a three-note tune on a long brass horn that elicited a stirring round of whoops and hollers on shore. More folk embarked the ship to take a gander at this new wonder, including, to Lucy's chagrin, her own little brother Tommy, being helped aboard by Ben Stephenson.

"Ho, young Thomas, there's your sister." Ben lifted him off the ladder and sailed him easily over the ship's rail before setting him down. Together, hand in hand, they ambled over toward the center mast where Lucy stood with Elzey and Winn.

"Sissy!" Tommy called. "We've got us a real pirate ship to play in!"

Elzey and Ben laughed, but Lucy wasn't in the mood to deal with Tommy's antics.

"It's not ours and it's definitely not a pirate ship," she said primly.

Elzey shook his head and added, "Piracy! Now there's a thought, Ben. Seems my little brother found us out." The two men shared a wary gleam as if entertaining the most dastardly deeds.

"What? You are going to sail this boat?" In the brief time since crossing the river Lucy had quite forgotten seeing Ben onboard earlier from shore. "We saw you at the helm? So, you are the captain? Certainly not a pirate?" She was babbling and must cease. He was going to leave Wellsburg. First Zack, now Ben—everyone was leaving her behind as always.

"No, not captain, not just yet, at least," Ben chuckled. "But I am to accompany the *Senator Ross* to its destination at the Port of Orleans by late spring. Should be a profitable venture for the trading post." He winked at Lucy and nodded in the direction of Elzey. "With your family's help, along with other investors, we'll have our own boat soon enough."

"So, you will be leaving? Going out to sea?" Lucy tried to keep her voice casual but feared the urgency sounded in a tight squeak.

"Out to sea?" Ben pushed back his cap and gave her a quizzical look.

"Now there's a thought.

Ah, yes. How does the song go?" With the wistful look of a young lad he whistled an unfamiliar tune and then struck up in off-key chorus with Elzey.

I that once was a ploughman, a sailor am now...
and to talk of such things as if sailors were kings...
that I left my poor plough to go sailing the deep.

Ending the fragmented song there, both men struggled to piece together the words until Ben settled the matter. "Alas, that's all I recall. No years before the mast for me. I'm only to accompany this tub on her maiden voyage as far as the Gulf. After that I should be back in a matter of a month or two."

"A month? Or two?" Hope raised in Lucy's heart as high as the flag on the ship. He'd return by summer time, but would that be soon enough? *Soon enough for what?* The strange thought struck her as if from some unknown voice deep inside her head.

"Yes, no more than a month or two," Ben addressed her question. She hadn't realized she'd even spoken it aloud. "River's not much navigable for large ships during the heat of the summer."

"Why not?" Tommy asked.

"Water's at low tide," Ben said stoutly as if Tommy were one of his crew. "Too many hazards like the Falls of the Ohio and sandbars to deal with."

"How you gonna get back without a ship?" Tommy looked at Ben as if he expected him to sprout wings and fly.

"Oh, there are ways, my good lad. I will most likely catch a keelboat on its way north. Bring back some goods to sell at the post, perhaps a few marbles or a compass for you or some pretty hair ribbons for your sister. If nothing else I can always walk the thousand miles or more."

"Walk back? No, you mustn't. Is it safe?" Lucy peripherally noted some black furry thing that Tommy scampered after across the deck.

"Oh, he'll do fine, Lucy," Elzey shook his head. "My babe of a sister, more an old woman, ever the fretful hen. I imagine the falls down toward Louisville will prove the ship's greatest trial, especially with the heavy rains we've had lately."

"Perhaps. Though as long as we remain at high water, it should be smooth sailing downriver. It's the poling and heaving north against the current that test a man's mettle." Ben leaned a hand on the ship's rail and gazed downriver. "Although, it's the Spaniards down toward the Natchez Trace and possible river pirates that trouble a ship's journey more these days, or so I hear."

"What's this talk of river pirates?" A man dressed in a double-breasted jacket with shiny brass buttons walked over from the port side with an older couple Lucy recognized as Kaspar and Wilhemina Briggs. "Good morning, Mr. Swearingen. Mr. Stephenson." Mr. Briggs tipped his hat to Lucy. "Ah, the little Miss Swearingen."

Lucy bobbed a slight curtsey to the couple reciprocated by Mrs. Briggs's smile and slight nod. "Lucy, where is your dear mother? "

"She stayed to home, ma'am," Lucy said. "She's not well today."

"I am sorry to hear that," Mrs. Briggs said. "I hope it's nothing dire. I was so hoping to speak with her about our next quilting bee. Do give her my regards when you get home."

"Yes, ma'am, thank you."

"Your brother is racing his horse this afternoon, I hear," Mr. Briggs said. "You as well, Stephenson?"

Lucy shot a wide-eyed look in Ben's direction. "You're racing too?"

The men chuckled. "Yes, there's a fine purse awaiting the winner," Ben said. "Josiah wanted to race Hercules but found the beast is more partial to my lead. If we win, we split the purse and put it toward our business venture." He patted the rail and nodded toward the tall center mast.

"Then the stallion is not yours?" Lucy mulled this over, thinking of the horse that almost ran her down along the road the day she and Van raced.

"No, miss, but I ride him whenever I get a notion." His eyes lit up at a sight beyond Lucy. "Someday I'll have a horse or two, some livestock, perhaps. But for now I've got a ship and this little pup to mind."

They all turned to see Tommy coming up from a lower deck holding a wiggling mop of black fur that looked more like a bear cub than a puppy.

"Tommy! Whatever have you gotten now?"

"It's my puppy." He let the whimpering mass of fur plop to the deck where it bounded over toward Ben. "Can I keep him, Mr. Ben?"

"'Fraid not, son." He reached to scratch the pup's ear. "This here dog belongs on the ship. He's kind of a mascot that came along as a bonus, of sorts. I'm supposed to see if some merchant seaman might want him." He rolled his eyes as he gave a hearty rub to the dog's massive head. "A sea dog, one of the crew, and he better well learn to earn his keep along the journey."

"What's his name?" Tommy asked.

"Name?" Ben arched an eyebrow, still crouched on the deck teasing the puppy's nibbling snout. "Hadn't thought about it yet."

"Can I call him Bear?" Tommy chimed in. "He looks like a little black bear."

"Tommy," Lucy chided, "don't be so impertinent. Mr. Stephenson should name his own dog. And Bear's a silly name for the dog."

"Actually he does need a name, come to think of it. Newfies do look more bear than dog." Ben stood, holding the pup, contemplating the prospect. "Bear. What do you think, ol' boy? Will that suit you?"

"Bear doesn't fit a sea dog," Lucy considered. "But what's a Newfie?"

Elzey shook his head. "Newfoundland, sister. It's a dog breed from

Canada. Water dogs is what they are, but they eat like bears. This one'll devour your entire larder if ya let him."

"Then why not call him Seaman?" Lucy spurted her suggestion while the two men continued discussing details of the voyage and Tommy took the squirming puppy from Ben's hold.

The men paused, stunned into silence at her suggestion. "Why, I do like it." Ben lifted the dog high as it licked a red velvety tongue over his chin and nose. "Seaman it is. You've officially joined the crew."

They all laughed and continued the tour of the ship, Seaman following on Tommy's heels until it was time to return to shore.

The morning drifted lazily along, as she chatted pleasantly with friends. Many people asked about her mother and she felt a bit uncomfortable telling them she was ill. She didn't want to tell the real reason for fear that her mother would be mortified, and, truthfully, she had tried to block out the reason herself. Folks in the settlement would know soon enough she surmised, and then what? The thought of having a baby brother or sister intrigued her. She loved caring for her little brother, who was now getting too big for her to pick up and carry about. Yet, she worried what would happen if her mother succumbed to childbirth. So many women in the county died in childbed that the graveyards were filled with the headstones of lost young wives and daughters. Mother looked increasingly pale and gaunt and spent entire days abed. A shiver passed over her as she thought of being left completely orphaned to the devices of Mr. Newhouse. Her thoughts shot back to the night of the cockfight. Van still wouldn't tell her everything he feared, only saying that Mr. Newhouse had access to their inheritance and could do as he pleased, being the head of the household now. If Mr. Newhouse had his own flesh and blood heir over the inconvenient stepchildren now living under his roof, her life would be like a ship navigating down a treacherous river.

She forced the thoughts to pass from her. It was easy to do on such a day. The excitement of being in the marketplace with the village folk smiling and full of gossip to share and goodwill to pass was all Lucy needed to lift her from her dismal life up the hill.

By afternoon the ship's horn blew again signaling the prelude to the race. First came an address by the town magistrate extolling the progress of the town of Wellsburg and welcoming visitors to the events. He talked of the Swearingen family and the contributions of their father, brothers, and Drusilla's husband, Sam Brady. A few local politicians gave long-winded speeches stumping their causes and encouraging people to move west and prosper to expand the United States into a great nation. Even Ben was asked to speak, and he reluctantly offered a few words on his upcoming riverboat excursion. He modestly explained the route he would be taking and thanked the investors who made the production of the schooner possible.

The horn blew again, and the order was given to line up the horses for the race. Van was nervous; Lucy could tell by the way he kept fidgeting with his horse's bridle and girth strap. She sidled up next to him and whispered, "Van, you're gonna do fine in this race. I know you can beat them all. Did you know that Ben Stephenson is riding too?"

Van continued brushing his horse as if he hadn't heard her, then pulled on the girth strap so tight Keeper let out a snort and flinched away. "Yea, I know so what of it? You think I can't beat him too?"

She moved in front of Keeper and stroked the white blaze between his eyes. "I didn't say anything of the sort. I just wondered if you knew is all."

Lucy watched her brother swing into the saddle. "Well, I just wanted to wish you good luck." She touched her forehead gently to the horse's long nose and scratched the loose flesh beneath his jowl. "There now, my fine fellow, you be swift but safe, run like the wind and make us all proud." She gave him a quick kiss before moving aside.

Van smiled. "Oh, he'll do fine. He wants this win as badly as I do. I can feel it." With a light tap of his heel he urged his horse toward the start line.

"Van, why is it so important to win they money?" Lucy bit her lip and looked to see that no one was within earshot. "It will help, won't it? Is it all for Mr. Newhouse? Maybe you'll tell me what this is all about?"

Van pulled on the rein and turned back to his sister before looking away. "Aye, you'll find out soon enough. Watch for me at the finish line."

Lucy looked for Tommy who was off playing marbles with a group of boys behind one of the cabins. "Come on, our brother is up first in the race. We'll watch from the schoolyard fence."

The racetrack extended from the edge of the settlement to the southern tip of William Engle's field, about a quarter mile down the road. Since only two horses could ride abreast along the narrow lane, the riders all drew straws in a complex tournament of elimination until the final victor on the fastest horse was declared.

People crowded along both sides of the road to get the best view. Men boasted about the surety of their favorites and surmised the odds of others. Lucy just prayed that Van would win so it would keep Mr. Newhouse in good spirits. Having found Tommy, Lucy caught up with Winn and Tobe and then headed toward the finish line where a rope was loosely strung across the road waiting for the first horse to break through.

Lucy could barely make out Van's horse at the start line prancing alongside Jacob McAdams's gray mare. She said a silent prayer that all would be well. Her fists were clenched into tight balls as if she could feel the smooth leather of the reins between her own fingers. She would have loved the chance to ride, but only men were allowed in such events.

Charles Dunlop stood near the riders holding a pistol in the air to signal the start of the race. A sharp pop of the discharged gun left a trail of smoke and the scent of burnt powder. The horses leapt into motion, a blur of sinewy flesh and pulsing muscle mingled with dust clouds. A tingle of excitement coursed through Lucy as the scent of leather and horsehide combined for a thrilling spectacle of speed, agility, and strength.

"Come on Keeper, come on!" Lucy shouted with all her might, in chorus with the pressing crowd. Lucy felt her knees shift in cadence with the pulsing of horse legs and the pounding of hooves. She could have ridden Keeper. She'd done it often enough before.

Cheers and shouts from the onlookers pitched in frenzied dissonance with the thunder of hooves against the dirt road. In a cloud of dust the two contenders flashed toward the finish. Lucy dared not blink. Was Van really still ahead? Just barely, oh just barely, but

McAdams's mare was all too close behind. The slice of time it took to race and win—a moment, a lifetime, an eternity—pulsed in sweeping motion.

The horses ran alongside each other keeping pace until Van nudged his horse into a longer stride that soon put him a half length ahead at just the right moment, allowing him to break through the finish rope just inches before McAdams.

Lucy and Winn shouted and cheered jumping in unladylike fashion, but Lucy didn't care. Van had won, but this was only the first heat with several more to go before a victor ruled the day. She kept her eyes on Van's horse as he slowed to a trot and circled back toward the crowd. When he caught sight of Lucy, he gave her a broad smile, reared his horse back, and let out a glorious "Yeeawh." Lucy laughed and shook her head at her outlandish brother, but many in the crowd responded with a resounding "Huzzah! Huzzah!"

The celebration was short-lived as two new contenders took their places at the start line. This time it was Huck Tanner on his chestnut gelding against Gabe Martin on his white stallion. Lucy judged it would be a few minutes before the next heat. She told Winn to stay with Tommy and then took off across the field to where Van stood talking with Elzey behind Engle's barn.

Lucy ran up to him and threw her arms around his neck. "Van, that was capital! You won!"

Van took a step back and tried to steady himself while keeping a firm grip on his sister. "Thanks, but it's not over yet."

"You got that right, my boy." The grating voice behind her sent a nauseating sting of bile up Lucy's throat. She looked back to see the gleaming eyes and crooked smile of none other than Mr. Newhouse.

"How endearing," he said. "The sister bestows her unmitigated delight at her brother's triumph. Such sisterly affection."

Lucy stiffened and released her hold on Van. She turned to face Mr. Newhouse standing with a gentleman dressed in an intricately embroidered, silk waistcoat and fine, black frock coat. He was dressed head to toe in shiny, crisp clothing that must be the new style from out east, for Lucy had never seen such finery.

"I am very glad he won, aren't you?" She tried to say this as sweetly and politely as possible and offered a winsome smile.

Mr. Newhouse assessed her a moment then gestured a hand toward her as he addressed the gentleman at his side. "This here is my wife's daughter, Miss Lucy Swearingen, and son Master Van Swearingen. Children, may I present Mr. Shepherd."

An interminable pause followed while Lucy realized a curtsey was expected. She quickly bobbed a slight dip then cleared her throat and looked sidelong to Van who followed suit with a jerky bow from the waist.

"Indeed, I am most pleased to meet you both." The man tipped his hat but never took his eyes off Lucy. At last he shifted his gaze toward Van. "Fine steed you have there, young man. That was excellent riding."

"Thank you, sir," Van said. He beamed at the compliment, but Lucy was not so easily taken in. She recalled the conversation from a few weeks before. The night of the cockfight. That was where she had heard it. This was the same man Mr. Newhouse had spoken with behind the tavern.

"'Tis a pity the steed is gelded." The gentleman surveyed Keeper with discerning eyes. "I should like such a creature for breeding with my mares."

"Do you live around here?" Van ventured his words cautiously. He sounded casual, but Lucy noted a fleeting look in her direction and wondered if he suspected what she did.

Both men chuckled lightly. "I'm from Shepherds Town."

"Then perhaps you know our uncle, Colonel Swearingen?" she said, flashing him her sweetest smile.

"I do indeed. Joseph Swearingen." He bore a fiery look into her that seethed with hatred and delight. "Your father's brother, I believe?"

"Yes," Van interjected, before Lucy could reply, "he is that."

"Little Mouse," Shepherd remarked. "Is that what they call you out here? I hear you are a girl who likes to speak her mind. John, I do believe I shall take you up on that dinner invitation before I bid my leave of your settlement."

Lucy bit her tongue to keep from saying it was now a village and nearly a town, no longer just a settlement. Something told her not to give him the satisfaction of seeing that she indeed liked to "speak her mind." She instinctively hated this man but had no real reason. It brought up an ire in her that tangled with guilt. It was childish, and she was determined not to be treated as a child by anyone anymore.

As the men continued to talk, Mr. Newhouse laughed nervously and shifted his eyes between the ground and those in their small group. "Ah, yes, well then, Abraham, let's say we go view the outcome of the next race, shall we?" Then turning to Van he said, "You make sure that boy of yours properly freshens Keeper for the next lap, mind you now."

He gestured to someone behind Lucy. She looked over her shoulder to spy Tobe standing beside Winn. She had quite forgotten he had even come along.

The afternoon continued with race after race. Van competed two more times—against Ned Billings's black mare and Sully Turner's dun stallion—and won. Lucy watched eagerly for Van and also noted how Ben Stephenson fared. She wasn't sure she should root for Ben and, above all, dreaded what his continued success would mean—that he and her brother would face a final showdown. If it came down to it, she would prefer Van to win, even if Ben had been kind to her lately and loaned her the book she enjoyed reading. Van had been so antagonistic toward Ben for reasons she could not fathom. The children's talk in the schoolyard along with what she overheard at the fort the day they buried Zack continued to haunt her. Ben probably only wanted the winning purse to fund his business, so he couldn't have any designs on Swearingen money or an interest in Phoebe. That's what she kept hoping, at least.

Lucy tried to block out all thoughts of this, focusing only on the fervor of each succeeding race.

The afternoon sun was waning when the final contest was announced. It would indeed, as Lucy feared, be a showdown between her brother and Ben.

A group of men gathered at the start line, conferring in serious fashion. Lucy watched as Elzey, William Engle, George Pritchard, and Josiah Gibson nodded and gestured between horses and field. Ben was off to the side rubbing down his horse's forelegs and checking the hooves. Van scowled on the other side of the field adjusting Keeper's saddle and talking softly to his horse.

At long last, George Pritchard stepped into the center of the road and called the crowd to silence.

"We're about to commence the last race to determine the grand champion winner of these festivities here today," George called in a commanding voice as a murmur filtered through the crowd.

"It has been determined by the officials conducting this here race that the final match will consist of a steeplechase of sorts." He spread his arms out and motioned toward the start line. "The race will begin here as before but will extend past the quarter-mile mark to cut around Engle's farm, down the path, through the woods. That will include several jumps to be taken by each horse. There's the Clifty Rock Creek and that old dead tree we've been meaning to move and anything else that gets in the way."

A chuckle rose among the crowd, but Lucy only felt a shiver of fear run through her.

"Judges will be posted at each point to make sure all jumps be taken in order."

Another murmur came up from the crowd. Lucy looked over at Van whose face was stony and unreadable. She glanced over to where Ben stood nodding and speaking with Josiah Gibson.

Winn moved over closer to her. "Miss Lucy what they mean by a steeplechase?"

"I don't rightly know, Winn." Lucy bit her lip and inhaled a deep breath. "I guess we'll soon see."

George quieted the crowd and resumed his explanation. "Once the path reaches the Coach Road again the riders will circle back along the southern edge of Engle's land and cross the field where there'll be the hay bales and the split-rail fence to jump before heading back into town and ending back here where the race commenced. All total we figure it to be about a three- to four-mile trek." George gave a long, hard look at both Ben and Van. You men figure you're up to such a race?"

Ben looked over at Van then returned a steady gaze at George and offered a curt nod. Van kept his eyes fixed on a point somewhere beyond the top of the nearest trees and said, "Nothing to it."

Satisfied with the responses of both riders, George gave a quick nod. "All right then. The final race will commence in one hour. When the boatman's horn sounds, all riders will be in position. Until then ye both can take a few practice jumps, walk the course, or head to the tavern for some ambition." A snicker erupted from the men, tempered by some shocked gasps from the ladies.

At the edge of the crowd, Mr. Newhouse stood exchanging an appreciative glance with his friend Abraham Shepherd.

Phoebe came up behind Lucy and placed a hand on her arm. "Why Lucy, just think, your brother in a steeplechase. I've heard of such things but to think we'd have one out here in Wellsburg."

Martha Gillespie, standing in the crowd next to Phoebe said, "I'm just as glad my William didn't win now. Think of the risk involved in such a sport, and all for a few paltry coins."

Lucy murmured to be excused from the ladies and made her way through the crowd to reach Van.

The hour passed quickly Van had tried a few practice jumps and sailed across both the rail fence and the hay bales. Lucy felt a bit better that Van would have a chance and come through unharmed. She watched to see how Ben did on his practice jumps and saw that indeed it would be a close race at best.

When the boatman's horn blew three clear, long blasts, the riders took their places at the start line, and the crowd took positions at various points along the track. Some crawled onto the top of the tavern roof, and others climbed up trees to gain a better vantage point for the race. Lucy wished it was not so undignified and she were not wearing a gown, or indeed she would have scrambled for such a prime seat. As she was watching those who had taken positions in the limbs of trees, she noted an unkempt head of ash-blonde hair and a pair of legs dangling from a thick sycamore branch.

"Tommy, what are you doing up there?" Lucy said. "Get down here this instant."

"But I can see clear down the road, almost past the creek," Tommy said. "I'll be able to tell you just what I see. You can come up here, too, if you like."

"Thomas Van Swearingen, now you know I can't climb trees in this gown." She pursed her lips together thinking through her options at the moment. "Well, all right, you stay there and be sure to let me know what's happening."

Tommy grinned and nodded vigorously, then settled himself more securely in the branch of the tree.

The signal of the pistol sent both horses leaping into action. Van's horse barreled ahead of Ben's black stallion as they flew toward the former, quarter-mile finish line. Had this been the culmination of the race, Lucy felt certain Van would have won, but this only signaled the beginning. From the quarter-mile point the riders veered left onto a path in the woods, and this was where Lucy lost sight of them. Some of the crowd ran along the road trying to keep up. Lucy strained to see as far as she could then turned to Tommy for his viewpoint. Before she could ask Tommy, a hand reached out to grasp her shoulder.

"Not now, Winn, I've got to keep up with the race."

"That is precisely what I had in mind." The voice wasn't Winn's.

Lucy turned to see Elzey looking at her with a sly smile. "Follow me. I'll show you the best seat in the house for this race."

Lucy followed her brother, with Winn and Tobe trailing behind, down to the river for the second time that day to cross the waters and board the ship. It seemed an eternity passed as Elzey paddled his way through the rippling river. At last she was aboard the ship and standing on the upper deck with a few of the sailors. One handed her a spyglass, which offered her a close-up view of the path through the woods. She couldn't see either Van or Ben at first, only the calm woodlands dappled in late afternoon sunlight.

Something moved across the glass, a blur of brown dashing through the newly budding green leaves. She focused and moved the glass a bit to the left. It was Van racing in and out of the trees. When he was on a high point of a hill she could see him clearly, but then he dipped behind some trees as he passed down a slope. Where was Ben? She wondered if it meant he was lagging behind or leading out front.

She moved the glass across the landscape hoping to find the answer.

"What do you see, Miss Lucy?" Winn stood on tiptoe squinting into the late afternoon sun. "Is Mister Van taking the lead?"

Lucy bit her lip and strained to see farther through the spyglass. Shouts from the men and boys sitting in the trees let her know they had spotted one or both riders. She felt a hand gently grasp the spyglass and turned to see Elzey. "Here, little sister, let me see."

She reluctantly forfeited the glass to him, and he positioned it just below the tops of the trees and turned the end piece. "Ah, there they be." He returned the glass to her bending down so as to keep the glass in about the same position. "It looks like Van is in the lead. Just there below Pine Ridge."

Lucy held the glass steady in the same position as Elzey had. She spotted Van then saw Ben close on his heels. They were galloping around another curve in the path and would soon reach the main road. Van's head bobbed slightly and his shoulders hunched forward, indicating he must have taken another jump. Lucy tightened her grip on the spyglass, every muscle tensed as if she felt the lurch of each movement the horse made over each obstacle.

She lowered the spyglass a moment and closed her eyes as a cold shudder coursed through her frame. "Oh, Van do take care." She knew the ridge they were taking. Hadn't she ridden Natty Blue through the pass often enough? Natty Blue knew how to scale any creek, log, or hedgerow along this pass. There was the old dead hickory log, scaled in perfect precision by each rider. Cutters Creek was just around the bend at the bottom of the hill. Lucy held her breath, her eyes still closed, feeling the wind on her face, the snap of every twig, and the muscle and bone and leather rippling beneath her legs.

Pounding hooves. Ben rocked in rhythm to Bronzer's gait, galloping at a speed that even he wasn't sure could be controlled. This horse wanted the win perhaps even more than he did. The lad was gaining on him. He heard the thunder of hooves behind, and Van's cries urging his horse onward. Three easy jumps so far had proved little contest for his stallion or Van's smaller chestnut. He should rein him in. Let the boy win. There were other means to fund his ventures. He never really expected to get this far. But this meant so much more. Perhaps the lad needed to learn a lesson in humility, curb his arrogance. He'd certainly been rude enough to him of late.

Another jump. This one trickier. Ben leaned forward, coaxing Bronzer to ease up a bit, just a bit. Longer strides—counting, one, two, three. The strong muscles pulsed beneath him. He flew airborne for a split-second of eternity. Was this what it felt like to fly? Sheer freedom. Every time felt new, undiscovered. Exhilarating. He was not much for jumping or racing, but this was pure pleasure.

A splash of hooves in a shallow creek bed ended the jump, bringing him back to earth. On the walk-through before the race, this had appeared the most unnerving of jumps, but Bronzer had cleared it. Another splash and hooves pounding a counter-cadence. Van managed the jump, too. *Don't look back. Press onward.* Ahead a band of folks cheered on the side, a blur of bonnets, beaver hats, and waved mitts. Onward, onward toward the last leg of the track. Van ran beside him, beating the crop wildly to the horse's rear flank. "Yah! Yah! Keeper go!"

"Easy, Bronzer," Ben willed his own mount onward. "Win or lose, we've come this far. Ease it along." As if the beast understood or merely couldn't abide the horse gaining on his flank, he lengthened his stride pushing onward, up the embankment, beneath the overhang of tree branches, and around the bend into the clearing that led toward the town and the cheering crowd. One final jump ahead and then the finish line.

Someone's hand clutched her arm. Lucy opened her eyes to see Winn staring wide-eyed and pointing in the direction of the town. "They comin,' Miss Lucy. They almost here."

Van moved onto the main road, appearing out of the trees, his horse, a thundering beast, cast reddish brown in the golden afternoon sunlight. Close on his tail, a black horse like an apocalyptic vision broke free from the tree-lined path kicking up clods of dirt that danced behind the horses' hooves.

They rounded the bend and headed straight down the road toward the town. All that was left was the two jumps across Engle's field.

Van sailed effortlessly across the hay bales. Now the rail fence, and he would surely win. Ben's horse was ahead, then behind. Van paced his horse at breakneck speed toward the rail fence. Lucy counted each pace, anticipating the jump with each tensed fiber of her flesh. Her teeth gripped her lower lip till she nearly tasted blood.

Something didn't feel right. A cold shudder rattled between her shoulder blades. Van glanced back. She knew it in the split-second it took for him to move his horse a bit off step. Paces counted one, two, three, before he slammed into the log rails. He had taken just a second to check Ben's position and perhaps gloat over his impending success, which was not to be. He and Keeper lay in a crumpled mass of logs and horse's limbs as Ben sailed in silky motion across the fence line and headed back through the heart of town and across the finish. The crowd erupted in cheers and victorious laughter, cut short as they also reacted to what had happened.

Lucy dropped the spyglass and scrambled to the ship's ladder not nearly quick enough. The sound of feet pounding across the deck followed in her wake. Winn and Elzey called after her. They joined her in the pirogue, though she couldn't say if they or the sailors guided her to the rough-hewn belly of the canoe. She didn't remember the trip across the short distance to shore, only that her feet flew across the landing toward the field where a group of townsfolk gathered.

CHAPTER 14

A bayonet fit into the end of a musket just so. Held between thumb and forefingers, a slight twist, and it locked in place. Zack had taught her that and the best way to sharpen and keep it tucked away until readying for battle. She had been seven then and couldn't imagine what a sharp knife would be doing at the end of a gun. Impaling the enemy was just one of its uses to a soldier while marching through the backwoods and surviving off the land. It was one of many lessons Zack had taught her, which she added to a small copybook for such things. She wasn't sure why that should come to mind now, though, sitting at the dinner table. The definition, along with the memory of him, kept her from screaming, and she wanted so desperately to scream. The ill-fitting gown was littered with pins nipping into the soft flesh under her arms and at the neckline. Mother had insisted she wear the silk fashion after digging it out of an old discarded trunk.

"It was my favorite when I was young. A fine, smoky rose and most becoming on me. Your grandmother hired a dressmaker from Philadelphia to sew it for me. I wasn't much older than you, the day we went to her shop. Such civility and propriety!" Mother had held it to her chest and twirled around, a sight Lucy had never seen before. It was a curious, if somewhat distressing, sight. The gown, creased and musty from years of storage, was not the high-waisted, simple cotton style Lucy had grown accustomed to wearing, but an older more fitted form, stiff enough to nearly stand on its own with an accompanying quilted, under petticoat to puff it out all the more. Still it was too large for her

and had to quickly be sized down for the proper fit. With no time to stitch it, pins had been the solution to nip it around her, giving the illusion she had more curves than her ten years allowed.

Now if she flinched even slightly the wrong way, she was sure to be in danger of impaling herself, like a musket's bayonet, she mused. Perhaps that was the point or at least she might end her suffering that way. Mr. Shepherd was expected for dinner, resulting in a flurry of commotion putting all to readiness from the time they arrived home from Sunday meeting. Servants were ordered about in Mother's gentle way. Tommy was banished to the second-floor bedchamber with Van, still convalescing with a broken wrist from his fall, while Lucy was primped and poked into a "fine proper lady."

Mother dictated her expectations throughout every tortuous step. "A lady smiles and speaks softly, pleasantly. A lady never rests against the chair back." A lady this, a lady that. Lucy never wanted to hear the word "lady" again. Her brown locks, combed and brushed to a sheen were piled high and painfully secured to her scalp with a few ringlets cascading down her neck. Could being scalped by the French and Indians be any worse? A terrifying image came to mind. Had it been real? She quickly dismissed it along with each ribbons chosen, then discarded, and another tried again to complement perfectly her eyes and hair. Blood red, saffron, robin's egg. Too many colors blending, shifting. Too many fingers had been involved in the process—mother's delicate, pale ones; Winn's sinewy, tawny ones; and even Ester's warm, brown ones that occasionally feathered her with soft, reassuring pats accompanied by sympathetic looks when Mother turned the other way. Fingers grasping, groping, bloodied, begging for mercy from a childish dream, a long ago time. No! Why think on that now? It was only a dream. Wasn't it?

The reasons for all this bother had been incomprehensible, but sitting now at the table listening to Mr. Newhouse and Mr. Shepherd kept even the smallest nibble of food in danger of emerging back on her plate in the most unladylike fashion.

"I do agree with you on that score," Shepherd said between bites of food, "England pushing toward abolishing the slave trade could be a concern, though it might enhance our market share in that as well."

"But with the insurrections in San Domingue," Newhouse countered, "what might that spell for us in terms of shipping?"

"Us?" Shepherd glanced again at her. Every time the term "shipping" came up, his gaze enveloped her like Shadrach pouncing on a spot of sunlight or a cricket on the kitchen floor. "No matter. Slaves will still be needed here for some time to come and as the nation continues to push westward, Congress will have less control as new territories are formed into potential states."

"And the Northwest Ordinance?"

"It only applies to future territories that as yet don't exist and perhaps never shall, at least not as is deemed so at present," Shepherd proclaimed. "Until then, we've set a steady course." Again another probing look in her direction.

The discussion brought back thoughts of her walk with Ben. If Zack were still here she could have asked him as she always did after listening in to the grown folks' talk, but then Zack would likely not have permitted the likes of Mr. Shepherd to their dinner table. If he was truly at odds with her family, what purpose did he serve here now? Zack always gave her answers she could understand about the ways of the world, sometimes more than she wanted to know, though she pretended to understand. Ben had been like that with her the day of Zack's funeral, though now she wondered if it had been such a good idea to trust him with so much of her thoughts and concerns. It frightened her the way she felt around him, and the strange nightmares and voices that seemed to have returned since the day of Zack's funeral. If Van had his doubts about Ben, there must be good cause. She had seen this man, her dead brother's friend, with these two now at dinner with her. That night they all had been there together, betting over fighting cocks and urging them on in fiendish delight.

"And as for this little lady," Shepherd addressed her now, calling her to attention once again, "she's a beauty as you said, John. Are you a clever one, m'dear?"

I'm not your dear. She balanced her fork between thumb and middle fingers, the lady way, though she wanted to hurl it at both these men. "Um...," she began and croaked another unintelligible response and tried again, prompted by Mother's silently mouthed words behind a discreet napkin. The next attempt resulted in a most unladylike belch that seemed to echo through the room.

A stunned pause and then an uproarious chuckle. "My kind of girl. Yes, she'll suit. A bit of honing, to kick the dust off her as we say back where I come from. But that's no matter."

"Suit for what?" Lucy felt the room pitch into swimming shades of color. "What do you mean?" she managed in a breathless stream.

Shepherd leaned across the table. "How about a school in Boston? Or perhaps even London? Oh, I'd pay for anything above the allowance in the trust, no doubt about that. A good investment. Perhaps a tour of Europe with a private governess."

"School? London?" Mother's eyes shone like fireflies on a moonlit marsh. "Oh, Lucy, just think."

"No." Numb fingers dropped the fork sending it clattering from the table edge to the floor. "I am to leave? No. Why?"

"I thought you said this was all arranged." Shepherd wiped a greasy napkin across his flaccid chin. "We've a deal, don't we, Newhouse? Didn't you tell the girl?"

Newhouse gritted his teeth in a scowl at Lucy. "Not as yet. But no matter." He slapped fingertips to the table's edge. "An arrangement has been made, daughter. You are to go live with Mr. Shepherd's family for a time, attend a fine school, learn to be a proper lady."

"For how long?" Lucy wasn't sure where the words came from. Did it matter how long? Her mind tried to wrap thoughts around all of this. "But I already attend school. I learn enough from Reverend Godbey."

"You'll learn more from a proper school," Mother patted cold fingers to her hand. "It's the best thing for you, for your future."

"No, it isn't." She pulled her hand from Mother's grasp and stood, tipping her chair backward with a loud clunk to the wooden planks. "I won't go. This is what it was about isn't it? What you were doing that night..." She clapped her mouth shut.

"What night?" Newhouse's chin wrenched in a baleful thrust.

"N-nothing, I didn't mean night...." She shouldn't speak. She should keep quiet, but her mouth wouldn't stop the thoughts that flowed forth. "You've been planning this all along. It's why you've come. You mean to send me away. I won't go. You can't make me. I'll never come back, will I?"

"Oh, please, dear," Mother soothed. "Don't be so dramatic. It's only for a year, two perhaps. Then you'll return a fine lady. But you'll be safe, away from the...well...from the dangers here."

"What dangers?" Nothing was making sense. These people were not her family or they wouldn't be doing this. Her family was somewhere else, in another time and place. In the place where the *nepi* flowed through the *mitik*.

"Mother? *Nikya?* Why? Why are you doing this?" She backed away from the table and somehow moved toward the stairs. Or should she head for the front door? Which would be safer? Neither really. Where would she run to? She didn't know but she had to run as the words, strange and sweet throbbed in her head.

"Lucy, it's for the best." Mother stepped toward her. "What are you saying? You're not making sense."

Newhouse stood while Shepherd sat studying her. If she was disagreeable he might not want her. Why should he want to help her anyway? The three of them continued to talk as if in some other place as her mind buzzed with thoughts and images too horrible to comprehend. The cockfight. Blood spattered feathers. A large, feathered monster. *Wennigah. Wennigah.* Children crying for their mothers in some dark place. Arms holding her, releasing her. A man in a soldier's blue coat, faded and crusted with beads and blood. His sinewy bare arms pulling her away. Her head ached and still other voices bled through in the here and now.

"What's wrong with her?"

"She'll be fine," Newhouse growled. "Eleanor do something. Take her upstairs. We'll settle all this..." His voice faded into garble like the gravel falling down a hillside.

"Is she mad?" Shepherd asked. "Perhaps an asylum for this one rather than a school..."

"No!" Mother's voice. "Please, she's just stubborn, a bit wild. She'll do well in a proper school. I assure you."

"I've no use for a wife such as this. Not for my son. Land or no land."

Wife? Had he meant her mother? No. Not her stepfather speaking. This was Mr. Shepherd. He meant her!

"I won't. I won't. I won't. *Ka. Ka.*" She kept screaming. *"Matchele ne tha-tha."* Her chest ached with fire. Her cheeks stung. Someone slapped her. Once. Twice. She wouldn't calm. No. She wanted to run, kick, anything to stop this as the words flowed like the *nepi*. It wasn't her. It was something else she couldn't stop. *"Psai-wi ne-noth-tu."*

"I'll get her to quiet down." Someone came at her with a fire iron. It gleamed hot and red inches from her nose.

"No, John. Not her pretty face." Mother's voice reached a pitch rarely heard. "Don't hurt her. Not like this."

"Shepherd, a deal's a deal. There's no backing out now."

"What the devil is that word she's saying?" Shepherd backed away.

Maybe he'd leave, like the others had.

"Is she mad or bewitched?"

"Neither. She's a spoiled, willful girl. It's all an act, isn't it now, girl? There. I'll burn that savage demon from her. It's for her own good."

"Wennigah! Wennigah! Grennah! Grennah!" The iron hovered over her arm. She wouldn't stop saying the magic word, no matter what he did—the one word that had saved her in the long ago time. The one that kept them back and brought help. How did she know that word? It was to be forgotten, left behind. Never to remember again.

"Never say that word again. I'll keep you safe. You must forget what happened here." He had told her that. But he had not told her to forget other things. How could she forget? It was too much, too terrible.

Her arm burned with a scorching pain. The word didn't work this time. He didn't come. Why didn't he come? *"Because he's dead. They're both dead, swallowed up and they can't hear you."* Some voice deep inside reminded her of what she didn't want to know.

Oh death where is thy sting?

Her arm stung, red and blotched. Was this death finally come for her? When she looked up, at last calm and dissolved into sobs, it was her mother's face she saw, standing over her and holding the hot poker.

CHAPTER 15

In the darkness of their bedchamber, Lucy shivered under the woolen blanket, wondering if she would ever feel warm or safe again. The house was quiet at last, after her peculiar and frightful ordeal at supper. Mr. Shepherd had left shortly after Ester was called in to calm her down and lead her away to bed. A soothing poltice on her arm, a cup of camomile tea, and a vinegar flannel wrap were the kitchen maid's solution to her every ache and pain, but some aches ran far too deep. The horrible thoughts that assailed her, the words she uttered without really knowing why or what they meant, all boded ill for the inevitable future she faced now.

"They're sending me away." She kept saying the words into the darkness as Van sat silently across from her at the foot of the bed. He said nothing at first, letting her come to her senses on her own. Did he think she was mad like everyone else thought?

"I heard most of it," he whispered back at last. "If my arm were not in this state, I'd have..." He clenched his fist and punched the feather pillow.

"You'd have been burnt too, or worse." Lucy held her arms tight against her ribs. "What a pair we make. Your left arm and my right now useless." Her jest came across distant and chillingly detached, almost as if she were far removed from everything and everyone around her.

Van held up a silencing hand with an eye toward the trundle below them. "Shush. No need to waken Tommy." Under his breath he added,

"I should have done something to stop them. Our stepfather did this, did he? "

Lucy felt the shock of the moment once again, but dare not tell Van the truth. She'd never tell anyone the truth of what happened. "I...was being a w-wicked child.... I sh-shouldn't have said...those things."

"No, sister." Van reached for her but she flinched away. "Never think that. He's a cruel, evil man. A liar and a thief."

Another involuntary shudder coursed through her. Why couldn't she feel warmth huddled under the bed woolens? Her arm still burned with fire, but inside she was ice. "I shouldn't have let that happen...the things I said... But they want to send me away...to school in Boston...or London. Why?"

"I don't think they really intend to send you to school."

"I don't understand what they want," she said, trying to make sense of the men's discussion and appraisal of her. Even Mother seemed eager to be rid of her. "But now it's all lost. They'll send me far away to some..." She couldn't bring herself to say the word. "Some place for wicked girls like me."

"They won't send you to a madhouse." Van filled in the word she couldn't bring herself to say. She bit her lip to suppress the cry welling within.

"Terrible places," her voice shook, "aren't they? I'll never get out or come home again. Ever. Will I?"

"Listen to me." Van gripped her hand and leaned in close, speaking in soft but clear whispers. "Shepherd isn't to be trusted and you were right to resist. He's up to no good and wants to see all of us fall. I don't know all the reasons, but it has something to do with Father and something between them from a long time ago, before we were born, before he married our mother."

"Is that why you copied the ledger? And we stole away to spy on him at the tavern?" She didn't know why he was bringing this up now, but it gave her something else to think on and that was more balm to her soul than Ester's poltice or tea.

" 'Tis no matter now," Van set back against the footboard post. "You need rest. We'll sleep on it all now and we'll see what happens come morning."

With the swiftness of a panther she lunged at him, her icy fingers grasping his wrist with a strength she didn't know she possessed. "No, tell me now." She growled more than spoke the words. "Come morning who knows what they'll do to me? Tell me now. Is this to do with Zack's death?"

"Ow!" Van moaned. "Not my sore wrist." He flinched, recoiling into the bedcovers. "All right. I'll tell you now, but be still." He nodded toward the trundle where Tommy turned and mumbled in his sleep. Van drew in a breath and in a barely audible whisper said, "Zack knew about Shepherd. He knew about Newhouse. I can't tell you more than that now. But he left it for me to put right. His death…it weren't no accident…and no fevers kilt him. I know it, I just don't know how to prove it."

"What do you mean?" Lucy swallowed, summoning the courage to say the next words. "He was like me, wasn't he? Mad. He heard them too, didn't he?"

Van shot a sharp eye back to her, having drifted his gaze to some soft, dark place in the bedding. "No, sister. Truth is…I ain't sure. Zack had the fevers. He was sick. We all know that. With you…it's different. You've a gift that none of us can explain."

"I'm mad." Her voice rose higher than she expected and then as quickly dropped back. "That's what you think?

But…have you known, all along?" Her chest tightened as if she breathed an icy wind. "I…hear things. I speak in ways that are…"

"Speaking in tongues?" Van shrugged. "Some say it's a gift, like prophecy or healing."

"And some say it's…witchery." Wasn't that what her stepfather had said? Wasn't that why she was burned? Branded? Would everyone know now? What would they think?

When Van did not respond she turned her attention to another thought. "Why does Shepherd want our land? My land? Or is it just me they want to see in ruin? But…why? What have I ever done?" She was babbling, making no sense. Where had this notion of the land come from?

"I reckon it is all about the land," Van spoke slowly, as if convincing himself. "At least that's partly what Zack thought. The rest? Well, he didn't get 'round to telling me all, not afore…"

"He died."

Van clenched his good fist as his entire body tensed. "It weren't no accident, I know it for certain, just can't prove it."

"What difference does it matter now?" Again her voice returned to the dull, unfeeling tone from before. "We're all doomed. There's no one to help us, or believe us."

"No, not here, anyway." Van spoke with a determination and conviction she had never heard before. "I'm going away, now sooner than I first thought. But no matter what, I'll figure something out and no matter what comes, no matter where you are, I'll find you. You got to know that and keep hoping."

"What? Where are you going? You can't leave me, not now."

"You promise not to tell, no matter what, not even if…if it comes out in another way." He meant her voices, the strange speaking in tongues. But how could she be certain of controlling them?

"What do you mean? Van, what am I saying when…when those things happen? Do you know?"

"Never mind that now." He leaned forward on his knees, crunching the featherbed where the folds of the bedding hollowed around them like two nesting birds. "Maybe it's better if I tell you, so at least someone else knows."

"What?"

"I'm heading out to Uncle Joseph's. It's why I needed the prize money from the horse race. I plan to take the ledger, and I've been storing up traveling supplies a little at a time."

"You'll take me with you now?" At last a bit of hope soothed her soul like a warm rain against frozen earth.

"I don't see how…," he stammered. "It won't work. I'll make better time alone."

"With your broken wrist? What if something happens? You could get lost, injured worse along the way, or even…" Images far too terrible to speak aloud taunted her mind. No, he would not leave her here alone. Who else would she have to trust now?

"I 'spect I have no choice."

"You've got to take me with you. You'll need me. We'll help each other, work together, and—"

"And they'll be looking for both of us then and it'll be harder to hide."

"I won't hold you back, I promise." She feared the same thing he did. What if she had one of her "fits" when they needed to be quiet and hide from danger or capture? But it was a risk she was willing to take.

"Will you shush now? We can't let Tommy know. He can't keep a secret, and we'll never get away, let alone make the journey to Uncle Joseph's."

A rustle of bed linens from the trundle below and Tommy's maize-colored curls emerged like a jack-in-the-box. "If'n you both are running away, then I'm coming too."

CHAPTER 16

The early morning mist hovered over the valley, settling on the town of Wellsburg with the haze of first light and muting the sleepy world in a soft blanket of glittering dew. Ben enjoyed this part of the morning best, the quiet before the world awoke and met the day. Another restless night, plagued by thoughts of recent events, had rousted him from his straw-filled pallet while the hours were still cloaked in darkness. By the reluctant spark of a single candle, he stoked the fire in the wood stove and set a pot of coffee to boil. While the fire popped and nudged warmth into the shop, Ben broke the thin glaze of ice formed over the earthen washbowl and sloughed away the remnants of sleep from his face. He donned his work clothes: a fresh shirt, linen breeches, and simple neckcloth. The events of the past few weeks compounded daily with as yet no clear resolution. He weighed the facts as he absently shrugged on his woolen waistcoat and jacket, combed his hair into a neat queue before checking the fire in the stove, and mulled over the prospects of cooking his solitary breakfast.

Over one of the hogsheads lay the ribbon banner proclaiming him champion of the horse race. It bore the seal of the county, embossed in gold leafing. Alongside was the discarded crown of dried ivy leaves that had been placed upon his head to the thunderous approval of the crowd. He had taken no glory in it, as he watched the Swearingens cart away his injured opponent. The lad could have won had he not got off count and pushed his horse quite so hard. Ben had even tried to ease up on Bronzer there at the last to give the foolish boy the edge. A few weeks ago Van could have seriously injured them all, including little Lucy, racing along a public road. And now this! He was damn lucky he had only broken his wrist, and not his neck, and had not maimed his horse.

Ben slammed the iron skillet on the stove. He wasn't much of a cook, but he could manage a few basic essentials to stave off hunger and keep him going through the day. Much as he hated to admit it, he missed the mornings he ate with Zack and Phoebe before starting the day here. The woman and the slave girl, Achsa, knew their way around a hearth. Phoebe would make a fine wife, had made a good one for Zack, until now, that is. But those days were gone now. He dared not go near that cabin after the last evening. Maybe he had drunk a bit too much after the race. Whiskey flowed freely at the tavern with those wishing him hearty toast after toast and ensuring his glass never went dry. Somehow Bronzer found his way clopping past Zack's farm. Just needed to check on her, make sure she was safe. That's all he wanted wasn't it? One brief stop to see how she was getting along and to ensure her continued silence in their conspiracy. She only wanted to talk, not be alone. Things had gotten out of hand yet again. The tears falling, her daygown unbuttoned, the bed awaiting. Lying with her beneath him, caressing her. He had stopped just in time—or had he? He remembered her cursing him again as he mounted his horse and turned tail home, far later than he intended. Damn her!

The pungent aroma of brewed coffee along with the smell of a few slabs of sizzling bacon filled the storeroom. He was down to the dregs of cheap coffee beans ground with chicory, but it would have to suffice. The next shipment should bring in a better grade from the West Indies, if the price didn't jumped again. There'd be enough to service local customers, some who even preferred the taste of chicory to fine coffee shipped in from the Caribbean. Ben didn't mind it much either, having grown up in an austere Presbyterian family on the frontier of Western Pennsylvania. Living a parsimonious life ensured all profits remained in the business or banked for his own growing cache of savings. There'd be time perhaps someday for luxuries and indulgences. For now there were pressing matters to consider apart from shopkeeping.

Phoebe still was bent on getting a child, if she hadn't already. Most likely not with Zack's heir, given his death occurred not quite a fortnight after their meeting in the woods that one evening. He had checked in on her a time or two since the funeral, making sure all was well and no one disturbed her. A young widow with her comely appearance could attract any number of wayward men. Should he care, though? Apparently that's what she wanted and perhaps had her choice of bucks to service her plan. It sickened him to think she would get her way, pass off a bastard as his friend's heir. But the alternative might be worse—allowing Shepherd a further hand in gaining leverage against the claim. It was all a tangle of lies, deceits, false documents, and stubborn pride.

He turned the bacon and watched the sizzling fat curl and melt into pools of grease sputtering against the gleaming iron skillet. The aroma played on his senses and spiked his hunger. Coffee. He craved the rich bitterness on his tongue to clear his head and warm his insides on this cold morning. After pouring a mug full, he topped it with a bit of whiskey to mask any lingering taste of charred iron in the boiled water. Hair of the dog, he mused. A thick slice of bread slathered with pan grease and topped with the bacon completed his morning meal. Breakfast out on the storefront porch this morning suited him, a chance to gaze over the river while the town of Wellsburg remained in a misty slumber.

He settled onto the stool, lingering over a sip of coffee as the steam cleared his head. Despite a layer of frost, the chilly morning had a refreshing hint of spring. The ship remained in dock, a hazy half-rigged ghost, like some relic from a pirate's tale. Another week and he'd be getting all provisions and crew in order to start downriver toward the Gulf. The first of many such voyages and the beginning of a lucrative enterprise, he hoped. Only time would tell.

First there was this business with Shepherd. If only he hadn't agreed to help the colonel, but he owed the man who had given him a new start and a chance to serve in the militia with Brady's rangers.

That and a recommendation to Gibson for a position at the trading post had been the only things that kept him going. Colonel Joseph Swearingen had served with Ben's father during the war, and the two were still longtime friends. Yet the man had risked that bond by aiding his friend's son, asking no questions of a young man desperate to flee his father's disappointment and wrath and a scandal that left him heartbroken and shattered beyond reason.

Shepherd knew of it all, had been part of it, too. He had as much reason to hate the man as Old Indian Swearingen had, though the old man wasn't without his culpability either. Land rights. Who knew who actually owned any of it? The native tribes had their way of reckoning it all, the law had another, and the men who toiled to clear trees for farmland and homesteads yet another. There were others, too, land speculators, who saw progress and towns—future cities with government trailing not far behind. Ben, as yet, had not a single acre to his name. He had no reason to be caught in the middle of another family's claim. What good could he do?

He knew the answer to that even before he could digest the last bite of bacon bread along with the thought. He set the mug on the porch planks at his feet. Phoebe wouldn't tell. She had as much to lose as anyone. What good would it serve? He hadn't told a complete untruth at the funeral nor in the days before. It was for the good of the family, for them all—especially for her, not Phoebe, the other one. The child. She had the Dutch Lady. He knew it, or he had his strong suspicions. But who else could it be? How to get her to tell him and what to do with that information was another matter all together. It was not good for her to keep it, though she may have a right to it. It was a valuable family heirloom, or so Zack had said, and no mere child's bauble to play with. The colonel's fears for his niece may indeed have credence. Several nights now Ben had made himself a visible presence at the tavern, conveniently keeping books for the cockfights or trying his luck at the card table. Bantering with the lads and locals was all part of the game as well. Newhouse, he learned, was thick with Shepherd ever since his appearance in the county. Was it only a coincidence Zack grew sick around the same time? His fevers fell into a certain pattern that was the way of it, but his delusions and madness...was there more behind it? A melancholia, perhaps. The chain of events, the escalation of his friend's condition, all seemed to fall too conveniently into the hands of Shepherd. Perhaps there were grounds to Phoebe's fears, though her motives were none too honorable either at the present.

After seeing Phoebe and her maidservant home that evening, he had returned to see Zack the next morning, only to find him missing. His distraught wife said he had slipped away early that morning while she slept. He had tracked his friend into the woods that day, alone at first, before anyone else knew the man had gone missing. Ben didn't want to alert everyone unnecessarily. Of course not. It all could have been handled neatly, efficiently. Why hadn't Zack cooperated? He was mad, deranged, when he finally found him. The woods were misty with winter snow that day, much like now, but colder.

At first he remained so still, Ben wasn't sure he had heard him, only a slight quivering, his feet dangling over the edge. It took his breath away. Something wasn't right. Phoebe had been frantic when he left her, bruises on her cheek and trailing down her neck, testimony to Zack's fierce and uncontrolled rage. He couldn't help himself, of course he couldn't. But to see a woman hurt like that was more than he could bear, even if his friend was in a fevered state beyond reason.

When Zack turned to face him, he barely recognized the wild, fixed eyes gazing at him, through him. Then the pistol poised at him cocked and aimed. "Get away, Blue Jacket. You'll not get her, not any of us."

"Zack, it's me, Ben." He swallowed and held empty hands high, beseeching. "I come to help you. You're not well. Let's go home."

"He'll come get us all." Zack's voice trailed into mutterings that made no sense—Wabash, lost friends, Blue Jacket's rampages.

"It's over, Zack." Ben tried yet again, soothing words. Remain calm. His friend would never hurt him. He believed that. "Blue Jacket's lost. Gone far away. The treaty. It's all done and the war's over for now."

A wry laugh, turned to something sinister, mad. "Ben? That you?"

"Yeah, my friend, it's me. Best be getting home." He took a cautious step closer, but Zack held the pistol steady at him again, having lowered it slightly.

"No, not 'til he gets her." Zack squinted. "You gonna help me? Blue Jacket should've kept her. Elzey was right. All of them were right. She's tainted

now. Been with them savages. The land, it ought to go to us now, not her. We're all cursed so long as she's still here and Blue Jacket won't give in. It's their way. Their evil, bewitching heathenish ways. They got to her and she'll never be right again, never be fit to live among us. Never be ours. Likely she'll turn on us all someday. It's why my head won't stop." He pounded the butt of his pistol against his forehead. "Please, stop it, the hurtin' is too much."

"No, Zack. I'll help you. Who's telling you this?" Ben knew. Softly he spoke the name only it didn't have the effect he expected. "Zack. No! Don't!"

Ben tossed his crumbs and the dregs from his coffee cup onto the ground before heading into the shop for another day's work. No sense rehashing what couldn't be changed now. Off in the distance a small ghostly shape bobbed down the hill through the mist. Ben squinted and blinked to determine if what he saw was real or not. For an instant his guard training alerted a need to reach for his gun. But this creature did not move with the stealth of an enemy or a vaporous apparition. Yet what villager would be up and about this early and alone? Still, a customer was a customer and the fairylike creature now appeared as flesh and blood as it emerged from a shroud of mist. A girl. Lucy Swearingen.

Ben raised his eyebrows and made a slight bow at the porch railing. "Well, good morning, Miss Swearingen. Pray what brings you here so early of a morning?"

Lucy stood there wide-eyed. Her lips were parted but all that uttered forth was something between a squeak and a sigh.

"Lucy?" Ben moved a cautious step toward her. "May I help you? Is everything well at home?"

"Um, yes, I mean no." She swallowed, winced, then took another deep swallow. "I came to…to return the book." She pulled the small volume from beneath her cloak and held it out to him.

"Ah, yes." Ben stared at her slim, pale hand holding the book. He had nearly forgotten, and it brought a slice of painful regret. "You've finished it already?"

"Yes." Her hand shook slightly at she held it out and let it dangle a bit as if it weighed heavy in her hand. "I read it. Twice, even. It was a fine story."

"Did you now?" Something in her demeanor made him suspect she wasn't speaking truthfully, or she had something more to say. Which it was, he couldn't tell just yet, but he was determined to find out. "And did you find Telemachus's adventures enlightening? Or, at the very least, amusing?" He crossed his arms playfully, one hand rubbing his chin as if contemplating a deep earnest thought.

"I...I thought the book quite a lovely read, full of adventure and..." She barely whispered and broke off to swallow as if her words were lodged too deep to retrieve.

"I must admit I wasn't quite as enthralled upon my first reading," Ben offered as way of keeping her engaged and to study out her reasons for coming by the shop so early. "I wasn't much older than you and found it rather dull."

Her brow beneath her hood furrowed, and she wrinkled her pert little nose in a most becoming way. "Why did you give me such a book, if you thought I would find it dull?"

She was a quick wit, that one, and certainly not averse to speaking her mind. Ben resisted an urge to smile at her expense. "I know your love of reading, or at least I presume to know. Perhaps I thought you'd be a bit more introspective than I. For myself? It was an acquired taste." He held the book and tapped it against his other palm. "I read the book again a few years later and couldn't put it down. It seems there's something undiscovered to be found each time I read it."

A grave expression turned childlike curiosity to something more poignant, or did he glimpse even a trace of despair? "You've read it more than once?"

"Oh, assuredly." He rubbed a finger across the tooled leather spine. "At least once a year since the age of fifteen. Your brother and I had many a fine discussion on its themes and philosophies. Some of the brightest minds of our age have sought wisdom and ideas from its pages."

The dimple on her chin deepened as she pursed her lips together, her eyes alive with curiosity. "And you, too, are a great thinker because of it? And so was...Zack?"

The last word hung in the air between them, heavy as a storm cloud. He held her in his gaze before bursting into a merry laugh and then scratched his chin, considering her comparison. "A great thinker? I'd hardly say so, and I do know some who would not place a wager on it, to be sure. Now your brother? Zechariah? He was... extraordinary. Always gave me something new to consider. I was more, shall we say...a student of philosophy...and science. And, perhaps of life. But your brother? Like your father, I dare say. They were great readers, both fine minds, much like another Swearingen I happen to know," he winked.

"Science and philosophy..." Her face brightened for the first time, a reminder of something past, a curiosity brewing beneath that tender gaze. "'Ode to Science'? Did you write the poem at the back of the book?"

Rendered speechless, Ben searched to understand what she meant. A blush rose to her face and she looked away. "I wondered is all." She closed her eyes and proceeded to rattle off the verse he now remembered scribbling on a blank page on the inside back cover.

"I copied it, but it's not my invention." He picked up the book and thumbed to the back page where he now recalled copying the verse. "'Tis a song I heard. A rather new one at that. You fancied it enough to memorize it?"

"No, I only read it once and committed it to memory." She turned away and seemed to be peering through the shop door for something to catch her eye. "I remember words, easily, especially in verse."

"Then you did find the meaning to the story."

She shook her head causing her hood to fall back and gather precariously at the back of her bonnet. She lowered her head thoughtfully before she spoke. "Telemachus is Ulysses's son. He goes in search of his father after the Trojan War.

"I didn't see much more to it than that."

"Oh, but there is." He leaned back and crossed his arms. She did wish to discuss the story as he hoped she would and perhaps he could yet turn the conversation to other matters he had not wished to broach the day of the funeral. "What did you make of Mentor? The conversations they had. I thought perhaps you'd find them even a bit diverting."

Lucy lowered her eyes to the floor then back to the book he now held in his hand. "Mentor?"

"Yes. The man who accompanied our hero on his journey to find his father." She absorbed the verse at the back but didn't recollect a key figure in the tale? She knew its premise well enough. It shouldn't bother him, given what she had been through, but it had been Zack's favorite book. He could no longer talk to his friend of the ideas presented forthwith between Telemachus and Mentor. How often had they taken turns debating the themes as their own version of the duo? What was he thinking, presenting such a task to one so young?

"She's got a keen mind and an ability to understand more than any of us can fathom. I must watch over her, Ben, and keep her from those that would seek their own gain." How often had Zack told him that? *"No one realizes and if they did, I shudder to think what might become of her. Father knew, but only saw her as an idle parlor trick. It's not a curse as some may say. It's so much more."* He had dismissed it all as a brother's devotion. But now it fell to him to see what may indeed lay behind that delicate brow and shining eyes.

"Well, I do thank you for returning the book, dear lady." He levied a dismissive bow. "It's a bit early to be discussing such heady issues." And rather early to be going to school. He turned to clear his breakfast dishes and noted that the schoolhouse was dark and vacant. The reverend's horse was not there as well.

She made no move to leave the porch. "It was actually Minerva, the goddess. Mentor, that is, was the teacher but really the goddess, Minerva, guided him all along. And he never knew it the entire time."

"Indeed it was." The light of understanding in her young face bemused him. "Minerva disguised as a man. Most remarkable, wouldn't you say? Rather a delightful twist? She represents wisdom. A more modern version of the tale has her named Sophie, which, as I believe, does mean wisdom." She had indeed enjoyed the book, though there seemed something more she hoped to say, but dared not.

"Our cook slave is named Sophie." A smile illuminated her face, a rare treat he had not expected. "I shall have to tell her."

"What is this other book that uses the name Sophie? I should like to read it to her and to Tobe."

"Tobe?"

"Ester's son, Tobe. Although he also has a secret name: Isaac. It's the one his mother gave him. Tobe is his registered slave name. But we call him Isaac when the grown folks aren't around."

"Ah! I see." Ben was amused by the secret. Perhaps this was the time to ask about another secret she may be harboring. Phoebe still had not found the necklace anywhere in the household inventory or anywhere she thought Zack might have stashed it away. Ben was about to gently broach the topic when she entered into a new thought of her own, her face brightening all the more.

"It was rather like a trick. Like the Trojan horse? Pretending to be something you're not." Lucy's face grew pale followed by an increasing blush that extended up her neck and across her cheeks. "I mean, Minerva, pretending to be Mentor and deceiving Telemachus."

"The Trojan horse?" A chuckle. Perhaps she had come merely to return the book, but he couldn't help thinking it was a ploy to something else. Perhaps there was something else she wished to render over to him. If Zack had given her something to hold, perhaps she was the one deceiving others. Did anyone in the Swearingen household even know she was here? Could this be a prelude to a confession?

"I...um...it's a story we're reading in our Latin lessons. I'm sorry to have troubled you. I thank you, sir, for the lending of the book." She set it carefully on the porch railing, bobbed a quick curtsy, and started to edge down the steps.

His hand accidentally crossed hers, brushing lightly as he accepted the return, causing her to flinch as if bitten. "No, 'tis I should be sorry for pressing you so. Please come inside and warm yourself by the fire. You came all this way on an early morning to return my book, the least I can do is offer you a cup of tea or a bit of sustenance. I warn you, cookery is not my forte, but you're welcome to a morsel on this chilly morning."

Her face twitched taking in the book resting in the misty air. "I've come early, for school. To meet with the reverend for an early music lesson. I figured you'd be wanting your book back. And...I do need some things...from the store...if you have time. He...he won't be expecting me for a while yet."

"I have all the time you need. You are my first customer of the day," he said, cocking his head toward the schoolhouse. "Reverend Godbey must be running a bit late himself. We'll watch for his horse from the shop window."

Ben held out a hand to bid her inside. "Please come inside. Never too busy to help a pretty lady and talk more of Telemachus. Come let's tell bad stories of sealing wax, cabbages, and kings."

She flicked a nervous eye over her shoulder, bit her lip, and climbed the top step to the porch. No one knew she was here, Ben surmised. Why had she sneaked off in such a way? Glancing toward the bare, dark schoolhouse told him no schoolmaster waited readying a lesson this early. The reverend was known for his exacting punctuality. She was lying and he would winnow out the truth from her somehow. Inside Ben crossed his arms after laying the book down and leaned back against the storeroom counter. "How is your brother doing? Van is recovering well?" Perhaps too direct a topic, perhaps not, but it seemed a polite, innocuous start at least.

"Yes, his wrist should heal in a few weeks. He's still abed with a sling, but already is trying to do much without it."

"Well, you make certain he gets his rest and proper healing." Ben turned to arrange a few jars on the counter. "He is quite the horseman and gave a good contest. I'm truly sorry for how things turned out."

"It wasn't your fault." Lucy shook her head and kept her eyes on the book he laid on the counter by his breakfast dishes. "You won fair and square. He understands that."

"I'm glad to hear it," Ben winked and tossed her an amiable smile. "He will be riding again soon enough. A good horseman like him, there's always another race to come."

The book still seemed to fixate her view, as if she couldn't bear to let it go. "What sorts of themes?"

"Pardon?"

"The book. Telemachus." She leveled a curious wonderment at him. "Mentor and Telemachus. You said there were some other themes in the book. I do remember many kings on his travels but it was not a bad story at all and there was no mention of sealing wax or cabbages." She wrinkled her nose.

"No," he chuckled as he spoke. "I quoted another tale by Mr. William Shakespeare. Or rather, badly misquoted it." He waved dismissively. "It is from one of the histories. *Richard II*, to be exact, but I once misquoted the line when reciting in school, when I was about your age, I suppose. And could never live it down thereafter."

"Bad stories, of sealing wax, cabbages, and kings." She mulled the words over on her tongue as if tasting some sweet morsel. "I like it," she declared. He hadn't the heart to tell her the true line was about "sad stories of the death of kings." There had been far and away too much death and sadness in this young lady's life.

She seemed to consider this thought further and then asked, "Why did you decide to read Telemachus again if you didn't like it the first time? And why the verse written at the end?"

"Excellent questions." Now perhaps he was getting somewhere. She had come inside and perhaps he'd have a chance to turn the topic to things she may know of Newhouse or Shepherd. At the very least she was showing the inquisitive mind he knew her to have. "I suppose I was too much a young boy, too restless for sitting and reading."

"But it is a boy's adventure tale. Perhaps not suitable for girls?"

"Is that what you think? Or has someone told you this?" Nelly. Her mother might not have relished such a book for her daughter. But she had indicated Reverend Godbey had taught them the *Aeneid*, in Latin no less. Surely there'd be no harm in this. Zack had read far more controversial literature to her and his younger brothers.

"I…rather liked it. The adventure, I mean. A journey to faraway places." She compressed her lips and elicited a slight shudder.

"Yes, I believe that was my take upon first reading and my disdain of it all. I wanted the adventure for myself. Not merely to sit and read about it." He had offered a cup of tea and should set about filling the kettle to heat.

"Reading is itself an adventure," she mused. "Especially in French. I enjoyed that far more. And Mentor was a most excellent teacher, but was rather hard on kings and common folk."

Ben looked askance at this latest comment, not paying attention to his task and spilling the coffee he had poured himself. He cursed lightly under his breath. "You...you read the pages in French?" He reached for a linen cloth from under the counter to dab at the coffee stains on his breeches.

She stammered a bit and swallowed, as if fearing retribution for some grievous sin. "I learnt a bit of French...from...school...and Mother taught me some. I only meant..."

"You read the English and decoded it that way, perhaps?" He helped her out, seeing her dismay, though something told him this child was far more extraordinary than anyone knew.

"Yes...of course." She sighed, relieved, and added a carefree shrug.

"You think Mentor was rather hard on kings?" Ben stoked the fire, which had dwindled to a few glowing coals and set about brewing a fresh pot of coffee. There was far more to his promise to Zack than he had ever known before. The things she had seen, things she knew, and things she had yet to learn. Was it even possible?

"Isn't that what you meant by telling bad stories?" Her words broke through his reverie. "Of cabbages and kings?"

"Not exactly." He spread his hands in a gesture of conciliation. "It's a saying, nothing more. Though the kings in every land they traverse are important. What did you make of them?"

"He...or rather...she—that is, Minerva-Mentor—seemed overly concerned with kings that do not do right by their people, govern so severely, and live in grand palaces while common folk suffer through taxing and poor conditions." She picked up the book and thumbed through it. "One part I did wonder about." She turned the book to him, pointing to a certain page he knew all too well.

"Ah! Yes. Idomeneus."

"He sacrifices his son." Her words levied deadpan and tainted in despair. "No true father would do such a thing. Yet Mentor seems to see it as the best recourse."

"He had no choice. It was most unfortunate. But he had made a promise and had to keep it." Ben recalled the scene. Perhaps the story was too shocking for such a young girl.

"It reminded me of Jephtha's daughter," Lucy said, "in the Bible. The Book of Judges, the eleventh chapter. Though he was no king."

"I'm afraid I'm not as well versed in that part of Scripture," Ben chuckled.

"It's the same story. A man asks God for something and vows that if his prayer is fulfilled, he will sacrifice the first thing he sees. When he arrives home, it's his daughter who runs to meet him and..."

Ben froze his hand midair as he prepared to dish up a measure of tea. He had forgotten that Bible story. It was all too familiar to the one in Telemachus. How very odd.

"I would not have gone to my death so willingly as did King Idomeneus's son nor Jephtha's daughter. I'd have...run away."

"Fenalon is making a point about kings and their relationships to the people they rule. It's called the Social Contract. I certainly don't think Fenalon is advocating the sacrifice of one's children. It was a mere plot device, I'm sure told for extreme example, to make a point."

"And to make for an exciting story, too? The kettle hissed on the stove and she reached it first to pour into the teapot he readied with the Oolong from the tea caddy. "You're saying it means kings should be honest and keep their promises, however difficult it may seem, even to their own loss. They should put the needs of the people and the country first and foremost."

"They should, but alas, they are human and subject to ambition and greed."

"Like our President Adams?"

"Ah! You've been dabbling in politics again?" He set out a fresh clean mug for her tea along with the sugar bowl. "Monsieur Fenalon wrote the novel some time ago. Long before our resistance here in the United States to England or France's rebellion against the monarchy."

"And long before President Adams and Mr. Jefferson?" She tossed her head with a twist of a smile. "It was a good thing we became our own nation, though, we still do not all live in harmony, even without King George or...is he talking about what is happening in France? Monsieur Fenalon is French, so is that what he is talking about?"

"You could say that. Some think he was speaking against one of the King Louises from a while back. I don't recall which one. The fourteenth or fifteenth, perhaps? Fenalon's views are a bit idealistic, though noble and worth consider—" Her arm drew his attention as she reached for her steaming mug. "Lucy, what's this?" He reached over to take hold of her wrist.

Lucy bit her lip as Ben noted with concern the blistering red mark on her inside forearm.

"Lucy, how did this happen?" He held her wrist gently and pushed the sleeve of her gown up above her elbow, inspecting the purplish fingermarks encircling the pale skin. She shivered and flinched ever so slightly.

He released the sleeve of her gown and peered at her. "Forgive me. Do you mind? Who did this to you, Lucy?"

When she didn't respond immediately he continued, "Those marks on your neck..." Distinct finger-shaped bruises lined the sides of her neck and tinged her jawline. With her hood fallen back he saw them now, no longer hidden in the shadows outdoors.

"It's...nothing. Just my clumsiness in carrying firewood the other day." Lucy affected a self-deprecating laugh that came out more like a nervous titter. He didn't believe her, fueling his impatience all the more. These were no bruises from mishandling firewood. Who would she be protecting and why?

"You are badly burnt." Ben bent down. "That's not from carrying firewood."

"I got too close...to the fire yesterday." She stammered looking down at the toes of her boots. "It's nothing. I shouldn't have been holding the fire irons. I was quite clumsy, I fear."

Ben released her hand and stood straight. "What the deuce were you doing so near a fire? You've got servants to tend to such things."

"Servants who have no choice but to do our bidding?" She raised her chin defiantly. "Would Mentor agree to treating others in such ways? Is that what you meant by the Social Contract?"

"We're not talking about a blasted story, Lucy. Nor world affairs. How did you burn your arm?"

"As I said. I was careless." She flinched away, raising a shaky hand to her mug.

"You know, Lucy, I did mean what I said that day, when I offered you this book." He laid his hand over the tome resting on the counter.

"You can count on me as a friend, whenever or however you need. If anyone has told you anything or made you keep a secret, I can help to ease such a burden. I consider your family very dear, your brothers, your sisters… And if anyone…anyone at all is causing you harm or distress, you need but…"

"I'm not in any harm. It's nothing." Lucy offered her prettiest smile and tossed her head. "I just came to return your book. I did not mean to trouble you. Thank you kindly for letting me read it."

"You mentioned some items needed?" He hoped a bit of shopping would ease her thoughts and keep her here longer. She would tell him more without his having to press. "What can I help you with?"

She scanned the shelves and twirled a finger through a basket of ribbons. "I was wondering…well…I could use a new haversack."

"A haversack?" Ben cocked his head and lifted one eyebrow appraisingly. "Now what would a fine young lady like you, need with a haversack?"

"Well, you see, it's for Van." Lucy hesitated and wracked her brain for a plausible reason. "With his arm and all, we figured he could use it to carry things that he needs like schoolbooks…and…"

"Of course, a most excellent idea," Ben shifted his head in an agreeable nod. "Then one haversack it is, coming right up my good lady." He turned and walked to a pegboard along one wall of the storeroom. Several sacks of varying sizes hung, all in heavy woven cotton. He scanned through a few before selecting one in particular. When he turned back around, she was studying a map on the wall. "Here we go, just the right size for your brother, m'dear. He should put this to good use."

He held out the sack, adding, "Fit for a journey across the continent, 'tis that. Are you set on a course as our young Telemachus was?" He nodded toward the map. "Or would you be the Mentor who guides the way?"

"W-what?" All color drained from her face that bespoke a rabbit caught in a trap.

Ben nodded toward the book. "I meant the story. You seem most interested in my latest purchase from Boston. This one updates the complete sixteen states and the redefined territories farther west. It's the most accurate to date. However, if things keep going as they are, I fear this printing will be obsolete before Christmas."

Another blush infused her neck and face, turning the bruises from deep purple to blue-black. "So many lines." Her tone was far too cheery, pitched too eagerly. "Are these all rivers and creeks? And the dots are towns and forts along the way?"

"Yes, more each day, it would appear. Surveyors can hardly keep up with it all." He traced a finger across the interconnecting lines. These are the river systems. Here is the Ohio and if you trace it thusly, it flows westward into this line—the Mississippi River, which flows all the way to the sea."

She pointed toward one corner of the map. "It says the maps are for sale. Do you still have one I could purchase?"

He cocked his head in mock suspicion. "So, you are planning a journey, my little Telemachus?"

"No," she returned sharply, "I should like to study the map. I could learn geography and...and..."

"Done. One map for my wandering friend who will someday take a grand journey, and so it is." He spun on his heels and picked up a neatly folded map from a bin beneath the wall display. "I'll add that to the haversack. Will there be anything else?"

"No, thank you. I should be going."

"Very well, then. Shall I put that to the Swearingen account?"

She parted her lips as if to speak then licked them and swallowed. "I had hoped to...to make a trade, if you please, sir." She reached into her pocket and pulled out a small comb and an ivory needle case. "These are mine to barter with. I hope they will be enough. I've taken care of them."

Ben tapped his fingers lightly on the counter. "I would not expect you to barter away your things. Your family has enough on account to make good with such a small purchase."

"No." Shaking her head vigorously, she held out the comb and case. "I want these to be from me. The haversack is for Van, but the map is for me and I'd...I'd like to make my own way of it."

"Very well, then, miss," he said, "you do drive a hard bargain."

"Please, don't tell I was here," she whispered hoarsely. "It's a surprise for Van. I wanted to help, in some way. I've also got money to pay with." She reached beneath her cloak to the pockets under her gown and pulled out a few coins. "Is this enough?"

"Aye." Ben counted the coins she laid on the wooden surface. "Here's your sack, m'lady. I'll not tell a soul. One haversack, fit for a journey of a thousand miles and a map to get you there." He meant to tease, but clearly she did not take this well.

"The items you offer are far too dear," he replied. "I'm afraid I would not sleep knowing I took advantage of your generosity. The needle case will do. The comb you'll have far more use of." He recognized the cherry comb as the one carved by the captain for his daughter. It bore her initials as well.

"Consider it our secret. Your company this morning has been payment enough, along with your review on the book." He handed the sack to her with the addition of the map and, without really knowing why, he slipped the returned book back into her bag.

CHAPTER 17

Lucy stepped onto the road in front of Gibson's Trading Post but didn't return home, nor did she head toward the school as she had told Ben. There was no schoolmaster waiting for her on this cold Monday morning. *One step closer.* That's all she could think on now. Mr. Stephenson seemed none the wiser and accepted her words quite well, including the reason for purchasing a haversack and map. She did feel a measure of uneasiness over her deception, given his good nature in helping her, the loaning of such a precious book, and his willingness to discuss it. She could remain there all morning talking about the story. There were so many parts she liked. Of cabbages and things. Of cabbages and kings. It was all she could do to contain herself. But if she had begun talking on any one point, she feared she would not be able to stop and a flood of words might reveal things she ought to keep carefully guarded for now. She couldn't risk telling what had happened the night before. Mr. Shepherd's visit and his plans for her. Those terrible things she uttered and the horrified looks on her mother's and stepfather's faces. A witch! Was she really a witch child as they said? She began to remember things and words that made no sense but were disturbing nonetheless.

Perhaps it was just stories she had read that brought up such terrible images. She wanted to ask him, but what if he should react like the others? She couldn't take that chance, not now with everything at stake. Only Uncle Joseph could help them now. But what if he didn't believe them or wanted to send her away too?

Grown folk always seemed pleased to get answers from children

—quizzing, testing, and cajoling. But then in the next breath they would tell her to "be a little lady." What they really meant was, "sit quietly during the grown folks' nattering." It seemed they were never satisfied with what they were told while still insisting on being told the truth. What good was being truthful when it only meant punishment or keeping secrets and lies when it served no useful purpose? Perhaps Ben was no different. Perhaps he meant to trick her into telling him something that could harm her or her family more. She had not forgotten the words she overheard between him and Mr. Gibson the day of Zack's funeral. Perhaps, as Van said, he was not to be trusted after all.

At the very least, she had not needed to delve into the coins in her pocket and could even have gotten off with no payment at all through the family's credit account. But the risk of alerting more notice was far worse—or later being accused of theft and giving their stepfather reason to withhold more of their rightful inheritance. That had been Van's concern as well and she heeded his warning. And Ben was quite satisfied with her barter of a mere needle case. Besides, she rather liked the idea of bartering her own way through a sale.

Gazing up the hill one last time toward the double cabin that stood watch beside her father's fort brought a tender unease and a rattling sense of dread. It was the only home she had ever known. She had never traversed beyond the boundaries of Brooke County or ventured farther than neighboring homesteads and surrounding woodlands. Uncle Joseph lived a good three or four days' journey east. While there were settlements and inns, could they trust who they'd meet along the way? Traveling through the wildwood could be even more dangerous.

With a sharp intake of breath, she ducked behind the store and skirted the path that led to the woods behind Engle's farm. She would cut across the trace and ford the brook toward Ojibwe Cave to their rendezvous point. Her brothers should be along soon enough. The ruse had worked so far. Van and Tommy would pretend to head to school but instead meet her here.

The sun eased over the horizon, peeking in and out of a hazy cloud cover. The mist that enveloped the world in the dim light of early dawn had now dissipated into the forest, merging dense shapes and apparitions of the night with the sentinels of the forest awaiting the renewal of spring. Lucy set down her sack and scanned the silent woods. Shaky fingers untied her bonnet and then removed her day cap. Next, to discard the short gown and petticoat. Underneath, she wore one of Van's old shirts rather than a lady's shift. She shivered thinking of Ben holding her arm and pushing back her sleeve. Had he investigated any further, he would have seen the cuff of Van's shirt. Fortunately she had rolled the cuffs up above her elbow. What might he have thought of her wearing a young man's shirt? Ideas about Telemachus echoed back. Minerva, the goddess of wisdom and science, disguised as a man—a teacher, named Mentor—guiding Telemachus on his journey to find his father. What would Mr. Stephenson think of the notions his book gave her?

It was both curious and confusing how easy it was to speak with Ben. She had wanted so much to tell him everything. *I saw you that night at the tavern, placing bets and baiting birds to tear each other asunder.* What would he think if she told him what Mr. Newhouse had said to Mr. Shepherd later that night? Perhaps he was already privy to it all and approved as he obviously did of such cruelty to chickens, and because of that, she must say nothing to him until they found Uncle Joseph.

Had she divulged even a smidgeon of what happened, she would also have to tell him the true reason for her burnt arm, the shameful way she acted, and the madness that overtook her. At least his questions about the story kept her distracted from other matters, and in the end she stayed resolute. She couldn't risk it. There was no taking back words once spoken. "The wise one uses words with restraint." Zack had taught her that. Uncle Joseph would know what to do. With Cousin Thomas so eager for their visit, Uncle would surely take them in and show mercy and pity for his brother's children. Van assured her the ledger would reveal everything they needed to prove Mr. Newhouse's treachery, though she still didn't understand what a few acres of her land had to do with anything and why that should be so important to anyone, least of all Abraham Shepherd.

She held the most valuable thing of all in her pocket, and no one had asked for it, since Mother's query weeks ago. But that had been easily appeased with a flat denial. Ben had not asked and he would surely want to give it back to Phoebe. She was still angry with her sister-in-law, though she couldn't really explain why—just an odd queasy feeling she had whenever the woman's name was mentioned and the way Ben sometimes looked at her.

The Dutch Lady remained inside her pocket. She brought it along, not sure what to do with it on the journey, but it seemed safer in her possession than to chance someone finding her hiding spot back at the fort. It belonged in Swearingen hands and perhaps Uncle Joseph would have a better idea of what to do, although she still wasn't too sure who to trust with Zack's gift. If it were indeed a valuable piece, they might even need to barter it away, should they run into trouble or need more supplies. She hoped with all her might that would never be the case. Van's stash of money was meager, even she knew that much, but she feared if she told him what she possessed, he might insist on selling it to fund the journey. No. Zack entrusted it to her for a reason and she would not fail him now.

Here alone in the woods, waiting on her brothers in the cool morning air, she couldn't resist one last peek at the gem. Though she was dressed in her brother's breeches, she still kept a girlish pocket tied about her waist with the necklace tucked inside. All the way down the hill to the store, it had thumped against her thigh beneath her petticoat that was now rolled up and stuffed into the sack. She draped the beads across her palm, letting the carved pendant dangle against her wrist. What was that ancient grandmother like who originally wore it? She tried to imagine standing before the Queen of the Netherlands and receiving such a rare gift. Had it been in some royal ceremony in a castle throne room? Or was it perhaps between dear friends over tea in a lovely garden? With mischievous delight, she glanced around the vacant meadow before clasping the necklace about her own neck. Why not pretend to be the venerable ancestor those many years ago in the court of the Dutch queen? There was no one here to tease her or think her silly. What was wrong with one last bit of frivolity before...before what?

In the end she shook off such errant thoughts and looked toward the brilliant horizon. With a resigned sigh she pulled her sewing kit from her other pocket and secured the Dutch Lady to the inside of her jacket lining. By the time the sun was nearing the tallest trees scraping the sky, Lucy heard the rustle of brush and footsteps. She held her breath a second. To her relief, her brothers climbed the hill.

"I was beginning to wonder when you'd get here." Lucy stood, hands on hip, and looked beyond to make sure there was no one following them. "Did you have any trouble getting away?"

Before either boy spoke, a crackling of twigs and crunch of gravel startled them until they saw who it was.

Lucy's heart beat rapidly even as she addressed this intruder. "Tobe, what are you doing here?" She looked about to see if any other house servants or even Mr. Newhouse or Mother were behind him.

"I reckoned you all were up to something." Tobe walked up to the mouth of the cave. "Miss Eleanor sent me to fetch you your schoolbooks. Mister Van done left his at the house."

He squinted wary-eyed from brother to brother to sister. "Looks to me like ya'll ain't gonna need no learnin' books today. You have a good 'nuff reason for shirking school today?"

Lucy looked into Van's stunned, sheepish eyes. In the uncomfortable silence, Tommy blurted out, "We're running away to Uncle Joseph's."

Tobe's eyes widened revealing whites stark as a snowdrop clinging to tree bark. The thin line of his brow arched high toward his curly hairline. "What ya'll wanna do that for? You gonna be in a whole pile o' trouble." He backed away as if their proximity contaminated him with their sin. Yet there was a gleam of envy for their adventure and escape followed by apprehension and concern. "And they's Injuns and wild critters out there. And the bad sort of white folks that you don't need to come across."

"It'll be worse if we stay." Lucy moved closer to take the books from Tobe. "At least for me that is."

Tobe crossed his arms and scowled at Lucy, assessing her head to toe in the way his mother sometimes did. "Miss Lucy, you dressed like a boy. That ain't right."

In spite of the serious nature of their circumstances, Lucy nonetheless could not help herself from bursting into a fit of giggles that infected the whole lot as Van and Tommy also doubled over in laughter.

"I don't see nothing funny about this." Tobe's brows sank most seriously, and his arms folded across his chest. "Noah said you was up to something but he couldn't say what."

The children ceased their laughter and now were the ones looking aghast.

"Noah?" Van shot an alarmed look at Lucy, then back to Tobe. "What do you mean?"

Lucy recalled Noah's odd look as he placed the cages of cocks back into the wagon. He had been speaking to Mr. Newhouse, but his eyes were fixed exactly on the spot where Van and Lucy hid in the brush. "He saw us there?"

"Ya'll was at the tavern t' other night, weren't you?" Tobe's arms crossed tight against his patched waistcoat, his face matching the accusing tone in his voice.

"He told you?" Van held his one free hand at his side. The vein on his neck stood out and his face turned red. "How can he be sure it was us?"

"Naw, Noah didn't tell me. I heard him talking to my ma when he got home. They thought I was asleep, but I weren't." Tobe thumbed his chest. "They always think I sleeping when I ain't. I hear lots o' good things that way from grown folks. Things I keep to myself 'til I needs them. Like now."

Lucy cocked her head to the side and gave Tobe a wary look. "So what did they say?"

"Nuh-uh, you ain't tole me why you dressed like a danged boy, when you should be in petticoats. I reckon ya'll gots more to lose. I just doing Miss Nelly's bidding." He casually slung the leather strap holding the schoolbooks.

Lucy sighed, "All right. But you have to promise not to tell anyone. Not Ester, Noah, and especially not our mother or Mr. Newhouse."

"I promise." A curt nod settled the matter, but his eyes held a devilish squint.

"No," Van intervened before Lucy could speak. "Not good enough.

You swear. Swear on something." Van leveled a look and took a step toward his slave. "You swear a solemn oath. A blood oath."

"A what?" Tobe recoiled with a grimace.

"You heard me." Van pulled a knife from his pocket.

"Van, no." Lucy hadn't seen the rosewood-handled knife since Zack's funeral when her brother and cousin tussled over it at bedtime. "That's not necessary."

"Yes, it is," Van snarled back. "We can't take any chances."

"I...I won't tell...nobody." Tobe inched backward but Van was quicker and grabbed hold of the slave boy's hand.

"You are my slave, or will be someday, if we can get all this put to rights. Unless you'd care to take your chances with Mr. Newhouse—or Shepherd and his plans." He threw a warning glare at Lucy as she tried once more to intervene. Tommy began to whimper, inching closer to his sister's side.

"I'm not gonna hurt you...much," Van said. "Just hold out your hand."

"Don't you cut me, sir." Tobe never called Van "sir," making Lucy even angrier with her brother.

"I won't actually cut you. See?" He pressed the knife blade into his flattened palm releasing a sanguine pearl against alabaster flesh. "Just a small scratch, enough to raise a drop. It'll heal in no time. We got to do things this way. A man's way."

Reluctantly Tobe held out his hand, wincing at the prospect of pain.

"Oh, that didn't hurt near as I thought."

Van smiled. "Not as much as the oath will, if'n you don't keep your end of things."

Pressing their hands together, Van held the knife pointed toward the sky. "Now, swear by all heaven and earth, all that is under the sky or beneath the ground that you will not tell our mother nor Mr. Newhouse nor your ma or pa..."

"I don't know who my pa be," Tobe persisted. "Not my true, natural pa."

"All right then, tell no other man, slave or free, what we here will say amongst these woods."

"I swear." He started to pull his hand away but Van held him fast.

"And if you do so much as tell any of them, you will be cursed forever and haunted by those who once held this knife and those that ever will."

"You means Mr. Zechariah?" Tobe darted a gaze to the woods beyond as if he half expected to see an apparition appear.

"Aye, and not just that," Van said. "I will see that you are sold to the worst possible slaveholder in these United States."

"Van! You can't. You wouldn't," Lucy spat back. "Our father promised him and Ester their freedom someday."

"If he doesn't tell, he's got nothing to worry about, does he?" Van shot a determined look between Lucy and Tobe.

"I swear," Tobe said as the boys shook hands.

"Good enough. Are we done?" Lucy crossed her arms, tapping one toe at the entire business. "We're running away to our Uncle Joseph's to flee our stepfather. He plans to send me to live with Mr. Shepherd and—"

"Mr. Abraham Shepherd?" Tobe's eyes opened wide before turning a wary frown to the dirt. "They say he a bad'un."

"What do you know?" Van said.

"Not much, just that he got something agin your pa." He shrugged at Lucy and Van's bewildered exchange. "Like I said, I hear things when grown folks think I'm sleepin'."

"And Van, he got a copy of Mr. Newhouse's ledger so we can prove he's a thief." Tommy yelled this so loud that all three older children shushed him in unison, echoing off every leaf of the trees.

"There's nobody out here to hear me," Tommy protested.

"Ya'll got any idea how much trouble you're in once everyone find you missin' and where you going?" Tobe shook his head.

"But they won't 'cause you swore." Van leaned in toward Tobe with a decided warning look. "'Tis true. We are leaving today to make our way east toward Shepherds Town, and no one need know nothing about it."

Tobe shrugged. "Suit yourselves. Ya'll are taking a mighty big risk going that far all alone. How you think you gonna make it without getting caught or worse?"

"We don't have a choice," Lucy said. "We have to make this work. It's for all of us. What Mr. Newhouse is doing is wrong and will cost us everything. We've got to stop him somehow."

"What you mean, he a thief? What he taken from you he don't already have?" Tobe squinted his face into a disbelieving grimace. "He done own everything, being massa and all, don't he? It all be his now."

"Not exactly," Van interjected leaving Lucy open-mouthed with words unsaid. "He actually don't own anything. You see, our father left everything to all us children in his will. Drusilla, Zack ,and Elzey all got their share being of age, but we three, we gotta wait 'til we turn twenty-one, as our father's will states. It's how the law works."

"Then what Mr. Shepherd got to do with all this?" Tobe scratched his chin and veered a skeptical eye between them.

While Van caught his breath, Lucy intervened. "That's what we've got to figure out. Mr. Shepherd seems to think he's got a stake in this too. Mr. Connell, our father's lawyer, was supposed to be looking out for us. That's what Zach always said. But since Mother married again, we haven't seen him and don't know what Mr. Newhouse has been telling him."

"And now Mr. Zechariah gone and can't help no more." Tobe seemed to be talking more to himself and recalling something. "So that's what they meant."

"What they meant?" Van shifted his weight to ease the rifle over his shoulder at a different angle. "Who's they?"

"My ma and pa. I mean, Noah." Tobe licked his lips into a knowing smile. "Well sir, I heard them talking as I said. 'Twas the night 'afore the town market day, it was. Pa had come home late as usual, and Ma was waiting up for him. I was in bed under the covers, supposed to be asleep."

Lucy grew impatient waiting for Tobe to hammer out his tale. "Yes, well, go on with it. What did they say?"

"Well, Pa he done seen ya'll over to the tavern that night." Tobe took a step back and rubbed his chin. His eyes squinted as he gazed off at a distant point. Lucy figured he was recalling what he'd heard that night. "Pa said, 'Yes'm, them young 'uns be at the tavern tonight,

Ester. They's up to something. Mister Van he there with some other boy I don't reckon I know'd who it be.' "

"It was our Lucy," Tommy chimed in and stepped closer to listen to Tobe's tale with rapt attention. "She was dressed in Van's clothes just like now."

"I reckon he might of knowed that, too," Tobe leaned back against a tree and picked at a patch of dirt under his fingernail. "He said he thought he saw Miss Lucy duck into the woods, while Massa Newhouse was a talking to that man from Shepherds Town. He told Ma, this is what he say, 'Ester, massa up to no good and ain't doing right by them chillun of Miss Eleanor's.' " Tobe's voice took on a deeper tone as he imitated Noah's rich timbre.

"What does he know about our stepfather?" Van said.

"Oh, he know plenty, I reckon." Tobe was eager to tell all he knew. Lucy wanted to hear but worried that they might delay their trip and risk being caught if they didn't leave soon. "My pa, he go off to the tavern most every night with Massa Newhouse. I don't just know what they do there, but it be some kind of gambling I do know that, 'cause Pa, he bring home with a coin or two for us most nights."

"You don't know what they do there?" Lucy felt a queasy sensation in the pit of her stomach thinking about the cockfights. Mostly she tried to block out the vision of Ben Stephenson participating in such things. "It's horrid. It's best you don't know."

"It's just some cockfighting they're doing," Van intervened, shaking his head at Lucy. "You know them prize cocks Mr. Newhouse keeps over to the north coop away from the other chickens, those are the ones he uses for cockfighting."

Tobe looked at Van with a nod of appreciation and understanding. "I always wondered what they be like. So, you got to see one for real and up close?"

Lucy cast a disgusted look at both her brother and his slave. "Oh, how could you think such things? Those poor birds. And no one was stopping it."

Both Van and Tobe looked at Lucy as if they just realized she was standing there. "Girls, what do you expect?" Van rolled his eyes and shook his head. "Well, if you are gonna dress like a boy I 'spect you best start acting like one and forget all your tender feminine ways."

"I'm still a girl even if I'm not exactly dressed like it." Lucy stamped her foot and bent to pick up her haversack. "And anyway, we best be getting on our way before folks come looking for us or Tobe for that matter."

Tommy, who'd been listening while sitting over on a large boulder, stood and clasped his hands together. "Say, why don't Tobe come with us? He could tell Uncle Joseph what he knows and be extra help along the way."

Lucy looked down at her younger brother and smiled. "You mean someone to do all the work for you. You're not getting out of toting your provisions neither."

With his free hand, Van tousled Tommy's hair. "No, Tobe can't go with us, Tommy. You know that. What if he were found? A runaway slave wouldn't do at all. And it would draw more attention to us as well."

"That's right," Tobe said. "I best be getting back now before they send someone to come looking for me."

"But, he's your slave, ain't he, Van?" Tommy looked between the two older boys. "Can't you take him anywhere you want?"

"Not if we're not supposed to be running away." Van must have wanted Tobe along, as much as she did, but they could not risk it. "He'd be seen as a runaway slave and that'd be far worse for all of us."

"No, Tommy," Lucy said. "It's best that he stay here. Three runaways is one thing, but a runaway slave might draw more attention." She wondered what that meant for their worth as three freed children compared to the value of a slave. Would there be more care and diligence in tracking this one boy over the three of them?

Turning to Tobe she said. "You will be sure to tell them nothing about us running away. Only say that we were on our way to school when you give Van his books, and that's all you know, even to Ester and Noah. No one should know where we are going, until it's all said and done. I promise you, we will return and see you are freed one day."

"Naw, I won't say nothing." Tobe shook his head and raised his hand in a gesture of compliance. "If'n I say anything about knowing where ya'll is, they probably gonna give me what for and I ain't about to let that happen, or maybe they won't even believe me. They might even blame me for the whole thing. No sir, I ain't getting on massa's bad side, and I can't afford to let Ma and Pa get there neither. Ya'll might own me but, my ma and pa, they owned by Miss Eleanor and that mean they owned by Massa Newhouse too."

"What difference does that make?" Lucy saw that Tobe was anxious about something and wondered why he suddenly resorted to such babblings.

"Massa Newhouse owe a lot o' money to folks," Tobe said, gravely. "I heard Pa tell this to Ma and they afraid that one day if'n things gets worse, Massa Newhouse, he gonna sell off some of us slaves and that mean I might lose my ma or Noah, whose the nearest things I got to a pa, and I sure as heck don't want that to happen."

Lucy realized just how far-reaching Mr. Newhouse's hold on them all could be. "Oh, Tobe, I hadn't thought of that." Desperately, she looked toward Van. "Do you think it's safe to leave them like this? What if Mr. Newhouse gets angry while we're gone and tries to sell Ester or Noah or even Tobe to pay his debts?"

"He could do that anyway, Lucy," Van said. "And like Tobe says, it'll be worse for the others if he comes along. We can't wait around to watch him bleed us all dry and then sell off everything in the long run. Unless you'd like to go live with Mr. Shepherd?"

The mere thought sent a chill down Lucy's spine, and it irked her. "Then I suppose we best be on our way. We'll be at Uncle Joseph's in only a few days, we figure."

"Then what you suppose gonna happen then?" Tobe raised one eyebrow in a curious look at Lucy. "You think they gonna send Mr. Newhouse to jail? What Miss Eleanor gonna think about that?"

Van pressed his lips together and gave a sidelong look at Lucy before proceeding. "Not sure, exactly. But we figure Uncle Joseph will know what to do. Hopefully it will just mean the court keeps him from dipping his hands in our inheritance. Zack told me what to do."

"Zack?" Tobe looked around his shoulder as if someone might be lurking in the nearby trees. "You been talking to your dead brother? I don't like the sound o' that."

"No, of course not." Lucy glared at Van. Clearly he still knew more than he had told her, but she would winnow out the truth before the end of their journey.

"Oh, so that the way it be," Tobe said. "I do wish I could go with y'alls but I best be getting back before they start looking for me too."

"No, Tobe. Wait." She flew at him, her arms embracing him with all her might. "Be safe. Be well. We'll all be together again soon enough." She pulled back to gaze into his sheepish, startled face.

"I...um...you be safe and well too, Miss Lucy." He nodded to her brothers beyond her shoulder. "You too, Mr. Van, Mr. Tom."

"And...and keep up your reading, Isaac." Lucy swallowed a choke and fought a tear threatening to spill over her lashes.

"You a boy, now, Miss Lucy." Tobe exchanged a smirk with Van. She knew this as certain as she knew her young student before her, even now as her back was to her brothers. "No cryin' for boys."

"And they don't waste time in long fare-thee-well's neither," Van chided. "You coming along or not?"

Lucy gave one last squeeze of Tobe's hands, squared her shoulders, and followed after her two brothers into the woods.

CHAPTER 18

"Come along, Tommy. We have to keep moving along." Lucy held her brother's hand and helped him over a large tree root. "You can't be stopping at every bug and critter, not this time."

"What will Phoebe think when we don't come to her place after school?" Tommy said.

"She won't know nothing about it." Van moved through the brushwood, steadying his balance with one arm still held in the sling, a flintlock and haversack full of supplies slung over the other. "We only told Mama that we were going to Phoebe's cabin for the night. They won't miss us for at least another day, maybe two."

Tommy's lip quivered slightly and he tugged at his ear, the way he had as an infant when he was fussy. Now that he was older, it only happened when he had done something wrong. Lucy took his hand and whispered soothingly, "It's all right. As soon as we reach Uncle Joseph's we'll send word that we're safe."

Soft rays of light bathed the woodlands in golden fire against the dark silhouette of trees, a sure sign the day was waning and they'd be alone in the dark once again.

"Should we see about setting up camp?" Lucy held Tommy's hand tighter as he tripped along at her heels.

Van made no change in his gait as he walked a few feet ahead of them. "Not just yet. We need to be as far away as possible. We've still got another two hours or so of daylight and we should make use of it."

"I'm hungry," Tommy wailed, "and my feet hurt."

As Tommy continued to mewl, Van came to a dead stop at the crest of the next hill and whirled around to his little brother. "You were the one who wanted to come along. You think my arm doesn't hurt? My feet aren't tired, too? And likely Lucy's as well?"

"Van," Lucy said, "he's only a wee baby. "

"I'm no baby," Tommy stomped his foot. "I want my supper."

Lucy reached into her sack to pull out a handful of parched corn. "Here, suck on this, Tommy-kins." To Van she added, "It has been a long time since we paused for dinner. Maybe just a respite and then we'll put more distance behind us before nightfall?"

A low rumble in the east was the last thing they wanted to hear now, but at least it settled the argument.

"I 'spect that means we'll be looking for shelter sooner than later," Van muttered, scanning the horizon where gunpowder clouds swirled against the soft rose of waning sunlight.

They managed to find shelter under an overhanging ridge before the swiftly moving storm overtook them. By nightfall, rain beat a pounding rhythm against the hills and woods, washing the path they recently trod into a muddy sludge. Scattered flashes of lightening cast them all in an eerie blaze before the darkness enveloped them once again. The journey would be more than some hundred and fifty miles from their home at Swearingens Landing, and there was no telling how far they'd come as yet. Perhaps ten miles, but with Tommy's dawdling, likely even less than that Lucy feared. How many more days would there be like this until they reached the journey's end. And would they even make it that far? She tried to dispel such thoughts as Tommy huddled closer.

"Maybe we should'a stayed home," Tommy sniffled. "I want Mama."

"Are you sure this is the only way?" Lucy turned to Van. "Couldn't we have..."

"We'll just have to wait out the storm and hope it's over by morning," Van said before another crack of thunder boomed and rattled the ground beneath Lucy's feet.

"Van, will we really get away with this, do you think?" Lucy reached a hand to feel the haversack at her side, laden with parched corn, some dried jerky, the compass, and an ax. Already, her stomach was pinched in hunger, but their provisions needed to last until they were able to hunt for more food.

"We'll hide here 'til the storm clears," he said. "This actually could work in our favor."

"What do you mean?" Lucy briefly saw his face illuminated in the flashing storm, eyes glittering with an idea.

"Well, if they think we are out to Phoebe's place for the night...and with the storm coming up..."

"They'll think we stayed over to wait out the storm..."

"Exactly," Van said.

Lucy's fingers lightly touched the necklace sewn into the hem of her coat. She was glad now that they had the compass to guide them. Van's rosewood-handled knife would be useful as well for fish they might catch or a rabbit or squirrel that might trap, as well. The necklace was the least useful item to cart through the woods, unless they needed it for trade, which she hoped would not be the case.

Another clap of thunder sent Tommy huddling closer to her under the wool blanket they shared. Rain dripped in silvery droplets from the overhanging rocks.

Van shifted to reposition himself away from the dripping rain. "What made you think of hiding the necklace in the blockhouse wall?"

Lucy leveled her eyes at him. "What? How did you know?"

He shot her a knowing smile, even in this darkness she knew by the superior tone in his voice. "You did bring it with you, didn't you?"

"Yes," she said, "but...no one was supposed to know. I promised. How...?"

"You talk in your sleep," Van said. "Sometimes I can't understand everything you say, but you've been talking about Grandmother's necklace."

"Zack gave it to me last Christmas. I've kept it hid ever since. Didn't even know what it was until I opened the puzzling trick box he wrapped it in."

Another clap of thunder and flash of lightening revealed Van's thoughtful gaze. "I'm glad you got it. Might be useful if we need to sell it to make our way east."

"You can't sell Grandmother Swearingen's necklace. It's a family heirloom," Lucy said. "And it's mine. Zack gave it to me."

"If it comes down to surviving the journey or parting with the necklace, you figure out which is best." Van sighed and then softened his tone. "I reckon we'll make it the ultimate last resort. Whatever made you think of hiding it in the fort in the first place?"

"That's where you hid my Clarissa when I was seven. I cried for days looking for her."

Van grinned. Even through the darkness Lucy could sense his mischievous gloat. "She was just an old corn husk twisted into a doll."

"Not to me she wasn't." Ester had made the cornhusk doll for her when she was seven after Mother had refused to buy her a wooden doll dressed in fine clothes from the trading post. It hardly seemed only hours ago, at break of day, that she was talking with Ben at the trading post. Now the sun had long since set, and they were to make their journey across the miles in hopes of reclaiming what was theirs.

"A fine thing," Van said, breaking her reverie, "here you are dressed in my old clothes and supposed to be a boy, and you're fretting over a necklace and a doll."

Lucy wriggled in Van's old breeches, shirt, and waistcoat. A brown wool cap of his completed the outfit, yet something was still not right. She stroked the long braid curled over her shoulder. It extended to nearly the middle button on the waistcoat she wore. Perhaps Van was right. If she was truly going to pass for a boy, she had one more adjustment to make. "Maybe there's something I need you to do, then." She swallowed and closed her eyes.

"What's that? You want me to carry the necklace? Or should I wear it round my neck?"

"No." A deep breath and a hard swallow aided her resolve. "I need you to cut my hair."

"What?" Van stepped back and let go of his knife. It clattered to the log floor. "That's not necessary, Lucy. I won't do that."

"Yes, you have to. I'm resolved." Lucy sighed and held her hair out toward him. "If I'm to pass as a real boy, I will need shorter hair. Just get it over with, please." She squeezed her eyes together.

"How am I supposed to do this one-handed and in the dark in the middle of a storm, no less?" Van pulled his hand away clenching it over his bandaged arm in the sling. "We'll do this later, in the morning at first light."

"No, it has to be now. I may not want to later. In the dark I won't have to see it so much, and the storm will distract me. In the morning it will be over with, and I'll have no choice but to accept things." She murmured the words to herself, the mysterious magic words that came to her, unbidden. Perhaps they would help garner the courage to accept her fate and will her brother's hand to be quick, clean, and sure.

"Just do it now, please."

Tommy placed his small hand over Lucy's trembling fingers. "I'll help, if you want me to."

Lucy smiled and gave her brother a kiss on the forehead. "I think that would be a fine idea, Tom. Van, let Tommy hold the hank of hair out and you cut through it just above where I've tied it." She unhooked her arm from around Tommy and turned her back to them as she stared into the darkness, the moldy dampness of the rock wall tingling her nose.

"Very well, if you're sure." Van pulled the knife from the leather sheath, and the cold steel grazed her neck. Lucy held her breath. "But if Mother finds out, remember this was all your idea."

Lucy sighed and let out a sardonic chuckle. "Van, we are running away and ready to prove our mother's husband is a thief," she paused and looked at him wryly, "and you're worried about a little hair?" She laughed.

Van had to laugh at this as well. He took a deep breath and twisted around to support himself on his knees as Lucy showed Tommy exactly where to hold the hank of hair. Lucy squeezed her lips as tight as she did her eyes, waiting for the inevitable blow. A slight tug on the thick tail at the base of her neck, a scritch-scratch of knife against strands of hair, then weightlessness let her know the deed was done. The clump of hair plopped to her side, still bound in its leather restraint.

"Is it done?" Lucy let out her breath slowly and reached tentative fingers to the place where once her hair hung in its thick, wavy glory.

Illuminated by the next lightening flash the brownish braid lay coiled like a miserable garden snake on the cold, wet ground.

They were careful to stay clear of the coach roads and main thoroughfares lest they risk discovery. The first night was spent hiding deep in the forest, a restless sleep upon the damp ground after the storm. The chill of early spring seeped into Lucy's bones, relieved only slightly by the few hissing coals they were able to spark after the rain. Ahead of them lay miles of wilderness dotted with the occasional settlement of cabins clustered together like the twisted knots of thread on the back of one of Lucy's samplers. *No more stitching, plain or otherwise,* Lucy thought as she walked down the tree-lined path through the woods. It brought little consolation, rather a twinge of guilt that her mother would be sitting at home alone to attend the mending, though she still had Ester to keep her company.

The miles of walking had at first been exhilarating, but now Lucy's legs had turned to heavy bands of iron with each move. She dared not complain though, lest Van chide her for being a mere girl who could not keep up. She must behave and act as a boy in order to maintain this ruse and prove she could fair the journey as well as her brothers. Lucy still felt a bit self-conscious in her brother's outgrown shirt and breeches and wondered if Mother would be mortified to see her dressed so and to know she had cut her hair. Stubbornly she put the thought out of her mind and resolved to keep going. After all it had been her idea to alter her appearance to throw off any suspicion and guarantee their safety. Three boys traveling would garner less interest or danger. And she had to admit that these clothes were indeed more comfortable and made travel less burdensome.

Van had walked along in stoic silence for most of the morning since their breakfast of dried apples and the last bit of johnnycake. They had gathered only enough supplies from the kitchen storehouse to get them started—a sack of parched corn, a hunk of cheese, some dried apples, and the johnnycakes Ester had made and would likely fret over missing. Might she blame one of the other slaves? Or would they figure out it was them who stole from their own family's kitchen? Still, it would only get them so far. They would have to rely on Van's skills at hunting and trapping the rest of the way.

His injured arm must be hurting, Lucy surmised, though of course he never indicated anything of the sort. He insisted on carrying the rifle, slung across his back. Lucy wondered how he figured he'd shoot it with one arm tied in a sling, but hopefully they would not have to find out. If need be, she could shoot, although the thought of shooting and killing a rabbit or squirrel was not appealing—even if she was raised on hunted game and slaughtered farm animals. To actually kill something was quite another matter, not like shooting at tin cans or glass bottles with her older brothers. On occasion they allowed her to shoot with them, when Mother wasn't around to object. But that had been with a pistol. A long gun had always been far too heavy to manage. Still, she was a bit older, taller, and stronger now.

"Van, if you want I could try to tote the gun a while, that is, if you're needing a little rest." Lucy tried not to sound too overbearing but knew by the scowl on Van's face that he did not like her offer.

"Naw, I'll be fine." Van straightened his shoulders and shook his head. "You just mind our little brother. Besides, you'd never be able to tote it very far."

"I couldn't do any worse than you with your bad wrist," Lucy spit out the words a bit too harshly before being filled with regret.

They walked in silence around the next bend of the trail, Tommy darting ahead to walk beside Van. "I can carry the haversack for you."

Van stopped and looked at his little brother with a warm smile. "You just want to pinch a few more bites of apple or cheese, little man." With two fingers he playfully pulled the boy's hat brim down over his eyes. "You've had quite enough 'til noontime, and we need to preserve our resources."

"How long do you figure it will take us now?" Lucy hitched her bundle a bit higher on her shoulder.

Van studied a spot deep in the woods as if calculating the proper answer. "I'm figuring about three or four days. Maybe more, since we aren't staying on the main roads, and if we encounter any more foul weather, it could be even longer."

"Couldn't we follow the main roads? At least once we get far enough away from Wellsburg?"

"Maybe," Van said, "once we get farther along Buffalo Creek. If we keep following as we've been, according to the map we shouldn't need to follow any roads."

"Did you find the one in the haversack I got from the trading post?"

Van turned to her with a self-satisfied gleam. "Don't need it. I found one in amongst Father's things still in his trunk of books. I remember seeing it once before and sure enough, there it still was. It's the one Pa made when he first come to Virginia from Pennsylvania." He produced a folded sheet of paper from his jacket. "I reckon if it got Pa west it could get us east to Uncle Joseph's."

Lucy came closer to look at the map, running her finger along the crooked lines that marked the creeks. "Shepherds Town, Martinsburg. That's where we're headed. Whereabouts do you figure we are now?"

Van pointed to a spot along the creek a bare finger's width from where Wellsburg was marked on the Ohio River. "I can't say for certain, but it appears we may be about here, maybe twenty miles or so along Buffalo Creek headed in the general direction of Shepherds Town."

"The general direction?" Lucy squinted skeptically while keeping a sharp eye on Tommy who wandered off to chase a baby rabbit.

"Best I can figure. So long as we keep heading east and follow the creeks, we'll be near enough. Once we get far enough away we can maybe stop at a cabin or settlement and ask directions."

Lucy pondered this and then plucked up courage to ask what had been on her mind all morning. "Van, do you really think this will work? We'll convince Uncle Joseph and win our case? I won't have to be sent away or end up married to Mr. Shepherd's son?"

"We'll have to try," Van said solemnly. "I think Uncle Joseph will see our side. I know he wasn't happy seeing Abraham Shepherd there at our brother's funeral."

"How do you know this? What else did Zack tell you to do?"

Van hesitated; his toe dug into the dirt making a small dent in the muddy road. "He said he never did like Mr. Newhouse, the way he courted Mother. Such a smooth talker he was. I guess he also was looking into his background. That's why he took that trip to see Mr. Connell last summer just before Mother's wedding."

"Who's Mr. Connell?"

"I told you this, Lucy," Van called over his shoulder as he forged ahead. A roll of his eye at her did not deter her one bit, no matter what he might think. "Mr. Connell is...was...our father's lawyer. He's supposed to look out for our property until we come of age."

"But you said Zack had gone to the courts. Was that to settle all this with Mr. Connell? How will that fare now that he is...that he can't now?" Lucy turned back again to walk down the road further. Tommy had wandered ahead and was chasing a chipmunk into a hollow log. She had better mind him or he would soon be getting too far ahead and lose them.

"I don't rightly know. That's why we need to get help from Uncle Joseph. He might know something of it."

"Then, if he knows, why didn't he do something when he came to Zack's burial?" Lucy's voice trailed away. She still didn't like thinking about that day and the mortifying occurrence afterward in the house or the chance meeting with Ben Stephenson later. She still feared she told him too much and wondered what Van might think if he knew. "He could have spoken to us or to Mother. He could have stayed to help."

"I don't think he knows everything or else he would have," Van said. "And who's to say he didn't try speaking with Mother. Remember, at the moment Mr. Newhouse controls everything—the house, the land, and, much as I hate to admit it, Mother."

"But he can't take what isn't his, Father's fortune, our inheritance. You said the law forbids it."

"I'm no lawyer." Van's voice was testy. He picked up a stick with his good hand and threw it into the woods beside the road. It skittered against a couple of trees before landing in a tangle of dead leaves and underbrush. "And neither was Zack, but Uncle Joseph knows a bit about these things and he knows other men who do. At least that's what Zack said."

"And he knows Mr. Stephenson's family. Remember, our Cousin Thomas said he was to apprentice for Mr. Stephenson's brother this summer. The one who works in the government, I think he said."

Van gave her a stern look. "I suppose."

"Then maybe Mr. Stephenson could help us, if he's a lawyer and works for the government, too."

Van spat on the ground with a sneer and a snort. "Aye, I'm sure he'd be right helpful and be sure his brother'd get all he could from our pa's land."

"What's that supposed to mean?" Lucy stopped in her tracks. Her heart skipped a wild leap. "Why don't you trust Ben Stephenson?"

"I got my reasons. Let's keep moving forward now. 'Nuff talk. Save your energy for walking."

Lucy wondered if she shouldn't have mentioned something to Ben before they left. Maybe he knew something of what Zack told Van. He had been their brother's friend too, but then the risk of him knowing too much might have been all the worse.

After two days of wandering through the woods, Lucy doubted her older brother had an inkling of where they were going. Her legs had long since grown tired of walking, draining her of hope with each step. She awoke each morning achy from sleeping on the cold, hard ground. Tommy was growing more irritable the farther they went and often had to be carried just to keep up. Van's broken wrist still pained him, though he tried not to show it. Lucy often saw him rubbing his arm in a grimace.

Lucy didn't want him to think she knew, so she often discreetly took the task of lugging Tommy on her back, saying he was accustomed to her carrying him about since he was small. At seven, he was getting to be quite a load as they trudged over hill after hill.

"I'm hungry," Tommy said when they stopped under a grove of ash trees for the noon meal. "I don't want to eat parched corn anymore. Why can't we find some blueberries to eat?"

Lucy popped a few kernels of corn in her mouth. "It's too early for blueberries, Tom. Here, why don't you just suck on some corn and imagine that it's blueberries?" Lucy knew this was not very helpful, but there weren't many options at the moment. They had hoped the provisions would last until they reached Shepherds Town, but the journey was taking a bit longer than expected.

"I want to go home," Tommy said as he reluctantly popped the corn into his mouth and made a face.

"We can't go home." Van grabbed the flintlock and stood up. "We've got to see this thing through. It won't be long now. We should be at Uncle Joseph's in just a day or so." He looked off into the woods and shouldered his flintlock.

"Where you going off to?" Lucy said. "We just got here and Tommy needs more rest."

"You two stay here." Van turned and headed off into the woods, calling over his shoulder, "I aim to get us some fresh meat for dinner."

CHAPTER 19

Ben reviewed the line of men mustered into formation inside the fort on an early spring morning. Were it not for the reason they were there assembled, it would have been a fine day for drilling and later, perhaps, an afternoon of fishing at the creek or a target shoot followed by a round of drinks at the tavern by evenfall. For the farmers it was the early planting season and many of the men now standing before him had left fields half tilled and waiting to be seeded. Instead, all had answered the call of duty when summoned to find three missing children. Thirty-two of Brady's rangers stood armed and capable of the mission before them. Most were fathers who did not hesitate to aid the call. Any neighbor's missing children would have elicited such a response, but that it was Captain Van's made the turnout all the more impressive.

"Men, you understand the purpose of our gathering." Ben paused at the murmurings between the corps before calling them back to attention. "We'll form posses of three to four men and scatter around the general vicinity first. It's thought that they may have gotten lost during the storm the other night. Hopefully they are just holed up in a cave nearby."

"What if it's the Injuns got 'em?" Henry Newell blurted out, causing another discontented murmur to filter through the line. "Blue Jacket's been rumored to be on the move again and up to his old ways."

Ben again called the men to attention, this time with a more forceful bark, "We have no reason to believe anything of the sort. There's been no threats since Greenville and no reason to think otherwise.

Let's not be stirring up trouble that isn't there. Do I make myself clear?"

"Still the only Injun, I say, is a dead Injun." Henry lifted his fist in the air. A few other men responded in kind, concurring with the sentiment. "For three little 'uns to go missing like that—and the captain's kin, no less

"Lookin' mighty suspicious."

Ben had thought the same...on quite a different level, but first he must set the search parties in motion and deal with his suspicions later. "Do I make myself clear?" he reiterated with a warning toward Henry and an eye toward the man standing up the hill toward the cabin. "Let's just be about our mission and get the young 'uns home safe and back to their mother. We've divided the area into sectors for each posse to search. We'll comb the immediate area first, alerting anyone you come across to be on the lookout. If you find anything to report, fire three consecutive shots in the air to signal the others."

"You mean, no matter what we find?" Abraham Shepherd spit a sluice of tobacco on the ground, narrowed his eyes at Ben, and worked his chin from side to side. "If you mind what I'm thinking, that is?"

"The storm left many a creek overflowing its banks the other night," Sam Butcher added. "The young 'uns might-a got swept up in one..." He dropped his head with a sorrowful look. "Ain't but little chance they'd survive, or we be likely to ever..." Butcher shook his head eliciting an ominous murmur from the ranks.

"They may not surface for days or even weeks," Shepherd eyed the man with interest from the sideline, ever so willing to finish the unspoken concern.

A few men shifted their eyes and looked at the ground. Ben cleared his throat. "Aye, three shots no matter what we find, though we pray they be found all alive and well."

Ben watched as the men who brought horses mounted and set out. Others on foot gathered in their groups and headed out from the fort. Elzey, Josiah Gibson, and William Engle drew near. The four would form a posse and ride out toward Zach's place again and see if the children had wandered away in the vicinity, though Phoebe had already said she never saw the children nor knew anything about their visit. This only irked him more. He had no reason to doubt Phoebe's word, but something about it bothered him. Why would the children deliberately lie about visiting their sister-in-law, unless they had planned a deception in order to run away? If they had done something this desperate and foolish, hopefully the storm delayed their course and they'd find three frightened, bedraggled children holed up in some cave afraid to come home and face their punishment.

His thoughts replayed the conversation with Lucy at the store that last morning. She had meant to return the book but seemed bothered by something else. He recalled her discomfort and the odd way she behaved when he noted the bruises and burn on her arm.

She had said she had been carrying firewood and was too careless around the fire, though Ben suspected it was not the case. Four angry, purple, fingerlike lines and that burn to her forearm were no mere accidents. He couldn't shake the notion that she had wanted to tell him something. He cursed himself for not seeing that and making her confide in him. The haversack she had purchased, was it really for an invalid brother? Or were the three urchins scheming to run away all along? He would never have expected such foolhardy behavior from Lucy, who for her tender years, seemed to have a good head on her shoulders. Van, too, for all his belligerence, knew better at his age than to try something so desperate or to lure his younger brother along with them, especially with his own bad wrist. What could have happened in that house to prompt this? He aimed to find out. More than likely they were just off at a neighbor's house or hiding somewhere in the woods. He hoped that's all this amounted to. Some childish game and they got lost in the woods and were huddled somewhere, scared and waiting to be found. Or perhaps they had found shelter with a far-flung settler who had taken them in. He ran each hopeful scenario through his mind to fend off the sinking dread. Another failure that was his fault. He couldn't let another death be on his conscience.

John Newhouse was putting on quite a front as the distraught father. He had insisted on going along and was hell-bent on finding them, especially Lucy. Ben had not missed the conspiratorial looks between him and Shepherd, same as he'd seen at the card table and cockfights of late. Eleanor was understandably distraught but had the aid of several womenfolk to comfort her, including the other Swearingen daughters, Drusilla and Phoebe—who was still holding her place in the wake of widowhood and the pretense she may be with child. He couldn't think on that now. He would find the children, no matter what it took. His thoughts wandered to those last words with Zack and the promise he'd made. He had also assured Joseph Swearingen that day at the store that he would keep a watchful eye on the three bairns. Yet, how had they so easily slipped through his fingers?

Ben was drawn from his brooding thoughts by William Engle. "Sergeant, we figure we'll head out toward Shawnee Ridge, if that fits with your plans."

"Private Engle?" Ben realized the man had been speaking to him all along and now looked at him with an inquisitive air. "Yes, of course. My thinking as well. Then we'll circle around and head down toward Wheeling and rendezvous back here by evenfall."

"We'll find them, sir." William's voice was low and soothing, but full of determination. "I know what the Swearingens mean to you."

"It's the captain's children we're looking for. That alone should mean a great deal to all of us." He dismissed the private and sought his opportunity to speak with Abraham Shepherd who was headed in the direction of the Swearingen cabin. "Mr. Shepherd, might I have a word with you?"

The man turned, his demeanor spoke marked irritation in being summoned just then, but he would have no choice in the matter. "Stephenson. What may I do you for?"

"As I understand it, you were at the Swearingens' Sunday last for dinner." A pause to see the man's blank response. Ben pressed further. "Am I to understand you were a guest?"

"I was, but I don't see what concern that is of yours, sir." Shepherd shifted his gaze to the rocky soil. "There's the children's welfare to consider—"

"And precisely my point." Ben stepped within arm's reach. "I wondered if anything happened. If you noted anything in the children that may have warranted their disappearance."

Shepherd screwed his eyes tight and jutted out his chin into a sidelong grin. "Now, why should I know that? I was there as a guest of Mr. and Mrs. Newhouse. I'm no child's nursemaid."

"I understand." Ben affected an amiable smile and subdued his tone. "I just figured you were there and among the last to have seen the children in their home...." He left the rest to an idle shrug, implying a need for the man's assistance.

"I can't say I saw nary the chit nor chip the entire evening," he lied with an unaffected shrug. "Must've been sent to bed early for all I know, as good children should."

Ben stood back, considering his next answer."Whenever I've eaten at the Swearingen table, the children were welcome."

"You accusing me of anything, Stephenson?"

"Not necessarily. Just making an observation." Ben drew back slightly, a blank stare masking his face in innocence. "Perhaps you saw or heard something. Might the children have had a reason to run away? Were they sent to bed early for a reason?"

"If it's anything to you, and I don't see how it is," Shepherd spewed, "the children ate apart from the adults, in the kitchen with the cook, maybe. I can't say I saw any of the little 'uns the whole of the time I was there."

"And just why were you there, if you don't mind my asking?"

"I do mind, sir," Shepherd gave an affronted jerk of his head. "And I don't see a need to continue this discourse."

"Oh, but I do." Ben smoothed the gloves he held and leveled his next words casually. "You see, I seem to recall seeing you and Newhouse riding down by the lower Catfish Creek the other week, just after you arrived. I can't imagine what you'd be doing on ol' Cap'n Swearingen's land, considering how things went between the two of you."

"That was a long time ago, lad." Shepherd shook his head as he studied the back of one flexed hand. "Different day and time. Ol' Swearingen, if ye haven't noticed, is dead and gone."

"Aye, but he is well remembered as are the things that went down between the two of you then and the land deal that went awry."

"You best not be making accusations about things you know nothing about." Shepherd eyed him shrewdly with a baleful grin. "There's more to the captain than most any of you here knows or remembers."

"I do mind your meaning," Ben whispered confidentially. "The captain had his wily ways too, no doubt about that. I'm not here to place blame, but those innocent children had nothing to do with this either, and if for any reason they've been made to suffer—"

"The sins of the father?" Shepherd interjected. "Is that your meaning now? Best be asking that of Blue Jacket and his horde of demon savages."

"I never said anything about Blue Jacket," Ben leveled the remark with an arched eye.

"It's what you meant. The boys already mentioned the possibility of savages, so it's no secret that's where this would have gone, and you figured I had something to do with him dragging the brats off again? I'd be very careful who you go around accusing, sir. Now if you don't mind, you've got a task to perform and I've got business of my own."

Ben nodded toward the woods beyond the cabin. "That section of land you were looking over with Newhouse, you have no claim to it and I aim to prove it. From what I've heard, that tract belongs to Lucy. If you had anything to do with the children's disappearance, if any harm does happen to come to them, you'll be wishing you never returned here."

"Are you threatening me, Stephenson?"

"Just making everything clear, sir."

"Well, then maybe you can make this clear, sir." Shepherd took a step forward with squared shoulders and a jutting chin. "Seems you're always in a position where one or the other Swearingens are getting themselves hurt or killed. You been hanging 'round the women folk too. Got your eye on a certain sweet young widow have ye? Or the little lass—you bein' the last to see her that morning?"

Ben took in this last bit of information, thinking of the mortified expression on Lucy's face as he examined the reddened blisters on her arm. He steadied his breathing, considering a new tack, and shrugged offhandedly. "She stopped by the store early yesterday morning and told me about the accident. Seems you might know more about this?"

"I had nothing to do with the hot poker burning." Shepherd clenched his jaw and shifted his eyes out toward the patrol of men heading out on foot and horseback. "Seems to me you'd best be out looking for those young 'uns rather than wasting time jawing with me."

"I never said I was accusing you of anything." He let the comment pass but noted the reaction. Lucy had never mentioned a hot poker. She had only said she burned herself while carrying firewood and getting too close to the fire. Shepherd was now caught in his lie. Had he witnessed the burning? Or done it himself? Ben steadied his nerves, resisting the urge to throttle the man. First, find the children and bring them home safe. Then hear their side of the story.

"Course not!" Shepherd cleared his throat and clamped his lips together as if biting back a cold smile. "Looks like the old Injun's curse is still playing out, not that I believe in such foolery. Still, it's a tragedy. Buried one Swearingen last week and here three more lost in one fell swoop. Elzey and Dussy best mind their heads, too."

That sounded like a threat, but Ben let it pass and turned a sharp eye on him. "More reason we need to get the children back home to their mother, wouldn't you say? The Swearingens have been through quite enough grief of late."

"Indeed they have." Shepherd eyed him cautiously. "And you seem to be always right in the midst when tragedy strikes, now don't ya?"

"Some might say the hardships only started once you returned to the valley," Ben offered lightly, but with unmistakable meaning.

Shepherd stepped closer...close enough that Ben could smell his foul breath behind yellowed teeth. "There's nothing you can do about what I'm here for, Stephenson. You, on the other hand, got a mighty lot of things to answer for. You were with the older boy when he was found near dead, I hear. Or was he already dead—and not by accident nor fever neither? And you admit to being the last one to see at least one of the children before they'd gone a-missing."

Ben tipped back his cap, taking the remark in stride. "If you're accusing me of something, you'd best bring your case to the sheriff."

"Just a word of advice, is all." Shepherd relaxed his tone as if chewing the fat over a game of draughts. "You ain't a Swearingen and best not to mix yourself up in their business. Go find the children. Bring 'em home to their ma, God willin'. Leave it at that and I might see a way to make it worth your while."

"I intend to fetch them home. And what I do beyond that doesn't concern you either, sir." Ben nodded his goodbye and turned to join his men.

As he readied to mount his horse, he spied a young slave standing off behind the well, watching the men leave. His eyes were wide with fear. Something made Ben stop and study the boy. Isaac, wasn't that his name? He had passed by the store while Ben was sweeping the porch that morning, just a few hours after Lucy left. Ben had seen him walking by with a couple of books under his arm, as if heading toward the schoolhouse, but then he veered toward the path that led beyond Zane's tract. Seeing this, Ben had called out cheerily to him, "Now, just who forgot their schoolbooks again?"

The slave had stopped dead in his tracks and then looked as if he'd been caught stealing. "I didn't mean to startle you, Isaac is it?"

"No, sir. Most folks call me Tobe." The boy pulled the books to his side and looked warily up and down the road. "Only my mama calls me Isaac."

"And Miss Lucy, at times." Ben added, though at the utterance of the girl's name the slave had frozen in his tracks and darted a look into the woods behind the store.

"Yes, sir, she do that sometimes." Tobe shuffled his feet. "I best be getting these here books off to the school."

Ben smiled and watched the boy go. The odd thing was, he had continued in the opposite direction of the school and disappeared behind the sawmill. The only thing back there was the trail leading into the woods through the eastern side of Zane's tract. Ben had dismissed the thought as the indolent behavior of a slave who preferred taking his good old sweet time following through with a task. Ben went about his work, figuring he'd leave the lad to his own devices. It wasn't his concern. Now he wished he had stopped the lad and pressed him. Perhaps this was the time.

Ben swung his horse around and headed toward the well. He called back to the other men. "Private Engle, you take the men on ahead. I'll be along directly."

Ben dismounted as the men rode down the path toward town. He walked to the wide-eyed boy who looked ready to turn tail and run.

"Tobe, I could sure use a drink of water before I head out. Would you oblige me, please?" Ben leaned against the well and pulled his hat off to rake his fingers through his hair.

"Yes sir." Tobe moved his brown, callused hand to the crank and began lowering the bucket. His arm jerked stiffly as he focused on his task.

"Don't be alarmed." Ben replaced his hat and kicked some dried mud from his boots. "I just mean to ask you a few questions, that's all."

"What sort of questions you be meaning to ask, sir?" Tobe's eyes shifted around to the back of the cabin as he continued to lower the bucket. The crank squeaked against the labored turns. "I don't know nothing about where Mr. Van and Miss Lucy be."

Ben kept his eye on the boy as the crank turned and the rope spun down. "Now, I hadn't quite asked you that, had I?"

"No, sir, I guess you didn't." Tobe backed away from the well and looked down at the ground when the bucket hit the water's surface.

"But you do know something more than you're letting on." Ben jerked on the rope to fill the bucket, but never took his eyes off the slave.

"What make you say that, sir?" Tobe fidgeted and tugged on the sleeve of his well-worn tunic. He reached the crank handle to retrieve the full bucket. "I just figured that's what all the fuss be about and you been askin' everyone." He nodded toward the fort as the men continued to file out and down the hill to the main road.

Ben nodded following the boy's line of vision to the departing militia detail. "Yes, indeed a lot of fuss for a very sound reason. I'm at a loss here and need to find answers anywhere I can. It would sure be a shame if one man knew something and didn't speak up to help his friends in need."

Tobe seemed uneasy about this last statement, but also Ben noted a flash of resentment in the boy's eyes. "I ain't ever gonna be no man, sir. I's just a slave."

Ben considered Tobe's situation a moment. "Well, being a man is a funny thing sometimes." He paused to see the effect this had on the boy. "A slave would keep his head low and protect himself. A man would help a friend no matter what the cost. It makes no difference whether you're a slave to someone else or a slave to your own fears and doubts. I do know that feeling well."

"You got a might strange way of putting things, for a white man, that is." Tobe looked warily at the house and ran his lower lip between his teeth. Beneath the lightly tanned skin, Ben noted the barest hint of a blush.

"I know things haven't been exactly the same lately, but anything you say will be between us only. You have my word as a ranger on that." Ben took the gourd of water Tobe had dipped from the bucket and sipped the cool water. "I know you didn't take those books to the school that day. I saw you disappear behind the store and head into the woods. The schoolmaster says the children never attended that day, and you never showed up with any books. I haven't made that known to anyone and I promise you I won't."

Tobe's eyes grew big so the whites gleamed brightly against the high color turning his dusky skin to a rosy tan. Those eyes in a face reminiscent of the young lass in his shop the day before. He had the rounded face of his slave mother but the almond-shaped eyes and slightly dimpled chin of a Swearingen—the ol' Indian fighter. The captain had made no secret of his dalliances. The Brown woman and one of Zane's daughters had each born him a bastard, and God only knew how many others. The silence hung between them while a flock of pigeons flew overhead.

Tobe scratched the back of his neck and twisted his mouth as if he wanted to say something. "Mr. Stephenson, you promise not to say nothin' to massa about any this? If'n they find out I get whipped for sure. Massa Injun Van he never whipped us, not bad anyways. Just a good slappin' when we needs it, is all. But now it be different. Miss Lucy, she say you's a good man, but Mr. Van...he think..." He stopped and clamped his mouth shut. "I's sorry. I don't mean to go on so."

"It's alright, son," Ben said gently. "I'm listening."

"Folks say I talk too much, I spect." He lowered his tone. "And think too much, too."

"And I do need you to talk to me now," Ben encouraged. "So just what might you be thinking on all that, Tobe?"

"'Bout what?" The boy drew in his chin skeptically.

"About anything." Ben leaned over the well and examined a frayed thread on the leather of one glove finger.

A smile played at the corners of his mouth followed by a snicker, more aghast than humored. "You're a curious one, Mr. Stephenson. Why you ask me what I think?"

Ben leaned back and laughed. "Curious one, am I? Now where'd you learn a word like that?"

"I...just...dunno."

"Miss Lucy's reading lessons have been paying off, I see." The slave hung his head but there was a sly grin twitching at the corners of his mouth.

"You've heard two opinions of me, what do you reckon it to be? Seems to me you got two choices and only you can decide. If you don't tell me what you know, it could cost the lives of your friends, possibly. Three innocent children who've not done you any harm."

"But if I tells you, it might cost them more."

"Aye, it might," Ben nodded. "Only you can determine that, Tobe. You have me at a loss with no real direction to take at the moment. So, it's up to you." He could tell by the glimmer in the lad's eyes and the crinkle of his brow, he had never been given such a dilemma—a choice to make that would control the destiny of others. It both vexed and intrigued him.

When a tight-lipped pause followed by a slight shake of the boy's head left Ben still at a stalemate, he pressed with the next tack. "Miss Lucy had bruises on her arm and a mighty bad burn. Van had a mighty bad fall from that horse last Saturday and is in no shape to be traveling out away from those who would tend to him. If the children ran away for a reason and you know where, it would sure help to be looking in a general direction."

"If'n I tells you, will you take me with you?" Tobe ventured this in a barely audible voice. "I'd like to help find them, too."

Ben shot the boy a look of new respect. "Aha! So you know your way around a barter, is it?"

Chagrined, he turned a deep shade of redwood dipped in sunset.

"I just meant…I mean…no disrespect, sir. I could help and won't be no trouble."

"No disrespect taken, my lad. You drive a hard bargain, but it seems I've no choice but to accept." Ben smiled and clasped the boy on the shoulder. "Aye, Tobe, I'd 'spect we best speak to Master Newhouse about the terms of renting me a fine young servant to help fetch and carry my goods." He drew a hand around the boy's shoulders and led him with a wink toward the Swearingens' cabin. What he was going to do with a slave boy in tow, he had no idea, but he hoped this young man would know something that would be useful in finding Lucy and her brothers.

CHAPTER 20

The thought of being lost kept plaguing her at every turn and passing foot of ground they covered. It hadn't been so bad when they first set out, full of hope and vigor at the prospect of freedom and adventure. There had also been the goal of reaching Uncle Joseph and seeking his help. Still, even with her trepidation she didn't want to say anything to Van who kept insisting they follow the map and "soon enough we'll find our way there." According to his calculations, they must be at least halfway to Shepherds Town or perhaps more than a hundred miles from home. One hundred miles from home! Lucy couldn't fathom where that actually placed them. She had never expected to leave the only place she had ever lived, let alone set out on a journey with just her two brothers as companions.

Thoughts of home crossed her mind at every turn, what Mother must be thinking, what Ester and Winn were doing. She even wondered if Reverend Godbey missed her in school and what lessons were being covered. At each stage of the sun's tilt across the sky, as they continued their journey, she ran over school lessons in her mind. Ciphering sums. Conjugating Latin verbs. Reciting the long list of English rulers from William the Conqueror to mad King George.

Willie, Willie, Harry, Stephen,
Harry, Dick, John, Harry three, then
One, two, three Neds, Richard two
Harrys four, five, six, then who?

It kept her pace even and steady, recounting each name to the marching tune her father had learned during the war, one that had been a jeering taunt by the British, but later the Continentals picked it up and embraced the term "Yankee Doodle." She found it worked quite well in remembering all the monarchs. Tommy especially loved the ending where she added a final verse of her own device, listing the two American Presidents.

...Charlie, Charlie, James again,
William and Mary, Anne the sad,
Georges one, two, three was mad,
Then we won independence.

Now we've had two presidents
Washington and Adams!
Who is next, we'll wait to see,
While we preserve our liberty!

When they'd tired of recitations, she was left to ponder what might be happening at home in their absence. At sunup she thought, *Ester is just stoking up the hearth fire for breakfast. She is humming to herself and putting the coffee on to brew.* At about ten o'clock she thought, *Winn is sweeping the kitchen and Mother is mending with her meticulously fine stitches.* It was Wednesday, the day for mending. *Reverend Godbey is listening to recitations and perhaps gazing at our empty seats on the benches.* Did the other children mull over their disappearance and invent stories of gruesome outcomes, much like they had about Ben that day they played fox and geese? Would their disappearance become the stuff of legends and songs?

Lucy shook such morbid thoughts away and concentrated on the journey ahead. The woods were thick with trees looming as far as the eye could see and nearly reaching the sky. They pressed along back roads and goat paths and avoiding the cleared areas where settlements cropped and where they might be found and returned home. She thought of the tales that were told to her of when Father first ventured into the backwoods of Virginia from Pennsylvania. Zack had often told them the stories of forging into the wilderness to stake a claim and build the cabin along with all those forts her father had overseen. That last day she remembered speaking to him of those times again, almost as if he knew that would be the last time and as if somehow this is where they would be in the days to come. She wished now she had paid more attention to what he had said.

Tommy grew heavier with every step Lucy took. "Don't hold so tight to my neck. You're choking me, Tom."

"I'm tired." Tommy laid his head against Lucy's shoulder. "I'm thirsty."

"I don't know why you're complaining of being tired." Lucy heaved his legs more securely around her waist and lifted herself to step over a large tree root. "I'm the one carrying you."

Van stopped and turned to look back at her. "Maybe I better carry him a while."

Lucy straightened to her full height, though her back ached. "No, I'm fine really." Her eyes rested momentarily on Van's sling.

"I can carry him better than you can, even with a busted wrist." Van lowered his flintlock and haversack to the forest floor.

Lucy let go of Tommy's legs and eased him to the ground. The sudden weightlessness gave her a moment of giddiness followed by sharp twinges of pain coursing down her spine and legs. She had not realized how much of a load she had been carrying.

Van smiled at her. "Bet that feels right good about now. You should have told me long before this he was getting too heavy for you."

Lucy didn't like it that Van had gotten the best of her and had made note of her inability to keep up. "I'd like to see how you are going to carry the flintlock and Tommy strapped across your back at the same time."

"Here then, you carry my haversack, and I'll carry the rifle in my good hand instead of across my back." Van looked up at the sunlight streaming through the trees. "Might be a good time to stop anyway and check the map to see how close we are to the next settlement."

"A town? Would that be safe?" Lucy looked hopefully at Van. A town would mean people who could maybe offer shelter and a comfortable place to sleep. They could have a proper meal, though the roasted squirrel the night before had been a welcome relief, if a bit meager to share among three starving youngsters. Lucy craved a fresh batch of cornbread, sugar-cured ham, or fish stew.

Would folks wonder why three young children were out wandering alone? She and Van had rehearsed what to say if such questions were asked in the event they crossed paths with folks from another settlement.

"Oh, you see, our poor mother died just a few days ago. Our pa he was killed by the Shawnee five years ago and our ma weren't never been the same since." Lucy thought back to the "rehearsal" she and Van had the first day they were out. It had passed the time and they had even had a bit of fun practicing their pathetic faces as lost waifs claiming to be on their way to find an aunt in Shepherds Town. Once they were close enough, they could ask around for anyone who knew Uncle Joseph, and how they hoped he would take them in. It wasn't much of a plan, but it was all they had.

Lucy contemplated all of this over the next few hours, up one trail and down another, through tangled, branched thickets until the woods opened up onto a main road.

"Where do you suppose this road leads?" Lucy squinted in the bright sunlight filtering through the trees. "Is it the one on the map?"

"I don't know," Van said. "But if it's the Cumberland Road as shown here, it will lead us to Shepherds Town within a day."

"Let's follow it and see." Lucy thrilled to the idea of being out of the woods for a change. Her legs were scraped from brambles and sticks snagging at her thick woolen stockings. "Surely it can't hurt to be seen now. We must be far enough away from Wellsburg."

Van let out a heavy sigh. "I suppose so."

"I'll beat both of y'all." Tommy let out a whoop and bounded toward the road with Van and Lucy following close on his heels calling after him. Tommy's short legs were no match for Lucy's smooth stride and Van's lanky form, even across the uneven surface of the forest floor. Soon Lucy overtook her little brother and together they tumbled out toward the road together, laughing and tripping over one another. Upon reaching the edge of the woods, they stopped short as Van came in close behind, nearly colliding with them.

They were not alone. Sitting on a log by the side of the road was a round, cherry-faced man in a patched gray coat and wide-brimmed felt hat smoking a tavern pipe, a book spread open in his lap.

"G'mornin' to ye, my fine friends." He tipped his hat to them. "Who have we here come out of the woodlands now? Three wayfarin' strangers? Pleasure 'tis to meet ye."

"Good day, sir." Lucy said. She first tried to drop into a curtsey until Van nudged her and cleared his throat. She had nearly forgotten she was not supposed to be a girl. Then watching Van, she mimicked his cordial bow.

"Ah, three fine gentleman, I see." The man took off his hat and rubbed his forehead. His receding hairline rimmed a moon-shaped face, accentuated by the severely tied queue at the nape of his thick neck.

"We're not all gentlemen." Tommy looked around back into the woods as if he expected to see some other travelers behind him. "We're just children on our way to see our Uncle Joseph on account of—"

Lucy cut him off with a nudge and answered for him. "What he means to say is we are on our way to our family in Shepherds Town."

"And are ye now." The man puffed on his pipe and narrowed his eyes and snapped shut the book he'd been reading. The smoke puffed like little clouds from the bowl extending from the narrow stem.

"Traveling alone? And where are your folks? Surely three young lads are not out to see the world on your own yet."

"No, sir," Van started, halted, and then started again. "I mean…yes, sir. Not really alone. We are orphans going to live with our aunt and uncle. They're expecting us in Shepherds Town."

"Three fine lads as yourself, and out to see the world with nary a mother or father to guide your way, is it?" He clucked his tongue, shaking his head. "More's the pity it is."

Van cleared his throat to add to the explanation but all that came forth was a croaky squeak. "Yes, that's the way of it."

Lucy broke in what she hoped would sound like a boy's voice. "We'd best be on our way, now."

The man raised his eyebrows as if considering this. "Well, it just so happens I'm on my way to Shepherds Town, don't ye know. 'Tis a preacher I am by trade and off traveling amongst the villages and settlements to spread the Gospel to all that are willing to listen. I'd be most honored to have three such fine lads along to accompany my way. 'Tis been a rather lonesome journey, that it has."

"You're a preacher?" Tommy cocked his head and stared at the sack sitting beside the rock on which the man sat. It was bulging with what appeared to be tinware and assorted tools. "Like our Reverend Godbey?"

The man let out a hearty chuckle and slapped his knee. "Well, m'good lad, I'm sorry to say I'm not acquainted with your good Reverend Godbey, though if he is as fine a preacher as I've been told I am you are most blessed to have had the benefit of his oration. So how about we all set a spell before we make our way to Shepherds Town together to find this aunt and uncle of yours?"

Lucy felt an uncomfortable lurch in her stomach. What if this preacher found out she was not a boy? Would he think it a sin? Or worse, alert the authorities that three runaways were found heading toward Shepherds Town? "I don't think that will be necessary. We can manage on our own."

Van looked at her as if she were being very rude. "I don't see the harm in it. At least for the time being. We don't want to be a burden, that is."

"Och! No burden at all." The preacher waved his hand dismissively and shouldered his bundle.

"Think nothing of it. I'll just be going my way and you'll be going yours. What of it if we just so happen to be going the same way. I've a mind to set up a camp meeting in nearby Martinsburg. Perhaps I'll take a gander at this Shepherds Town, ye say? I'm certain the good folk of the area would do well to be enlightened by the Word of the Lord and hear a fiery sermon the like they have never heard afore. Or so I've been told. I could use a lad or two...or three." He patted Tommy's capped head and motioned for them all to proceed down the road. "And, perhaps there'd be a bit of coin for ye to take to your auntie and uncle or to help ye along the way."

"You would pay us? To travel with you?"

"Aye," he called over his shoulder with a wink, "if you've a mind to follow the callin'. Could use a lad to help set up, get the word out, and pass the hat once the preachin' is done."

Van gave Lucy a wary look, then shrugged, and stepped in behind the tinker. "You are sure you know the way to Shepherds Town?"

The man turned and looked askance at Van. "Didn't I say I was heading there myself? Ye think I'd be going a place I'd not know the way to?" He arched his eyebrow in a mischievous way that made Tommy laugh but made Lucy's stomach lurch again as if she were once more feeling the sting of the iron to her arm from the hand of someone she trusted.

CHAPTER 21

Tommy skipped along the path beside their new companion. Aside from a sniffle and an occasional cough, he seemed back to his boyish ways again and rarely complained of a sore throat as he had earlier. A boundless bundle of energy, Lucy's little brother no longer asked to be held. Rather, with the preacher traveling along with them, Tommy seemed even more determined to keep up the pace on his own. For that, Lucy could be grateful, but she was worried that maintaining the ruse of being a boy might prove difficult.

For the time being, Robert Weedon, or simply Preacher as he preferred they call him, accepted their story and her role as the third brother in a trio of orphans on their way to seek help from relatives. After all she had grown up more in the company of the men and boys in her family than the women, hadn't she? Thus, it should be natural to assume such a role. Other than her mother, the slave women, and the few settlement girls that attended the Wellsburg School, she had almost exclusively spent her younger years trailing after one brother or another as they hunted, fished, and explored the surrounding woodlands. And then there were the occasional militia musters where she watched the men march and drill.

This made her think of Ben and the lies she had told him that last morning at the trading post. She gingerly patted the inside of her arm where the burn had continued to blister until the raw skin broke free leaving tender new skin beneath. Whenever they stopped for a rest she bathed the wound in cool water to relieve the sting. As the water droplets splashed across her reddened forearm, she recalled the tingle of Ben's touch against her skin that last morning. His concern seemed genuine when he asked her how it had happened, more than a mere polite, passing inquiry. A twinge of guilt continued to fester in her mind for having lied to him about the cause of the burn. It was wrong to tell a lie, and perhaps he could have helped them had she told Ben of their plans. Yet, he was an adult, a friend to many in the valley, and perhaps Van was right Ben could have alerted her mother or Mr. Newhouse and even supported them in the idea of sending her away with Mr. Shepherd. Hadn't she seen Ben talking with their stepfather and later to Mr. Shepherd at the graveyard? And then there was the talk she overheard between Ben and Mr. Gibson after the funeral luncheon. She still hoped to learn more of what Van knew, but now with the preacher along, that was not possible.

They continued on a steady course, the weather being favorable and warm, and soon they would be in Shepherds Town, where all would be handled by Uncle Joseph. Perhaps then Van would reveal more of what he seemed determined to keep secret until handing over all the "evidence" as he called it, to their uncle. The day was clear with a spring breeze wafting through the trees tingling Lucy's face and neck. Tommy danced a jig around Preacher Weedon who blew a tune on a pennywhistle produced from his breeches pocket.

"Will you teach me to play, too?" Tommy jumped and clapped his hands in time to the lively melody. His golden curls bobbed in the sunlight. He looked like a miniature scarecrow flailing about in the spring breeze, gaunt and loosely jointed in clothes that now seemed a bit too large for him.

As they walked up and down the winding paths, the preacher spoke of the many places he had traversed from Connecticut to the Carolinas and across the rivers winding westward.

"Oh, the folks of Connecticut liked my preaching well enough, they did," he offered unsolicited. "And a fine lot of believers we brought into the fold that day when I visited their church."

"A revival?" Tommy chimed in. "Is that what you said they call it?"

"Aye, laddie." He paused and looked heavenward. "And a righteous fine thing it is to be called into the Lord's service, spreadin' the Gospel message to all who would hear. Scatterin' the seeds is all I do. The rest is up to the Lord to see it falls on the good soil to grow into fine fruit yielding Christian folk like yourselves or, alas, among the rocks and thistles to be choked out."

"Rocks and thistles sure ain't good for seeds, are they?"

"Of course not, Tommy," Lucy caught up to them and grabbed her brother's hand. "Now stop asking so many questions."

"Oh, 'tis a fine thing to ask questions, Lukey." Weedon wagged a jovial finger at her. "That be your name, laddie?"

She blushed, feeling the heat rise high from her neck to her cheekbones, another festering lie and one told to a preacher, no less. Lucy still felt uneasy about having him along and now she knew why. It was as if he could see into her soul and knew every sinful thought. But revealing the truth at this point could fare worse for them. With a curt nod of affirmation, she added, "Yes, Lucas, but…Lukey…or… Luke to my friends."

"And I should hope to be considered among your friends, me lad."

"Will we be to the next settlement soon?" She turned away from his gaze and focused on the road before them.

Van continued to study the map with quick glances toward the direction of the waning sun. "As far as I can see the map says to go east. It looks more like we are headed north, in the opposite direction of Fort Hindley."

Weedon stopped dead in his tracks and looked askance at Van. "And what would you be needing a map for my fine young man, when ye have the world's most well-traveled preacher in yer midst?" He stood tall, one finger pointed toward the heavens. "He shall lead his flock like a shepherd, and I'm here to see ye safely to your aunt and uncle. But first, I'm heading to a small burgh, only a stone's throw from your destination, a place called Fort Bliss. You've heard tell of it?"

"No," Van said, still studying the map as he walked. "You say it's near Shepherds Town?"

"Aye, that it is," Weedon assured them. "A mere stretch of the leg up the creek, it is."

"I don't see it on the map," Van murmured.

"And you did say your father drafted that map some time ago?"

"Y-yes," Van admitted. "It is dated some ten years ago."

The preacher chuckled merrily. "A good deal of geography can change in a decade, me lad. Especially in the way folks are heading westward these days." He picked up his pace and gestured onward with his walking stick as if he were Moses leading the children of Israel across the Red Sea. "Have no fear little flock, and we'll be there in no time a'tall."

Van shifted a look at Lucy then folded the map and, with a final shrug, stuffed it back in his knapsack.

"Now that's more like it." The preacher's eyes shone with a satisfied gleam followed by a drooping of his head with a pained expression, as if he'd forgotten something. "Alas, lads, I have been remiss in not telling ye all I'm about as we've traveled together. And I do think I owe ye that. Aye, indeed I do."

"I know what it is, Mr. Weedon. You haven't finished your story!" Tommy skipped forward, not minding at all the new direction they were headed in.

"Indeed I have not, and 'tis that has troubled me soul long enough." He rubbed his chin as he led them forth along the winding road. "And it's there I'll begin with the camp meeting in New Jersey where I met the good Reverend George Whitefield when I was a wee lad not much more than yourself." He offered a kindly pat to Tommy's head, as if measuring his height against his own youthful stature. "It was there I first heard the calling."

"I thought it was Connecticut, where you were born and raised." Lucy stepped over a rough patch in the path and kicked away a couple of small stones.

"That is true, but I was a roving lad even then, from a roving family." He shot the comment back a bit sharper than Lucy expected. "There have been a fair number of camp meetings since that one. I'm quite the busy preacher these days tending to the lost lambs of his kingdom."

"Like us?" Tommy said.

"No," both Lucy and Van chorused together.

"We're not lost," Lucy added.

"I've still got the map." Van patted his pocket.

"And so ye have, m'lad." Weedon screwed his eyes as if he were looking straight through Van to find some hidden meaning to his words. "And it'll serve ye well someday. But back to me tale, I do have one small favor to ask of ye, and what I mean is that it be the Lord askin' of ye as well. Are ye ready to meet his call, young friends?"

Lucy and Van exchanged a baffled glance. "What do you mean, sir?"

"Before ye come a bounding out of the woods this morning, I had been settin' a-prayin' for some inspiration, if ye will, somethin' to keep me pressin' onward." He put a fist to his chest with a quick smote. "Oh, 'tis ashamed I am to tell ye, but the dark plague of discouragement fell over my soul, it did."

"What?" Tommy wrinkled his nose, trying to understand the preacher's words.

"He means he was sad, Tommy-kins," Lucy whispered.

"Aye, sad indeed! Preachin' is a hard and lonely life at times. And I was like Job, not wanting to heed the Lord's call to Nineveh."

"Wasn't that Jonah?" Lucy interjected, but then regretted correcting a preacher.

Taking it in stride he nodded. "And I was wondering who would be the first to catch me mistake. Quite well-versed in Scripture! 'Tis what I knew about ye, but had to test it to be certain."

"Certain of what?" Van asked as all three children hovered in closer. "What's our meeting this morning got to do with anything?"

Weedon shook his head and adjusted his cap. "I know it sounds like a great burden to ask of you, but remember, it's the Lord askin' and not meself. Still...I can't be expecting three young lads to take up the cross I've been carrying these long years. But would ye consider accompanying me to the next town for a camp meeting? The Lord will bless you on your way thereafter, forevermore. I am as certain of that as I am me own name."

Lucy looked at Van who stared back before darting a glance at Tommy who shot huge innocent eyes back in return. "Well...I really don't think...," Van began before Lucy interrupted.

"Shouldn't we be on our way to our aunt and uncle's farm?" Though even as she said it, she knew there was little use of resistance. Tommy's eyes lit with childlike faith and Van, too, seemed uncertain of going it farther on their own.

"Oh! I'll see to it ye get there personally," Weedon pressed on. "And indeed, I would be taking you all there this very minute, I would. But ye see, I've got me promises to keep and the Lord's bidding to do. And yet, how can I leave three wandering souls to fend for themselves? Not now that the good Lord has seen fit to bring our paths together. And I've been a wrestling with what He has in mind. That I have. Two tasks lay before me now and I see that perhaps, 'tis all for a divine purpose." Here he again glanced heavenward.

"You want us to help you in preaching at the camp meeting?" Van asked, skeptically. "What could we do?"

"I had the same thought meself, the day the Lord called me." Here he paused and lifted hands and face toward the open sky. "'Lord,' I asked, 'what am I but a weak sinful man, slow of speech and slow of tongue, just like Jonah was back in the days of old.'"

"Moses." This time it was Tommy who piped up with the correction. "Not Jonah. Moses said that at the burning bush."

"Ah! Ye've passed the test again," Weedon recovered his thoughts as easily as before. "And that is precisely why I'm needing such fine eloquent lads to accompany me. I could use your help with the singing, the passing of the hat, and teaching the Good Word. Many a soul will be saved and others well instructed with your fine example to lead them."

When they stalled a bit more, the reverend agreed the two older children should discuss it among themselves while he entertained Tommy with another tale. Together, Lucy and Van tossed around the idea of striking out on their own, leaving them open to who knows what other strangers they'd encounter, perhaps not as kindly as this preacher. Was it such a small matter to spend another night or two away from home? She had begun to lose count of the days already. There was no telling what kind of reception Uncle Joseph would give them or if he'd send them back home where they started—and where disaster loomed especially for Lucy.

In the end it was agreed to follow Reverend Weedon, especially when he dangled the prospect of earning a few coins from the collection. "A minister is worthy of his hire, or so the Good Book says.

We can't expect to muzzle the ox while it's stamping on the grain. 'Tis all in doing the Lord's work."

Van eyes gleamed at this, and Lucy knew they could use the extra money if they had to run away again, should Uncle Joseph not take up their cause.

Lucy hung back with Van as Tommy and the preacher strode ahead, the old man continuing his story much to the young boy's delight. Van looked at the map as he walked along, pausing to scan the horizon pensively.

"Van, do you suppose it's all right to be letting Mr. Weedon come along with us? All the way to Uncle Joseph's, I mean?" As she spoke she kept her eyes peeled down the path.

Van looked up ahead and shrugged. "He seems harmless enough. I'll keep a watch on him, though we have little he could want, other than our help in a little preaching and singing." He sidled in closer to Lucy and bent his head down to whisper in her ear. "But I'd move the bag of coins out of the haversack and to a place a bit safer."

"Where might that be?" Lucy ran her fingers on the haversack slung over her shoulder. The necklace bobbed easily against her leg, still sewn in the hem of her shirt, which was tucked into her breeches. At least that was safe. But where could she move the sack of coins? Most likely they were being too cautious. She again felt a twinge of guilt for not trusting a preacher, of all people, and one who had worked so hard sharing his faith among so many.

"You have the set of pockets that tie under your lady's gown. Wouldn't they do for tying 'round your waist under your breeches?"

"And just how am I supposed to get them tied on underneath my breeches?" she hissed back under her breath.

"Well, maybe you'll have to say you need to go off in the woods to make water. You're gonna have to go sometime, and you can't do that like a boy now can you?"

It wasn't right that he should talk about such things as lady's underthings. It made her blush to hear him describe such an intimate task, but she was dressed as a lad and there was no room for modesty on this journey. She said no more as they walked, lest it attract more attention from the preacher who had seemed to perk his ear in their direction at Van's last statement. But Mr. Weedon continued his story unabated and perhaps hadn't heard what they said.

The cool evening air settled in over the children as they made camp for the night. Mr. Weedon kept a happy prattle up all afternoon as they traveled along the path. "Now, ye do know that the best way to find the nearest settlement is to just let me lead the way. Ye'll have no use for a map that is nigh on far older than all of ye fine lads put together."

Van had sheepishly put his map into his knapsack since turning away from the creek and had not pulled it out again since. At least Mr. Weedon readily accepted that they were indeed all lads, or so she hoped. They had adapted her name from Lucy to Lucas along with the more familiar Lukey and Luke—easier to explain in the event Tommy made a slip, as he had done more than a few times already, though their companion and guide seemed not to notice or was polite enough to allow for the childish slip. She rather liked the sound of her new name and even found herself quite comfortable fitting in with her male companions. She hardly gave a care to what Mother might think should she ever find out about her deception. No matter, soon they would be in Shepherds Town and she would have time enough to change back into her shift and gown before meeting Uncle Joseph. Hopefully, Mr. Weedon would be on his own way by then. She did long to be herself again and was surprised that she missed the feel and swish of a fine silk gown trimmed in ribbons and lace.

"Now the bogeys, there's a terrible lot that allus brings the worst terrors in the dead of night." Mr. Weedon was delighting them with his tales again, especially Tommy who sat in rapt attention. "That's why ye should never go to sleep without sayin' your prayers."

"Ester always makes us say our prayers," Tommy said in the midst of a yawn.

"Ester?" Mr. Weedon arched his eyebrow. "That be your ma?"

"Nuh-uh. She's our slave that puts us to bed and cooks for us—"

"N-no," Van swallowed. "What he means is...we used to have a slave...but..."

"She ran off after our parents died," Lucy said, inventing a story as it came to her, "...of the fever...and we were left alone."

Weedon clicked his tongue in sympathy. "More's the pity, ye children have had a mighty cross to bear. I'll assist ye with your prayers if that be to your liking."

Tommy nodded eagerly and folded his hands as he did every night.

"Dear Lord..." Reverend Weedon began a litany of petitions asking for everything from the conversion of the unbelievers to stirring the faithful to more piety and a host of other things that included words Lucy had never heard before. She resolved to look up those she could catch and remember—words like "pestilence," "temperance," "schisms," and "tribulation." If only she had her copybook with her to write them down. Instead she let them play on her tongue, tasting them like wild honey stored in the combs of her mind, to be shared later with Tobe and Ester. Perhaps tomorrow she would ask the reverend what they meant while they traveled. Finally he resolved the prayers with a petition for a peaceful night's rest and Godspeed on their journey and one more she was familiar with. "And from ghoulies and ghosties and long-legged beasties and things that go bump in the night, dear Lord preserve us. Amen." They all joined in chorus on this last petition and readied for a peaceful sleep at last.

"We saw something go bump in the night already." Tommy looked back at Van who sat poking the fire with a stick. "Didn't we, Van. It was a real long-legged beastie. A panther, wasn't it?"

Van looked over at Lucy then back to his younger brother and shrugged.

Seeing little response from Van, Tommy continued with his own tale unhindered. "It was a panther. It almost ate me, but Lucy...I mean Lukey, he jumped up and punched him straight in the nose with his bare fist, and that ol' panther he took off a running."

Mr. Weedon arched his eyebrows and shot a curious look at Lucy. "Did ye now? Struck him clean in the nose with your bare fist, ye did?" A knowing smirk played at the corners of the preacher's mouth. Lucy knew he didn't believe little Tommy and even in the dim light of the campfire could see the amused appreciation in listening to Tommy's tale.

"Well, it wasn't really at all like that." Lucy drew Tommy close, hoping he'd bed down and have sleep overtake him soon. "I never actually struck him."

"But you did scare him away, or Van shot him." Tommy chewed on his lip and narrowed his eyes as if trying to recall exactly what happened. "It all seemed like a dream at first. Something big and black…like a bogey came to our camp the other night and tried to steal our food."

The preacher's bushy eyebrows arched and an appreciative smile dimpled his plump cheeks. "Ah, so ye've a tall tale of your own, my fine young lad. I'm wondering if I should be believing yours as well."

"Yes, it did happen." Tommy shot his head up again. "Didn't it Lucy? She threw something at it—a big rock, I think—but it scared that old bogey panther away for sure. Then Van fired a shot and it run clean off in the woods."

The preacher eyed the flintlock leaning against a tree. A rapacious gleam flickered in his eyes; he ran the tip of his tongue along his thin, lower lip. Tommy had slipped and said "she" and called her Lucy when referring to her deeds with the panther. Had the preacher noticed? He seemed more interested at the moment in the flintlock against the tree, and then his gaze traveled to the knapsack at Lucy's side. When he saw her watching him he smiled and quickly turned his attention to the penknife he held, and he scraped bits of dirt from under his fingernails.

"Ye shall not fear the terror of the night nor the arrow that flies by day," Weedon recited.

"Psalm 91," Lucy said. "I know that one. It's one of my favorites. 'Nor the pestilence that stalks in the darkness,'" she finished the following verse and finally felt safe enough to sleep. "G'night, Reverend."

"And right ye are, m'laddie, about the verse that is." Weedon leaned back against the tree and slumped down comfortably. "Go to sleep, my children. We've a good ways to go come morning. Good night."

Tommy yawned and rubbed his eyes. He squirmed over to Lucy and nuzzled against her. "Mr. Weedon will you tell us just one more story?" He looked up at Lucy, his eyes a deep cobalt in the flickering firelight. "Remember how Ester always told us stories at bedtime?"

Lucy put an arm around her little brother and looked at Van who situated his cloak on a pile of moss and leaves. The song of early spring frogs croaked a hypnotic cadence along with the preacher's haunting pennywhistle tune. He had put aside his penknife and as if by magic conjured the flute to lull them into blissful slumber.

CHAPTER 22

The dark *mist spreads through the woods enveloping her in its thick cloud. She is alone and struggling to find someone, but who? Where is she? A menacing presence looms above her, behind her, something dark and foreboding. Its wings rumble in a low thunder with each stroke. Where is Tommy? She tries to call, but her voice is choked with the suffocating darkness. She tries to run, but the fog thickens against her so her limbs are heavy as tree logs stuck to the forest floor.*

The screech of a panther echoes far into the distance, then splits through her, as if the creature were near enough to feel its foul cat's breath against her ear. A faint light emerges and she calls for Van who is moving up the hill carrying his flintlock and the knapsack that contains the necklace. She must get it back.

"No, don't go. Please Van, come back. Don't leave us." Lucy lunges toward him but for every step up the hill, Van only seems that much farther away as if everything moves backward from what it should be.

"I'm going to get us some meat, Lucy," Van calls back. "We'll have panther for dinner." Van holds the flintlock high over his head, and she hears the click of the lock close to her ear. Someone looms above her now with fingers fiddling with the buttons of her waistcoat and wanders down to her breeches. The face of the beast breathes over her, speaking a language only she can understand.

"Be of sober spirit, be on the alert." The preacher's voice breaks through, while the hum of singing reverberates around her. "Because your adversary the devil, as a roaring lion, walketh about, seeking whom he may devour."

"Amen!" The crowd echoes as women weep and hands are raised. She is standing in a wooded glen as the preacher delivers his message. Tommy dances around them, holding a tall hat for collecting whatever coins or bank bills the people have to give.

"And heed the words of this young lad." He turns to Lucy, now positioned upon a rock. "The gift of tongues, this one has. A rare and wondrous gift that only comes from the angels. And I, his humble servant, am given to interpret."

She opens her mouth and tries to speak. "W-what's that you're saying?" This voice is different—husky—and warbles from one single voice to sounding like a multitude.

"What words are those, laddie? Or are ye a lassie. Tell me true?"

She tries to explain, but the words are nothing he understands. "Keewagluskabewahkee." *The Great One, who is never far away, always at her beckoning, hovers above the preacher and carries him off into the darkness. The great winged beast soars into the thundering clouds, the preacher in its talons. He makes one last grasp at the buttons of her waistcoat, snapping one off as he accuses and screams into the darkness, "You're no more a laddie than me mam is."*

Morning haze filtered through the trees awaking Lucy's senses to the reality of another day in the glen where they had made camp after a strange and chaotic day. The hellish nightmare now faded into the soft glow easing across the hills. It had all been just a dream. The panther, the fog, and strange noises were all the shadows of tormented nightmares, a conglomeration of the happenings of recent days. Still it felt oddly real in ways no other dream had before, almost as if she could still feel the hot, moist breath of the panther against her ear and the fingers at the buttons of the waistcoat she wore. It had been a mere dream brought on by the panther who had drawn near their camp a few nights before and the preacher's frenetic revival meeting they had participated in, compounded by the weariness of the journey. That was all it was. They had followed Mr. Weedon to the settlement where they had helped him preach and sing, and Tommy had indeed passed around the hat. If there were any doubts about the preacher, she should have been assuaged by his willingness to divide the collection between them.

"A fine lot of ministers of the Word, ye were," he had said, handing them a handkerchief tied with coins amounting to sixty-seven cents. She had felt a thrill when leading the assembly in singing a favorite hymn, and Tommy had played the part well of a formerly crippled child, now able and dancing about.

"'Tis no lie," he had said to Lucy's objections of having her younger brother pose as a former cripple. "Why, didn't our good Lord tell a few tall tales himself, about a certain man beaten by thieves who found refuge in another's kindness? Do you really think that be a true enough fact? 'Tis no different now. I'm delivering a message of hope and a lesson for others to embrace."

It did seem a harmless fib for a greater good and in the end the four had left the town full of hope, and they basked in the adoration of the people there. Thankfully, no one recognized them or asked about three missing children, so perhaps wandering a bit astray with the good reverend hadn't been such a bad plan at that.

She twisted into a sitting position to assure herself that Tommy was still curled up beside her. He was indeed, but Van's spot on the other side of the smoldering coals of the fire was vacant. Something was not right. Where was Preacher Weedon? The spot where he had been sitting the night before still held his impression in the soft dirt, but there was no other sign of him. Lucy shot a look over to the tree where Van had set his flintlock. It, too, was gone. She stood and stretched, relieving the achy bones and muscles from another night on the hard, cold ground. Van and the preacher must have gone off hunting this morning or perhaps scouting a new route to Shepherds Town. Well, she had better be about getting things prepared for breakfast, though there was little left in the way of provisions. It was just as well that the men went hunting. Lucy laughed inwardly thinking of her gawky older brother as one of the "men," but at the very least it felt good to have an adult presence with them.

An alarming chill gripped her when she spied the empty place near one tree where she was sure they had left their two knapsacks. Now why would Van need to take both knapsacks along hunting and leave nothing for her and Tommy to eat? It was strange enough for him to take off without any notice. She ran fingers through her short, mussed hair and stepped into a sheltered area of the woods to attend necessary things. At least she would be able to relieve herself as a girl without fear of being found out. Still she kept a keen watch should the men return and find her squatting instead of standing as she had sometimes spied Van or Tommy doing. Odd that her waistcoat had a button missing and another was undone. She recalled the fitful dreams of the night before and chalked it all up to restless slumber. But then a chill went through her thinking of the preacher's voice and strange fingers grasping at her buttons as the Great Beast flew away with him.

She returned to the campsite and began tending the fire. The meager coals would not be enough to start another fire and the flint, striker, and char cloth were in the knapsack. She would have to wait until Van and the preacher returned. A rustling in the trees behind her caused her to turn as she refastened her breeches. Just then Van bolted out of the woods toward their campsite. A fretful look lined his face.

"Van, there you are. I've been wondering... Van, what's wrong?" Lucy's heart thumped in her chest as her brother lunged toward her and grabbed her arm.

"Where is he? Did you see him?" Van's eyes were filled with wild fury, as he looked frantically around the campsite.

"Who? Mr. Weedon?" Lucy hardly recognized her older brother. "I don't know...I..."

"Yes, that damned thief, he's gone. He's stolen our things. Everything is gone."

"What? No!" Lucy began to tremble and a cold fear clutched around her lungs, stifling her breath and turning the world into a fiery red haze.

"It's all gone. He's nowhere to be found. I've been searching since before daybreak. He's nothing but a thief, and I trusted him. How could I let this happen?" Van released Lucy's arm and rubbed the back of his neck as he paced around in a circle.

Only then did Lucy realize how painful the grip of his hand had been. She rubbed her sore arm where the burning fire iron had left its mark only days before. "Van, your rifle...the knapsacks...the ledger...the sack of coins." Trembling hands flew to her mouth and she felt a sudden urge to retch.

"He took everything." Van stopped his pacing and looked at her with a hopeless despair that mirrored her own fear of knowing their world, once tethered to solid shore, was now set adrift in futile misery.

"Not quite everything." Lucy felt for the shirt hem tucked beneath her breeches. "The Dutch Lady. We still got that." She felt for the necklace through her breeches to the shirt beneath. It wasn't there. The hem had been ripped clean away as if by a knife. "It's gone. The Dutch Lady. Grandmother's necklace. Oh, Van!"

"Then he did take everything," Van moaned.

Clouds like unwashed wool sullied the sky. The early spring warmth had been only a cruel tease of a season still too timid to repel winter's savage rage. Now a northerly chill, only a fleeting threat a few days earlier, came forth with full vigor as the sky released cold droplets onto the three children trudging up the woodland path.

Lucy forged ahead against the lagging weight at the end of her arm. "Come along now, Tommy. We must keep moving." She gripped his hand and tried to smile though chattering teeth. The rain stung against her frozen cheeks.

"I'm cold and I want to eat something." Tommy dragged his feet along the wooded path. "I'm hungry."

"I know, Tommy, but there's nothing to eat." Lucy heard the irritation in her voice. This had been the hundredth time she'd had to tell him this. She, too, was hungry after having only a little johnnycake and jerked pork the night before. Then this morning—nothing.

She shook away the disturbing dream she had had and the even worse reality she had awoken to. Mr. Weedon, the preacher who only yesterday had befriended them in the woods, had stolen away during the night and taken all their possessions. The knapsacks with remaining provisions, the compass, the rifle, and even the map Van dutifully followed to find their way to Uncle Joseph, all had vanished into the darkness of the night along with this mysterious man. All they had now were the clothes on their backs and each other. Lost and forsaken they were determined to find their way to the nearest settlement to gain shelter and perhaps learn how far off the track the devious preacher had let them wander.

Tommy's hand was like ice against Lucy's fingers. Rivulets trickled over his cap and down his red cheeks, glistening on his lashes and freckles. "Where are we going?" His eyes held a lost look of fear that Lucy hoped was not mirrored in her own. She squeezed his hand, but her fingers felt numb.

Van walked ahead up the path, still muttering and brooding, he had avoided speaking with Lucy all morning. She hesitated, debating the wisdom of yet again venturing to learn her older brother's intent now that all their plans had run afoul.

She swallowed as a low rumble emanated from deep under her ribs. "Van, couldn't we stop just for a bit? Tommy is so—"

"No, we can't." He stormed to a dead stop and turned on Lucy. "I've already told you, and I won't say it again. We won't get anywhere just sitting still pining away at what happened."

Lucy met his anger with a steady gaze. "Then we'll keep going, but you might have to carry Tommy again so we can cover more ground, or else we'll have no choice but to stop and rest. We've gone all day with nary a morsel."

Tommy huddled close to Lucy who put a protective arm around him. "I'm cold, Van. My head hurts. Can't we stop?"

Van's mouth twitched as if he considered what to say next. His eyes wandered between Lucy and Tommy and then looked up through the trees where the rain continued to pelt down on them. "It had to rain too," he said, "as if losing everything wasn't near enough."

"Why did Mr. Weedon have to take everything of ours?" Tommy said. "He's a bad 'un, ain't he? Just like our stepfather?"

The childish sentiment was just what Lucy had been thinking all morning, but to hear it put so bluntly only made her twinge with a sour feeling. "Hush now, Tommy. It isn't fitting to say such things about people no matter what they've done." Lucy thought about the lovely necklace that had been her grandmother's, so carefully kept since the day Zack died, now gone to be sold or squandered by the likes of Mr. Robert Weedon.

"Aye, Tommy, he's a bad 'un all right." Van's face softened a bit then hardened with determination. "That's why we gotta keep going and find our way to the next settlement or fort. Even a homesteader's cabin would be fine at this point."

"But what if they find out about us?" Lucy drew her cloak closer to her and shivered again against the cold, biting rain. "What will we tell them?"

Van shook his head and drew his forehead into a knot beneath the brim of his hat. "We'll just have to take that chance. 'Tis better, at least, to try and recover our rightful possessions." He looked away across into the piney forest. "Maybe someone will know something about that blasted preacher."

Lucy shook her head and tears stung against her eyes. "We won't ever get our things back, Van."

"You don't know that. There's always a chance. I'm not giving up yet." His eyes blazed with a lust for vengeance that sent a jolt through Lucy making the ground beneath her feet feel unsteady and misshapen.

Lucy remembered again that also hidden within Van's knapsack was the ledger he had so diligently copied by candlelight each night after Zack's death. The ledger was the only evidence that could help prove their stepfather's deceit in trying to confiscate their rightful inheritance. It might not have been enough, but without it, they had no proof at all.

"Van, why does everyone keep taking what is ours?" It was a pointless question, but one Lucy had to voice. She received no answer from Van but continued to ponder their plight as once again they trudged up a hill through another rain that finally began to slacken to a slow drizzle. A glint of sunlight caught the corner of Lucy's eye. She turned to see a small patch of blue sky peeping through the clouds. At least the rain was stopping. But there was still a long road ahead with no means to keep them safe or fed.

CHAPTER 23

Ben kicked his horse into a trot down the trace heading east along Buffalo Creek. There were only three now in the search party: Ben, Tobe the Swearingen slave boy, and Elzey Swearingen. They were well along the meandering creek that snaked its way to the Ohio River from its source in Western Pennsylvania, a place Ben remembered from the simpler times of his youth. At most every outpost and cabin, they had stopped to ask if anyone had seen the three children. But no one had. Four days now had passed since their disappearance. No sign of them was to be found in the vicinity of Wellsburg, and no one in the surrounding area had reported seeing them. One child disappearing into the woods, falling into a swift moving creek, or being taken in or captured by a band of peaceful Indians was likely and had happened on occasion before to settlers. How three children could slip away so easily and so unnoticed without a trace, was perplexing. But these three were determined to run away with a purpose and that was most disturbing of all. With the information the slave boy had given him, there was no point in detaining the entire patrol from their farms and homesteads any longer. Thus, he had no choice but to thank the men and send them home and immediately set on a course east for Shepherds Town, hopefully finding the children alive and well somewhere en route.

Ben shifted his seat in the saddle. Riding all day up and down the hills was a far cry from his usual duties at the trading post. He at first had his doubts the youngster riding beside him could keep pace, but he seemed well suited to riding and even perhaps, as he did, relished the chance to be out wandering free across the hills and creeks. Ben indeed felt the boy's delight at every new discovery and the adventure that lay before them, even amidst the concerns for their young friends.

Elzey had been companionably silent for the most part, but as they paused to water their horses late in the afternoon, he seemed bent on having his say. "Looks like we won't get too much farther now that we've come a ways into Pennsylvania. We'd best set up camp for the night or...I seem to recall a fine establishment up ahead at a settlement along Cross Creek. Or, we could maybe make it down to Waynesburgh about another hour south. There's a couple of young gals there I'll bet you'd like, Ben. Tomorrow, or the next day, we could head toward the main roads rather than following this crooked creek."

Ben studied the sky and gauged the line of the sun, making its descent westward. "There's still plenty of daylight, and I don't see any reason we can't keep searching at least another three or four hours. We've got no time for socializing. We'll make it as far as we can, bed down for the night, then be on our way first thing in the morning."

Elzey chuckled and pushed back his hat. "Folks sure are making good time in coming toward western lands. Won't be much longer and these hills will be dotted with all sorts of settlements on their way to becoming full-fledged towns."

Ben nodded and looked over the rolling valley that only a few years earlier he had crossed on his way west to Wellsburg, which made it all the more strange and frustrating that no one had spotted three runaway children who by now should be lost, frightened, and hungry, if they'd made it this far. Looking across the landscape he pondered the progress of tilled fields spreading where once there were dense forests. Mill ponds nestled in areas where creeks had coursed freely through woodlands into rivers and streams. When he last traveled this path it had been a different time in his life, a time he had hoped to put to rest, though it still haunted him, even now. Some things had not changed and only served to dredge up the memories of why he had escaped as far west as he had stamina and ambition for at the time. It had been at a spot on a creek just such as this, he'd vowed he would never return home again with all its shame and suffocating ignominy. No. Not after what he'd done and what his father had told him. Colonel Joseph Swearingen had been his only salvation then, and for that reason, among others, he had a debt to pay. It was best not to dwell on anything but that and keep to the task at hand.

Out of the corner of his eye he saw Tobe was riding on the horse the young Swearingen boy had raced against Ben only a week before. "You look right easy on that mount of Van's, Tobe."

"Yes, sir. He sure is a good horse. Noah, our stableman, he lets me help groom and tend him most times."

"Why do I get the feeling you do more than just tend him?" Ben eyed the boy with a wry grin. "Something tells me Mr. Van has been letting you ride him some as well."

Tobe looked a bit befuddled and shot a sheepish, unsettled flicker toward Elzey. "No, sir. Mr. Van he don't let me ride Keeper much at all. I guess I just learnt enough watching him ride. But Sergeant Stephenson, sir, you is the finest rider with the fastest horse in these parts." He paused and shifted in the saddle as he rode along. "That is, after the last race, if you don't mind my saying so, sir."

Ben let out a laugh and shook his head. "No, Private, I don't mind you saying so. Now you wouldn't be trying to change the subject on me would you?" The lad had taken seriously his role as a "soldier" on their expedition, and Ben willingly played along.

Tobe offered a look of feigned innocence. "Me, sir? I don't know what you mean, sir."

Ben leaned over to pat his horse's neck. "It was a crying shame that Van had to take a fall like he did." Ben thought about Lucy's words at the store that morning.

"I was wondering... well... I could use a new haversack. Well you see it's for Van. With his arm and all, we figured he could use it to carry things that he need...."

She wasn't telling the complete truth and he should not have let it pass so easily. Perhaps it was the lost, yet resolute, look in her determined eyes—the color of dew-drenched moss on the side of a hickory tree. He should have seen it for what it was, a lie by a child frightened as a hunted rabbit. But there was something else there too—a strength and perhaps even a steely-cold purpose that was far beyond one so young and sweet. Why hadn't he pressed her for more details or watched closely as she left so he could determine exactly where she was headed off to? His promise to the colonel ate at his conscience. If they did find their way to Big Springs, Joseph Swearingen's estate, and the children weren't there, it would mean explaining another tragic loss. This time two young nephews and the man's beloved niece.

"Been a long time since I've been back this way," Elzey mused as they rode. "Big Springs. Uncle Joseph's farm. I must've been about this boy's age." He gestured good-naturedly toward Tobe.

"He's got quite the large spread, as I understand," Ben added abstractedly.

"That he does!" Elzey smiled, shaking his head. "You hail from around Martinsburg and know my uncle, you ever been to his place?"

"Once." Ben patted his horse's nose. "The horses have rested long enough now. Best be moving along."

"Oh, yes," Elzey replied, but not quite responding to Ben. "We Swearingens are land rich and will be a hundred years from now."

Ben murmured his agreement, still considering the next course to take and keeping his eyes peeled for any sign of the children as they remounted and moved on their way.

Elzey let out the rein on his horse and leaned forward toward Ben. "It's a crying shame that little brother of mine had to entice the two young 'uns into going along on this madcap escapade." He looked over at Tobe. "And, boy, you did nothing to stop them? You knew all along and just kept tight-lipped? What were you doing bringing them supplies? I could have you—"

"Easy there, Elzey." Ben reacted with full attention now. "He's just a young 'un put in a bad situation and felt honor-bound to keep a promise to a friend, and, from what I hear, they had good reason to be fearful and run away."

"Friend?" Elzey snorted. "He's nothing but a slave. I still don't see why you asked him along."

Ben turned a wry smile toward his companion. "You're just now bringing that up? Maybe you ought to lay off the whiskey flask I keep seeing you nip when you think no one is looking." He meant it in an easy, light-mannered way, but the look on Elzey's face spoke otherwise.

"What I do and the reasons I came along are nothing to you, Stephenson." He leaned from his saddle in a threatening posture. "You mind what I say?"

"We're in this together to find your brothers and sister, Elzey," Ben stated carefully, still wondering if this was some sort of ruse or if the man had lost his wits. From the corner of his eye, he saw the young slave ease up his horse to keep a subservient, and perhaps safer, distance behind them. The boy appeared to be lost in his own thoughts, but a look in his eyes also spoke of his wariness and cunning in surmising the situation, perhaps better than Ben had all along.

"I'm beginning to think we're on a fool's errand here is all I'm saying, Ben." He rode around the other side to where Tobe hung back behind. "You think you've got us bamboozled, boy? Think you'll see your young master again, who you seem to think is your friend? Or are you leading us into some sort of trap too?"

"I...don't...I...didn't...," Tobe stammered, wide-eyed. "No, sir. I hope we find Mr. Van, Mr. Tommy, and Miss Lucy.""Leave him be, Elzey." Ben veered his horse closer, still trying to maintain his composure. "He's under my orders now."

"Your orders! Seems to me he's Swearingen property by rights and mine to order about."

"It never seemed to be an issue before." Ben tried to make sense of this outburst. "And currently he's under my charge, since I contracted his services from—"

"John Newhouse? Or you mean my stepmother, Nelly?"

"If you've got a problem with any of this, you could've said so before we left."

"I've been biding my time just long enough to see if we could've found some evidence of my kin. I've got the family honor to uphold, after all." Reaching out to grab Tobe's horse, he added, "But seeing as how we've been coming up short and this here young whelp's not helping us any, I'm aiming to take him back home.

"That fever mad brother of mine," Elzey said, sardonically, "it wasn't right for Zack to alarm the kids the way he did no matter how sick he was." He jerked the reins, preventing his horse from taking a nibble of sweet, early spring grass."

"Let's not get into this now, Elzey. Your brother had his reasons. You well know that."

"That lawsuit again. Shepherd's land claim. I told my brother long ago to settle matters with Shepherd. There's enough land to go around, maybe even more now."

"More?" Ben jerked his head around, a strange chill working its way through him. "What's that supposed to mean?"

"You think Shepherd has no claim?" Elzey followed with a cruel, menacing laugh. "You don't know the half of it."

"We'll leave that to the courts to decide." Ben did not want to get into this now, but if Elzey pressed it further, he would have to. "Your pa had his reasons and you know good and well..."

"I know what I know," Elzey spat back. "What do you know of my pa's interests or intentions? You only got in on the tail end of the Injun Wars along the river and saw him as the grand hero. When he first come to the valley, how do you think he went from a few acres of government bounty land to amassing pert-near half the county and then some? Shepherd's got his reasons. I'm not saying I'd agree with his methods, but there may be ways to settle all this without dragging it through the courts."

Ben drew in a breath and glanced at Tobe, who appeared to be trying his hardest to ignore the conversation of two white men.

"Yeah, that's about what I thought," Elzey continued with a smug smile as he bit off a nip of chew from his pouch. "You think you're one of us, but you're not. My pa never had his hands completely clean of those land deals."

"I made a promise and I aim to keep it." Ben turned his attention ahead, hoping that would be the end of the matter for now. "We've got your brothers and sister to find so let's keep our aim steady and sure."

"Promise is it?" Elzey laughed ruefully. "Sure, that's the way of it. That'll do for now. I know how my family can be about honoring promises. But you owe us nothing, Ben. Just bear that in mind. I'll just drink a toast to family honor and to the success of our journey."

As he spoke he pulled the flask from his pocket and took a swig.

Ben chose to ignore his last taunt as he had the many others the man had tossed about over the last hour or so. He clicked Bronzer into a trot and pressed ahead of the other two riders. Something among the trees just off the trail ahead caught his eye—an odd shape and a splash of color that didn't quite belong there.

"Where you going in such an all-fire hurry?" Elzey called after him. "Was it something I said?" He chuckled at his own joke.

"I thought I saw something," Ben yelled. "Tobe! Stay back. I'll call for you if I need you."

"What? I don't see nothing." Elzey lagged behind, grumbling under his breath between swigs.

A few yards from the edge of the clearing, Ben dismounted and strode through a patch of scattered trees, his breath seized with the heavy thumping of his chest. He held his gun easily at his side but was ready to aim if needed as he scanned the surrounding woodlands. The thing he saw when he was a few feet back looked barely human and seemed more a part of the tree. Seeing it now, it was unmistakably the mutilated remains of a man propped against a tree, almost serenely, with his hat scrunched down over his brow as if he was just taking a snooze on a warm spring afternoon. But the pool of blood coating the grass and dripping from his hands and clothes meant this poor soul had met with a bad end.

"You reckon it was the Injuns got him?" Tobe's wavering voice reminded Ben of his tender age.

"I thought I told you to stay back, boy," he warned, holding up a cautionary hand. "This isn't a sight for your young eyes."

"I've seen more'n a few things most young 'uns ain't supposed to." He straightened to his full height and stepped closer to stand beside Ben.

"I did warn you." Ben knelt down to remove the man's hat and examine him closer. "I don't know that you're prepared for this. Not sure I am either."

It wasn't as if he hadn't seen a scalped man before. The years spent fighting Indians with Sam Brady's brigade and old Indian Van Swearingen had offered plenty of such grisly sights along the Ohio.

This corpse, like so many others, stared wild-eyed, bearing a blood-soaked skull where the hair had been savagely ripped away. Only a bare fringe of the man's queue remained held at the back of his neck by a frayed black ribbon. Beside the body an open Bible lay just within reach of bloodied fingers. Three were missing, cut off at the second knuckles. The pages flapped in the breeze, as if frantic to relay the tale of the man's fate or mournfully keen this forsaken soul.

He turned to see the frightened, brown face of the slave gawking at the dead man. Tobe's mouth formed a perfect "O," but he remained stalwart taking in the grim sight.

"Who you suppose that be, sir?"

By now Elzey approached the scene with equal surprise. "Damn! Shawnee at it again? I figured it wouldn't be long. There's been talk of a certain chief getting things riled up." He glanced furtively around the surrounding woodlands as if half expecting a tribe to come charging out any moment. "Poor devil."

"I don't know about the devil part. Looks to be some sort of itinerant preacher," Ben muttered, lifting one cold, blood-soaked hand. "Powder burns. Maybe he tried to fight back, but it's hard to tell who might've started things or if this was possibly a random murder made to look like an Indian attack." He muttered to himself, logging the evidence as a way to keep his own fears at bay. What would this mean if Van, Tommy, and Lucy met up with a similar roaming band? Or a pack of cut-throat thieves?

"Looks to be an Indian attack pure and simple. Probably Shawnee. Looks like they've broken the treaties and we could be headed for another war."

"If it truly is an Indian attack and not just staged as one." Ben knelt beside the man to inspect his pockets hoping to learn his identity. "However, let's not jump to any conclusions just yet. No one we've talked to so far has seen any sign of trouble, unless the tribes were provoked first. It could be this was a murder or he attacked first."

"They're Injuns, ain't they? They killed one brother of mine, tried to kill my sister, and now likely have captured her and the other two as well." Elzey leveled his weapon. "Best be ready, just in case."

"I think if the culprits were still about, we'd know by now or likely not still be here to talk about it." A trail of blood coated the grass, winding its way into the wilderness underbrush. "It appears someone else was injured and either carried or drug away. Might have been one of their own shot by this one here before they got to him, or he provoked them."

"Could be they took hostage this poor devil's family or companions. You say he's a preacher? What preacher would attack a peaceful band of Injuns?" Elzey pulled the rag from the lock and aimed his gun into the surrounding woods. "He's a man of the cloth. Dirty heathens massacred him and took off with his family more than likely."

Ben stood and followed the trail a few feet. "First things first. We alert the next town over and see if anyone knows who this man is or if he has any next of kin in the area. Maybe they'll also have word on the kids. It's worth a try at least."

Mulling over the evidence, Ben steadied his nerves, considering his next move. A band of thieves posing as Indians didn't make matters any better, especially if it incited the local settlements and got things stirred up again.

"Maybe it'd be best if we set for home instead," Elzey said. "Nothing more we can do here, and we need to warn the others in Wellsburg of what could be coming next."

"Not until we find the young 'uns." Ben gently laid the man's hat over his face. "We'll need to notify the folks at the fort we just came from and let them tend to the man's burial. They'll alert the magistrate who'll see to things from there."

"Aye, that's what we'll do." Elzey wormed the rag back into the gunlock and headed toward his horse. "We'll alert the authorities and warn the good people at the last settlement and then we'll head home."

"Not so fast, Elzey." Ben stood watching Elzey's reaction, as if he were glad to find this poor massacred man and wanted any excuse to avoid finding his kin. "We've got a mission to complete—your brothers and sister to find and fetch home."

"It's all as it should be, as it should have been years ago."

"What's that supposed to mean?"

"Don't you see?" He held out his hands as if that settled the matter.

"It's some sort of sign, a warning to stay away. Maybe the Shawnee have been watching us all along. Maybe they got Van and Tommy and Lucy and they meant us to find this as a message to turn back now."

Ben scratched his head and looked incredulously at his companion. "And just how would they know we'd be passing this way and then just happen to kill this poor preacher for our benefit?" He shook his head. "That makes no sense."

"Maybe not," Elzey tightened the girth on his horse's saddle, "but I'm not sticking around here to find out. We'll get this man a proper burial and alert anyone who may know his kin. Perhaps someone will find the culprits who done this."

"And we're still heading east to the colonel's place and hopefully we'll find your brothers and sister there."

"Sir?" Tobe called from somewhere in the distance, as Ben dealt with Elzey's change of heart.

Elzey grinned. "Ben, you are being 'Benish' as usual, a chub. I know you got your own interests in our land, but it's over. Let her go."

"What are you saying? This has nothing to do with my interests in anyone's land."

"Oh, don't it now?" Elzey said as he lazily played with the horse's reins.

"You know good and well, she's gone. I've been feeling it since we left Cross Creek. You've lost your right to everything, but it doesn't matter. We've still got a chance with the shipyards. It's better this way."

"How is this better? We can't just leave them and not try. What will you tell Eleanor? Your uncle? And the rest of your family?"

Elzey faced Ben with a knowing smile. "Leave it be. They should've kept her then and maybe they've got her now."

Ben struggled to maintain his control with measured breaths. Somewhere in the distance, he heard Tobe but did not heed his call. "I don't know what you are talking on about. They could be nearly to the colonel's by now. Your uncle would surely take them in. We'll head there soon as we rule out interference from any local camps."

"Was it your idea to send them there?" Elzey tossed the question with a curl of his lip and then turned on the slave like a menacing wolf. "Or was it the boy's? Curious how you cozied up to the boy, Ben, and insisted he come along."

"You're as mad as the rest of them."

"But not as mad as she was…or is."

"I don't believe that."

Elzey paced back toward his horse calling over his shoulder. "Believe what you want. She was there that night. You saw what they did, what she saw, what she said. Like something possessed, she was. Where'd she learn to speak like that? What sort of demon from hell was she calling?"

"She was just a child," Ben called back. "A babe in arms. You can't really have expected to leave her there."

"I told you then, it was for the best, but you and that soft-hearted brother of mine wouldn't listen." He shouldered his long gun and scanned the woods to the other side of the road. "Pa's little wonder. Always teaching her things. Then Zechariah and you took it up, too."

Out of the corner of his eye Ben saw Tobe cross the clearing to a spot at the edge of the woods. Would the lad try to run? He couldn't blame the boy for wanting to be rid of all this, but first he needed to tend whatever it was Elzey had up his craw. "Elzey, we'll settle this all later. Let's get back to matters at hand."

"She's tainted now." He turned like a flash, the gun spun and ready to aim. "Blue Jacket cursed us all and it's never going to stop until he has every Swearingen heir, one way or another. Maybe getting the three young 'uns will be enough to appease him once and for all. A sacrifice to their heathen gods, mayhap."

"This is nonsense." Ben stepped closer pacing off each step with each word.

"And another thing, Pa shouldn't have married that Nelly. Shouldn't have rutted out three more brats to divide the property and shoulda just been happy with his other whores. It's enough he had two bastards and included them in his will." Motioning toward Tobe he added, "And that one. Even coddled his darky bastards, too."

"You're drunk, or mad. I don't give a bugger which, but you'll see this through if it's the last thing you ever do."

"Is that what you did to Zechariah? Did you shoot him, too?"

The words sent a ringing into Ben's ears that echoed through his heart. "You don't know what you're saying."

"Don't I?" Elzey snarled in a low voice. "Been hanging around Phoebe, ain't ya? It's fine by me. That lawsuit my brother and you started, it might work in our favor. I know the way of it. She told me everything."

"What did she tell you?" Ben hoped his bluff would work. Something told him Phoebe would not tell Elzey of all people. She had as much to lose as anyone, maybe more. Surely she wasn't that desperate to get with child. Elzey hadn't said anything that wasn't part of the rumor mill of the town. "Go on. Tell me just what you think you know. More rumors? I could quote a few myself. Nothing I haven't heard at the trading post. So you just tell me what you know."

Elzey's silence and shifting feet told Ben what he needed to know. "That's what I thought. You coming with us or heading back on your own? Your choice. But I'm heading to their camp."

"You're a damn fool then," Elzey said. "Should have left that little sister of mine with them when we had the chance seven years ago."

"You don't really mean that." Ben lowered his voice, trying to keep calm. "You can't mean what you're saying. She's a little girl, innocent."

Elzey rambled on as if not hearing him. "Not a day goes by I don't think of it. She's not one of us now. Never has been. That's the way of it."

"She doesn't remember."

"Oh, but he does," Elzey signaled with a nod toward the thick forest. "It's their way. He could even be one of us, who knows? Pa thought so, hoped it was his cousin, Marmeduke gone savage. Some whisper he is, and he wants revenge for what his own folk done to his savage kin. Maybe it's him speaking through her now."

"That's utter nonsense."

"Is it? Can you explain how she knew those words?" He paced into the meadow toward Tobe. "None of us can. I'm taking my slave home now, and you can do whatever you want. Go see Uncle Joseph. Tell him you killed his one nephew and lost two others along with his precious niece."

"I'll tell him his other nephew is stark-raving mad, too. Shall I do that?"

"Go to hell for all I care." Elzey kept an even stride toward Tobe, who stood stock-still. "C'mon, boy, we're heading back now."

"Your pa was wrong. We know that now, but it was worth a try." Ben did not want to get into this now, but the effects of the drink were taking their toll. Elzey didn't really mean what he said. Or, was this his true nature beneath the surface? He should have stopped him and taken the flask when he had the chance. "All that matters is getting them back. We saved your sister then and we will again. Are you coming or not?"

A pained look in Elzey's eye offered the possibility Ben had broken through whatever drunken state possessed him.

"Sir, they's something over here you really need to see." Tobe held something in his trembling hands.

Slowly Ben turned away from Elzey and headed toward the spot where Tobe stood stunned, looking around uneasily from tree to tree.

Elzey followed behind Ben. "There's no use staying here. I'll fetch you home to your ma where you'll be safe. Get your horse and we'll be off."

"Sergeant Stephenson?" Tobe gave him a helpless, pleading look.

"Boy, I told you to get. That's an order." Elzey took a menacing step toward the lad and grabbed him by the elbow. "Get back to your horse now, I say."

"Leave him be, Elzey." Ben continued toward Tobe, realization mingled with disbelief as he saw what the boy held in his hands. "If you aim to leave, then go. I'll tend to the lad and see him home."

"He's Swearingen property not yours, Stephenson. Worth more than you make in a year shop-keeping." Elzey released Tobe's arm and swung at Ben. Catching him off-guard, he landed a blow beneath Ben's cheekbone.

Eyes watering, Ben regained his footing only to find the end of a barrel pointed square at him. "I'm taking the negro back. You coming along? Or you gonna join that feller as buzzard feed?"

Ben relaxed as he held a hand to his throbbing face. A conciliatory smile and a nod might be his only chance. "Aye, Elzey. If that's what it means to you." From behind his opponent, Ben saw Tobe walking toward them holding a book-shaped object in his hands.

"Please, sir?" His eyes were bright with alarm—or was that the glimmer of a tear he saw? "I think you better come see this. This here say it Swearingen pro... pro-per-ty," the boy sounded out the word as his finger grazed across the item in his hand.

The distraction gave Ben just the moment he needed. Elzey lowered the gun barrel a bit and turned to Tobe. "What you say, boy?"

In one swift move Ben kicked away the gun causing it to discharge into the air before landing still in the grass. He wasted no time in returning the earlier favor to Elzey with a punch that landed the sodden man flat on his back. Ben quickly pinned Swearingen with the quick point of the knife he'd drawn from his belt.

"Now, Elzey, do we understand each other?" Ben seethed through clenched teeth. "Are you going with us or not? I don't want to hurt you, but I'll not see your brothers and sister come to harm either. Not if I can help it. Understood?"

"Aye," the quivering man spoke barely above a whisper as Ben held the knife close to his gullet. "Do what you want. Keep the nigger and the girl. Get all yourselves killed. What do I care? The land goes to next of kin—the eldest—and that will be me and no one can stop that. Not Shepherd and not Newhouse. The courts will see to that."

"Fine." Ben let the knife up a fraction. "Then you best be on your way, and the boy and I will go our own."

"Oh, but didn't you know Shepherd's plan?" Elzey gloated as he slowly rose to his feet, Ben's knife still at his throat. "If you bring them back, Lucy goes with him. So what's the use, then? Shepherd gets the land and gets my half sister, and we've lost the prime tract to build a shipyard on. You'll lose your stake in it, too. Would you rather see that bastard get her? Or Blue Jacket scalp her and butcher her like he did the others that night? Or maybe they'll keep her and turn her into one of their Indian whores to breed more savages. Think on it. Savage half-breeds with her fine honey-colored hair and pretty green eyes. Wonder if they'll get her quick-witted, addled mind as well."

Ben took all this in as the man continued to rave unabated. "And what makes you think Shepherd'll even keep her? She'd fetch a fine purse for any Indian tribe or French trader willing to take on a prime article like her."

"You're drunk and raving mad. What are you even saying?" Ben kept an eye on Tobe's find but needed to sort out this man's meaning and intent too.

"I'm saying I know the reason you drove us into the camp that night." He took a deep breath as a incensed grin crossed his face. "You had your own interests in my baby half sister, didn't ya?"

"For a piece of goddamned land?" Ben returned the pressure on the knife. "She's your sister. We went to save them all. Zechariah and your father knew what we were in for. So did you."

"I'm saying we could have it for ourselves," Elzey shrugged. "No girl for Shepherd to marry, the land comes to me. You'd help me see to that with your legal double-talk. It solves everything. It's still a long shot we'll even find any of them at this point. You gotta know that. You'll be in and won't have to wait till she's grown. You could even have Phoebe now, if that's your fancy. A fine-looking woman, a homestead, and a profitable shipping business. It'll all be yours"

"Is that what Shepherd and Newhouse had planned?" Ben's blood boiled, recalling Lucy's arm and Shepherd's admission he was there when it happened.

Elzey laughed. "Aye, it changes things don't it?"

"Sirs," Tobe called, "please, this might be important."

The slave stood above them, holding a leather-bound ledger marked with gold letters across the cover—Property of Swearingens Landing. In his other hand he held a crumpled haversack spattered in dried blood. Ben took it after letting up slightly on his prisoner. The bottom corner of the sack bore the stamped emblem, Gibson's Trading Post, Wellsburg, Virginia. Inside was a map that bore the name Captain A. Van Swearingen—1782. With a trembling hand, Tobe held out a bloodied hank of braided hair. "And I found this here lying out in the grass."

Elzey blew out a low curse. "Now how would you say that old preacher got my pa's map and our family ledger?"

When Ben didn't respond, didn't trust his voice to speak, Elzey pressed further. "Looks like Blue Jacket's got her for sure, now, Ben.

Done scalped her and who knows what else they done to her. Still wanting to go chase them down? Or you ready to return home and call it a day while we still got our scalps?"

Ben held the braid tightly as he gazed absently at the trail of bloody leaves in the distance. "You can leave, Swearingen. Might be best if you did. I'm going to keep searching and head toward your uncle's place."

"I'm coming too, sir." Tobe stood tall and saluted as Elzey lumbered off toward his horse.

Returning the salute, Ben replied, "Remount, soldier, we've a fair piece to go and three friends to bring home. Let's get moving. There's still another three hours at least till sunset." He turned to see Elzey swing into his saddle and head in the opposite directionn.

CHAPTER 24

Lucy wasn't sure exactly what she saw first—whether the trees took on the shape of the Indian standing there unnoticed all along or if he had crept silently from the depths of the forest for some cruel and deadly purpose. She had been apart from her brothers who were downstream fishing while she searched the woods for roots and tubers nestled under the forest floor. She was so hungry even the new spring soil began to look appetizing as she scraped up patches of early moss and lichen from rocks and tree bark in the shadowy, wet woods. It wasn't much but would have to do as an accompanying dish to their main course of fish should Van net his catch, or it would be the only thing to sustain them along their journey. A patch of winterberries caught her eye, and she stooped to reach for the irresistible red gems.

It was just then when she stood up with the meager handful of lichen and berries that the Indian boy appeared ahead of her. When he didn't move, she let out a sharp gasp, time hanging in the balance like a fish caught on a line between air and water, damnation and salvation. 'Twas merely another dark vision like those that plagued her dreams. But never had they seemed this real, as if she could reach out and touch the soft linsey-woolsey shirt or wide beaver hat trimmed in bright beads and eagle feathers. The same breeze that traced the lines of her face even rippled the strands of his reddish-brown hair escaping the long plaits dangling behind his pierced ears.

"Are you real?" she whispered, blinking back fears of capture or worse, if this was flesh and blood, against the more terrifying thoughts of madness. "Or...are you a mirage?" That's what the French traders called them, those figments induced by a mind fraught with hunger or thirst or simply lost to madness or witchery.

"Stand down!" Van's firm, frantic voice broke the moment's indecision into cold reality as he sloshed through the stream and straddled the rocks, creating a barrier between her and the threat of danger. He stood, armed with a birch stick. "Lucy, back away. Take Tommy and run, fast as you can. Just keep running no matter what."

"Van, I don't think he means any harm." Lucy clutched Tommy to her side. He had been right on Van's heels with a smaller stick of his own, a meager, pitiful defense against the sharp tomahawk the Indian shot from the belt of his buckskin breeches to the firm, sure grip of his right hand.

"Go away, you bad Injun," yelled Tommy.

"No! Please!" Lucy pushed her little brother down behind her and ducked under Van's stick that was ready to strike. "Stop! Please. Tommy, shush. We don't know he's bad just yet."

"And I don't aim to give him that chance for us to find out one way or t'other." Van gripped the stick higher. "I'm warning you, we'll fight and won't go down easy."

"Van, put the stick down. He may not even speak English."

Lucy thought this must be real if Van could see it, too. In spite of the dire stakes, knowing that brought her some relief, even with this new threat. That was her next concern as time seemed to move forward between a snail's pace and the swiftness of a rifle shot.

"I'm warning you," Van hissed breathlessly again, "we want no trouble with you. Let us pass."

"Van," Lucy said, "please, I don't think he means us any harm or something tells me we'd all be dead by now."

The Indian boy lowered his weapon a bare inch, but with the easy smile of idle curiosity. "Mirage?" he said, startling them all.

"You...you speak French?" Why she asked such an obvious question sent a giggle rippling up from her beating heart. Could he have understood her before?

He darted a wary look between them. *"Vous voyez un mirage?"*

"Er...parlez-vous français? Parlez-vous anglais?" She moved one cautious inch closer with an outstretched hand.

"Have a care, Lucy." Van stepped beside her, stick still in hand. "What did you just say?"

"It's the first words our schoolmaster had us recite in French," she said. "I think he speaks French. He knows the word I said earlier, "mirage." Maybe he knows a little English, too." She repeated the question in French again. Whatever she said seemed to please the young warrior whose smile broadened with an assuring nod of his head.

"Ah! *Oui,*" he said, followed by a stream of words too fast for Lucy to clearly comprehend. But why should she? She had only learned some catch phrases in French from the few lessons at school and from hearing it spoken among the militiamen and traders.

"W-hat's he saying? What're you saying to him?" Van gave a perplexed look to Lucy and the brave. "Jumpin' Jerusalem! What kind of hell-hatched things did you just say to him?"

"Van! Mind your words, brother!"

Slowly Van lowered the stick and took a step back. "As if anyone out here is gonna hear us? Or that anything matters now? Is that Frenchie you're speaking?"

"Oui, mon frère." Curious, she had meant to respond in English to Van, but instead it came out French.

A light of curious caution lit the boy's face. *"Ah! Oui! Très bien! Je parle français. Vous aussi?"*

The question was accented by a gesture toward each of them and a beckoning hand.

"He...wants us to follow him?" Van uttered, aghast. "Did you understand all that?"

"I think so," Lucy mouthed barely above a whisper. "He asked if you know French too, and he wants us to follow him."

"It's liable to be a trick. There's probably more of his tribe out there. By the look of him he must be Shawnee. But he also looks...not quite like an Indian. Maybe a half-breed or a captive?"

"A good many tribes know French," Lucy shrugged. "'Tis not so peculiar. His tribe has probably traded with the Canadian fur trappers, up toward the English Lakes. Or he's been taken into some tribe. Maybe we should follow him."

"Ah!" The Indian boy beckoned again with a firm nod. *"Anglais. Mon père parle anglais. Venez!"*

"The English Lakes? Aren't they far, far away? Are we so lost now?" Whimpering, Tommy squeezed Lucy's hand all the more tightly.

"No, no, Tommy-kins. That would take many more days than we have traveled."

"Toh-mee-kuns? *Non, non?"* The boy cocked his head at their little brother, sidestepping Van to get closer to him.

"You just stand back." Van threatened with his stick, causing the boy to wield his tomahawk at shoulder level, aiming for Van's head.

"Non! Non! S'il vous plaît, arrêtez! Stop!" Lucy lunged between them as she had done once before between brother and cousin in their bedchamber only a few weeks before. Why were boys so much trouble? The tomahawk cut into the air where Van's head had been. It likely would have cracked his skull had he not ducked just in time. With his one good arm he aimed a decisive blow of the stick across the Indian's shins, driving him to his knees. Lucy had been thrown free in her attempt to intervene as the two boys wrestled. She now sat plopped in an inch of water at the creek's edge.

"Van! Stop! Let's at least find out who he is and what he wants. Maybe...he can help us."

Surprisingly, her brother had gained the upper hand, even with the agility and strength of this native and despite Van's disability. It was almost as if the Indian boy wasn't trying his hardest and thought it more a game than a fight to the death. The discarded tomahawk and stick lay a few feet clear of the two boys who punched and kicked their way to gain an advantage. A trickle of blood oozed from the corner of Van's mouth after the Indian scored another blow that flattened him to the ground. Her brother lay helpless as a rag doll, his bad arm twisted under him as his adept opponent straddled him and then pinned him to the rocky edge of the creek.

"Non, s'il vous plaît, arrêtez! Arrêtez!" It would do no good to plead with him. They were doomed and all because of Van's impudence. "Tommy! Run! Don't look, just turn away and run as fast as you can and try to find help!" She struggled to her feet, not sure how she could get to one brother when the Indian pinning down the other

became the barrier. She had to do something to stop him. The tomahawk! It was within easy reach if she moved carefully, and so long as the two wrestlers remained focused on each other. She had just about reached her goal and wondered if she'd have the strength or stamina to actually wield it at the brave—but she had to try. She was about to grab it as she watched the brave increase his pressure on Van, who moaned in pain beneath him, when suddenly the fight was over. The boy stood, releasing his hold on Van and giving them all a satisfied smile.

"Vous vous battez bien," he said, shaking off the gravel and mud from his arms. He extended a hand to his defeated opponent who was still gasping for air on the ground. Offering a curt nod to each of them, he added another stream of French words, looking pointedly at Lucy as if she must understand him.

"Lucy! Hand me the tomahawk and I'll…finish him." He gasped the last words, as he writhed into a sitting position.

She locked eyes with the boy, whose tomahawk she held at her side. When had she picked it up? He held out his hand in a beckoning gesture and an assured expectancy. "He wants his tomahawk back."

"Of course he does! He's going to kill us all now. Hand it to me, sister!"

The boy blinked curiously at Lucy. *"Soeur?"*

"Not sister! I'm…a boy. Remember?" She stood, chest puffed out, the grip on the tomahawk ever tighter, squeezing her eyes to conjure the words. "No hurt my brother," she said, in the best French she could muster. "Help. No bad. No harm." Again in French, the words seemed to come, however tenuously, without her really thinking about what they meant.

"Pas de mal," the boy returned with a slight shake of his head. Holding out his opened hand, he took a step toward her. *"Donnez le moi."*

He wanted his weapon back. He could have killed Van with his bare hands, but he didn't. If they provoked him further, they might not be so fortunate the next time. Slowly she moved forward, lifting the tomahawk, handle first, toward his outstretched hand.

She could hear Van yelling "No!" as he rose from the ground, Tommy's feet splashing toward her from the left. But still she was drawn toward the Indian whose eyes met hers in an understanding. He took hold of the smooth, carved handle as Lucy released her grip. A shower of pebbles bit at her upper arm and neck, pelting them both. Lucy lunged just in time to stop Tommy from his next shot. "No! What are you doing? No more fighting." She scooped up her little brother, kicking and flailing against her.

"He hurt Van," the little boy repeatedly yelled. "He's a bad Injun."

"No. No. He's not. This is not helping." She was so weary of the morning's events, the lack of food, the fatigue of travel. "Please, we're sorry. *Pardon,"* she said first in English and then in French.

He made a wave of his hand and a slight shrug of one shoulder. Was that a sign all was forgiven? She couldn't tell, but he watched as Van, limped over to them, and made another sign, moving hands through the air in some meaningful way. *"Mon ami."*

"He's wanting to be friends, isn't he?" Van said. "I know that much French. I suppose I did start things and he could have finished me off, could have done in all of us, but...didn't." He waved his hand back in a similar gesture, saying, *"Mon ami."*

"It's about time," Lucy pointedly scolded. "Pity you didn't figure that sooner."

Van shrugged. "We fought it out, came to an understanding. It's done."

"That's it?" Lucy screwed her face, incredulous. "Just like that. And now we're all friends? I'll never understand boys."

"Well you are one for the moment, anyway," Van teased. "And it would be better if he thinks you are, until we know where he's taking us and who we chance to meet there, sis...I mean...brother."

Lucy blinked incredulously at him. "Why the sudden change of heart? You were fighting him, and now you want to follow him? It can't be that simple."

With a despairing sigh, he explained. "I'm hurt bad now. It pains me even to say it, but this one gave me quite a whooping and could've killed me, could've killed you just now, but didn't. And I know you and Tommy are weak with hunger."

"And you aren't?" She put hands on hips to emphasize the point. "If you hadn't fought him, he might have let us go easy. Now we're...in his debt, aren't we? Because he spared you? Isn't that the way of it?"

While she and Van argued the means to contend with their situation, the brave followed their every word as if hoping they would break into French again. For a moment, Lucy wondered if he did indeed know English better than he let on.

"Venez vous les amis." He beckoned, this time commanding and hearty. *"Venez!"*

"What other choice do we have but to trust him, for now at least? Maybe he'll lead us to someone who speaks English," Van said. "But till we find out, you have to try speaking to him, letting him know we aren't going to go easily if he, or his tribe, tries anything."

"And how will that help?" Lucy said, continuing the discussion even as they followed their new guide, hoping he would not lead them into yet another trap. "As if we can do anything to stop him or anyone he takes us to." The creek bed twisted over the next rise where a patch of blue swirled with spun wool clouds. "He has to know we're defenseless. So, even if I could tell him, which I can't, I won't. What would it matter?"

Another steep hill loomed before them. "Talk to him, Lucy," Van said. "Let him know our plight. See if he can help us find our way to Uncle Joseph's or knows someone who could."

"Van, I...don't know if I can." Tears welled in her eyes and she wanted to grab the stick Van now used for walking and beat her brother for making her remember. Her burnt arm, crusted with delicate new skin, seethed again with Mother's fearful warning. "It's an abomination. Wickedness. I'm...wicked." He couldn't know those other words she kept trying to squelch. Something about this boy, the way he looked at her, as if he knew something about her and could read her thoughts. She began running lists through her mind again to stem the tide of words. Sixty-six books of the Bible. All the crown heads of England. The twelve apostles.

"You are not wicked. Maybe, it is a gift after all." Van faced her with a determined hopefulness that frightened her more than the dangers of the unknown—of savages in the wilderness or whatever lay ahead.

"Please...don't make me."

"You were speaking fine with him before," Van encouraged, taking hold of her hand. "No one else ever need know about this. If we ever get back...that is, *when* we get back, I'll never tell anyone about this and neither will Tommy." He turned stern warning eyes on their younger brother. "And I'll always take care of you and protect you from whatever and whoever tries to hurt you."

Lucy swallowed the words rattling in her head and threatening to ooze off her tongue. She squeezed her eyes tight, surrendering the internal battle and letting the strange tongue have its way. "I suppose... We don't even know his name yet. And he doesn't know ours."

"Maybe he's a runaway too?" Tommy exclaimed, then ran ahead to walk alongside their new companion. He extended his hand. "Good morning! I'm Thomas. I'm a friend." Looking back to his sister, he asked, "How do I say that in Frenchie?"

"B-bone...joor," Tommy stumbled through, mangling the words to Lucy's chagrin. "Zah... swee...Thomas. Ay-meee." Perhaps it would be better if she did all the talking and translating.

"Good idea, Tommy!" Van said, "We should have thought of that before. Ask his name, Lucy."

They walked along a little farther while Lucy summoned the rudimentary French phrase, "What is your name? *Votre nom?*"

Their guide stopped in his tracks and turned with a chagrined slap to his head, seemingly realizing his remiss in manners. *"Oh! Mon Dieu! Pardon. Je suis Auguste Dubois, fils de Auguste Jean Baptiste Dubois, de la tribu, Weyapiersenwah, Et vous?"*

"Auguste," she relayed to her brothers. "That's his name... I reckon he's named for his father...whose name is...Dubois. And his mother might be Shawnee...or Ojibwe. I'm not certain." That Indian word was familiar, yet disturbing in the tangle of words buzzing like bees in her ears.

"You're doing fine, Lu," Van said. "Tell him our names and where we're headed. See if he can help us."

"Not so fast!" In exasperation, she returned the introduction, staring first with Van, then Tommy, and then herself. "And I am..." She stopped herself just as she started bobbing a curtsy. Boys did not curtsy. Auguste raised his eyebrows in confused surprised, almost as if he realized her faux pas. Changing to a gentlemanly bow, she cleared her throat and with a deepened voice said, *"Je suis Lucas."* Why hadn't she remembered to bow first instead of curtsy? As if proper social protocol—bow or curtsy—really mattered out here in the wilderness. She smiled inwardly at the thought.

"So, he's got a frog name and must be more French than Injun," Van said.

"Good thing he doesn't understand you, Van," she retorted. "Would you like me to repeat that back to him?"

"Dépêchez-vous," Auguste interjected, apparently overhearing them, he motioned for Lucy to walk with him.

"He wants us to make haste," Lucy replied to Van's anticipated, quizzical gaze.

"Hurry?" Van looked warily about the surrounding woods. "What's to hurry for?"

"Perhaps he's expected home." Lucy paused for his next words then relayed them to Van. "He's offering a place to stay and food from what I gather."

"Food?" Tommy gleamed eagerly. "What kind of food? Bacon? Roast chicken? Queen's cakes? Sally Lunn?"

"I don't know, Tommy," Lucy said, absently. "We'll have to wait and see, but stop talking about food. You're making me hungry."

"Sah-lee Loon, eh?" Auguste turned around with eager eyes. *"Oui! Sol et lun. Ma mère fait cuire sol et lun. Mmm très bien."*

To her brothers' questioning faces, she explained, "He seems to know what Sally Lunn is and says his mother makes it. And...he prefers it."

"An Injun making Sally Lunn?" Van sneered. "Must have a French mother then too."

"Well, he does speak French. And Sally Lunn may indeed be an old French receipt." She pondered a memory of the kitchen slave and her mother preparing an old Virginia receipt. "Ester once told me Sally Lunn was actually an old French receipt that means sun and moon, *sol et lun."* She mused this more to herself, her stomach rumbling with thoughts of the sweet cake with dark crust and a soft center as white as the sun. The mesmerizing thought of soon finding such delicacies, after days of deprivation, spurred her along.

"Oui! Sol et lun," he said, *"Gâteau sucré délicieux."*

"He says it's..."

"Sweet, delicious cake," said Van smugly. *"Oui,* I understand that much French, or at least his manner of liking good food." He imitated the same lip-smacking, ravenous gleam of their guide. "Or maybe I have the gift of tongues, too." An upturned twist to one corner of his mouth was a rare sign of humor from his otherwise stoic demeanor. "Ask him if his mother is French and if he's a captive," Van urged. "Might be that's how he knows the way of making cakes...er...*gâteau."*

"At least ask him again where he lives and what he means to do with us. We have a right to know that."

If nothing more than to appease her older brother and keep him from grabbing her arm at every turn, she asked their guide again, *"Où allons-nous?"*

"Vous verrez. Venez avec moi." Again he motioned and pointed ahead. *"Tout est bien."*

"He just said to keep following and all will be well." She shared one more wary glance with Van as they trudged through the trees. Her brother seemed to relax a bit to their new situation even though he still walked with his hand resting on the sharpened stick tucked in his waistband.

A short while later, Auguste led them to a clearing that opened to a small cabin nestled on the edge of the woods. Outside were various traps and a few furs stretched across frameworks. An axe was wedged into a large tree stump a few feet from the cabin door near a pile of firewood. The cabin had only one window and it was covered in oilcloth.

At his insistence, they followed him inside where a petite woman tended the hearth. She appeared more Shawnee than French, bearing little resemblance to Auguste. Her long, silky black hair was tied in twin plaits, and she dressed in an odd mixture of styles. A yellow, checked short gown was cinched over a faded-blue, silk petticoat that looked like it was once finery fit for a proper lady rather than one tending a log cabin hearth. A pair of well-worn, deerskin moccasins peeked out below the frayed hem of the once elegant petticoat.

"Ah! Ma chère maman," Auguste greeted the woman with a kiss to

her plump cheek, followed by a flurry of words that Lucy feared she could not do justice, regardless of Van's intent look begging for her translations. This strange capacity for words seemed to have a will of its own and she both dreaded its continuance as well as its departure.

The woman paused in stirring the pot and looked up at the intruders after a quizzical smile to her son. Her demeanor was nonplussed, leaving Lucy to wonder if Auguste routinely brought strange children home with him.

Though she didn't completely understand the exchange of words between mother and son, it was obvious he was telling their tale of meeting in the woods. One at a time he motioned to them, stating their names, to which the woman offered no response, placidly taking in the information. Then Auguste made a grand gesture to Lucy and said, *"Celui-ci parle français.* This one speaks French." Everyone in the room stared at her as if expecting her to perform. Van nudged her with his elbow. "I think they want you to speak."

"Er... *bonjour, madame."* Lucy offered a stiff bow, making sure to resemble a proper boy.

"What are you doing?" Van whispered. "I don't know that Injun squaws go by *madame."*

"Quiet," Lucy hissed back. "I'm just being polite. She knows French. It never hurts to be polite. And I'm supposed to be a gentleman, remember? What else should I call her?"

Auguste motioned to his mother and seemed to be saying her name. Some long Indian word and then in French, *"Pégase. Mon papa l'appelle* Peggy," he added. "So, Peggy?" He nodded as if that settled the matter.

Peggy was much easier to pronounce and remember, though it didn't seem to fit the sober-looking woman stirring the concoction bubbling in the pot. Lucy repeated the woman's name as a nod of acknowledgement and appreciation for welcoming them into her home. Van and Tommy followed her example.

The aroma of the stew was intoxicating and served to remind Lucy of just how faint and hungry she was, though her light-headedness also seemed to stem from the dizzying array of words swirling in her head. English competed with French, which seemed to generate from a place she had no control of. Auguste motioned for them to sit down at the long, rough-hewn table in the center of the room.

Tommy tugged at her sleeve. "They're gonna feed us now?"

"I think so, Tommy." Lucy put a protective arm around him, holding him back. "I'm sure he means for us to sit down."

Peggy nodded in assertion that they were to follow Auguste's instructions and spoke in quick, harsh-sounding words. She further underscored this gesture by filling bowls one after another with the savory-smelling stew and placing them on the table with Auguste's help.

"Asseyez-vous," Auguste motioned once more. *"Mangez. Bon appetit."*

"Merci," Lucy replied, then turned to translate for Van. "He's saying we should sit down and eat and enjoy our meal."

Tommy needed no more invitation than that and scrambled upon the long bench to partake of the first decent meal he'd had since the preacher left them destitute.

The stew was the best Lucy had tasted, but she chalked it up to also being so hungry anything would have sufficed. Still, it had a flavorful, unique taste unlike anything made from the Swearingen kitchen. Auguste's mother bustled about the table and offered them helping after helping. Lucy tried to maintain a polite demeanor and only partake of one serving, but the Shawnee woman seemed perturbed by this and was pleased when Tommy wolfed down seconds and then thirds of the flavorful concoction. Lucy noted bits of venison, turnips, onions, corn, and some other vegetables appearing to be similar to Ester's succotash, but seasoned with some herb she could not detect.

With bellies full and the sun sinking lower on the horizon, Lucy began to feel a bit drowsy and noted that Tommy's eyes were drooping along with his curly head. The cabin had been silent all through their supper save for the occasional grunts and brusque words between mother and son. They frequently looked at the door as if awaiting someone to enter. Lucy wondered who, and then was rewarded with the sound of a clopping horse outside.

Auguste looked up with a smile lighting his face and headed toward the door. *"Mon père."*

The door swung open and a robust man wearing buckskin leggings and a linen shirt topped with a dirt-smudged waistcoat entered. He wore a greasy leather cap, which he swiped from his head revealing gray-streaked hair tied into a long queue that trailed down his back. He spoke a greeting in French to his wife and son, before stopping dead in his tracks at the sight of three strange children sitting at his table. Lucy tried to discern what the three said to each other in the next few exchanges but they spoke too fast to be understood. Van looked at her beseechingly as if he expected her to translate it all. She looked at him and shrugged. Lucy caught one word spoken several times—*anglais.* The man finally turned to them and sat down at the head of the table to a steaming bowl of stew, placed there by his wife. He chomped down a few bites before addressing them. "So, you are English children. *Américains?* Where are you from and how do you come to be traveling alone, eh?"

Lucy was both shocked and much relieved to hear him speak fluent English and didn't know quite what to say at first. For a second she almost didn't recognize her native tongue, so surprised was she. He had certainly taken long enough. Van jumped in at this point. "You speak English?" The relief was apparent in his voice and echoed her own ease. "Well, sir, me and my brothers, here, are Kentuckians on our way to visit our grandfather in…Martinsburg, Virginia." He paused and seemed to be considering what to say next. "Our parents died last winter from the fever and we have nowhere else to go…so we have to make our way to our father's brother…who is our only next of kin."

The man seemed to consider all this as he stood and walked across the room to fill a cup of coffee from a pot warming over an iron trivet. "Kentucky? Quite a ways south from here. You are a far piece from home, no?"

"Well…you see, sir," Van stalled, as if trying to grasp the next plausible lie. "We did live in Kentucky, but our folks, they moved to Pennsylvania a few years ago. We've been trying to make our way east to find our uncle in Shepherds Town, now that they're dead and gone."

He paused, coffeepot in hand. "I thought you said you were headed to Martinsburg…where your grandfather lives."

"Er...yes...Martinsburg," Van fibbed. "He...actually lives somewhere in between."

"Your uncle?" He set down the pot. "Or grandfather? Which is it?"

"We're not sure," Lucy interjected, hoping to do a bit better job of fabricating their past than her befuddled brother. "He's like a grandfather to us. Our mother's uncle, who raised her. So...he's our... granduncle, I suppose."

The man returned to the table and creased his brow, considering all as he proceeded to shovel large spoonfuls of stew into his mouth. "My son tells me you were wandering alone and without provisions in the rain." He spoke between mouthfuls, arching his eyebrows in expectation of the truth.

"Well, uh...you see we had a bit of hard luck." Van hesitated and Lucy knew he did not know how to tell them about all they had endured and the recent setback with the preacher.

"There was a nasty old man who stole all our things. He pretended to be a preacher. But I don't think he was," Tommy blurted out, bits of stew and gravy dripping off his chin. "We've been walking in the cold rain ever since and had nothing to eat for days."

"It's only been a little over a day," Lucy corrected. "It just seems longer. And then Auguste found us."

The Frenchman looked first at Tommy and then at Van and Lucy. "So he said. And you have had a bit of the *mal chance*, eh?" He seemed to consider this a bit then looked at the Shawnee woman and the young man standing near the hearth. He spoke something in French to them. Lucy's head began to ache trying to puzzle out all the rapidly spoken foreign words. She figured he must be saying something about their situation but how it was interpreted between these family members made her squirm uncomfortably.

The man returned his attention to them. "My name is Dubois, Jacques to my friends. And this is my wife, Peggy, as you've been told, I'm sure. And our son, Auguste, you have already met. Maybe you start by telling us your names—your true names. My son says you are Thomas, Van, and...Lucas?"

Van swallowed and took in a deep breath before confirming their

Christian names. "As I said, we're trying to get to our uncle's house in Shepherds Town."

Dubois surveyed the children with raised eyebrows and lips pressed into a thin line. "Who might your uncle be? Perhaps I know him. I have been down toward Shepherds Town. Martinsburg. You know it?" Dubois motioned toward Peggy who stood over the fire stirring the pot of stew. "My woman's people once lived down that way."

"No, no, sir," Van affected a light chuckle. "I don't think you'd know him at all. He doesn't mingle with society much. We'd be obliged if you could set us on the right path and help us get near enough. Our uncle would gladly repay you...once we find him."

He weighed the idea with a twist of his head as he picked a piece of meat from between his yellowed teeth. "You are a long way from Shepherds Town...or Martinsburg, whichever. Perchance we may be of help."

"Oh!" Lucy gasped, excitedly. "We'd be ever so grateful."

"Two brothers you say?" He let out a chuckle and looked at Peggy, continuing to speak in the strange Indian tongue that sent the bees circling dizzily in her head. All three—the woman, the man, and their son—let out a merry chuckle, at Lucy's expense, she feared.

Peggy came over to Lucy and gestured to her bowl saying something in French Lucy figured must mean she was offering her more stew. Lucy shook her head and said, *"Non, merci."*

The woman gently took hold of Lucy's chin and lifted her face to scrutinize her features. Van started on the opposite side of the table, but Jacques motioned for him to be still. The woman shook her head and made a clucking sound with her tongue, then turned a knowing look on her husband who nodded. Peggy inspected Lucy's jacket then threw up her hands in an exasperated gesture, saying something in French. Auguste snickered as he moved to the table with his bowl of stew and sat down next to Van.

"What's so funny?" Lucy blurted out, feeling more than a little perturbed atbeing the brunt of a foreign joke she couldn't understand.

Auguste cupped his hands around his face and made a gesture Lucy thought must be some sort of irreverent Indian slur and repeated part of what his mother had said. *"Le garçon est joli en tant que fille."*

They all laughed again at Lucy's expense she feared.

"What exactly is so funny?" Van's face was growing red by the minute. "What are they saying?"

Dubois wiped a tear from his eye and chuckled. *"Ah, mon petit.* My wife and son think for a lad you have a pretty face more, shall we say, like a...how you say...like a lass."

Auguste looked at Dubois again and made the same gesture. "Ah, *oui.* Pretty lass."

"Now see here. I am no lass." Lucy sat up a little straighter and tried to speak in a deeper, outraged voice.

Dubois was bemused and skeptical. "Perhaps you would rather have us prove what we already suspect, *mon chèr?"* His gaze raked over her before sharing a knowing leer with his son.

At this, Van rose abruptly from his seat. "You touch her and I swear I'll—"Dubois let out a hearty laugh, echoed by his son and put up a conciliatory hand. "Be still, *mon ami.* I think we have proved our point, no?"

Lucy felt her face flush and tried to change the subject. "What was that she said about Van? I know you were talking about him, too."

Dubois looked at her with narrowed eyes. "My son says you speak some French?"

"Yes...er...that is... *Oui, je parle française un peu."*

Dubois nodded appreciatively. *"Bien, c'est bien."*

"But I'd prefer speaking English, sir," she added, "if it's all the same to you."

"Anglais. Français." Jacques weighed them equally between empty hands. "I speak both and assorted *langues tribal* of the native peoples."

Auguste cleared his throat and uttered another stream of French toward Lucy. His father turned to him with a decided shake of the head and firmly stated, *"Anglais, mon fils. En anglais."* Turning to his three guests he added. "You must excuse my son. He knows English far better than he makes us believe. He says you had quite a *combat magnifique* out in the woods, eh?" Dubois pounded his fist on the table, shaking the bowls and horned spoons as he spoke harshly to his son in French again. Lucy started and instinctively drew Tommy near as he whimpered against her.

"Yes, sir," Van muttered, "I mistook your son for…a…that is to say an…"

"Un savage?" Jacques prompted, with a probing arch to his brow.

"Auguste is no savage," Tommy chirped. "He's our friend. Mon ahmee. We just didn't know if we could trust him. Not after the thieving preacher."

Jacques studied them a long moment before breaking into laughter that spread to his son. *"Mes amis.* And so you two fought and now are friends." He shrugged. *"C'est la vie! Non?* My son needed a good sparring and some boys his own age to match him. He usually loses to the others of his kind, *non?"*

"Papa!" Auguste lamented, clearly understanding their conversation, which made Lucy a bit uneasy thinking of all that was said between her and Van on their way here.

Her mouth felt suddenly dry. Her heart beat heavily in her chest. She scanned the walls of the cabin and noticed the odd mix of crude items gracing this humble abode. Kitchen tools of cast iron and wood hung from the mantle. Pelts of various animals dangled from the rafters while bone fragments littered the dirt floor. Everything she would expect to find in a fur trapper's cabin; yet, along one wall stretched a leather strap bearing long hanks of hair in varying shades from the darkest walnut to honey-colored shades even lighter than hers.

She felt like there was an iron trap clamped around her lungs in a death grip of fear. These were human scalps, taken from the heads of unfortunate, and now unknown, settlers. Among them were a few auburn shades like the color of the McTavish girls' hair and some the fair color of corn silk. Her hands shook and she tried to clench them tightly in her lap. Till now she had kept her fears at bay; memories held back now flooded over her with the cries and screams of long ago. Had she known any of those whose hair now graced this cabin's walls like flowers Mother arranged in vases each spring or vines she tucked around the mantle each Christmas? She breathed in air in sips and kept her eyes on the table.

This Frenchman had lived among the Shawnee and married a tribal daughter. Could they have heard of her father's exploits, or possibly taken part in the battles against English and American settlers long ago? There had been the Seven Years War some now called the French and Indian War. And then there was the War of Independence. She had grown up hearing the tales from her brothers and the militiamen who gathered about the nearby forts. They could never know who they truly were or it might be their doom.

The conversation drifted peripherally around her, Van telling of their great loss of everything needed for their journey and squelching Tommy's attempts to spill too much of the truth. If they could only sneak away, perhaps during the night... But they'd still be left with a long journey to make and no resources. What if they never found Uncle Joseph and he never learned the truth of their stepfather's treachery? Everything would be lost. And there would be no proof to show in court. How could they face everyone? They couldn't stay here and yet they couldn't return home. Not now.

Peggy came over to the table with a bowl of stew and sat down to eat across from Lucy. She pointed to Lucy and spoke in very rapid French then shot an accusing look at her husband. With the clear understanding of what was said ripening in her mind, Lucy froze from the inside out, tightening her arms at her side.

Dubois nodded in reply to his son and turned to Lucy. "English girls are not supposed to wear men's clothes, *non?* My wife keeps wondering why you are a girl dressed as a boy."

Somehow she knew that was not all the woman had conveyed to her husband, not by the intense, cold gaze she received. Perhaps this was one lie she needed to rectify. Lucy cleared her throat and sat up very tall. "We figured it would be safer...and less burdensome...if I dressed as a boy."

"It was my idea," Van said.

"It's really not that unusual. And gowns are not easy to travel in through the woods." She realized she was speaking very fast and probably wouldn't be understood. Already Auguste was concentrating closely on her face as if trying to decipher each word, then turned to his father seemingly awaiting a translation. Jacques spoke something in French to his son who then turned back to Lucy with a nod of understanding.

"Lucy, you don't need to tell them anything." Van rose from the bench and took hold of Tommy's arm. "Thank you, sir, for your kind hospitality, but we will take our leave now."

"Van!" Lucy wasn't sure what he was doing but felt his rudeness was not warranted. She did not wish to forsake a warm, dry bed under a real roof for at least one night.

"It's obvious they won't help us and we are not welcome here," he whispered under his breath. "And we can't keep up this ruse."

"Relax, *mes amis.*" Jacques motioned for them to sit down and gave Lucy a look of understanding. "You dress like *un garçon,* like a lad, to move through woods easy. *Bien sûr!* Of course!" He slapped his hand on the table and stood up. "You children are most welcome to stay the night here. In the morning I will see how to help you on your way to Shepherds Town…or Martinsburg. Your grandfather…uncle, who must be very worried by now, will want you safe, eh?"

Van smiled weakly. "Yes, I'm sure he will. Thank you…er…*merci beaucoup.*"

"Please, sir," Tommy added, "is there a way to find out about our stolen property, the things that the preacher robbed away?"

"Tommy, no." Lucy's turn to whisper under her breath. "Those things are long gone to us."

Dubois stood and scratched his chin, "A preacher you say?" He let out a heavy sigh. "I will see to it in the morning and ask around if anyone has seen such a scoundrel. Such are known to make their way here." He shook his head as his mouth curled into a sneer, growling something Lucy didn't recognize. "The travelers we call them. *Les gitans. Les scélérats.*

"For right now, my wife will see to your bedding and you can rest safe here for the night." He motioned to Peggy and spoke again to her in that strange tongue that sent ripples of nausea in the pit of Lucy's stomach.

Peggy turned to clear the table and pointed to a dirt-stained mattress at the far corner of the room. She gestured to Lucy. She then moved to the other side of the table, motioning to the two boys and spoke to Auguste who indicated for Van and Tommy to follow him up a ladder to a loft area.

Van hesitated and looked at Lucy. "I rather think it better if we all sleep down here. We can't let them separate us. Lucy, tell them."

"I want to stay down here too." Tommy ran over and clung to Lucy while Peggy tried to steer the boys up to the loft area.

"I don't think we have a choice, Van." Lucy tried to smile bravely but felt too tired to care anymore.

Van sighed and walked over to take Tommy's hand. "I suppose if they were going to harm us they would have by now and wouldn't have wasted their food on us. We will see you in the morning."

Tomorrow, perhaps, with the help of Jacques Dubois and Auguste, they would find their way back toward Shepherds Town even if they could not regain their things. At least they wouldn't be sleeping on the cold, hard ground tonight, Lucy thought as she snuggled under the woolen blanket.

CHAPTER 25

The night *terror comes once again. She walks—no, she floats—through a wooden glen cloaked in heavy blackness. This is where they brought her in that long ago time, when she was smaller than a rain barrel, when strong hands lifted her up, allowing her to see the pooled water dripping from the spout by the barn. She should have hidden in the rain barrel or under the table the day they came. That's where she had been playing while the women wove their magic threads across the clouds above her. Needles through cloth, lacing in and out like spiders spinning their fairy webs. She must have cried then, or did she shiver in silence? One was a dream, one not a dream. Even now she could not tell. The screams silenced her tears, her infant cries, or were they merely drowned out, forgotten? She won't cry now, as she had then, an infant, too small to reach the rain barrel. She must be silent as the darkness, still and thin as a mouse's whisker so no one will hear her.*

Inside a cabin, she knows this place, not anywhere else but in this dream. How does she know a place she has never been? A woman, dressed in beaded doeskin under a faded yellow short gown, stirs a pot of stew over a hearth, flaming with heat and spitting fire like dragon's breath.

"Wendigo. Wendigo." The woman speaks to the rhythm of her stirring. Lucy echoes, softly at first and then as she stirs their voices raise higher and higher as the flames spit and writhe. The woman nods approvingly before her face turns into the face of a lion with large teeth and the horns of an elk. The yellow short gown she wears becomes a man's jacket, dark blue, stained in blood. A soldier's coat.

"Paghllissa, paghllissa, *Cautantowit* paillissa weydagnohyahtn."

She stands in the darkest of forests, alone once more, calling the words that bring both life and death, salvation and destruction. Drums beat around her, above her, behind her eyes inside her head.

"*Wendigo,* paillissa, *wendigo,* paillissa, chanoooahweyapaglebemu." *She tries to say the words that call the beast, the Great Mystery, to her aid, but the Blue Jacket man holds a finger to her lips. Cooling, gentle.*

"Sweet sister, do not fear," he whispers.

The face is Elzey, her brother. Around her lie strands of hair—honey brown, cornsilk, tawny, wheat, coal black, rusty red. All the colors of those she knows and once loved. Scalps tinged in spatters of red that drip from her fingers. She tries to run, but her legs are iron sinking into sand. Then it comes, the eagle winged Creature with the face of a man, the tail of a snake, clearing forests in one writhing swish. Punishing and saving, Devouring and *delivering. It lifts her in its talons and carries her higher, higher into the brightening sky. The great bird, the winged horse that rides the sky and hovers over the seas. Higher and higher, over the rocks and cliffs they soar together where the beast has its lair where the Great Rivers meet and Cautantowwit is there to greet her. Cauntantowwit, who hovers over the waters, formed the land, and is the One Great Comforter to all. There she finds shelter. There she is safe.*

Lucy awoke to the tickle of the musty, woolen blanket's fringe against her nose, the cool earthen floor beneath the fur pallet, and the soft padding of moccasins somewhere in the room. The dream had faded into murky memory, fragile as morning dew on a spider's web, even though she still felt the comforting wings of some great bird. Her hazy mind tried to hold on to some shred of what she had seen and heard, but no words seemed adequate. Still in the sloth between sleeping and awaking, she tried to grasp the meaning, even as the visions faded into the darkest recesses of her mind. She was lost but had found a place of refuge flying on the back of some great thing. An eagle? No. It had been terrifying—familiar and yet nothing she knew in this existence. And it had four legs, not two. She was sure of that, but talons like an eagle, perhaps? She remembered the dream ending in a place of safety only to awaken now to uncertainty and strangeness here in predawn darkness of Jacques Dubois's cabin. Only the present reality of this room roused her body to the new day.

The footsteps moved toward the hearth where in the dimly glowing embers, Lucy made out the hazy outline of Auguste's mother. She stirred the fire, adding kindling and fanning the glowing embers enough to ignite one candle. After setting it on the table, she turned to Lucy, wooden spoon in hand pointing toward her then back to the pallet. She should tend to her own bedding? Was that what this woman meant? Peggy—that was her name, but not a diminutive of Margaret, like Peg Weller whom Zack had fancied before he married Phoebe. What had the Indian boy called his mother? *Pégase.* But that was not her Shawnee name. *Pahglissa.* That is the name Auguste first mentioned when introducing his mother. It had slipped into her mind and became part of her strange dream, but oddly it seemed more familiar than that, as if from some long-forgotten place.

Again the woman at the hearth uttered a command, more forcefully this time, "Tend to your own bedding. I am no slave." She wasn't speaking French or English, yet Lucy understood somehow. It was almost as if she wasn't speaking at all, as her lips barely moved. Yet Lucy understood her meaning. She couldn't be reading her thoughts. Gazing at the mussed bedding, the soft fur, the wool blanket woven in pleasing striped patterns, she thought of home. It was Winn's duty to tend the bedding each morning, but it wasn't as if she didn't know how to do chores when needed and be a courteous guest. She obeyed willingly and eagerly. It was the least she could do to repay their kindness and would have gladly tidied up Peg's bedding as well, if the woman hadn't already taken care of this. She went about her task, the woman giving her a quizzical look as she rolled the blanket and furs into a neat bundle.

Upon finishing she faced her hostess with a smile and a croaky, *"Bonjour, madame,"* followed by an awkward attempt to ask if she needed help with preparing the breakfast. Clearly, she did not use the correct words, for the woman gave her a blank look and pointed the spoon at her chest then toward a pile of clothing laid over a chair. The words were guttural gibberish at first, but even by the signs, Peg's meaning was clear. The chair held a cotton short gown and petticoat neatly folded over a well-patched, linen shift. Atop these articles was a pair of cornhusk moccasins, similar to the ones Peggy wore, but with no beaded embellishment. She lifted each item feeling a bit sheepish at being found out and instructed by this woman to don the proper clothing of her gender. It would be something her own mother would do, though probably not as stoically as Peggy had. Rather, Mother would either scold her mercilessly on proper conduct and how dreadfully scandalous it was for her to be wearing Van's old breeches and waistcoat, or she would have taken to her bed with another headache, leaving Lucy to her own devices or for Ester to tend, as she had for most of Lucy's memory. But then, wearing boy's clothing was the least of her worries at the moment. She had run away and had been taken in by a French fur-trapper's family and had slept on a dirt floor next to a Shawnee woman who was now ordering her about like the wayward child she was. Whatever would Mother have to say about that? Perhaps she was a wicked child for running away, for wearing boy's clothing, and for disobeying her mother. But even if she was a guest in this woman's home, she did not wish to wear clothing that was not hers. One item at a time she folded and stacked them neatly on the chair.

"Thank you kindly," she said, "but I'd much rather wear my own clothing." She patted her rumpled waistcoat for emphasis, though the woman's frown and tightly compressed lips were enough to show she understood and was not pleased. *"Non, merci,"* Lucy added, in case there was any doubt.

A slight shrug and returned attention to the cook pot told Lucy the matter was settled. Relieved, she wanted now to see her brothers. They should be waking too. Perhaps it was best to let them sleep. The dream still disturbed her, and, more to the point, she also needed a chamber pot. Seeing none—and not quite knowing how to ask—she headed toward the front door to seek out the privy or at least a discreet place in the woods.

Just as she reached for the door handle, Lucy jolted to a stop at Peg's harsh guttural command. "Wait. Take this with you." That's what she understood it to mean, somewhere in her head the words jumbled into understanding. She turned to see Peg holding a bucket and something in her hand. A comb! She motioned as if using the comb to smooth her hair. Gingerly, Lucy felt the tangles in her cropped hair. She must look quite the wild thing and did need a good combing. But...the bucket? Did she mean for her to use it to relieve herself? It was a water bucket, not a chamber pot. As if she understood Lucy's confusion, Peg made signs of filling the bucket and washing her face. It made sense to Lucy, who hadn't taken time to properly groom herself in days and there had been no mirror in which to properly see her reflection. She gratefully took the bucket and comb and headed out in the direction Peg pointed to, hoping to find the water source. *Nepi.* Water. River. Spring. It wasn't clear which she was to find, but the direction to go was certain, down the path that led from the cabin. A well or spring couldn't be far.

The sky bloomed from deep indigo to rosy pink as the sun glinted over the hills and ignited the dew-drenched trees into sparkling gems. The world was refreshed in another new day and Lucy took a moment to bask in the beauty and tranquility. A solid meal from the night before and a refreshing night's sleep, save for the strange dream, had made all the difference. Yet there was still the uncertainty of finding their uncle's home and proving their stepfather's false purpose. There were other things to consider too. If they could not prove their family's case against Mr. Shepherd's claim, would she ever be free from the likes of all who would govern her life? Could he take away everything from them and would her only recourse be to marry into his family someday? Hadn't that always been the way of things? Everyone telling her how to behave, how to dress, how to do what was proper, even how to speak and what not to speak, all because she was to be a fine lady someday destined to marry a fine gentleman. But what gentleman would ever want her now if he saw a grubby-faced girl with tangled hair, who looked more like a wild boy?

It was peculiar that Peg insisted on speaking only to her in the Shawnee language, as if she, of all people, should understand it. Last night at supper, Jacques and Auguste had conversed in French to Peg. And he was kind enough to speak English to them, which relieved her of having to conjure the French words. Van had called it a gift and insisted she spoke strange words in her sleep. Were they the same words she heard in her dreams last night? She had heard those words from her earliest memories, somehow she knew this.

"You must never speak those heathen words again. Be a good little girl. You be our good little girl."

Someone had said those words to her, once long ago, when she was very young. The memory came mottled and jagged as the scattered patches of sunlight through the budding trees, brilliant and blinding but also hazy as the fog coating the distant hills. Mourning doves and robins chirped their lively tunes proclaiming the new day and chattering away their woodland gossip, as if encouraging her to remember, or perhaps to forget, in their own cheery way. Lucy attempted a birdcall back, one that she had seemed to always know. Zack had liked to make birdcalls and must have taught her—or had it been someone else?

She hadn't gone far when the sound of a gurgling stream rippled through the trees, and the sweet smell of rain-drenched rocks indicated a spring was near. She followed a winding path through the trees and over a rocky incline to a small cavern where the gurgling echoed bright and clear. At the entrance a shallow pool bubbled from a cleft at the back of the cavern—water clearer than any she had ever seen. Lucy positioned herself on the ledge and tried to reach the narrow falls that poured down over the rocks and fed the spring like a natural pitcher into a basin. The water was so clear she should have been able to see her reflection in the morning light beaming through the rocks, but the waters were not still enough and her reflection undulated in strange shapes making her grubby face even more distorted and unseemly.

Tenderly she daubed a finger into the cool inviting water, then leaned down for a delicious scoop to splash across her cheeks and forehead. The blast of water hit her like the slap of a reprimanding hand, taking her breath away and tingling in its refreshing vigor. She scooped another and then another and lapped huge mouthfuls of drenching sweetness down her parched throat. After recent attempts to filter whatever murky water they had managed to find along their route through gravel and sandy soil, this tasted of something so sweet and pure it brought tears of joy.

"Oh, marry, I know I must look a fright but could it really be all that horrid?" She said the words to no one in particular as she stared into the rippling pond, thinking of Peg's offer of a comb along with a motherly, reproving eye. Sheepishly, she retrieved the tortoiseshell comb tucked into the sleeve of her shirt.

"I 'spect my hair could use a good combing." Her voice echoed in the cavern against the tinkling strains of the stream. "Hello," she called out to no one in particular. Her voice resonated in full chord back to her. *"Bonjour,"* she tried again practicing her French. It would be easier here with no one to hear her. "My name is Lucy Eleanor Swearingen. *Je m'appelle Lucy Eleanor Swearingen."* As she practiced other words and phrases, the dream words seeped into her thoughts like the pure stream before her gurgling up from the depths of darkness. *"Nepi,"* she said louder, giving her voice another go at her newest word. Then in a deep breath she called in full voice, *"Wenigah."* She offered in singing tones, *"Pégase. Paghlissa. Keewahwahkweeung."*

With senses now fully awakened, she would allow herself just this one bit of play with the hollow of the cavern before returning to the cabin—the first real chance in days to be alone with her own thoughts and free to wistfully sing whatever pleased her. The tune she chose was one she'd often heard the militiamen singing, one that Mother always found unseemly.

"Oh, soldier, soldier, won't you marry me, with your musket, fife, and drum..." With the gurgling stream her only accompaniment and the cavern walls her concert hall, she abandoned herself to the singing of each verse telling of a young maid who sought out pieces of a wardrobe to placate the soldier at his bidding, hoping to become his bride. Sadly, in the end the young woman discovered the rogue had deceived her all along. She recalled how the militiamen always had a good rousing laugh over the final line:

"Oh, no sweet maid I cannot marry thee for I have a wife of my own."

A lonely chill passed through her as she bent beside the spring to fill the bucket with water. Perhaps it was just the coolness of the cavern and the underground stream, but she shivered involuntarily before dipping the oaken bucket into the crystalline ripples. She scooped enough water to nearly fill it and then set the bucket on the rock ledge and waited for the water to still before gazing into her makeshift mirror as she worried out the well-rooted snarls in her shortened locks. In the morning sunshine that streamed through the cavern entrance, her face looked much as she recalled before leaving home, only dirtier, and her hair was a rat's nest of snarls and frizz from sleeping outdoors on moss and dead leaves. Auguste's words at dinner came back to her. "A pretty face, indeed." How could he possibly have thought that from the image staring back at her now? She brushed a dirty finger across her nose and cheek in an attempt to clear away the smudges. With a heavy sigh, she worked handfuls of water vigorously to cleanse her face of all grime. She needed a cake of soap to do justice, but for now the spring water would have to suffice. The last real bath she had had was at home the evening before Mr. Shepherd came to dinner.

She sat still on the ledge, shaking off thoughts of that dreadful evening. The sound of the spring accompanied by the cheerful song of the morning birds soothed her thoughts as she mulled over what lie ahead. Monsieur Dubois had sent them to bed last night with the promise of finding out on the morrow the whereabouts of the preacher—but likely it was just another grown folk's attempt to soothe them off to bed for the night. It still did not set well, this idea of trusting yet another stranger to help them, especially a French fur trapper married to a Shawnee with a half-breed son who spoke little English. The sight of the grotesque scalps dangling on the log wall and the disturbing dream only served to make her feel more uneasy. Clearly, Jacques Dubois did not believe their story and had winnowed out most of the truth, even if he chose not to press them further. Perhaps he was biding his time till he scouted out more about them. Perhaps he knew too much about them already. What if he learned they were runaways? There may be a reward out for finding them and every reason for him to profit by it. She should dally no longer and return to the cabin to find Tommy and Van. How could she have left them there?

"We are Swearingens," she called into the hollow cavern. Thinking of another song, she started to hum,

"The gloomy night before us lies, the reign of terror now is o'er."

She sang out the words the militiamen often marched to, a song about freedom and victory,

"It gags inquisitors and spies, its hordes of harpies are no more."

Steadying herself to her feet, she balanced on the spring ledge and tapped her feet to the lively jig tune before bending to hoist the bucket of water.

"Rejoice, Columbia's sons rejoice! To tyrants never bend the knee,

But join with heart and soul and voice, to Swearingen rangers and liberty."

As she finished the last rousing line of the refrain, she turned toward the cavern entrance, to see Auguste standing before her. Startled and gasping, she dropped the bucket full of freshly drawn water. Had he stood there listening all this time? Indians had their ways of moving silently. Yet with the constant gurgle of the underground stream echoing against the cavern walls, accompanied by her raucous singing, perhaps it wasn't such a feat of Indian skill after all.

"Oh, Auguste!" Flustered, Lucy bent to pick up the rolling bucket while frigid water tore at her ankles, soaking into her stockings and shoes, chilling her to the bone.

"Bonjour."

"W-what are you doing here?" Her hands began to shake with the realization of what he must have heard, and the bucket slipped from her hands, oozing water over the rocks and into the earth. "Oh, fie!"

Auguste looked at her with an amused grin. "Oh, fie? *Ah! Merde!*" He laughed mockingly at her.

"What?" Lucy scrambled after the bucket before it rolled into the sunken pool.

Auguste reached it first and snatched it from beneath her grasp. *"Essayez encore."* He handed her the bucket and nodded toward the spring.

Lucy stood there a moment. She knew he meant for her to refill the bucket, but was he trying to encourage her or mock her, she couldn't say. With a toss of her head she smiled. "I suppose it was rather beetleheaded of me." She grasped the rope handle and turned to refill the pail.

Auguste stepped in close behind her. "Bee-tahl hawd?" He poked an index finger toward his brow and crossed his eyes. He understood her.

"Yes...*oui,*" Lucy mimicked the same gesture, as if to confirm her stupidity. "Beetlehead." She knelt down on the rock ledge and dipped the bucket under the clear, running water. "Think what you like of me. I know you understand English better than you claim."

Lucy took hold of the bucket with both hands across the handle and stepped carefully down from the rocky ledge toward the back of the cavern. "I suppose your mother is waiting for the water." She repeated in very stilted French the words for mother, *maman,* and water, *l'eau,* holding the bucket up.

Auguste nodded, then frowned and cocked his head in sing-song fashion uttering, "Oh, suhl-chair, suhl-chair. You sing. *La chanson, non?*"

The bucket slipped again from Lucy's hand as she realized he was trying to sing her soldier song. He must have been listening outside the cavern, but for how long? How many verses? Which also meant he had heard her singing the other song about Swearingen rangers and liberty, invented by the militia to honor her father and his service to their settlement.

"It's just a silly song." She steadied her hands on the bucket handle and ignored his attempts to hum the tune as she concentrated on a way to get past him. He stood between her and the cavern entrance. "I'll have to fill the bucket again and...your mother, *votre mère,* must be wondering where I am." Behind her the cavern wall formed a shell with the only escape a small hole from which the underground spring emanated.

"Le chanson concerne un soldat? Non?" Auguste moved a step closer and reached for the bucket handle.

Lucy concentrated on refilling the bucket. "Yes, I was singing about a soldier. And if you indeed understood, you should speak English, which is better than my French, *non?"* She tossed him an accusing grin.

Leaning against the cavern wall, he seemed to consider this. "Lucy. Your name is Lucy? *La jolie."*

"Julie? Who? Oh...*jolie*...pretty. Er...yes. Thank you. *Merci."* She wasn't sure if he meant her name or her appearance, but she accepted it politely, even if it was bit impertinent for him to address her here alone in such a manner. At least he seemed to have moved from the topic of her singing and was speaking some English. It still didn't quell her unease and her hands shook as she tried unsuccessfully to fill the bucket.

"Venez! Come!" He said, bending down to her level. "I help you."

If he tried to do anything more than that, she could splash him with the water and run. She braced herself for this next move and offered a pleasant smile. *"Oui, merci.* Er…thank you."

"I show you… er…*une technique."* He seemed to search for the right word. "A…trick?"

"A trick? A technique?" Lucy replied saying the word with an English spin rather than in the less guttural French. "What is it?"

"Oui! Yes! You see." He took the bucket and deftly walked on the narrow, slippery ledge. Straddling the pool, he reached the water's source at the far back of the small cavern. A stream of water pouring off the rocks was too far for anyone to reach without falling in. But by balancing precariously across the narrow, rocky ledge, he stretched out and aimed the bucket under the natural waterspout.

"I fill water all the time like this for *Maman,"* he said, as if it was the most natural and easiest of things to do.

"It's a wonder you haven't fallen in," Lucy chided, aghast at his antics, yet curiously envious of the wondrous ability.

"Non, I never fall in." He shot a mischievous grin over his shoulder, causing him to slightly lose his balance and spill a bit of the water.

"Mind your step!" Lucy called. "Or you will fall in."

"Ah! Just a bit more." The bucket was nearly full when he eased back to his full height, presenting his accomplishment. "There! *Voila!"*

"Huzzah!" Lucy laughed and applauded as he inched his way off the ledge, not spilling a drop.

"Huzzah?" He stood beside, leaning so they looked eye to eye. *"Votre père était un soldat, oui?* Your father was a soldier? Your brother, he too like to fight?" When Lucy didn't reply, stunned by his question, he licked his lips and started singing fragments of her song earlier. "To tyrant never bend le knee. To Swearingen rangers and… *liberté."* Ending in an off-key flourish, he pronounced the last word in the French manner, just as he had "tee-rahn'" instead of the English way.

She swallowed a hard lump, her heart beating wildly against her ribs. "You don't know anything about my father. 'Tis none of your concern. He's long dead. And...and you were threatening my brother. We didn't know you weren't going to harm us." She wasn't quite sure where this conversation was going, but she was sure she did not wish to be having it out here alone. She took hold of the bucket he offered and turned to go.

Quick as a weasel, he blocked her path. With a keen eye skimming her from head to toe he tugged on his own shirt and then gestured toward her. "You dress as *un soldat...un garçon.* Not *like une fille... kweewa...*" He swished his hands as if wearing a long skirt and gave a most clumsy curtsy. "A lady."

Lucy barely suppressed a giggle that erupted as a snort. "Where did you learn to do that? *Oui.* I'm dressed as a boy," she replied in broken French. "But I'm not a boy nor *un soldat*...a soldier, and neither are my brothers—yet, that is. I just don't want to wear lady clothes at present."

He nodded as if he understood. "Someday you marry a soldier?"

She blinked, wondering if she heard him correctly. "No. I don't know. Why do you ask that?"

"*Le chanson*...eh...the sol-chair marching song." He mimicked her singing earlier, high-pitched and quite out of tune. "Won't you marry me with musket, *fife et un drum.*"

"It's just a silly song." Lucy steadied her breathing to quell both her temper and her fear. "I...liked hearing my voice in the spring. Now let me pass."

"Someday, you marry," he pressed on, still standing in her path. "Maybe, *un soldat.* Maybe he kill many in *la bataille.* Maybe he kill many Shawnee?"

"In battle? Kill Shawnee?" Lucy scrunched her face at him. "What a curious thing to say. Why would you say such a thing? You just met us and can't know anything about us. How should I know who I'm going to marry? That's years away."

"*Maman,* she know many things." He said the words thickly and slowly as if every word mattered. "You say French words but know others too, *non?*"

"If your *maman* knows so many things, then why won't she speak

English?" Lucy wondered if he was mocking her for her song or merely trying to be friendly, in his own misguided way. Perchance, his understanding of English was not as adept as she presumed—but then how did he understand her singing? "If you know English well enough to understand my song, then why did you not speak to us yesterday? You were being an eavesdropper."

"Ayvs-draw-pair?" He shook his head, confused.

"Someone who listens when they shouldn't. It's impolite." When he continued to give her a blank look she summoned the French. *"Oreille indiscrete."*

"Here, I carry." He reached for the other side of the bucket handle and cocked his head toward the path. The full bucket was getting heavy and at last he was ready to head home. Perhaps it was his manner of ending things well. "Or, we can carry together. Share load? Two strong boys? Maybe not so strong, but stronger together?"

She hadn't released the handle immediately and wasn't sure why. Maybe she did want to prove something. Maybe he did not want to take the task completely away from her. Either way, the eager kindness in his eyes softened her will, and she offered a meek, *"Merci."*

They had walked a few paces when he broke the silence, returning to their prior talk. "*Maman* Peg know English. Could speak as well as Papa Jacques. But she think English *mal*...er...much bad."

"Why?" Lucy kept her eyes forward, keeping pace with her bucket-carrying partner.

"English kill many from her tribe and most of her family. Then she marry *mon papa.*"

"But your father speaks English. Does that bother her?"

"She knows Papa Jacques must speak the English for his work. But at home, we speak *en français.*"

Lucy thought of the woman's words to her upon rising that morning. "You said she knows something about me. She wouldn't even speak in French to me. I don't know her Shawnee tongue."

"She say you do."

"What does your mother know about me?" she said, with an idle laugh, then shook her head and tried to quicken their pace wanting this time to end. "This is stuff and nonsense. We should move faster to get the water back to your cabin. Your *Maman* Peggy is waiting and likely to scold us for taking so long."

They walked a few paces in silence then came to a slight incline that made carrying the bucket in tandem difficult. Lucy let go of the bucket as she scurried down the slope and Auguste inched his way behind her. "No, *Maman* not scold. She say you may be soldier's daughter. The Indian Fighter's daughter, *non?*"

"N-no." Lucy lost her footing on this last statement and skittered to the bottom, stubbing her toe and landing on her knees.

"She know you speak the old tongue, *le Shawnee,"* he said, as if not paying attention to her. "You a *kweewahkwahesepaillissa,* like *Maman."*

"A…w-what did you say?" The cold wet stockings gripped her ankles like icy fingers, sending a chilling grip up through all her bones intensifying the sting of rocks against her knees when she fell. The word he said bounced in her head with unsettling images conjuring from her darkest dreams.

"La bête. The Ogre who live in forest and eat man." He made a horrible face and lifted his arms high in the air with hands like menacing claws, as she stood up on her own. Any gentleman would have helped her up. But then again, any proper lady wouldn't be wearing breeches. She didn't need his help.

"There is no such thing," she primly replied, standing and brushing off the dust and gravel. "Monsters are not real."

"Wendigo. *Chenoo. Keewahkwee.* The Ogre go by many name among many tribes." Those were words she had heard before, but didn't want to think about. "You know these names?"

She turned, her heart pounding hard from chest to ear. "W-what? No, certainly not."

"Maman has seen them. Wendigo lives in forest and is hairy like the bear, but face like a man." He looked at her curiously now. *"Paillissa!* Ah! That is another kind of beast. The sky horse that has horns like the stag and claws like eagle but four legs like a panther, and like the wendigo, some call *chenoo,* is said to eat flesh of man."

"Whatever are you talking about and why are you telling me all this? There are no such things." They had traversed together far enough in this course for her liking and soon would be back at the cabin, but not soon enough. "If you are trying to frighten me, I'll have none of it. I have chased away a panther. I'm not afraid of any primitive savage monsters—flying, crawling or otherwise."

"Oui!" He turned excitedly toward her. "As I said, *Maman* knows you are like her. You understand. She knew you were to come. Is why I wait for you by creek."

She shook her head, weary of the discourse. "You are making no sense and I don't wish to talk of this anymore." At last, the cabin was in view. The trip back seemed longer than her quest earlier for finding the spring.

"You carry bucket now." He held it out to her, his face an unreadable mask. Was he angry with her now for not believing his stories? In spite of the bruises and stinging knees from the fall, she would show him what she was worth. With a curt nod she took the bucket and turned back down the trail.

They walked along in silence toward the clearing where the cabin came into view. Auguste made no attempt to relieve her of the water bucket, and she stubbornly refused to show him that it grew heavy for her to trudge up and down the rocky path. When they reached the clearing to the cabin, he spoke again but to her surprise, he attempted a bit of English. "My father...go to village de Shawnee... You stay here...I stay here. No leave."

Lucy puzzled over this. She couldn't tell if he were asking her if she wanted to stay or was relating a command from his father. Perhaps Monsieur Dubois would explain once they returned to the cabin. She nodded but said nothing.

"Where have you been?" Van burst out of the cabin, wild anger mingled with confusion and relief. "What were you doing with my sis...with Luke."

"Van, they know I'm a...I'm not a lad. He knows my name is Lucy."

Her brother looked from Auguste to her before stepping between them. "Stay away from her, ya hear?" A shove of his hands square into the Indian's chest seemed not to disturb him.

"Van, stop. Not again. No more fighting."

"Your brother?" Auguste cocked his head accusingly. "The Indian Fighter? *Non?"*

"No, Auguste." She corrected him before addressing Van.

She pointed toward the bucket. "I went to fetch water. I thought it only polite to help with chores this morning." She reached for the bucket, which Auguste held up as explanation to Van. "How long have you been awake?"

"Not long. I was talking with that Injun woman, at least that is, as best I could make out. She won't speak French or English. Just some...gibberish. I've been worried sick wondering where you'd gone off to. Tommy's been fussing for you. Dubois's gone and we didn't know what to think."

"Apparently," Lucy said, "Monsieur Dubois headed out this morning to find out about the preacher."

Van pulled her ahead and whispered close to her ear as they walked toward the door. "We can only hope. I don't think we need to stay around here much longer. I don't like the size of things."

"They don't seem to mean us any harm, or they would've by now. Don't you think?" Lucy gazed over to the wall adorned with the scalps and said a silent prayer as she sat down to the table where the woman dished out bowls of something that smelled like cornmeal mush. Tommy was already fast at work lapping up mouthfuls of the steaming porridge.

"I honestly don't know what to think. I just reckon we ought to be on our way soon as we can."

"But we have no provisions still. Maybe Dubois will find out something and be able to help us."

Wendigo. *Paillissa.* The words stirred in her mind like the swirling brew under her spoon. It was a magic word that had saved her once upon a time, perhaps only in a dream, where strange flying beasts carried her to distant lands where unstill waters meet primal forests. She didn't know how, but it had. Perhaps it might again. She held the words on her tongue like a prayer—the heathen prayer it probably was. But Auguste had said his mother knew of her strange way with words, and she also knew of her father's past as an Indian fighter. Lucy would find out for sure what it all meant before they left this place, if they ever could leave.

CHAPTER 26

"We can't stay here forever, Lu," Van whispered as they helped with the outdoor chores after breakfast. Once again it was good to have eaten a full meal prepared over the hearth and served at the table. Lucy had helped Peg wash the wooden bowls and tableware afterward, while Tommy brushed crumbs from the table and Van swept the floor, best he could using his good arm. They all worked in silence, even Tommy who sensed Peg's sullen demeanor and followed Lucy's lead.

Auguste had left the cabin abruptly after breakfast, without so much as a word to anyone and now sat outside on a log stump a short length from the cabin, fast at work fleshing a beaver pelt with a two-handled knife. A long day stretched before them, as they waited on Jacques Dubois's return. After roaming the trails and creeks, scrounging for food, and scouting their next course for days on end, this time of lingering idly was maddening for Lucy. It gave her too much time to think and thoughts could be worrisome, disturbing, and deceitful. Perhaps Peg somehow understood her need for some occupation, or maybe she was bent on making them servants. Either way, Lucy was glad to be put to the task of weeding the garden with Van while Tommy roamed the yard picking up kindling sticks, when he wasn't pausing to chase after a chicken.

"Soon as we can," Van said, squatting to pull another weed from the packed earthen plot, "we'll have to leave and head to Shepherds Town. We're not welcome here. I don't like the way she keeps looking at us and treating us like we're servants." Van veered a surreptitious gaze toward the cabin where Peg kept watch over them all as she sharpened a knife on a whetstone.

"How do you propose we'll get there with none of our things and no map?" Lucy scraped the hoe across the clods of dirt. "They took us in, gave us a bed for the night, and *Maman* Peg fed us supper and breakfast. A few chores is the least we can do."

"*Maman* Peg?" Van arched a quizzical brow.

"That's what Auguste and Jacques Dubois call her."

"We're not getting too close to these people, Lu." Van struggled with one stubborn weed.

"They're not our family." He turned toward Tommy who left his chore of picking up kindling sticks and sidled over to watch Auguste at his labor. "It ain't right being here. What exactly were you doing with Auguste this morning? He say anything else?"

"I went to fetch water like I told you," Lucy shrugged. "Just being helpful and polite. He must have been sent to check on me and see if I needed help."

"More'n likely he was making sure you didn't run off or nothing," Van snorted and yanked at a particularly deep-rooted stem. "Not likely we could, given how well they keep us under *Maman* Peg's watchful eye."

Lucy ignored his spiteful tone and kept her focus on the blade of the hoe. "Monsieur Dubois left this morning to find out about the preacher. At least, that's what Auguste said. And his father told us as much last night. Maybe he'll bring back some clue as to where our things are."

"Or maybe he'll figure out who we are and alert the local authorities who'll take us home. We'll never see our stuff nor that damn thief again."

"Or maybe they'll believe us and take us to Uncle Joseph's," Lucy smiled hopefully in spite of the fears coiling like night crawlers in her stomach.

"There's other things they could have in mind, and I don't aim to give them a chance at." Softening his voice a notch lower, he looked warily at Auguste. "Though I swear he understands us better than he lets on, and I just don't trust them. What did you two talk about out there at the spring?"

Lucy smiled and offered a slight nod to Auguste who paused in his work and glanced their way before repositioning the pelt, almost as if he somehow knew they were discussing him. "Oh, he means well, I believe, and I think he's trying to understand our words as best he can. I'm not doing so well with the French either." She shrugged. "Sometimes I wonder just what I might be saying to him, but he seems to accept it all well enough."

Van snorted derisively, "Huh! I'll just bet he does."

Leveling a sharp eye at her brother Lucy said, "Just what does that mean?"

"You sure took your time fetching water. He had to have said something." Van's intensity startled her. "He's an odd one, that. What else did he say?"

"Nothing much." Lucy held a finger to her lips as Auguste perked his attention toward them. "You may be right, he does understand more than we realize. But there are reasons he prefers speaking French, even to us, and there are good reasons *Maman* Peg won't speak English."

She paused, gathering her thoughts as Auguste showed Tommy the art of scraping bits of flesh and blood from the underside of a pelt. "He just mentioned some things. Asked if I were a soldier and—""A soldier?" Van laughed. "You?"

"Considering how I'm dressed, perhaps it was his way of making a joke," she said with a toss of her head and a hand on her hip. "And I was singing that song about the soldier and the maid when he came upon me and must've overheard. He liked my singing and was just being friendly."

"Did he now? " Van grimaced skeptically. "That the one about the maid who wants to marry the poor sot and brings him all manner of things? You always did like that one. What else did he say? And just how friendly was he?"

"Nothing much." She leaned on the handle of the hoe, words starting to swirl again in her head. Images of things she couldn't describe.

She took a deep, settling breath to soothe her disquiet before speaking. "Van, what did you mean when you said I had a gift for speaking French and…other strange words?"

"You're rather clever…for a girl, I'd say. Everyone always thought so." Van stepped across the row and dug a trench with the heel of his boot. "You talk in your sleep. Not so unusual, is it? You sleepwalk too, sometimes. But you've always learned words quicker than any of us." He paused, skewing his mouth to one side, as if weighing his next words carefully. "I never was much good at reading and writing English, let alone some Froggie tongue or Injun gibberish. But if our friend over there knows English, then maybe best we speak that and then you won't have to fret over it."

"You're not telling me something, Van." She gauged her brother carefully as she dragged the hoe down one row of crumbled earth, making a trough for sowing seed. "You fetched us all out here and now we're lost."

"Whoa! As I recall you and Tommy asked to come along." He held up a defensive hand. "On my own, I'd a maybe made better time and be at Uncle Joseph's by now."

"Even if you'd met up with the same thieving preacher?" She stood tall, bracing a hand atop the hoe. "And of course you'd have known just how to speak with Auguste when he confronted you in the woods without my intervening or Tommy's way to win friends easily."

"Perhaps," Van said, defeated again. "But you still haven't told me what you two talked about out there in the woods. You come back all dirty, skinned knees, and holes in your stockings, like you'd been… tumbling or some such mischief."

"Tumbling? Mischief?"

"Never mind." Van's color rose high. "So, you were singing a soldier song about wooing a maid and he comes along and…then what?"

"Oh, I don't know." She twisted the handle of the hoe, debating whether he would want to hear about her dreams and the strange words that keep playing in her head. "Auguste talked to me. That's all. We just talked. And he showed me a trick for filling the bucket way far back of the spring where the water flows in."

"And he spoke in English all that time?" Van faced her, blocking her view of Tommy and Auguste. Did he think the two of them could hear their talk? In a low whisper he spoke while pretending to weed a patch he had already cleared down to bare dirt. "What's that you were saying about his mother? Something about her not wanting to speak English?"

With a slow, drawn breath, she collected her thoughts, sorting out the voices competing in her head. "Peg doesn't want to speak English because of…us. Our people did something terrible to her tribe before she married Auguste's father." She glanced back at the cabin and the shadow of the Indian woman moving across the oilcloth window now that she had returned inside. "He said I'm…like her. She… understands things I know. I can't explain it."

From across the yard, Tommy squealed and jumped around the makeshift workbench where the pelt lay stretched. "Lookey! I did it! I scraped it all clean." He started to say something else but was stopped by a cough and a swipe of his sleeve across a runny nose. "Ach! The smell makes my nose and gullet all itchy!" His antics made Lucy smile and doubt Van's concerns.

"It's well they don't find out our true name," Van muttered more to himself. "We best make our leave quick as we can, if they feel that way about English soldiers."

Realization struck Lucy once more like the cold water from the spring. "Oh, Van. They may suspect who we are. I was…singing another song. The one the rangers sing about Papa. I think Auguste may have heard that too. He did ask if our father was an…Indian Fighter."

"What did you tell him?" The look in Van's eyes spoke of recognition and a wary concern, as if she had said something truly dire and obscene. "You didn't tell him about Father, did you?"

"No. I merely said our family was none of his concern and that our father was long dead."

Seemingly satisfied with her answer, Van drifted into his own sullen thoughts.

"You do know what he meant, don't you?" Lucy squared her shoulders and faced him. "Could…could our father or his rangers have been part of such terrible deeds?"

"Many bad things happen in war, Lucy, be it with the French, the English, or the Injuns. They can't hold all of it against us. If our folks did anything bad to them, they done far worse to our kind. After all look what they did to you and—"

"To me?" Something in his eyes, a look of dread for having said too much, sent the blood rushing through her ears. "Whatever are you talking about?"

"I just meant…all those times we hid in fear. You remember." He sighed and headed toward the shed, their gardening task complete. "Just what I've heard from the other lads at school, and what Zack told me."

"I don't remember any of it," she lied. It had all been a terrible dream, hadn't it? She wanted to believe that, but if Van had the same recollections too… "Tell me what you remember. No one ever wants to talk about it. No one will hear us over here, and we can still keep an eye on Tommy." Behind the shed they took their time arranging the tools while Van began his tale.

"Aye. Lots of folks have heard of our pa, so it's mayhap they'll recognize his name. He's the reason many say we can rest easy now, 'cause of the treaties. He defeated the mighty Shawnee chief that tried to unite the tribes and caused all the trouble. Pa was a major part of that. Something we can all be proud of."

"What happened to the chief? Could he have been part of Peg's tribe?"

"Why would you ask that? There were lots of tribes this chief united." Van shrugged and shook his head. "They called him Blue Jacket. But he's long gone now. Likely dead, we can only hope."

"Blue Jacket?" Another image. Another word. *Weyapiersenwah.*

"Aye. He was known to wear the coats of dead soldiers he slew and that's how he got his name. He even wore the coat Injun style with sleeves shorn off and all decked out with the scalps of the men he killed."

Lucy shuddered and swallowed back the dizzying colors floating around her. Scalps tinged in blood lying everywhere. She must have heard this story once before. Was it only in her dreams? Or real?

"How do you know, Van?"

"Oh, the lads at school talk," he said, with a slight smirk. "And some stories aren't for young ladies to hear."

"But you're telling me now, and I'm glad of it."

"You aren't looking quite like a young lady now are you? You wanted to be treated like a lad and...," he sighed sadly, despairingly, "I reckon not much matters from here forward. We either find our way through this, or..." Clearing his throat he adopted a merry bravado. "We will find our way through. We gotta believe that."

"I do remember some things—they're all just foolish nightmares —but sometimes they seem so real." She couldn't bring herself to say more, brushing aside a wisp of hair like an errant thought, hoping Van would fill in the rest. "What else do you remember?"

Van squinted; his eyes grew dark and glazed into a distant point. "Not much. Just...there was one thing that happened when we were young. But no one ever talks about it now."Mother was always afraid," he said, "still is, I suppose, but it's understandable. Pa built the fort for folks to gather whenever there was a hint of trouble. His men were always around with guns, much more than they are now. But it was a rough, unproven country along the Ohio River then." He shook his head. "We holed up in the fort many a time. I was young, but I do remember. You cried, sometimes. Tommy was a baby, I suppose. I remember Mama holding him...and crying."

"Yes, I remember," she said, vague images filled her thoughts, "some things...." She drew in a breath.

"What sort of things?" Van squinted at her curiously. "That...fit you had...before we left? Those nights when you kicked the tarnation out of the bed linens and spoke in gibberish? Was it something you remembered then? You were saying those strange Injun words the night before we left. Is that why Newhouse burnt you?"

"I...think so." A chill shuddered through her, and she felt an uncontrollable urge to run or scream. She quickened her breathing and tried to keep her head clear. "Van? Did any Indians ever attack our home? Did...did something terrible ever happen there?"

Van's eyes widened then narrowed into slits. "Zack told me never to mention it, especially not around Mother...or you. It's something awful. I once overheard him and the shopkeeper, Stephenson, talking about it. Then not long before that last fever, he told me a story and said I should know the truth, but the way he told it didn't make sense. Something about Blue Jacket and how we were all cursed."

"Van, you must tell me now."

"What I overheard twixt Zack and Stephenson was years ago. I was not much older than Tommy. I don't really remember." He scanned the woods as if the memory was there to be found, as if it would come barreling down the path. "Zack's ramblings made no sense. So, nothing I know for certain and I sure wasn't going to ask anyone else." Van firmed his jaw and his mouth curved bitterly. "Don't forget we lost a brother to Injuns. Zack did tell me that." His gaze wandered over to their giggling little brother jumping among the weeds and logs. "Don't you ever wonder what the other Thomas might have been like?" He twisted a piece of grass between his fingers. "And how strange it is that we keep losing the menfolk in our family? First Thomas, then Dusy's husband Sam, and next Zack. Now it's just Elzey, Tommy, and I."

The ring of childish laughter drew Lucy's attention toward the impish lad twirling along the woodland path with Auguste following behind. She felt a surge of ardor, like a mother bear must feel in protecting her cub, as she watched Tommy prance along the sun-dappled trees. Had anyone protected her then, in that long ago time when they hid in the fort? If mother held Tommy, and Pa and their older brothers were off fighting, who held her and Van safe and close? The feeling of being ripped away from her cradle became startlingly real in her mind.

"I wonder sometimes, but I don't remember our departed Thomas. How could I? He died before I was even born. It's like he never existed."

"But he did exist, a part of our family, and he was killed by murdering savages, possibly by the likes of those we're staying with now." Van dropped the bits of shredded grass he had picked from the edge of the shed. "One of us, gone, just like Zack and Father, and we never had the chance to know him."

"But, if Papa killed Indians too, what does that make him? Someone killed Peg's family—maybe one of her brothers or her entire tribe. Could it be Pa or his rangers did the same?"

"They were just doing their duty as soldiers. Protecting us all."

"But isn't that what Shawnee braves might have been doing as well? And here the Duboises have taken us in." Lucy had followed Van across the backside of the shed to where several pelts, once living creatures freely roaming the wild, were now scraped, beaten, and boarded to dry.

"That's different." He glared at her with a look of fire and venom. "Did you see those scalps hanging on the wall? Only savages do that kind of…" He clamped his mouth shut as if he'd said something terribly wrong. "I'm…sorry Lucy. I shouldn't have said that."

"Why?" Lucy caught another glimpse of Auguste and Tommy studying some small creature crawling on the ground. "They must not think too badly of us. Why else would they be so willing to help?"

"We still don't know all there is to this," Van said as if that settled matters. "Injuns are a tricky lot. You can never trust them. We can't talk like this around them. We must not let them separate us for any reason again, not even at night. And if we abide by their ways, we might find our way out."

"You saying you want me to keep talking to them? To…keep using my way of understanding their words?" It disturbed her to think of giving into this, like falling into a raging stream and being swept away into darkness.

Tommy spun around and skipped back toward Van holding a smooth, glittery pebble in his hand. He looked at Van then at Auguste. "Lookey what we found. *Un…un…caillou.*"

"Ah, *très bien.*" Auguste ruffled his hand across Tommy's head.

"*Très bien,*" Tommy parroted back. "That means I did well."

"*Oui*, so it does, Tommy." Lucy offered a grateful smile to their new friend, hoping that this bond she had begun to feel was something true and noble and not another lie or deceitful trick. It seemed her life had been filled with far too many lies and untrustworthy folks and words that had no meaning.

CHAPTER 27

It wasn't until long after supper that evening when the sound of footsteps outside signaled the approach of the master of the house—but it wasn't just a single set of footsteps. Dubois burst into the cabin followed by two Indians.

"Ah, the children are still here." He looked at Peg sitting in one corner of the cabin weaving woolen threads on a hand-held loom as Lucy carded a matted tuft of wool. She had only seen this task done a few times, by Mrs. Carter, who kept a few sheep and goats for their wool. She knew Peg was not happy with her efforts by the way she kept frowning. But she said nothing to correct her. Actually, both mother and son had grown rather sullen and quiet as the evening sun went down. It was as if they knew something was to come, judging by the furtive glances between them. Van had actually begun to relax a bit and helped Auguste in combing out a few pelts along with Tommy, who gloried in every aspect of the new craft. Yet they had all eaten supper in an uneasy silence until the door finally opened and Dubois entered.

At her husband's entrance the woman did not look up but uttered a brusque greeting in her Indian language. Dubois responded in kind and then sat down on a stool and offered seats to his guests. Lucy quietly set down the paddles and wool and slipped across the room to huddle on a bench with Van and Tommy along one wall.

The men commenced speaking in rapid French mixed with the Shawnee dialect. Dubois said something to his wife who immediately rose from her work to fetch clay pipes and tobacco from a shelf next to the mantle. She laid them on the table and quietly returned to her corner but shot a wary eye at the Swearingen children. The men began to fill their pipes and lit them from a long stick Dubois sparked from the glowing embers of the hearth. They sat silently for a while as dusk shadowed the room with mingled wisps of smoke, an interminable length of time in which Lucy felt her heart thud a rapid rhythm in her chest wondering what might soon befall them. She exchanged a furtive look with Van who sat stone-faced. Tommy between them swung his legs back and forth like a pendulum. Every now and then his heels thudded against the back of the cabin wall or brushed against the bottom of the rounded puncheon log, once a mighty oak but now their penitents' pew.

The sins of the father shall be heaped upon the son a thousand times.

The words came to Lucy from where, she could not tell. Only that they were brought to mind. Why had Dubois brought these Indians here? What had he told them of their situation? Her eyes wandered to the leather strap on the opposite wall. The room flickered with odd shapes cast from the glow of the hearth and a few earthen oil lamps. Grotesque shadows of the Indians with their feathered heads and Dubois, all sitting at the table, danced in undulating images against the log walls. Why wasn't Dubois telling them what he had found out at the Indian village? The two braves sitting at the table puffed small circles of smoke from the ends of their pipes. They were discussing the children; Lucy knew it from the cautious glances thrown their way.

Van kept his eyes staring ahead in stoic silence. Tommy slowed his swinging legs and leaned a heavy head against Lucy's arm. She cocked her head down to rest her cheek atop the soft curls on his warm head—too warm for her liking. From the shadow cast on the floor, she saw his arm crook as a thumb entered his mouth, the only comfort allowed him in this godforsaken place.

Children should be seen and not heard. How often had she listened to adults say such things? Children, obey your parents in all things. Were Shawnee and French children raised with such words?

Yet Auguste readily entered the conversation with these men when addressed and accepted the pipe when passed to him, even as he continued his work sharpening his blade on the whetstone.

She would speak out, even if Van would not. Parting her lips, dry and cracked as drought-infested earth, she formed her words. The rifle crack of the cabin door opening startled her into silence and wrested a moan from her sleepy little brother. In the opened doorway, silhouetted against the lantern, there stood a tall Shawnee man in soldier's coat, devoid of its sleeves and encrusted with beads—a blue jacket.

CHAPTER 28

She must have fallen asleep or slipped away into some dark abyss, for the next thing Lucy recalled, the room was spinning in swirls of color and misshapen forms. The men at the table laughed, and pipe smoke rose in thick heady clouds throughout the room. There were four of them now, including the tall man in blue. Peg sat in the corner of the room working at her weaving. Dubois and the Indian braves jabbered on in a mixture of French and the apparent native language of the three men. How long had they been sitting there on the bench, huddled together before she drifted off? Lucy labored to keep her breathing steady against the pounding of her heart. The sweat poured down her armpits, and she trembled in silence fearing what might soon befall them. She must remain vigilant or she might find herself torn from her brothers.

Something jolted her awake again, as if a pike had been thrust up her spine. She realized she had nearly fallen off the bench. Tommy moaned and fidgeted into a more comfortable position at her side, the heavy warmth of his body and deep, regular breathing, reminding her to stay alert. It seemed silly to sit so still here on the bench. No one had told them to, yet since Dubois's return, neither had anyone bothered to say anything to them.

Van sat next to her rubbing the thumb of one hand against the palm of the other. Lucy tried to get his attention by nudging him with her elbow and whispering in his ear, "What should we do? I don't like this."

The look of warning silenced her. He veered his eyes in the direction of the men at the table. Lucy slowly turned her attention there as well. The younger Indian stared at her, unblinking as if trying to work out some remembrance. Lucy shrank back against the wall. The rough edges of the logs poked against her back, but she sat motionless, until the brave turned his attention back to Dubois. He had resumed the conversation with the blue-jacketed man who had to be some sort of chief by the way the others revered him.

What had started as short sporadic phrases between long pauses as they puffed on their pipes, quickened into long, elaborate conversations with frequent gestures, sometimes directed toward Van, Lucy, and Tommy and sometimes toward other things in the room. Dubois's face was difficult to read; he seemed deferential toward the Indians but kept a face hard as stone. His eyes narrowed as he stroked the bristles covering his chin and jowls. With the bowl of his pipe clenched between his fingers, he motioned to things around the room just as the Indians had done. Dubois appeared to be negotiating some sort of trade by the way he bobbed and cocked his head to one side or shook and gestured his pipe toward various places around the room, sometimes toward Lucy and her brothers.

At last one of the Indians, the tall blue jacket, rose from his seat and walked over to the bench where she sat with her brothers. Lucy averted her eyes to the floor then peered up quickly at Van when she felt his hand reach over and grasp her trembling fingers. What had Dubois told these braves about them? Toward the end of the day, Peg and Auguste had been strangely aloof, even brusque, as they completed their chores and were fed supper. She recalled the words Auguste had said to her that very morning at the spring,

Would Dubois have brought these Indians here to trade them away? Such tales had been told. Sometimes the captives were returned, sometimes not. The memories Van shared earlier mingled with the terrifying dreams. She had not been truthful in saying she didn't remember those fearful days her father's fort teemed with women and children all huddled together. Someone often held her close when she cried or trembled in fright. Someone had taken her away one day. Not from the fort. No. It had been somewhere else. The bloodied glen. The wisps of scalped hair and that word—wendigo. It came to her clear as the crystal water from the spring that morning. She had survived when others hadn't. Why had no one told her? Auguste said wendigo was evil…some sort of monster. Was it this man? Or was it a magic word that held him at bay?

She bit her lip until she tasted the metallic tinge of blood. Blue Jacket inched nearer; the odor of gamey fur, leather, and oily sweat underscored the pipe smoke. He would kill them all now, finish what he had started once long ago. How she knew this she couldn't say, but she knew. The word could save her, but her mouth wouldn't move. Van stirred and tensed as if ready to strike. She squeezed his hand and leaned in to him, willing him to do nothing. She could save them. She had done this before, long ago. Or, someone else had been her protector, her savior. Who?

The arms she recalled were a vague sensation, more like a gentle summer breeze upon her face than a memory to which she could put words and a sense of time. Was it Mother? No, she would have been holding Tommy, who was a tiny baby then. That's what Van remembered too. It might have been Elzey or Zack, but often, of late, in dreams strange and haunting, she saw a different face that felt singular yet familiar with arms comforting her.

"There, my sweet Lucy, be not afraid. Nothin's gonna harm you, not while I'm here." In certain dreams of late, the voice was there. The breath, sweet and comforting against her ear, was none other than that of Ben Stephenson. Whether these dreams echoed childhood memories or more present yearnings, neither served to be of much aid to her just now. He was not here. She had lied to him that last day at the trading post. Why should he want to help her?

"Hush little baby, don't say a word. Papa's gonna buy you a mockingbird."

Someone sang that song to her once. Mama? Ester? Papa? It could have been anyone.

The Indian stood before them now, only inches away. Lucy stared straight ahead and tried to look past him. Van's grip on her fingers tightened. His other arm drew around her. She in turn held Tommy ever closer. Still heavy in slumber, he somehow managed to stay blissfully oblivious to each dire moment of their sojourn, Lucy both resented and blessed the moments that allowed her little brother these respites.

Blue Jacket moved slowly past each one of them. He touched a ruddy finger across Tommy's cheek, then across the top of Lucy's head. Van flinched and his breathing slowed. His fingers dug into Lucy's palm, squeezing her fingers into a vise. Then just as slowly as he approached, the chief turned around to gaze for a moment at Auguste scraping bits of flesh off the underside of a beaver skin on the other side of the room. He spoke something to him that sounded only like a guttural murmur. Auguste paused in his task to motion toward the children and comment in return. The Indian nodded while puffing on his pipe and then made a slow return to the table.

The other men continued to converse with Dubois. Lucy strained to understand even a single word to learn their fate. She wished they would leave so perhaps she or Van could speak with Dubois—unless he, too, was not really out to help them. Perhaps the point all along was to trap them here, sell them to the Shawnee, never to see their home or family again.

More gestures between Indians and Frenchman, pointing at them, shaking their heads, laughing, arguing. More strange gibberish wafted throughout the corners of the room along with the haze of smoke that swirled in hypnotic curls. Choking fingers clutched in a menacing primordial dance taunting them as the firelight cast grotesque shadows on the rutted walls.

Peg stood, setting aside her task, and spoke to the Indians in lilting tones. She still held a knife in her hand from cutting the threads of her weaving from the loom. She then turned to her son and spoke to him, gesturing with the knife and pointing toward the children and then the loft. He dutifully put down his tools and beaver skin and yawned, crossed the room, and climbed the ladder. Peg returned to look at Lucy and Van and motioned to them as well. When they did not move, she padded over to the bench still holding the knife and tried to lift Tommy from Lucy's side. Lucy closed her eyes and clung ever tighter to him, fearing the worst and preparing for the end of everything. Perhaps they were to be taken away now, or was only Tommy to go with these men? She would not allow it. She would not entertain anything worse than that. Not yet. No.

Van must have sensed it too, for he released her hand and threw an arm across both Lucy and Tommy, creating a barrier between this woman and his family.

"No, go away," he shouted. "You can't have him. Leave us alone."

Lucy turned and curled around little Tommy, tears streaming down her cheeks in great heaving sobs. She wanted to grab him and run, but where would they go? Between their seat and the sole door of the cabin was the table with the three men.

Someone else was speaking loudly. At first it didn't sound like her voice, then she realized it was her own.

"Wendigo. Wendigo." Words tumbled from her mouth, strange and wanton, unbidden, like a stream of cooling water pouring from the earth. She began to kick her feet and batter the bench. Van encased her in her arms. His whispers warmed her ear, incomprehensible but there, mingled with the dull moans of being thrashed against. At last, Van's arm relaxed and Lucy opened her eyes. Tommy stirred at her side and clung to her.

"Lucy? What's happening?"

Peg backed away. The Indian braves rose from the table and walked toward the door with Dubois without giving them a second glance. At the door Blue Jacket paused and turned to face them again. He shook his head with a quizzical smile before turning to leave.

Dubois spoke briefly to the men outside before Lucy heard them mount their horses and ride away. When the fur trapper returned to the cabin he held a small bundle. A mischievous smile curled his lips. "Are you children planning to stay up all night? Peg has asked you to retire, and still you persist in sitting there. This little one is already asleep." He pointed to Tommy. "And you, *ma chérie*, must be quite exhausted after that little...ah...episode? You had my guests quite amused by your antics."

"What?" Lucy looked at the man incredulously.

"Well if you insist on sitting on a cold, hard log all the night long," he shrugged and shook his head, "who am I to say otherwise? Suit yourselves. It has been a long day. We will talk tomorrow."

Van stood. "Sir, we thought that…those Indians… Why were they here?"

"You wanted me to learn of *le rogue* who left you and steal your things, no?" Dubois arched an eyebrow and inclined his head toward them. The bundle swung lazily by his side. Lucy saw it was a deer-hide sack cinched together at the top with a leather thong.

"Yes, sir," she said. "We want very much to know, but we thought…" Lucy wasn't sure how to explain the ordeal she had just been through. It seemed insulting to imply such evil intent. Her face was heated from the odd behavior and fears still haunting her thoughts.

Dubois looked a bit puzzled then his face brightened and he let out a hearty laugh. *"Ah, mais oui.* You children think I let Indians scalp you, no?" He made a guttural sound in his throat and slashed a finger across his neck. "Or, maybe you think I trade you off to them, never to be seen again, eh?"

"Umm." Van and Lucy looked at each other.

Tommy yawned and stretched. "You wouldn't do that, would you Mr. Dubois, sir?"

Again he flung his head back with a hearty laugh and swung the leather pouch lightly at his side. "Non, *mon cher.* I would not do such a thing. Here, catch." He threw the leather pouch toward Van who caught it easily.

"What's this?" he said.

Dubois inclined his head toward them. "Take a look. It won't bite you. I think you will be rather pleased."

Van cautiously loosened the drawstrings and peered inside. The expression on his face changed from reticence to incredulity and finally to joy. Slowly he pulled from the leather pouch a string of blue and white pearls with a pendant bearing the likeness of a woman carved in the stone.

Lucy drew in a quick breath, unable to speak. Tommy clapped his hands. "Lucy, it's Grandma's necklace. The Dutch Lady!"

"Is everything else there, too?" Van looked sidelong at Jacques and then at Lucy. "All the other things we'll need?"

"See for yourselves." Dubois inclined his head with a wink.

Van reached in again and brought out a round brass object, the size of his palm. "The compass! My knife! And..."

"Papa's map." Tommy jumped up and threw his arms around Lucy and then Van. "We can find Uncle Joseph now?"

"But...not the copy of the ledger," Van muttered, hopelessly. "Without that we'll have no proof to show Uncle Joseph."

Lucy held out her hand to claim the necklace. "But we have all we need. Maybe the proof doesn't matter so much anymore. Or... we'll find some other way. There's always another way." She held the Dutch Lady to her chest and offered a grateful smile to Jacques Dubois. "Thank you, sir." She tried to swallow, but her tongue still felt thick and dry. "Who were those men? That one man...in the blue tunic."

"Ah! You mean Chief Weyapiersehnwah? *Oui*, some *do* call him Blue Jacket."

Van and Lucy exchanged a wide-eyed stare.

"You know him? *Excusez-moi*. I should have introduced you." He chuckled and grimaced as if in self-deprecation, though the glint in his eye said otherwise. *"Je suis négligent.* I am...as you say remiss?"

"He didn't look any too friendly," Van said. "We do know who he is."

"Ah, I imagine you would. His fame is quite known, as is your father's, no? The great Indian Fighter, he. No?"

"Y-you know who our father was?" Lucy ventured.

"Oui, mademoiselle. Le ranger Brady. Capitaine Van Swearingen. I do know well their dealings." He made a tsking sound with his tongue. "Such terrible things done in those days. My Peg," he gestured toward her his wife with a warm smile, "her family was lost to a terrible battle. The camp destroyed. Blue Jacket fought to save them but alas..." His words drifted into a shrug.

"Our father did that?" Van spoke barely above a whisper.

Dubois sighed and sank into the chair by the table. "It was a terrible time. Many horrible deeds and too much killing. Blue Jacket had his ways too." He picked up a knife from the table and started to put it back in its sheath but paused to gesture it toward Lucy. "But I think you remember this, no?"

The knife might as well have slashed through her, for the almost tangible tear she felt in her soul. "I think so."

"Wendigo?" He squinted at her. "Where did you learn such a word? And the others? You speak very good Shawnee."

"I...was speaking Shawnee?" Lucy's mouth hung open.

Van took a step back. "Is that what that was? It sounded like Latin ...but not exactly. Just some sort of gibberish."

"*Oui*, there was some of the Latin mass mixed in there too. Though I admit, it has been some time since I heard the words of our Mother Church. Far too long, I suppose. *Dona nobis pacem?"*

"Lord, grant us peace." She had been saying that prayer, the Latin prayer, that Reverend Godbey had taught her. But where had the other words come from?

"We're no Papists," Van stood tall, defensive.

"Quiet, Van," Lucy warned. To Jacques she turned a questioning look. "I don't understand. Why?"

After putting the knife in its sheath and returning it to his belt, he started gathering the discarded pipes and tobacco from the table. "There is a tale among the Shawnee, *ma chérie*, of a maid who came to these woods some years back. A young thing captured by *le Blue Jacket's* men. The purpose was to...," he paused as if to check his words, "well, perhaps it's best not to know."

"They stole her away?" Van finished. "They tried to kill her? My sister?"

A slight incline of Jacques's head and a squeeze of his eyes affirmed his words. Lucy felt the floor shift. Her head swam in smoky colors. "You knew?"

"I didn't...not for certain." Van rubbed his head. "Zack told me never to say, warned me even, that should I ever say, they'd..."

"What?" Lucy clenched her fists, rage building again with a primal desire to pummel him with her fists, anything to get the words kept from her for far too long. "They took me away? And no one did anything about it? I was to be a...a...""We got you back, didn't we?" Van recoiled back as her foot swung toward his leg. "Somehow... I don't really recollect. But we must've. Hey! No need to hurt me."

"Eh! *Mes enfants.* Children. *Assez.* Enough." Jacques held a hand between them to stop the scuffle. "This one is a little fighter, no?" He wagged a finger at Lucy, who hung her head. "It is what the chief remembers, too."

"The chief?" Van and Lucy both chorused.

"Remembers me?" Lucy whispered. "Please, Monsieur, what was the tale you started to tell? The one about the maid. It was me?"

"Oui," Dubois said, tenderly. "I don't expect you remember. The Shawnee were on a raiding party that night, bent on killing and taking as many of the white man's tribe as had been taken from theirs. Chief Weywapiersenwah, the one some call Blue Jacket, was leading them. They gathered many from a settlement, women, children... Most were slaughtered save for one wee little maid. She fought back, spoke in the most fluent of Shawnee and called upon a terrible beast to save her."

"The wendigo?" Lucy barely moved her lips, but Dubois heard her.

"Yes, *ma chérie.* The wendigo."

"But, Auguste said it was something evil, *mauvais,* horrible." Lucy shuddered thinking of the beastly face her Indian friend made earlier that morning. It seemed a thousand years ago now.

"Perhaps," Dubois weighed with his hands. "But there is another legend of a young Shawnee maid who stood up to the wendigo that came into the camp of her family and scared her brothers away. Only she remained calm and welcomed him to her fireside, called him her grandfather and gave him shelter in their tent. Well, so surprised was this monster so pleased to be at last welcomed to someone's home that he became flustered and sat beside the fire." Dubois leaned in, clearly pleased at captivating his small audience of listeners. "As you see, it was a cold winter's eve and sitting there by the fire he began to melt and below his beastly facade was indeed the girl's grandfather."

"But that's just a story, a fairy tale," Lucy insisted. "It can't be true." But how could she have known perfect Shawnee? It was impossible.

"Ah! But is it?" Dubois spoke with a mischievous gleam. "Do you know why the chief spared you when he did not spare others? Why he came here tonight?"

Lucy shook her head, not sure she wanted to hear, and yet she did.

She couldn't think any more of those who were not saved but wanted to make sense of why she alone was spared.

"It was our father's men who saved her," Van spouted back proudly. "He would have done anything to bring you home, Lucy. And he did."

"'Tis true some say he was there that night, the great Injun Fighter, *non?*" Dubois conceded. "All that matters is that the chief saw that you were brave, that you were a wise and clever child. That you were not afraid to call upon *les chiens d'enfer*, the hounds of hell, the *chenoo*, the *paillisa*, and the wendigo, if necessary, to save you. He knew the legend of the other young maid, and he was fearful you may indeed be some special child protected by her spirit grandfather or by *le grand Cautantowwit*, who watches over all. He would have taken you in, raised you as his own, had it not been for those who intervened. I do not know exactly who, but I suppose someone from your settlement did. You were returned and never seen again, until now."

Was it her own father who had saved her? She considered Jacques's story and a sense of comfort, as if strong arms held her close, whispered in her ear, *"All is well, all is good."*

"There was another word, besides the wendigo, I keep remembering," she said, thinking of the great horned beast that spirited her away in its talons, flying across the sky. "It has a name similar to Peg's."

Dubois's eyes widened in surprised understanding. *"Les Paillissa? Oui!* My Peg is named for the great flying beast, the sky horse. In French we say *Pégase*. And so I call her Peg, *ma chére*, Peggy." He tossed an affectionate smile toward his wife. "Much easier to say, *non?"*

"Pégase? Sky horse." Lucy puzzled out the words. "Like a Pegasus? A horse with wings?"

"Oui!" Jacques said. "But, more fierce, a four-legged bird, *n'est-ce pas?* A terrible, strong creature, with the steadfast horns of the stag, the brave nobility of a lion, and the strong protective wings of the eagle. When provoked, it can be a most fearsome thing and most dangerous. But those who seek to understand its ways will find a true and loving protector. 'Tis much like my Peg." He winked affectionately at his woman.

And like me? Lucy wondered if she would ever truly be as brave, strong, protective, and beloved as this woman, who had lived up so admirably to her name.

"But you did find the preacher?" Van asked, impatiently. "The thief who took our things? How did you?"

"He happened to come across a band of Iroquois. They managed to...acquire a sort of trade with him." Dubois shrugged. "It does not matter the details. We have returned your possessions and all is as it should be."

"Blue Jacket came to trade them with you...for us," Lucy said. "Didn't he? He wanted...us in return?"

"Ah, you are indeed a clever and perceptive child. But then you know Shawnee, *non?*" Dubois gave her an appreciative gleam. "He drives a hard bargain, that one. But in the end I persuaded him to take my beaver hat, a side of pork, and a blanket Peg will weave for him. In exchange your things are returned to their proper owners."

"Thank you," all three children echoed in unison.

"You are most welcome." Dubois patted each one on the head in turn. "Although, life among the Shawnee is not so bad. You all would have been well cared for. Even now, my Peg would take you in. Auguste has wanted brothers and sisters. My woman would like a fine daughter. What do you say, eh?"

The short gown, petticoat, and cornhusk moccasins remained on the chair in the corner of the cabin. Guilt washed over Lucy for having misunderstood the woman's intentions. Could it be so bad to have worn it for even a day? With eyes still peeled on the untouched clothing, she asked, "Is that why she wanted me to dress as a girl?"

"Ah, *oui, mademoiselle.*" Dubois slapped his knee and winked again at his wife. "It is the Shawnee way. To accept their clothing you take on a new life, become a member of the tribe. She has wanted a daughter ever since...well, no matter now. Such things are in the past and not for telling on such a happy day." He shared a wistful smile with his wife that made Lucy wonder what they had lost, but she did not feel it right to ask.

Van and Lucy exchanged a silent understanding. To live here, among these people who had taken them in, cared for them when they had no reason to, and accepted them completely for who they were, asking nothing in return but to become one of them, gave her pause. "Mr. Shepherd or Mr. Newhouse would never find me here," Lucy observed, with a soft laugh.

"No, I don't suppose he would," Van retorted. "But then, you'd have to marry an Injun someday. Is that what you'd want? We have our own family, Lucy. Our own people."

Lucy crossed her arms. "Who says I have to marry anyone?"

Dubois wagged a finger at them. "Now, don't say such things. It is not so bad to live with us."

"No, it can't be worse than Mr. Shepherd. I'd sooner marry a wendigo." Lucy made a fierce face. "Or live with *paillissa* in its lair."

They all shared in the laughter and more stories about the strange creatures that lived farther west beyond the Great Rivers before retiring to bed.

CHAPTER 29

"Can't we stop here? My head hurts."

Tommy did not appear to be getting any better. Since leaving the Duboises' cabin, his cough was noticeably worse. This morning Lucy felt his flushed face only to draw back her hand at the intense heat in his once plump cheeks. After a week of wandering with little to eat, he had grown far too thin and pale. Surely they would arrive in Shepherds Town soon. Uncle Joseph would see to proper care for them all, including Tommy. Uncle Joseph could hear their story and help their cause. This thought alone kept her hope alive and feet moving forward.

But Shepherds Town was still miles away, close to a day's journey or more by Van's estimation. Jacques and Auguste Dubois had traveled along as far as Springer's Creek, then set them on alone. The Frenchman had assured them that if they followed the creek it would lead to the road to Shepherds Town. The long road stretched before them. Lucy wondered if perhaps remaining with the Dubois family might not have been such a bad idea. She steeled herself against such thoughts and tried to focus on finding a way back home and facing their problems bravely.

Tommy rubbed his eyes and tripped along behind Lucy. Not even the occasional forest creature or unusual rock formation could amuse and divert his attention now. Last night the wind had turned, bringing in a northerly chill. Though it was now April, it had been known to snow even after spring planting had begun. Lucy scanned the sky noting the swirling soup clouds overhead. Perhaps they could make it to the next settlement before nightfall.

"There now Tommy, mind you keep up." Lucy's cheerful, light tone belied the fears she fought inside.

"I wanna stop now." Tommy rubbed his eyes, stumbling along behind Lucy. "Please, can't I just lie down for a bit?"

Van stopped and studied his younger brother carefully. "Just a bit farther, Tom, and we'll be to the next settlement. Maybe someone will put us up for the night in their barn."

"He's not well, Van," Lucy's voice echoed the concern on her older brother's face. "He needs to rest now."

"He needs a warm bed and some doctoring, too, Lucy, but not much chance of finding that out here. No, we gotta keep pressing onward. It can't be more than ten or twenty miles to Shepherds Town. There may be a good size settlement or at least a homestead not far ahead." Van paused as he looked down the road. "Maybe even a surgeon to tend him."

"Maybe we should have stayed a while longer at Mr. Dubois's cabin." Lucy pushed the curls away from Tommy's forehead and brushed her fingers across his flushed, clammy skin. "He did say his head hurt. Maybe if we had paid more mind to him then."

"No use in looking back now. It was time to leave that place. We stayed two days longer than we should've." He squatted down to lift Tommy onto his back. The boy let out a weak, grateful moan. "I don't think I could've stood it much longer."

"If we hadn't been fortunate enough to find our way there...if Auguste hadn't come upon us when he did...," Lucy drew in a breath. "They did help us get our things back and offered us hospitality."

"Some of our things, only." Van hoisted Tommy higher on his back and strained under the load. "T'would have been better to have the rifle, the axe, and..."

"The ledger?" Lucy spoke the words she knew Van wouldn't say and just as soon wished she hadn't.

Van's face clouded. "And everything else that was rightfully ours."

"Mr. Dubois did try." Lucy picked up the discarded sack filled with meager provisions from the fur trapper and his wife. "He parlayed with the Shawnee and went to great lengths to convince them to return even the map and Grandmother's necklace and our sack of coins. I think he figured these things would mean the most to us."

"Aye, so the Injuns kept my rifle, our food, and...everything else." He whirled around at Lucy. "Oh, but we got our bit of coin and your precious necklace, as if that could help us out here, as if that could make Tommy well so I wouldn't have to carry him. The map's the only truly useful thing we have now. And that may not help much." He turned worried eyes toward the sky and drew his coat tighter around him.

Lucy stared at her brother not knowing what to say next. "When we get to Uncle Joseph's house, all will be well." She said this more to convince herself than Van, though hearing the words aloud had little effect in either case.

"He *is* mighty warm, Lucy." Van cocked his head back and adjusted the small boy's flushed hands. Tommy grasped his brother around the neck.

"Just a mite." Lucy tried to sound matter-of-fact, but her voice came forth in an abrupt snap. "It was just the chill last night is all." What was that plant Mother always brewed into a tea when they had a fever? If only she had paid more attention, though there was little chance of finding it in the woods this time of year.

Lucy trudged alongside her brothers. Tommy moaned softly, falling into bouts of sleep with ragged breath. A thick drool slobbered out of the corner of his lips and trickled down Van's woolen sleeve.

Timepiece or no, it was clearly midday and time for a rest. Van had continued to carry Tommy without complaint.

"This here's a good place." Van nodded toward a small clearing off of the path. A large sycamore tree offered a shady spot, and a thick twisted root beckoned to them as an inviting place to sit and rest their weary backs.

Lucy breathed a sigh of relief and let the knapsack fall in a thud at her feet. Her body felt so achy and then weightless, followed by an imbalance at letting go of the counterweight, and she nearly fell over onto a patch of dry leaves and grass.

Van had not seen her stumble as he was letting go of his own burden at the time. Lucy quickly regained her composure and helped settle a drowsy Tommy to the soft mossy ground at the base of the tree. She felt his forehead again and frowned at the heat emanating from his skin even before she made contact. She stared at Van, who met her eyes with a look that registered hopelessness and frustration before he turned away to set up camp.

"You mean to bed down here for the night?" Lucy trusted Van implicitly but wondered what he was thinking.

Van thought a bit, his brows knitting into a furrowed twitch. "I'd like to make it a bit farther, but we may not have much choice."

Tommy let out a whimper and grasped a trembling hand to his throat. "I'm cold…hurts…wanna drink."

Lucy pulled the water skin from her shoulder and tried to offer a few sips to Tommy's burning mouth. He drank a little, but Lucy knew from his wince that it was painful to swallow.

"Do you think he has the ague?"

"No telling what he has. He's sick, that's for certain. We've got to get him to shelter and out of the night air." Van was looking at a distant point beyond the spot where they rested beneath the sycamore.

Lucy scanned the dense thicket beyond the clearing but saw only trees. Then her eyes caught a ridged shape covered with bracken and overgrowth deep within the trees. "Van, what do you suppose…?"

Van chewed the inside of his lip a moment, the way he always did when he had an idea. "Looks to be a homestead. I'm gonna go see who lives there. Maybe they can help us." He rested his hand on the knife tucked at his waist and set off in long strides across the clearing and disappeared into the thicket.

Lucy turned to ease Tommy's fretting and sat close so his head rested against her shoulder. He shivered and complained again of being cold, despite the heat that radiated from his body. It felt like hot coals searing against Lucy's flesh. Lucy kept her sight focused on the distant grove of trees into which her older brother had vanished.

The afternoon sun had begun its lengthening of shadows from the trees when Lucy heard a rustle from the direction of the cabin. Van's lithe form appeared from out of the thicket and strolled over to their spot.

"Well, what did you find? Was anyone at home? Will they help us?" Lucy was relieved to see him but disappointed that he had returned alone. Perhaps no one was willing to help three stranded children, one sick maybe with the plague.

"It's an abandoned cabin, but it will do to give us shelter and allow Tommy to rest for the night."

Lucy parted her lips to say something, but Van interrupted as if reading her thoughts.

"We've got no choice, Lucy. We gotta stop here. Tommy needs a proper roof tonight. It don't seem anyone lives there now or has in quite some time. I reckon we'll be safe."

They gathered their belongings and headed toward their lodging for the night. Lucy and Van each held one of Tommy's hands and coaxed him along between them. Closer now Lucy could see that this was indeed an abandoned cabin, perhaps built by some long-ago settler who grew weary of backbreaking frontier life and decided to return to the security of some eastern town. Or perhaps a fur trader or adventurer bravely forsook this woodland hollow to forge deeper into western territory down the Ohio. Lucy mused over these things as Van dug out his knife to hack away at the brambles covering the doorway.

"Wonder who lived here?" Lucy picked at the vines and twigs with her hands.

"Who knows?" Van shrugged as he made some headway at clearing the area around the door. "Maybe some poor family got carried off by Indians. Seems likely no one's lived here since before Methuselah, so I don't 'spect they'll be coming back anytime soon."

"Not all Indians are bad, Van. We'd still be lost had it not been for Auguste and his family." Lucy still marveled at all the years she had been taught to fear and hate Indians only to learn things look different from another's point of view. "He saved us from the likes of Mr. Weedon. We'd have surely lost everything had Auguste not come our way. That preacher was certainly more savage than Dubois and his kind."

"Not all Indians are like Auguste or Peg. Not all white men can be trusted either, else we wouldn't be running from John Newhouse."

Van spat out the last few words as if they were putrid meat. Lucy was surprised to hear her brother refer to their mother's new husband by his given name. Till now, he had been either Mr. Newhouse or Stepfather to them. Perhaps her brother was growing into a man before her very eyes. After all they had taken on more responsibility and shouldered more burdens than most children their age tackled on the frontier. Had she likewise changed so much? She paused in picking away a tough bramble root and flicked away a strand of her short hair from her face.

Once most of the dead brush and overgrowth had been cleared from the doorway of the cabin, they were able to pry open the front door. Little Tom lay still under a wool cloak nestled by a hollow log. His breathing was growing increasingly raspy and labored. A deep cough had settled in his chest.

Van heaved him onto his shoulder and carried him into the cabin. Inside, the smell of a dirt floor and mustiness met Lucy's nostrils. The single room was about half the size of the Swearingen kitchen. One narrow window covered with tattered oilcloth permitted the only real light source, and small streams of light filtered through tiny holes in the worn cloth. Opposite the window stood a hearth covered in ashes with remnants of a few bits of charred wood from the last occupant's fire. Although the mud chinking was deteriorated in places allowing pinpricks of light to filter through, the cabin remained a sturdy shelter. The dwelling was bare, save for a lone puncheon bench crudely constructed from a half-hewn log and a rusted iron kettle hanging from a hook over the hearth.

Lucy busied herself with arranging a bed for Tom while outside Van sought suitable kindling for a fire. Soon the cabin warmed with the glow of the hearth as twilight settled in the woods. It felt good to be sheltered once again in spite of the mean conditions. Only a few miles more to Shepherds Town, Lucy hoped. They might have arrived at Uncle Joseph's that very night had it not been for Tommy, but Lucy pushed that thought aside.

The older children continued to ready the cabin in silence. The only sound was Tommy's restless babbling and fevered moans. Lucy willed herself not to think about the consequences if they did not find help in time or Tom continued to get worse. Finally, she broke the silence as she portioned out their meager supper of small bits of cheese, biscuit, and parched corn—the few rations Peg had packed in a sack before sending them on their way.

"Will we try to get started early in the morning? Maybe a good night's rest will break Tom's fever and—" Lucy spoke as she handed a piece of cheese and biscuit to Van who interrupted before taking a bite.

"Lucy, we need to get help for Little Tom. I reckon I can make Shepherds Town alone in about a day." Van went back to poking the fire with a long stick as he mulled over a plan. "Thing is you'll need to stay here with Tommy. I'll leave you enough supplies to get by for at least a day or so." Lucy looked at him with alarm. The thought of staying here alone with a very sick little boy gripped her in fear.

"Mayhap you needn't go all the way to Shepherds Town. If there be a settlement or cabin along the way... Mayhap we could..." Lucy ventured this thought trying hard to steady her voice. She would not have Van thinking her not brave enough to stay behind, but what if Tommy got worse? How would she care for him alone?

Van shook his head and leveled his look at his younger sister. "Near as I can reckon Shepherds Town is the nearest settlement. We've got to chance it. It's the only way." He stood up from the fire, now blazing. It cast a soft golden glow around the dark cabin. Outside creatures chirped a cheerful cadence as nightfall descended on their woodland dwelling. "Both of us staying here won't make Tommy any better. What if he should—"

"Don't you say it!" Lucy spat the words out and jumped at Van, her fists clenched in balls. She wasn't sure how she would stop the words that echoed her thoughts. He was abandoning her and she'd be left with a sick, possibly dying, little boy. She wanted to plug her ears to shut out the words or clamp his mouth shut before they were even uttered.

"Don't be afraid, Luce. We've come this far, ain't we? I got Zack's map and the knife. I'll lay low in the woods like we've been doing and get help back here soon as I can."

"I'm *not* afraid!" Lucy lifted her chin sharply and straightened herself to her full height. "And don't say ain't. Use proper gentlemen's English."

A sardonic smile eased across Van's face as he shook his head and laughed. "Little Lucy Locket, you are a puzzlement. We've run away from home, stolen our stepfather's ledger, defied our elders, nearly got ourselves captured by Injuns, and you're worried about proper grammar?"

Lucy saw the nonsense in her reaction but was fighting for some sense of control in a situation far beyond her element. She felt anger flooding up from deep within and wanted to lash out at someone… anyone. With her fist still clenched she raised her right arm to strike at her brother. But Van was quicker ducking just before her thin knuckles hit him squarely in the jaw. With his left hand he grabbed her wrist firmly deflecting the punch and twisted her arm safely down to her side. To ensure that she did not try again with her left fist, he reached out with his right hand pinning both arms securely at her side.

"Lucy, STOP! This won't make any difference! Lord Almighty!" he yelled as she tried kicking him with the toe of her boot. Now the helplessness of their situation, the desperate peril they had thus far survived, and the despair over losing so many loved ones loomed before young Lucy: Zack, Father, now possibly Tommy. Van was planning to leave her. Ben Stephenson, too, would no longer be there when they returned home. Why thoughts of him occurred at this moment only angered Lucy more. Then there was their mother's increasing distance and Mr. Newhouse's cruelty, suddenly all the events tumbled down as if the logs of this shabby cabin were crumbling on top of her. Van's strong, roughened hands kept her wrists pinned to her side. Her wrists ached from his pinching hold but not nearly so much as the sharp pain that stabbed at her chest as she tried to keep sobs from escaping and opening the floodgates of so many tears held back far too long.

Van's eyes softened with understanding and compassion. "Whoa there, Lucy," he spoke soothingly as if he gentling one of his high-spirited ponies. For a moment his voice sounded strangely older, deeper, with confidence and authority. For a moment, only a brief moment, Lucy thought she heard an echo of Zack's voice calming her when she was a small child, or her father's own voice from some distant and more primeval memory. Finally, the floodgates could hold no more and her slim body shook with heaving sobs. Tears streamed down her face, hot and stinging. Not since that moment weeks ago at the creek the day Zack was buried had she relented to her pain and despair—that day when she had been walking with Benjamin Stephenson.

Van slowly released his hold on her wrists and wrapped his arms around her holding her close to his chest. She melted against him digging her small, dirty fingers into his wool vest. After a few moments of wracking sobs she pulled away wiping her face with her hands. Van looked at her helplessly as if not knowing what to say.

Lucy brushed her hands across her face and shrugged. "You are right, Van," she looked over at Tom again as he stirred and moaned. "It's the only way." She bent down to tuck the cloak around her little brother. "I will look after Tommy. Just you mind your way and come back to us safe and sound."

Van was awake before daybreak preparing for the day's journey ahead. Little was said between brother and sister as they ate their meager rations of cheese and dried biscuit. He had found a small stream near the cabin and was able to catch a couple small fish expertly using a hook and line. Then he headed off through the woods toward the road leading to Shepherds Town. Lucy watched from the path they had cleared in front of the cabin only the day before. When she could see him no longer she turned her attention to the day ahead.

First she tended the fire making sure it stayed lit through the day. She and Van had spent several hours the day before collecting a pile of wood and kindling now contained in one corner of the cabin near the hearth. Next, she turned her attention to the fish, cleaning them with the small piece of flint kept with the tin of char cloth for starting fires. When she checked Tommy she was startled to learn that his fever had not gone down and he was hotter than ever to the touch. Keeping a cool cloth on his head seemed to soothe his restless thrashing but did little else for him. Van was right, he needed a physician and needed one quick. Lucy mumbled a silent prayer that Van be safe and return swiftly with help.

By late afternoon Tommy was drifting in and out of fevered sleep. He babbled incoherently and did not seem to know where he was. He called for his mother over and over and did not seem to recognize Lucy. She quieted him the best she could with singing and recounting their journey and relating Van's plan to find Shepherds Town and return with help.

When she could think of nothing else to say she began to tell him stories. First she retold the tales he had always loved before bedtime. After that she recounted the story of the wendigo and the Indian girl that Dubois had told them. Having finished that she searched for another tale to describe. She thought of the book Ben Stephenson had loaned her about the man who traveled to such strange places.

"There once was a man named Telemachus who set out on a quest to find his father." Lucy affected her cheeriest voice, the one that always delighted Tommy so, even though just at the moment she didn't feel cheerful.

She wished she had a book from her father's collection or one of her favorite books: *The Persian Tales*, *The Vicar of Wakefield*, or *Robinson Crusoe*. Finally, she chided herself for such nonsense, wishing for novels to read. If any books were available surely something on herbals to treat fevers would do her and Tom more good right now. But the season was too early anyway to find enough growing plants to be of use, and the thought of leaving Tommy for any length of time, was not pleasant.

Thus Lucy passed the afternoon keeping a watchful eye upon her youngest brother. By nightfall his fevered delirium was growing more fretful and his breathing was increasingly raspy and labored. He refused to take any of the sips of broth she had boiled, left from cooking the fish Van caught. Propping him up she made him breathe the steam from the boiling liquid in the cup to soothe his raspy throat. She wasn't sure if this would really help, but she remembered her mother doing this two winters ago when Tom had the croup.

She thought about the surgeon's common treatment of bleeding. She did have a sharp piece of flint. Did she dare try to ease the fevered blood from her little brother in order to purify his weak body? She studied the sharp piece of flint in her hand. Somehow she could not bring herself to do that.

Long shadows crept across the cabin floor and seeped into the darkening corners. The pinpricks of light filtering through the oilcloth on the window diminished like candle flames slowly dying into the recesses of the wax nubs. She wished for even one small candle to hold and stave off the encroaching darkness. The hearth fire provided the sole source of light and warmth.

An uneasy feeling swept over Lucy as she thought of the long night ahead being alone with a very sick little brother. She thought of the dangers the woods might hold—the panther that stalked their camp only a few nights ago, the strangers who lurked in the shadows. All these silly childish terrors began to take hold and she pushed the lone bench against the cabin door as the only barrier to outside peril. But the fear that gripped her heart the most was the one inside the cabin, the fear of falling asleep only to awaken to a little brother lying still and dead.

Lucy sat as a faithful sentinel beside her younger brother keeping a cool, wet cloth on his head, singing him songs, and reciting Psalms she had learned by heart.

"The Lord is my light and my salvation, whom shall I fear. The Lord is the strength of my life in whom shall I be afraid?" Lucy whispered the words as she wrung out the warm cloth that had absorbed the heat from Tom's fevered body. Dousing it again in the bucket of cool water she pulled back the cloak and wiped the cloth over Tom's flushed chest and neck.

"One thing have I desired of the Lord, that will I seek: that I may dwell in the house of the Lord all the days of my life..."

Lucy thought about the cabin that sheltered her and Tom. She thought about the spacious home their father had built and wondered if she would ever see it again.

"For in the time of trouble He shall hide me in His pavilion, in the secret place of His tabernacle..."

Perhaps providence had led them to this cabin in the woods at just the right moment. What hand had guided them here offering just what they needed—a place for a proper fire, a pot for cooking, and a stream full of fish?

"And now shall mine head be lifted up above mine enemies round about me..."

Mine enemies. Mr. Newhouse, the preacher, the panther, and all those who had brutally attacked and killed friends and loved ones about her, these were her enemies. Even the very sicknesses that claimed the life of her brothers, first Zack and now Tommy, they stood against her. Helplessly she was alone facing that lonesome valley, standing her trial.

"Teach me Thy way, O Lord, and lead me in a plain path because of mine enemies..."

She thought about all the lessons she had learned about strength, about trial. She thought about the Reverend Godbey who had taught her to sing, taught her French and Latin. She thought about Mother gently guiding in her in the art of stitchery. She thought about Noah, Ester, and Tobe, all her friends, and she longed to be back in the warm, cozy kitchen again with Tommy playing his bilbo catcher game and Van and Tobe teasing him. If only all their trials were as simple as trying to place a bilbo ball on a spindle. And yet life was just that precarious, always just missing what we longed for, with happiness and peace just beyond our reach.

She felt like that bilbo ball, swinging out of control, flailing wildly in the air, spun around at some arbitrary divine whim. Again she focused on the Psalm in her head.

"Hear O Lord, when I cry with my voice. Have mercy also upon me and answer me... When my father and mother forsake me, then the Lord will take me up..."

Ester always said the Lord heard her prayers even if she didn't get the answer longed for. Ester, though a slave, always seemed connected to some source of power greater than her own and listened to that small inner voice that guided her ways and always led her on a plain path. Lucy longed to talk with Ester now, but somehow she knew what the wise woman would tell her.

A warm calm melted over Lucy, and her eyes began to droop even as she fought the urge to curl up and drift off to oblivious sleep beside Tommy.

"Hear, O Lord, when I cry with my voice... Hear, O Lord, hear, O Lord... I had fainted unless I had believed... I had believed...wait on the Lord, be of good courage...of good courage...wait on the Lord..."

The red brick house loomed before her across the lush green field. A small garden just off the back door was framed by a picket fence and filled with every savory herb and summer's finest bounty. She was dressed in a clean linen gown walking up the path toward the house. Oh, if only she could reach that house. All would be well.

Someone was waiting for her in the doorway. Someone she knew but did not recognize at first. He was smiling and calling to her to welcome her home. But this was not her home. This was not Swearingen Landing. Yet she longed to enter the house as she had been denied so often before in her dreams.

As she drew closer she now recognized the man in the doorway. It was Mr. Stephenson! What was he doing here? Inside the house was filled with people, some she knew from home some she knew only in her dream. The inside of the house was beautifully decorated with elegant furnishings and painted walls. Everyone seemed to be enjoying a family gathering and all bid her welcome.

Two rooms extended from the entryway. The parlor stood to her left where several elegantly dressed people laughed and chatted. To her right a formal dining room beckoned with a table laden with fine china and delectable foods. She was so hungry. The food smelled delicious. It was just a few feet away. If only she could reach it. Someone was calling her name. At first she thought it was Zack and then it took on a deeper, huskier tone. The walls of the elegant brick house melted and became a forest glen alone. No. She wasn't really alone. Around her were other children, clothed in white, their skin as pale as snow and glowing like the sun. They emerged from the trees like vapor flitting between the shadowy branches. Sometimes a face emerged from the ghostly shapes that she almost recognized as someone she ought to know, but she wasn't quite sure.

"Paillissa, Piusa," the ghost children chanted over and over. "He comes. He comes. Do not fear. Wendigo. Wendigo."

A clap of thunder echoed across the sky and sent the ghostly children hovering back into the trees. She must find shelter from the coming storm too, but her feet would not move. The rain did not come, but the thunder grew louder and then ceased as the great beast she knew from dreams before, landed in the open glen before her. It had the face of a bearded man, antlers like a stag, and a long serpentine tail. Its great red wings were what made the thunderous sound, and its scaly, green body rattled like the sound of rain.

"Red as vengeance. Black as eternal night. Green like the spring that brings hope again," sang the children of the mist, all around her, above her. The beast's massive body and wingspan melted as the man's face lost its beard and the features grew softer and more handsome. An Indian chief stood before her dressed in a...Blue Jacket. He said nothing but swept his hand wide across the stream that now surged through the glen. Another clap of thunder. The children's chanting faded as a sight more horrible emerged. Zack lay dying by the stream, an arrow in his chest, blood pouring from his head. Behind him stood Ben Stephenson holding his musket, powder smoke trailing in the air.

Light filtered through the dingy oilcloth window and fell on Lucy's face. She was still in the abandoned cabin in the woods. Someone was knocking on the door and calling her name. Van was here and others were with him.

"Lucy, wake up. We're here! Uncle Joseph and his man, Phineas, are here to take care of Tom. We're all here now."Uncle Joseph was here. They were safe. Help had finally come for Tommy. Tommy! Where was Tommy? Had he faired the long night? Oh, why had she fallen asleep? What if he had slipped away from her forever and she had not kept her watch?

"Tommy! Where's Tommy?" Lucy bolted up grabbing frantically at the form beside her. The small tow-headed body of her brother was still under the cloak. Lucy's heart leaped into her throat. "Oh, Lord, please God, no!" Her lips moved in silent prayer.

"Lucy, dear! Open the door. It's your Uncle Joseph. I'm here to help you."

Lucy backed away from the still form on the floor, a gray wool shroud with a pair of boots peeking out as the only evidence of her baby brother. If he was truly gone and she'd let him slip away under her watch, she did not want to face the truth alone. With shaky hands she moved the puncheon bench away from the door and lifted the latch. Van's face thrust through the crack. The door burst open emitting a bright stream of daylight followed by the welcoming faces of Uncle Joseph and Van. To her great surprise, also in their wake was Tobe and—of all people—Benjamin Stephenson.

Lucy fell into Uncle Joseph's arms trembling and sobbing. "He's gone. Tommy. His fever was so great...he's not moving. I tried to keep him safe."

"It'll be all right now, Lucy. We're here." Uncle Joseph's voice soothed her. He had dropped his cane and held her close, one hand smoothing her cropped hair.

"He's a mite better, I'd say, and resting right fine," Van's voice washed over her in waves of relief.

She turned to see Ben stooped next to Tommy. He lifted the cloak to reveal a little boy peacefully sleeping with thumb in mouth. "Not a lick of fever as I can tell." Ben winked his eye. "But then never let it be said I know anything about doctoring."More on the order of finding wayward children, I'd say though." Ben knelt beside Tommy and gently moved his hand across the boy's back.

Tommy roused out of his sleep and rubbed his eyes. "Uncle Joseph, Mr. Stephenson, what are you doing here?"

Lucy pulled out of Uncle Joseph's embrace and rushed to the boy's side. She leaned down to touch his rosy face. His breathing, though still a bit labored, was steady and deep. His skin was much cooler and his shirt was drenched in sweat. He was going to be all right. Uncle Joseph was here and their long journey had ended. Somehow she knew this just as Ester had always told her—the Lord had been her light, her salvation. He had tarried with her through the night, with Tommy too. She felt strength and joy welling up inside of her.

Uncle Joseph tended to Tommy while Phineas and Tobe laid out fresh baked bread, milk, and cheese. Uncle Joseph explained that a wagon awaited to take them all back to the Swearingen home near Shepherds Town.

Ben eyed Lucy suspiciously. "I see we've adopted a new style. Is this what is fashionable for fine ladies in the West these days?"

She remembered she was still dressed as a boy in her brother's outgrown clothes. Feeling awkward and exposed with her gangly legs shooting out beneath knee breeches, she looked down at the floor and dug the toe of her boot into the dirt.

"Near as I can recall, the last time I laid eyes on this fair lass she was standing in my storeroom purchasing a knapsack for a maimed brother to tote around." Ben squinted at her with his arms folded across his chest, but the corners of his mouth curved in mischievous delight. "You got any inkling where that young lady might a gone off to?"

Uncle Joseph shook his head. "Well I never would have expected this niece of mine would've come from a fine lady like Eleanor, but she sure is cut from the same Swearingen cloth as her pa, as I can tell."

"A Swearingen's a Swearingen, be they lass or lad," Ben added with a teasing grin. "'Tis not the first knobby-kneed lass I've seen in breeches, to be sure."

Both men chuckled, releasing a ripple of laughter that echoed throughout the room. Lucy blinked in surprise, wondering just what other lass he might be referring to.

"Stop it now!" Lucy stamped her foot and pulled the coat close around her. The men might have their fun and make light of her odd attire and knobby knees, but surely her mother would have a thing or two to say once word got back, as it surely would. If only the preacher hadn't stolen everything, including the gown she had intended to don before reaching Uncle Joseph's house.

Lucy looked over to see Uncle Joseph smiling with a twinkle in his eye. "Well, I'm certain my Biddy will find appropriate raiment for my pretty niece. In the meantime, you seem to have been well suited for trekking the wild wood, as you three brave adventurers have done thus far."

Lucy was greatly relieved to know that all matters were to be tended to in due time. Uncle Joseph would be in contact with a lawyer friend of his and see to the business of securing their fortunes. But somehow the concerns of keeping land and inheritance seemed to pale in the wake of Tommy's dire illness. What good were possessions if one lost the most priceless gifts of all, those we love most?

Still all would be righted. Uncle Joseph's good friend James Stephenson was a powerful lawyer and politician in Virginia. He would know exactly what to do to handle this situation.

At long last, the weary group arrived at the Swearingen farm. The housekeeper, Biddy, flew out of the cabin door the instant the carriage rolled into the winding drive, flustering about with two serving maids following her. Her orders barked in rapid fire to "get the chil'uns outa those filthy clothes" and "have cook serve up some nice hot broth" were instantly met with a flurry of feet scurrying in every direction.

Under the woman's direction, two valets, not much older than Van, attended to the boys in the springhouse while a housemaid scurried Lucy off to the kitchen for a proper washing and fresh garments.

"Ain't none of you children coming into master's parlor before ya'll are properly washed and free of chiggers, lice, and nits," Biddy decreed, supervising the entire operation like a militia drill sergeant.

Lucy endured quite a scrubbing from the girl set in charge of her. She giggled over Lucy's choice of attire, gingerly picking up the soiled, tattered garments that she had grown rather fond of on the journey. Nevertheless, the touch of freshly laundered, lavender-scented linen against her well-rubbed skin was heavenly, once the entire ordeal was done.

Scrubbed clean of all dirt and grime, her skin glowing red with the vigorous effort of her attendant, there was still the problem of appropriate dress. All of her clothes were left behind at Swearingen Landing, and the short gown and petticoat she had kept tucked away on the journey was long-lost, perhaps now worn by some young Shawnee girl. That might have been her, in another place and time. She mused over all this, while the serving girl toweled her hair and skin completely dry. Biddy appeared in the doorway of the kitchen with a lace-trimmed bed gown.

"This will have to do until we find more fitting attire." Biddy inspected Lucy to be certain every vestige of dirt had been removed. "Mister Joseph say he gonna send over to the Lane's place for to borrow a gown from one of their girls until we sew you one of your own. He done ordered two whole bolts of cloth from over at Harpers Ferry Mercantile for to make you some new clothes. Mizz Lane's girls be just about your age."

"What you want done with these here things?" The tall serving girl, called India, pointed to the basket where Lucy's breeches, waistcoat, and dingy shirt had been tossed. "You wants us to clean them for the two young misters to wear?"

"Lordy! No! Take them out and burn them. We got more'n enough young gentleman clothes from young Mister Thomas." Biddy stood with hands on hips giving Lucy an appraising look. "Mizz Winn, she shore have a thing or two to say 'bout her niece that for sure if'n she were here, Lord bless her soul. And her own Swearingen niece puttin' the whole family to shame! Here, now. Put this on."

After all she had endured—the dusty trails, rain, cold, near starvation—stripped of everything they had to survive and nights of uncertainty with the Duboises and then nearly losing Tommy, she didn't mind the scolding or the poking and prodding. Just then she knew more than ever she missed Ester, Tobe, Noah, Mother, and everything to do with home.

CHAPTER 30

The days were bright and warm as April eased its calm breath over every hill and valley around Shepherds Town. Lucy reveled in the teeming, new life everywhere she looked, grateful to at last be in a place of comfort and peace. Big Springs was what Uncle Joseph called his estate. Though there was a spring on the land, Lucy wondered if it wasn't named during just a month like this when the lush green, purple clover, yellow dandelions, and coltsfoot covered the land, and the trees sprung to life breathing fragrant blossoms along the Virginia hills.

Three days had given her quite enough time to settle comfortably into the world of Uncle Joseph's farm. Tommy was still weak but recovering from the fever with the aid of the local doctor and the attentive house staff. After the rigors of living on the open road, Lucy enjoyed the spacious stone manse that boasted seven rooms including a kitchen in the cellar and a formal dining room. Though Van had insisted they had all been here before, she could not recall such a memory, yet something about this house beckoned to her and welcomed her into its homey atmosphere. Perhaps it was the ease of the servants and the way they fussed over her, finally having a lady of the house to care for in the absence of her aunt who has passed some years earlier. Perhaps it was due to the trials she had sustained, though in some odd way she missed the Dubois family and even the cabin where she had spent that harrowing night alone with Tommy. In odd moments a flash of recollections came back to her like whiffs of lavender or lemon balm in the breeze as she toured the gardens. Peg's nimble fingers weaving at her loom while humming some haunting Indian chant. Auguste scraping a beaver hide, delighted at teaching Tommy a new word in French or Shawnee. Jacques's merry laughter and the sight of him in his smock, musky with the scent of pelts and tobacco. These were images she would keep, not the terror or the uncertainty that still lingered.

Though they were safe for now, nothing truly had been settled about her future and she still faced the frustration of once again being helpless, at the mercy of the older folks to find a solution. And so it was that on the third morning of their stay at Big Springs, Uncle Joseph called them all into the parlor after breakfast to hear in full their tales of adventure and formally take them to task. At least that was how it seemed.

"My dear children," Uncle began, standing by the hearth, "I am yet not certain whether to award you medals of honor or roundly thrash you each for your folly, your waywardness, and insubordination."

Lucy sat on a wooden chair, ramrod straight, wearing a borrowed day gown and stays from one of the neighboring Lane girls, whichever one must have been smaller or long outgrown the stays, for they pinched under her arms and the busk dug into her ribs. The gown was finer than any she'd ever worn. All she knew of the Lane girls was that they were daughters of some important magistrate a few miles across the state line in Maryland. What must they think of such a wayward, woodsy girl wearing their cast-off finery? She imagined them tittering over her tale of adventure as they dug through their old gowns for something to send a runaway with only her brother's old breeches to wear. Van and Tommy received their cousin Thomas's castoffs and now sat like young gentlemen on either side of her. Thankfully at least their cousin was not present to witness more of their shame. However, Benjamin Stephenson was, further adding to Lucy's mortification. She focused on her breathing, in spite of the binding stays, and on the lace and pintucks trimming her fashionable bodice.

"I'll not say I can't see the reason for your impetuosity," Uncle's stern gaze moved between them, "but after hearing your stories, is there anything else you wish to add before Mr. Stephenson and I confer on the matter at hand?"

"No, sir," they chorused. "We're very sorry to have been so much trouble." Lucy kept her eyes on the tips of her pump shoes pinching her toes. That sort of pain was easier to take than her uncle's disappointment and she could only hope it would end soon.

"We…that is, I…," Van croaked out the words. "It was all my fault, sir. My idea to copy the ledger and to run away. After we learned of Mr. Shepherd's scheme, after…what happened to Lucy…we didn't know where to turn, who to trust."

"And you didn't think to ask your departed brother's dearest friend?" Uncle gestured to Ben who stood placidly by the window. "Did I not tell you all at your brother's funeral whom to turn to and whom to trust?"

Lucy exchanged a bewildering glance with Van, who cast a steely gaze toward Ben, cross-armed and composed, leaning against the bookcase.

"And as I understand it, my dear niece, you happened by the store the morning your little scheme took root. And did you not think to tell Mr. Stephenson of your troubles? Of your mother's three children, nay of all my brother's children, I would've thought you the most sensible and discerning."

"Colonel, sir," Ben broke in with a conciliatory hand, "have a care. The children had their reasons. It couldn't have been easy, these past few months. They've shown their mettle against great odds and provided the evidence that may prove needful in court."

"Even so, Stephenson. 'Twas a most fortuitous turn of events that brought you and the children safely here." He walked a line in front of them as if he were reviewing his troops. "Do you realize the time and resources you have cost many? Sergeant Stephenson here, having to leave his shop and forego a much anticipated business trip, and…I shudder to think had the worst happened and you all were lost to us forever."

"Evidence?" Van jerked his head high, accusation and wonder competing in his widened eyes. "Mr. Stephenson, sir, what do you mean? The ledger is…"

"In our possession." Ben's demeanor remained as placid as before, except for the slightest gleam in his eye. "We happened upon it—your young manservant and I—while searching for you. The ledger and other things of yours as well."

"How? Where?" Van and Lucy chimed in unison, a sudden rush of air filling her lungs. "That's...not possible."

Ben cocked his head in a light, carefree smile, sending another rush of warm air and sunshine down to her shoe-pinched toes. "Well, now, you young 'uns aren't the only ones with a bit of good fortune. It seems destiny has been on all our sides this week."

"You...you found the preacher thief?" Van broached the question, more as a statement, confident of a candid response.

"And my...hair?" Lucy whispered.

"Yes, it's in safe keeping along with the ledger."

"Did you 'rrested him and toss him in jail?" Tommy bounced his question, nearly tipping his chair over. "Or did ya shoot him on the spot 'twixt the eyes to get our ev'dence back?"

Amusement wavered against prudence in Ben's easy smile, one finger smoothing his temple. "No, Tommy, I didn't shoot him, but I believe he has learned his lesson and won't be bothering anyone in such a way again."

Lucy knew in that instant, the preacher was dead and gone, just as she'd known the day she and Mother rode onto Zack's tract to find Ben waiting at the end of the lane. Then as now, he would never tell them exactly what happened. Had he killed the man, or found him dead? How many men had he killed? Now was not the time to ask, but someday, when she was older, when this present trial had passed, she might find a time to ask him again, and maybe he'd find her not so much the child who would not understand.

For now it was enough that he defended and even commended them for their resourcefulness and bravery, at least she hoped that's what she saw in Ben's eyes. Why this should matter, she checked herself constantly and shooed away the thought like a fly buzzing in her ear, whispering nonsense.

"We'll settle all matters from here, children," Uncle Joseph said, with a tap of his cane against the carpeted floor, as if to regain his ground in the discussion. "All will be well." The silent, wary exchange between the two grown men as the children were dismissed brought a brisk chill to the previous spring of hope blooming in Lucy's soul.

They had the ledger and even commended Van for his diligence and foresight in copying it. Now it was the waiting time again as Ben locked himself away in Uncle Joseph's library poring over the ledger, only to leave in haste with a leather portfolio and no word of where he was headed.

"Now, don't you worry your pretty little heads, my dears," Uncle Joseph assured them day after day. "The truth will come out, all in good time, and you'll be home again soon enough, when we're certain all is put to rights."

Truth was, she wasn't certain home was a place she really wanted to be anymore. She wasn't really sure where home was or even what it really meant. Was home being with her brothers walking the wooded pathways and huddled around the campfire each night? Was it listening to the preacher play his tin whistle or speak a Psalm against the terrors of the night? Was it a rough cabin nestled deep in the woods where a Frenchman fur trapper lived with his Shawnee wife and son? In each of these places she had not been home, but a stranger in a strange land. Yet there had been a sense of belonging, a sense of knowing herself and what she was capable of, a sense of who she might be or hope to be. Waiting here, helpless, behaving as a lady should, was not home, but the house still held a lure for something greater she couldn't quite grasp. Part of her wouldn't mind remaining here with Uncle Joseph, being a fine lady and tending his home. Another part of her wanted to be back out on that wilderness road ready to face whatever came around the next bend. Waiting was maddening, worse than sitting huddled on a bench in the fur-trapper's cabin while the men smoked their pipes and discussed her future.

She sometimes wondered what life would have been like living among the Shawnee. Dubois had said it wasn't so bad. There Blue Jacket and his men had spoken in tongues she could not decipher, yet she had spoken perfect Shawnee, not just at the trapper's cabin but also a few weeks earlier at dinner with Shepherd. It was what alarmed her mother that night and caused the retaliation with the hot poker to her arm. She had also spoken it that long-ago night that had been more than just the stuff of childish nightmares. It had all been true, as real as her journey across the hills and woodlands and her time here at Big Springs where she waited.

Here it was silence she faced. The silence of a closed door and a preoccupied man in her uncle's library penning notes in a means to find legal recourse to free her from some tangled web she still barely understood.

When she could stand it no longer, she offered to relieve the kitchen maid of taking Ben his mid-morning coffee. With one arm bracing the tray and a shaky hand at the door, she knocked three quick raps.

"Yes, Hattie, come in."

Ben sat at the cherrywood secretary, a pile of books stacked on the desk and a few on the floor at his feet. He leafed through a thick tome and referred back to the ledger and then back to the tome, pausing to scratch a few notes with the nib clenched between ink-splotched fingers.

She steadied the tray. He didn't look up at the clink of the cup when her nervous hands shook, nearly spilling the steaming brew over the delicate rim of the fine china. Another step toward the desk with a clearing of her throat startled him into awareness.

"Oh, it's you! I figured..."

"Hattie had some...uh...something to tend to in the garden. I offered to bring you...this."

"Ah! Just in time." He smiled with eyes bright and clear. "I've been hankering for a cup of Hattie's fine brew."

She nodded and set the tray down on an end table. "You've...," her voice cracked and she winced, clearing it again. "That is...how are things progressing?" *Stand straight, voice low yet sure and firm—he must see a proper lady.*

His brows lifted and eyes crossed as he sat back, rubbing a finger across his temple. "Ah! That is the question, is it not? We are making progress. Not to worry."

"Oh, I'm not worried." She willed her clammy hands to be still.

Don't spill coffee on him. He's trying to help. He already thinks you to be a befuddled fool for running away.

"Here, I'll do that." He stood and lifted the fragile cup as she bent to place the tray. "Could use a good stretch after sitting so long." Taking a sip he breathed in the steaming brew and flexed his writing hand. "Nothing beats a good rousing cup to clear the senses. I was past due. Feeling a bit sluggish."

Lucy backed away toward the door. "Well, I should go then. I only wanted to bring you the coffee, seeing as how Hattie was rather busy with the...gardening and all...." She checked herself again. *Why is this so hard?* She had spoken to him many times. That last morning in the store, at Zack's wedding the summer past, all those stories around the militia campfires, their walk in the woods on the day of Zack's funeral. Somehow, something had changed. She wanted him to see her as more than that little girl, more than a wayward child running from home, more than the scrappy little tyke, muddy and disheveled, lost in a woodland cabin.

He took another sip and gestured his cup toward her. "It must feel mighty good to be back in familiar grounds again and dressed in fine clothing. I say, you clean up rather nice."

"Um...yes, I suppose," she shrugged. "Though I don't really recall being here at Uncle Joseph's before this, and these really aren't my clothes."

"Not to worry. As I understand, the colonel has a fine lot of gowns on order for you."

"I suppose that means I'll be staying here a while?" *Perhaps a bit forward to ask?* She hoped he might take the meaning of her hint well enough.

He paused to set down his cup and returned to his seat at the desk and bid her to remain. "Sit, please. I do believe it's time we spoke, and I could use the company. I imagine you do have some unresolved questions?"

"No...I mean...yes...well...if it's not too much trouble."

"Trouble?" He rounded his eyes with a mischievous lurch of his head. "Let's see. I've had to leave my shop, round up a troop of militiamen and take them from their homes and farms, rent a slave from your estate, and high tail it in a wild-goose chase across two states and half of Virginia to find you, and you think taking a moment away from a tedious list of text and figures to talk to a pretty young lady, is any trouble at all?"

Heat flamed her face. *He thinks me a pretty young lady?* "I do thank you...for all that you've done... For Van and Tommy too." She studied a blooming dogwood tree out the window beyond the secretary piled with papers and books. "And for Tobe. It was kind of you to bring him along. It was an adventure for him too. "

"Adventure?" Ben leaned back with his cup. "One I'd not care to repeat. And I believe our man, Tobe would agree, for all his love of roaming and fine horsemanship. You three put him in a terrible position that could have gone very differently for all of you."

"I'm sorry. I know I've been more trouble than I could ever imagine."

"Lucy," he said, her heart skipping and then sinking to her feet, "I'm jesting. I really haven't done all that much yet." He waved one idle hand toward the heap of books at his feet. "I've almost got this thing mastered. We'll be meeting with my brother tomorrow."

"Your brother? The one whom my Cousin Thomas will apprentice for come fall?"

"Yes, James. He's the lawyer and will know more ways around these sorts of laws."

"The lawsuit, you mean? Mr. Shepherd's claim?" She hoped he would simply tell her without having to ask, fearing she would pose some stupid questions.

"Mr. Shepherd. Huh!" He shook his head. "You could have come to me sooner, told me what was happening. That morning at the shop. Why didn't you?" His voice reverted to a sternness that made Lucy draw into herself, not certain what to say. She could endure anything except his disappointment and low opinion of her.

"Could you truly have done anything?" She felt her mettle return. How could she have told him? What proof did she have of anything? Yet she didn't dare say such impudent things. She only held a steady gaze, her chin set firm. He may not wish to continue helping her, but she would not be scolded anymore.

"I do see your point. In your situation, I'd have probably not done much different. Lord knows I've no room to scold anyone on that score, and at least you have the excuse of complete innocence in all of this."

His face darkened leaving her to wonder again what the children gossiped about in the schoolyard. Those days seemed ages past now. "You've run away too? When you were a boy?"

He shook his head and waved dismissively. "Not important. We all do some foolish things in our youth. Though I wouldn't say your attempt was all that foolish; it has proven fruitful in the end. You are right, in that there may not have been much I could have done back in Wellsburg. Having you here, well, it may give us some leverage."

"Because, they won't be able to find us?"

He weighed his hands like a balance scale. "I haven't sent any word as yet, not until we determine what's best. The courts will decide if Abraham Shepherd's claim to your family's land is valid. But from what I can see, it's clear your stepfather has been abusing his privilege as caretaker of the trust set up for you and your brothers." With one finger pointed straight in the air, he gave the impression of a politician stumping his cause. "That is one legal recourse we do have and reason to petition for a more forthright custodial administrator."

"Like Uncle Joseph?" *Or you,* she wanted to add, but instead amended her thoughts. "Or Mr. Connell?"

Ben rolled his eyes. "Ah, the dubious Mr. Connell. Your father placed a great deal of misguided trust in him. He seemed reputable at the time, but he's the sort to be easily led and..." He paused as if he'd forgotten she was there then checked himself. "I shouldn't say, really."

"It won't be Mr. Newhouse, then? Looking after our affairs any longer?" She dug a toe into the carpet under her chair. "And I won't have to go live with Mr. Shepherd or...anything?"

Ben lifted his chin with a confident air. "No, most assuredly not. No one can make you marry anyone you don't wish to. Not now and not ever. I do want you to know that."

"Girls don't usually marry so young, do they?" She said this without realizing what she meant and then amended it quickly. "I'm not so young, am I?"

"That would depend." Ben rolled his shoulders and stretched. "The law in Virginia allows age of consent for maidens reaching their tenth year, can you believe that?" He chuckled lightly. "A relic from some less-enlightened, medieval time, I suppose."

"Is ten really so young?" She sat straighter, not certain why she wanted to challenge this, but his tone made her feel small and infantile. "It means I could choose to marry, if I wanted?"

"Well, providing you had a proper gentleman declaring his intentions and suit, I suppose." He chuckled, propping one elbow on the secretary with a skeptical glance. "I was given to understand a certain young lady had no interest in matrimony."

"What else am I to do?" she muttered, eyes downward

He leveled a dubious grin at her. "Are you saying you'd prefer to marry into Abraham Shepherd's family? Say the word and that can be arranged. It seems the offer is pending. Though as your counselor and friend, I would not advise it."

"He...never intended to marry or do right by me, did he?" she said.

He sighed resolutely. "I suppose we'll never know for sure, but I do have my suspicions."

"Van and I...heard something, that night, at the tavern." She swallowed hard before making a full confession. "We were there. I saw you...in the room before Mr. Newhouse spoke with Mr. Shepherd about...me...and my land."

Ben nodded. "I know. It's part of the case and I regret not making myself aware of it fully. But I want you to know, there is nothing to fear ever again of anyone taking you, or anything that belongs to you, away. I'm here to make very sure of that."

"But, then what..."

"Are you to do?" He finished for her. "I'm thinking a school far away from home. Provisions were made in your father's will for it, and I do believe he meant for more than the settlement school in Wellsburg."

"A school? I'd be sent away? Where?" Her heart skipped a beat as she took in the shelves of books around her. It might not be so bad, perhaps not bad at all.

"Haven't quite worked out the details as of yet, but there are some possibilities, with your approval of course. Somewhere secure, a good place. It would only be a year, maybe two at most."

"I can decide?" she gulped. "Where? For truly?"

"That would be agreeable?"

She managed a nod, not trusting her voice for fear of it wavering.

"First, this blasted court case. Then we'll talk more. As I said, all will work for the good, for yours and your brothers' welfare. I will promise you that, no matter what."

"All's well that ends well?" She hoped her quip would lighten the mood and sound more assured and grown-up.

"Reading Shakespeare again, are you?" He shook a finger in the air before tasting the coffee again. "You've a fine library to choose from here to get you started." He glanced around the room. "If I wasn't such a slave to the law books at the moment, what I wouldn't give for a chance to peruse some of your uncle's fine collection."

"It's the finest in three counties, or so I've heard Mother and...others, often say."

"Yes, Zack you mean." He looked tenderly at her. "I miss him too. Not a day has gone by in these last weeks that I haven't thought of him. When you all disappeared...well...you can't imagine what I must have thought. I made him a promise, you know."

"To watch out for us? Tommy, Van, and me?"

"Yes, but especially you."

"Because I'm a girl and therefore, need more looking after?" she blurted out. She had not meant to, but there it was.

"From what I've seen, you are quite capable of looking after yourself." He leaned in with a confidential air that set her back a pace. "It took great bravery to remain alone at that cabin with Tommy and care for him as you did."

"I'm a good soldier then?" She sat a little straighter. "One my father would have been proud of?"

"Most assuredly." He snapped her a smart salute. "I knew that the first time you stood up against Blue Jacket. You do remember, don't you?" He squinted at her as if searching her for clues. Or was he perhaps being cautious, lest he incur another of her fits?

"Yes," she said, dropping her face from his gaze. "I think so. Could you...could you tell me what you know...of that night? The Frenchman we met said Blue Jacket was angry with Papa, wanted to seek vengeance for wrongs done to his tribe. Is that true? Was it Papa who did those terrible things?"He paused, releasing a long slow breath as she held hers hoping he wouldn't use her minor age against her as everyone seemed to thus far. But ten wasn't so minor after all. It was the age of consent. That is what he just told her.

"You have to understand a few things. First, your father was a very great man. The finest soldier I have ever met, but times were...difficult. The stakes were high and tensions between settlers and Indians were...not good."

"Was I captured?"

He was stalling as all grown folk were wont to do and she would have no more of it.

"Yes."

There it was. A blunt response, true and delivered with the precision of a marksman's bull's-eye. "You were three...or four...I suppose. The women were all at a quilting bee at a neighbor's farm. Your mother was there with a servant girl and you, of course."

"And Tommy? Van?" She shot her eyes to his. She needed to see the honesty there, know for certain he wasn't coloring the truth in any way. "They were there as well?"

"I don't recall. Perhaps Tommy was. He'd have been a baby. Van, I'm not sure. I s'pect not, though or..."

"He'd have been taken as well? But it was just me. Wasn't it?"

"A raiding party of Shawnee came by and...captured some of the women and children, along with you."

"And my mother? Tommy?"

Ben's head shook. "They escaped somehow, or were not selected. The Shawnee are known to spare some and take others. Who knows why? Perhaps because your mother held an infant, and they didn't want to be bothered with such a young one. Or, maybe she was able to hide before they came."

"But I was taken? Along with others...who were...killed?"

"Tell me what you remember. Perhaps that might be best." He was afraid of telling her too much. She knew this and it frustrated her, but she also knew to get to the truth she had to mind things in his manner and say just the right words. Is this how it was in a court of law? Perhaps it was best she did remain here and let him face a judge on her behalf.

"I remember being under something, a table or quilt frame…ladies sewing…thread. Needles, I suppose. Screaming. I was afraid. A baby cried."

"Your brother, perhaps? Though given there was a group of ladies, there were any number of infants of varying ages, of course. Please, continue."

"I remember a forest…a glen…Indians…a man in a blue coat or tunic. That was Blue Jacket?"

Ben nodded with a silent gesture encouraging her to remember more.

"Then, someone held me, carried me to safety. For a long time I thought it was Papa, or Zack, but now I think…not. It was you, wasn't it?"

"Aye." He said this quietly, almost imperceptibly. "The captain, your father, wasn't there that night. He took off with another band of Brady's rangers to look for you. Your brothers and I formed a separate search party and looked for the next two days. We found the band that had a remnant of the captives."

"A remnant? Others were killed, weren't they? You can tell me. I won't have another fit. I promise." She lightly fingered the sleeve of her gown. Beneath was her scarred, but healing, arm. "A word was spoken by me, but I don't understand why, really. Wendigo?" She held his gaze firm and sure, which he returned with wide recognition and a hint of admiration.

A soulful smile prefaced his next thought. "You do remember. Your father always did say you were the keenest and smartest of the lot."

"I spoke more as well…a strange tongue. Shawnee. It happened at the cabin, too." She swallowed. "With Blue Jacket. The Frenchman said it was perfect Shawnee, but I don't know what I said, exactly."

Another deep breath exhaled let her know she had perhaps told him something she shouldn't have. "I suspected that. It was…peculiar. None of us could explain how…or why. When we came upon the camp, the Indians were performing some sort of ritual…slaying. Blue Jacket held you. I had him in sight to blow his…" He cleared his throat. "To do him justice. Then you started screaming, pointing toward the forest as if you saw something. You spoke in perfect Shawnee. The wendigo. You called for it to help you. I'm not much for the Indian tongue, but I could decipher that much. We were all at a loss to explain how...or why. It's quite possible you put the fear of God in that old warrior, or, you charmed him."

He lifted her chin and looked deep into her eyes, as if to make clear the thoughts he meant to say next. "I want you to know something. I could have killed Blue Jacket that night, but I didn't. It was you that stayed my hand from the trigger. Something in the way you looked at Blue Jacket and he looked at you. I can't explain it."

"Dubois told me the story of the wendigo, and of another creature, the *Paillissa* or *Piusa*. But how did I know it?"

He shrugged. "It was a tale we told at that time, the wendigo. An old Indian legend of a monstrous man-eater. It goes by many names. *Chenoo. Keewahkwee.* Every tribe likely has a different name for it. But...this *Piusa?"* He frowned, scratching a finger thoughtfully to his cheek. "That I've not heard tell of."

"Then how did I know of it?" Her voice trembled. She sucked in a breath to gain composure. "I did know it, from a dream before Monsieur Dubois told me."

"But how, at that precise moment, you recalled it and the language just at that moment...some might call it a miracle, others a curse, and some more scientific-minded would say a genius of sorts—a keen awareness of nature and its wonders that we have yet to discover."

"But what do you call it?" She wanted to know his mind, to know he didn't think her peculiar, or tainted. Somehow her family had made her feel that way, and for all these years she had never really known it until now, until her time in the cabin had confirmed so much that she vaguely recalled.

"I'm not a man for flagrant myths or supposition, though I do like a good yarn now and again. I prefer to deal in truths, in justice, proven facts, if you will." He pressed a hand across the opened law book on the secretary desk.

"I prefer it, too." She clutched her hands together and studied the ruffle on her borrowed gown. "I don't want to be...special...or peculiar...or..."

"Mad?" Ben said the word she feared most. "Lucy, you are most definitely not mad or peculiar. There's not a speck of insanity in you."

"But Zack was." She swallowed a dry lump. "Those last days, he was not right." She grazed a tentative finger across her temple.

The pained look in Ben's eyes prefaced another carefully laid thought. "Zack was dangerously ill. It comes with the fever. We don't know why. I've seen it before among the soldiers. It affects a goodly number of folk in these parts, and farther west, I hear."

"Do I have that same fever?"

"No, hopefully you never will. It is a terrible plague among us. Some say it's due to the night air or the foul swamps near the rivers. Just when you think it's gone, it appears all over again."

Just like those terrible nightmares? she wondered. "Swamp fever, it's called, isn't it? Or yellow jack? That's what he had?" Terms whispered once between Phoebe and her mother last summer, and at too many funerals along the Ohio.

"Some do, yes. It goes by other names. Bilious fever, ague, malaria. However, yellow jack or yellow fever is altogether different." Shaking his head he turned to some far distant point. "That is one plague I do hope you never encounter." He leaned forward. "It was not Zack's fault, anything he said or did. I want you to know that above all. We must remember the good. He was a devoted husband, a fine brave soldier, a dutiful son, and the kindest of brothers to you and Van and Tommy."

"And he was your friend," she said. "You did all you could for him." It was both a question and a statement. She still hoped for answers.

"That he was. Like a brother. And that's just what we must remember most. The rest, is just...circumstances we can't control but must accept." He turned and faced her fully, taking her hands into his. "Lucy, I know you want answers, but just now...I have none to give. Someday, perhaps, I will tell you all, but just now..." He drew breath and cleared his throat, his eyes as misty as hers must be. An ever so slight shake of his head settled the matter. An image from a dream flitted in her mind, replaced by another one far brighter and more pleasing.

She rose from her chair to take her leave. "I thank you, Mr. Stephenson. And I won't mind going to school, not at all, wherever you choose. I trust you fully in this."

He needed to be about his work and discuss no more. For now she had her answers and would wait until the courts decided where her fate lay. His interest in her was no more than a promise made to defend the younger sister of a dear friend and fellow soldier. She knew that now...but perhaps in time?

CHAPTER 31

Joseph Swearingen's incessant drumming on the ivory knob of his walking cane fueled Ben's nervous energy. Twenty minutes had passed, according to the clock ticking on the wall in his brother's law office in Harpers Ferry. It seemed more like hours and yet in those twenty minutes they had managed to weave through a tangle of legal issues in hopes of protecting one little girl and her fortune. The result would be a potentially life-changing course for her and possibly for him. All the while the colonel's fingers played along the cane's head. Ben looked between James pouring over a stack of documents splayed across his desk and Joseph Swearingen adjacent in a matching Windsor chair.

Ben broke in, "You're sure it's the only way."

"Well, my brother, I would say so." James sighed and peered at him over his spectacles. "Certainly not the only way, but quite probably the most expedient, if you are so determined to help this girl, that is, and keep her out of the madhouse or lost in the woods to the savages again." Ben held his brother's fixed gaze, before James broke away to the older man thumping his cane on the wooden floor.

"We're here to see to my niece's welfare," Joseph said. "I will not have Lucy dallied with nor see her rightful fortune squandered by the likes of Newhouse or any other greedy land speculators, least of all Abraham Shepherd. And no kin of mine will wind up in an asylum. I know we are asking a great deal of you, Ben. It is unusual, but not without its precedents. If I could attain custody of her... But my hands are tied." His eyes filled with a look of fleeting desperation. "She is fond of you, you know. A delightful child, though perhaps a bit willful—fanciful, some might say. But she's a good girl. In time, with proper guidance, she could grow to—"

"No," Ben shook his head and chuckled wryly. "I won't concern myself with the whims of a child and I'm most certainly not looking for a wife at this time, especially not one I need to...*guide* into marriage in due course. I only want to do what's best at present for all concerned. She deserves a chance at being young." He drew in a deep breath, looking away. Childhood was far too brief as it was. "We'll let the future take care of itself." *With time on our side*, he thought, but chose not to add.

Joseph threw a puzzled glance at James and then placed a hand on Ben's shoulder. "Admittedly, I had once hoped that a match between my Thomas and Lucy would secure their combined landholdings and create a strong financial future for them both. It's what my brother and I hoped for...once. I knew nothing of this last agreement or the codicil naming you, if it is indeed legally binding." There was something else brewing behind the creased brow of this military tactician and former county magistrate. Ben had not considered Thomas as a potential match for Lucy.

"My brother most certainly had his reasons, and I'll abide by that," said the colonel. "Thomas is too young to offer her the legal protection just now—that a man of age could provide." He nodded toward James. "With your family's connections, she'll be well represented, for the time being. But am I hearing you to say you have no interest in a future marriage to my niece at all?"

James exchanged a knowing look with the older man then turned a bemused grin at Ben. "Have a heart, brother dear, are you so opposed to marriage cutting short your days of independent bachelorhood? Still fancy yourself out West, do you?"

Ben gave his brother a warning look, "I would hope to court a young lady properly and be ready to offer her a fortune of my own, in due course of time. That is, if I ever choose to avail myself of such bliss again. Certainly not a marriage of convenience to an infant orphan, isn't that the legal term?"

James shook his head. "I would have thought you'd learned a marriage is not built solely on affection or desires of the flesh. A wife of means will suit you better, and one young and malleable enough to..." He spread his hands outward before pressing them flat against the desk blotter as if drawing validity to his words. "I know what this will mean to you, Ben. Do consider." His arched eyebrows and piercing gray eyes drew Ben's ire. James gave the impression of their father more every day; an irritating thought he did not welcome clouding his judgment. This bit of news had best not reach their parents. They already thought his choices till now were nothing but capricious folly.

"Do consider what?" Head erect, Ben cocked a leveled gaze across the barrister desk. "A young, malleable wife with a fortune? A mere child? Is that what you think suits me? I suppose you believe I need the time to mature as well? That I am not capable of otherwise courting a suitable wife to the altar?"

"Brother," James interjected, "no one here thinks lesser of you. On the contrary, your motives are noble as well as practical."

"And just what am I supposed to do with her in the meantime? Do you have any practical solutions?" Ben leaned forward in the chair, then stood and paced toward a standing globe near the window.

"We already discussed the possibility of my niece remaining at Big Springs," Joseph tentatively offered. "Are you now saying...?"

"All that matters is a promise I made to a friend," Ben said, giving the globe one revolution, "and I will hold to that alone. We're here to discuss what's best for Lucy." He let his fingers play lightly across the continents as the globe spun, illuminated in the shafts of light filtering through the window. Absently, he traced great rivers of the world on their course to the sea. "I'll not have her held to the same sorts of promises I hold myself to. She shall be free to grow unfettered by responsibility except for her schooling, of course."

James eyes narrowed and softened with a look of remorse. "Still, perhaps at this point, a practical marriage does have its merits, Ben. If the colonel is agreeable to having her remain with him and—"

"Let her be raised as her cousin's future wife?" Ben interjected with a joyless chuckle. "Meaning no disrespect, sir, she has expressed an interest in her education, which the captain's will allocates."

"Of course, Ben," James concurred. "I see your meaning now. Certainly, it will be years before this girl is...," he cleared his throat, "suitable to the duties of a wife. In the meantime you're at liberty to..."

"To do what? Bide my time and wait for her fortune? Whore about until I've sewn my last wild oat? Is that what you believe I've been doing these past years?" Ben slapped his fingers down on the globe, stopping it in its revolution. He cast a cold, steady gaze at his elder brother. "Oh, yes, dear brother, I am being practical. This is the most practical of business ventures yet. It buys all concerned a commodity more valuable than land or property." He paused in the space of time it took James to raise an eyebrow in the interrogating look of a courtroom barrister.

"And what might that be?" James cocked his head with an air of impatience and that bemused grin that Ben recalled from childhood.

"Time, brother dear, time, as you've always said, is the most valuable thing we all possess. Time and opportunity. Her financial assets and welfare are secure, whatever the future holds. No one dare touch her dowry, her land, or otherwise, so long as I hold the contract. Is that not so? It gives both of us options and the freedom to choose our own destinies in time, especially hers." He paused to consider his next words carefully, one final trace of a finger across the globe's North American continent. "Therefore, I have but one condition: Lucy will know nothing of this match...this arrangement...until I deem it necessary to tell her. I will make that decision and no one else."

"Certainly, we can arrange a meeting as soon as possible. I do believe it would be best presented by you. I can file the proceedings in court while you to return to Shepherds Town and—"

"No, we'll make all the arrangements as soon as possible, and I plan to appear in court to see all goes as we've discussed here. Make it plausible with the courts. Do what you must, but she will have no knowledge of the proceedings until the proper time, when she is old enough to understand and to make her own decisions, until, as you say, she is suitable to the duties of a wife."

The two men stared at Ben, wide-eyed. "Little brother, just how do you propose to contract a marriage to the girl without letting her know?" James chortled and shook his head. "I certainly hope you inform the little woman sometime before your first child is born." He chucked lightly before clearing his throat and restoring order. "Guardianships in the cases of infant orphans, while uncommon, are not without precedence and quite often resolve into an amicable and mutually advantageous marriage, even in our enlightened age."

Ben let the words hang in the air along with the whirring of the globe as he spun it again. "I've watched you work the law to your advantage. You're the congressman with the judicial mind to find loopholes in the law to suit your purpose." He returned to the desk and sat in his chair. "Surely there is some legal recourse that would work to everyone's advantage. The pending lawsuit will show I have a claim to Swearingen land as well. That's really the purpose of securing her fate and fortune at such a tender age. As the colonel indicated, my majority and legal connections will give weight to the suit, not to mention my sworn declaration that it was the captain's wish for such a marriage."

"Nothing necessitates a loophole here," James said. "It's a simple matter, benefiting all concerned, except those contesting the land claims, namely one Mr. Abraham Shepherd. And of course, Mr. Newhouse's handling of the children's inheritance will be far more closely monitored from here forth. I really don't see—"

Ben held up a hand in counterpoint. "All we need is my name on the suit, a mere paper filed in court. Is that not so? It would seem there's little concern for her welfare, beyond what she possesses in land holdings. If I choose to tell her or not, is of no consequence to anyone, once the dispute is settled. This marriage will be in name only, a legal document filed with the courts for her protection. We will tell her nothing. Only that, I am to be her...," he flailed his arms in search of the proper legal term, "her guardian, so to speak." Her trusting eyes gazing at him the week before in the Big Springs' library, he had told her as much then and would see it through now.

"I will look after her estate and her brothers' as well, if possible. They're children and will know nothing else but what we tell them. We'll keep the contractual arrangement discreet for the time being. Arrange all the legalities as you see fit, brother. It certainly is not the first arranged marriage under a guardianship, and certainly not the first to be dissolved—so long as I alone maintain complete leverage over her estate and dowry. "

Joseph Swearingen grabbed the arms of the chair, his knuckles turning as white as the outmoded periwig he wore. "You're saying you would cast my niece aside? Just like that? Take her land...her holdings? It all goes to you? Benjamin, I...can't...believe..."

James frowned and nodded in confusion, "Ben, do you realize what you are saying?"

"Yes...yes, I do." Ben brightened as the idea began to germinate, sounding better in words than the thoughts he had previously mulled over before arriving in Harpers Ferry. "I have no intention of casting anyone aside." He leveled his gaze between the two men. "I will remain her guardian and see she is properly cared for. She will attend school for the next few years. The provisions are there per her father's will, so long as Newhouse cannot access them. And we're making damn sure that doesn't happen."

"A school?" Joseph rubbed his chin and gave a half smile. "The Lanes are considering such a place for their younger daughter. She is about Lucy's age. I have planned a meeting between them before summer. It would be a fine place for her, a year or so should be enough."

"Precisely." Ben relaxed in his chair. A Philadelphia school would keep her far from Eleanor, Elzey, and Newhouse. His long-held suspicions were now a hellish reality. None were above trading her off to any man, Indian or white, for their own selfish gain. The colonel's interest lay only with her suitability to marry his son, her own cousin. If she were secure in school, she might have the chance and hope of something more...a life of her own choosing. Or at the very least she'd be out of harm's way while he managed his own affairs until such time as he...

"Quite a sound scheme, my brother," James said wryly. "Seems you've thought of everything. But what happens after the year or two of schooling? She'll be nigh on to fifteen, quite a few changes can occur in a young lady's life in that time."

"We could extend her tuition, renegotiate terms at that time. Until then, no one will know any different," he pressed further. "When she is of age, or completes her education in proper order, she will have the option to make her own decisions as to her future, be it marriage or otherwise." He gestured toward Joseph, "If she wishes to marry your son, so be it. I'll not object."

"You understand what you are saying?" James leaned across the desk and peered at his brother. "Arranged marriages to minority heirs, or infant orphans, as the law considers her now, have a long history in English Common Law. A temporary guardianship can be arranged but usually with the understanding that a marriage indeed will take place at the proper time when both parties deem agreeable. It is a binding contract as to the property. We'll put that in place. No court or church can force her into a marriage against her will. Therefore, if either party does not carry through their intent, all properties will be forfeit."

"Precisely," Ben pointed an emphatic finger at his brother. "Just as I read the law as well. Should she refuse, I keep the dowry, the land, everything. Should I refuse, she's free to go her way."

"With a ruined reputation?" The colonel thumped his cane louder than before. "You'd forsake her? A compromised woman? With no property? No dowry?"

"I'd tend to agree, brother. What you're suggesting, it's highly unorthodox. I wouldn't advise—"

"Then it is possible." Ben met his brother's stare with a challenge. "I do not plan to leave her ruined, hence the need for complete secrecy. Let her think she's a ward of the courts, that you, James, are her court-appointed guardian. When she is older, she will understand better what we've done here for her welfare."

James sighed and removed his spectacles, buffing the lenses with a handkerchief pulled from his waistcoat pocket. "You could make such an arrangement. But what will you do about Mr. and Mrs. Newhouse? How will you keep this from them…from the rest of the Swearingens? Her parents must agree to the marriage at the very least. You're planning quite a deception, Ben. How do you propose to keep such a thing from the girl?"

"James is right, Ben," Joseph said. "My niece is a bright young lady.

She'll not be trifled with. And what makes you think Newhouse and Eleanor will go along with this and comply with your demands?"

"Oh, they'll go along with it." Ben flicked a miniscule piece of lint off his coat sleeve. "I'll see to that. Lucy will be away at school for the next few years, as her father wished. I'll keep her affairs in order and Newhouse will get his gambling debts paid. I'll personally ensure that." Ben's strategy of outsmarting Newhouse at cards would work in his favor now. It had worked before over a few coins and would work to his advantage even more now. The rogue was not the bluffer he pretended to be when dealt a hand. "He'll keep quiet. He has far too much to lose. He's made it clear he cares little what happens to her, so long as his accounts are settled. Mrs. Newhouse follows his lead in all things. There will be no one to object. I believe they will be just as glad to be rid of the chit."

Joseph wrapped his fingers around the top of his cane. "Then, it is possible she could marry my Thomas someday? You would agree to this Ben?" He turned to James. "This could be done legally, without scandal? Marriage is a sacred bond. I just don't know about this."

James fixed his spectacles over his nose and exhaled through his teeth, pressing his lips together before speaking. "Yes, it can be done. Such arrangements do have their precedents. It's merely a legal contract over your niece's dowry at this point. The codicil to Van Swearingen's will makes it clear. Her tender age would necessitate a deferment on the actual consummation of said marriage, and of course she would have to give consent, which, under Virginia law, she could even now." James refitted his spectacles and inspected a leaf. "As I understand it, she is past the age of ten?"

"Twelve," the colonel corrected. "My niece insists she is twelve." Shaking his head he added, "Can hardly believe it myself, but there it is."

"If she is clever and the beauty I've heard tell with a fortune in land," James said, provocatively, "and if she is the least bit fond of you, Ben, then what's to prevent..."

"If you were not my brother, James, I'd demand satisfaction for such words." Ben's nostrils flared, and he balled his fists on his knees. "I'm not about to take a child of twelve or any age remotely near it."

"Of course not," James said, not looking down to his papers. "There is no question of that. Without a ceremony and vows before witnesses, it isn't a legal marriage as of yet, only a contract for her property with the provision for a future marriage. You'd both be free, so long as the marriage is not...so long as nothing untoward occurs, you understand, which is in your legal rights at any given time, with her consent. That's all I'm saying. It would therefore imply a...ahem... a marriage de facto...by implication." Both men looked at Ben.

"Upon consummation, you mean. I'm aware of the law," Ben's gestured dismissively. The stacks of legal books in the library, a young maiden gazing at him, trusting and soulful, nothing would hinder his purpose in aiding her cause. He had made a promise first to her father, then to her brother, and now to Lucy.

"She's a child, of tender age, no less," he said. "All the more reason to secure her in a proper school, where there shall be no doubt to her virtue." He turned to Joseph. "Until such time she is allowed to set her own course, to have the freedom to flourish unaltered when she is of proper age. She's been through enough already, and I won't betray her trust." *Wendigo. How had she remembered that after all these years?* He had protected her then and would continue to do so.

"Well, Ben," James leaned back and picked up a quill. "It sounds like you've thought this through very carefully. It's highly irregular, but possible nonetheless." He shook his head. "You'd make quite the lawyer, yourself, if not a shrewd politician. Still reading the Blackstone I lent you?" He dipped the nib of the goose feather into an inkwell and began to write. The scratches of the quill marked time with the ticking clock, the only other sound in the room.

Ben sat back in his chair. "No, brother dear, I shall leave the law work to you. One politician in the family is quite enough for my taste. I'll see to my surveying and river boating to get by."

James paused in his pen stroke to peer at another document. "You're aware that, as her betrothed, or 'guardian' so to speak, you will be responsible for her upkeep, but equally entitled to the one-third portion set for her dowry according to Andrew Van Swearingen's will, the remainder to be endowed when she reaches her twenty-first birthday. The codicil provides for an additional land tract and monies, with the provision she marry according to her father's wishes—that being you, as I understand the reading. The girl has a sizable dowry, including at least one slave, a girl named Winn, and possibly another though it's not specified by name. You are aware of that?"

"I'm well aware of her holdings," Ben's tongue rolled the words with precision. "But I am no speculator, at least not with an innocent child's fortune. I'll do what I can to help manage it, see that it grows and offers her the best future possible."

James raised his eyebrows, causing lines to form along his receding scalp, and dipped the quill in the bottle of ink again. "Still, it's yours for the taking, and you'll be a slaveholder." A glance over his spectacles implied a challenge Ben wasn't ready to address.

"My stance on slavery is as yet undecided for the time being." An image rose before him of Tobe standing obsequiously by the well, but underneath he could see the lad's lust for adventure, for freedom. He had enjoyed his time with Tobe and would hate returning him to Newhouse.

"Still, yours for the taking. And you might consider how to invest your portion. At the very least you are entitled to a tenth as manager of the estate until she reaches maturity. It's what Newhouse claimed as his and quite a sum more, it would seem. I could set it up that way for you as well. It'd help with your business ventures and make a good return for Lucy's future, whatever that may be."

"I'll leave the details to you, just be sure all is done with her best interest in mind, and keep me informed." Ben stood and met his brother's eyes. "I'll be leaving for New Orleans in a few weeks, once I see that she is enrolled in a proper school."

James nodded and continued writing. "Mr. Connell will continue as executor as set by Van Swearingen, Sr. Though now under my consultation in all matters. I'll see that he holds to the requisite annual report to the courts on the status of the two brothers' holdings as well. In the case of the sister, that will all be in your hands, the dowry portion, at least, the rest to be conferred upon her reaching her majority, which I shall oversee on your behalf."

"Then there will be no chance for Connell, or Newhouse, embezzling any more property? No more rents paid to the mother?" Ben leaned forward on the desk, his knuckles bearing down on the smooth hardwood.

"Not without your permission. As Lucy's intended husband you have full rights and as brother-in-law to Van and Thomas, reason, at least, to ascertain their assets as well, on your wife's behalf, so to speak. I dare say, Connell won't try any more of his tricks, if he plans to continue practicing law in the state of Virginia." James exchanged a smile with Ben. "It'll all be presented in court along with the suit against Abraham Shepherd. I do think the court will rule in our favor."

Ben mulled over the plan as he paced to the window. Parting the draperies he caught sight of a liveried coach and four trotting past. On the back a young Negro boy stood erect with a most forlorn look, much as Tobe had looked that day beside the well. "Then this can be done? A marriage presented only to the courts, nonetheless legally binding, yet not exactly so either?" He could indeed make this work, and all would be well. "I will be her guardian with the option to marry her, for all intents and purposes, should I, and more importantly, she choose, at the appropriate time."

"Rather on that order, yes," James frowned, lifting another document for review. "If that's how you want this. Still, I must say, Ben, consider carefully. The girl will be a young woman in but a few years. A wife with a fortune would make a good match for you both. Perhaps it's time you think of your future as well as hers. If she is fond of you now, you may both grow to—"

"I know what I'm doing," Ben said. "I expect nothing from her. A young woman's heart can be most fickle. I know that better than most. For God's sakes, I'm nearly old enough to be her father. There will be no regrets." He looked pointedly at Lucy's uncle. "She will be allowed to choose for herself, at the proper time, without any coercion or obligation from anyone. Make no mistake on that."

Joseph leaned toward Ben, hands crossed over the top of his cane. "Thank you, Ben. I can't begin to express my gratitude. I'll personally see to it that you are adequately compensated. I understand the great sacrifice you are making here. You realize this binds you to my niece, with little recompense. You'll not be free to marry anyone else for, possibly, another four or five years at the very least."

Ben closed his eyes, exhaling a long slow breath. "That is the least of my concerns. Let's just get on with this."

The worn, skin ball flew up into the air and made contact with Lucy's paddle in a sharp thud of leather to wood. She released her foot off the lever of the trap that had propelled the ball to meet her aim and ran to the designated stone base. She touched one foot on the stone then turned for a mad dash back toward home. Van lunged forward and caught the ball firmly in his grasp. He lobbed it to his cousin Thomas who tried to reach the trap's home base before Lucy returned across the grassy field. With a squeal Lucy darted in a race toward the goal only to be intercepted by her cousin.

"Ha, ha! I have you." Thomas raised the ball in triumph after touching his foot squarely on the trap. "That's another point for our team."

"Oh, fie!" Lucy laughed and stamped her foot in mock protest. "Well, that still puts you three points behind Tommy and me."

Van approached the trap and picked up the paddle. "Only because we were easy on you, considering you're a girl, and Tommy's been ill."

"Oh, so you think we couldn't beat you otherwise?" Lucy stood arms akimbo and thrust out her chin, glaring at her brother and her cousin.

Both older boys laughed. Van shook his head. "Dear sister, I know it to be so."

Little Tommy came running across the meadow. The scent of clover and new grass mingled in the warm breeze of the April day. Lucy inhaled the essence of the moment and reveled in the carefree feeling of a season full of new life and possibilities.

"We won, we won!" Tommy jumped and skipped his way to where Lucy stood. He threw his arms around her in a firm embrace. "Lucy, we won! Didn't we?"

"I wouldn't say that." Van caught the trap ball as Cousin Thomas lobbed it across. "We still have another round to play before game is called." He lobbed the ball up and down in several strokes of a one-handed catch.

Lucy turned her gaze toward the road down the hill from where they played. No sign of horse or rider yet.

"What are you looking at, sister?" Van tossed the ball once more in a catch and release then threw it toward Cousin Thomas.

"Hmm? Oh, nothing. I just...," Lucy absently chewed on a tag of peeled skin from her lower lip, then realized she had lost track of the game and the conversation.

"They won't get here any faster by staring down the road." Van threw the ball into the air and swatted it with the paddle. Tommy ran to retrieve it.

"Who?" Lucy felt her face flush. She well knew the reference to "they," but didn't want Van to think she was that anxious.

Van reached out to catch the ball as Tommy threw it back, but was intercepted by Cousin Thomas.

"I think Van means my father and your Mr. Stephenson." Cousin Thomas lobbed the ball toward Lucy in a smooth, effortless stroke. "They'll be here all in good time."

Lucy threw a hand instinctively at the ready, but just missed the leather sphere as it grazed her fingers and bounced in the grass a few feet away. "He's not my Mr. Stephenson. More likely, your Mr. Stephenson, as you'll be working for his brother come fall."

"As a matter of fact, I shall. The Congressman James Stephenson, and from what I hear, he can be quite thorough." Thomas scanned the sky, shielding his eyes from the bright rays filtering through the clouds. "I shall have my work cut out for me this summer as his clerk."

"They've been gone quite long enough, though. Don't you think?" She bent to retrieve the ball. "Surely it can't take all that long to discuss a few legal matters."

Tommy knelt down on the grass and examined a few blades, choosing two to hold between his thumbs. "Will they force Lucy to marry that odious, old man?" He blew through them in an attempt to create a grass whistle.

The children all laughed.

"Odious? Tommy, just where did you get a word like that?" Lucy bent down next to her little brother to help him adjust his hold and create a clear, crisp pitch. "Here Tommy, like this."

"I heard you say it to Van and Cousin Thomas. You said that Mr. Shepherd was an odious old man and you would sooner marry a billy goat than him or his son." With a full intake of air he blew across the grassy reeds. "When can we go home? I miss Mama."

Lucy clapped her hands at her little brother's next attempt, a clear bright tone. "There, Tommy-kins, that's much better. And I miss Mother, too. We'll see her soon when this is all over and done with." In spite of everything, she did miss Mother, even the sewing lessons and the gentle prodding, but more she missed Ester gently tucking them into bed each night and the smells of the Swearingen kitchen. Yes, she did miss it.

"Will she be cross with us? Will Mr. Newhouse punish us for running away?" Tommy took in a deep breath and blew through the blades making a weak, bleating sound. "Drat! I want to make that other sound again."

"No one will be mad at us." Lucy sat back and pulled her knees up to her chest. She looked again down the road past Uncle Joseph's house below them in the valley. "Mr. Stephenson and Uncle promised to fix the matter."

"You know, there is one way we can fix this matter ourselves." Thomas flopped down on the grass and picked out two blades. He placed them over his mouth and blew a clean, clear whistle, once, twice. "I've been thinking… But, it will mean something a bit diabolical." He blew another whistle and peered with a devilish gleam.

"Diabolical!" Van swished the paddle through the grass. "Couldn't be any more diabolical than stealing our stepfather's ledger and running away. Or Lucy hoarding our family's jewels that should've gone to Phoebe." Van grabbed two blades of grass and blew his own whistle.

"Or Mr. Newhouse charging us rent to live in our own mother's house, from out of Father's estate." Lucy made a snooty face and then looked cross-eyed at Tommy. "Or, more diabolical than marrying me off to Abraham Shepherd's son and packing me off to Boston or London."

"If that is what he intended," Van warned skeptically.

"I don't want to consider the worst," Lucy said, recalling what they had overheard from the stairs when Ben and Uncle Joseph argued well into the night over her situation.

"You'd rather believe that than the possibility they might have traded you to the Injuns?" Thomas leaned up on one elbow from his reclined position in the grass.

Van followed his cousin's lead with a sly grin. "I thought you liked living with the Shawnee family. You already know the language, and Blue Jacket had an eye for you. I could tell."

Lucy hugged her knees as she followed the line of drifting cloud wisps. "I suppose you are right. Mr. Dubois did say it was not a bad life." Since Ben mentioned the possibility of schooling, her thoughts had wandered to the idea of seeing great cities like Philadelphia, Boston, or even London and studying there. What sort of libraries might they contain?

"What's 'di-bow-licle' mean?" Tommy giggled when his sister made another silly face and reached to tickle his ribs.

"It means you're a silly little addle pate of a brother, that's what it means."

"I have been thinking on all of this." Cousin Thomas lay back on the grass, his arms tucked behind his head. He kept his eyes intently on Lucy. "You see, I'm to apprentice to a politician soon, and, from what I hear, the best way to outmaneuver anyone is to beat him at his own game."

"And just how are we to do that?" Lucy cocked her head and gave her cousin a wary look. "The men are at the courthouse now, tending to our estate and making sure all is secure. What can we do?"

"Your Mr. Newhouse wanted to prearrange a marriage between you and this Abraham Shepherd, correct?" Thomas turned his attention toward the sky. He took a piece of the grass he had used for a whistle and worked the end between his teeth.

"Yes," Lucy eyed him suspiciously.

"Well then, we beat him to it with our own prearrangement." Thomas sat up with his head held high, looking quite pleased with himself.

"And just what does that mean?" Van looked at Thomas then back to Lucy with a puzzled frown.

"It means, we do a handfasting between Lucy and myself." Thomas held out his hands and clasped them firmly together as explanation.

Lucy looked at her cousin as if he had gone completely mad. "And what exactly will that prove?"

"All it means is that we make a promise to each other to someday marry. In the interim, until we are of the proper age, no one can dissolve our union. It's the law."

"But I don't want to marry you, Thomas. I'm too young. You are too young."

"Not right now, you silly," Cousin Thomas shook his head. "But we can do a handfast and make a pledge to be true to each other to wait, and someday, when we are older we will wed. It's what our fathers wanted."

Van and Lucy stared at each other, open-mouthed.

"How do you know this, Thomas?" Van said.

Thomas shrugged. "Father's always talked of it. He's quite fond of you, Lucy. I think he wishes he and mother had a daughter as well as a son."

"Our papa wanted this too? How do you know this?" Lucy held her knees tight against her chest.

"Father told me once, that after you were born, they had an idea brewing that if they matched up their children in marriage, it would unite the property and leave a large legacy for future generations. Since Uncle Van had a daughter, *c'est vous...*," he gestured toward Lucy, "and Father had a son, *c'est moi...*," he poked his thumb at his chest, "and we're both near in age, it just seemed logical, I suppose."

"You're four years older than I," Lucy protested. "I'd hardly call that near in age."

Thomas shrugged. "Now, it seems a wide spread in years, but someday it won't. Years have a way of doing that. I know you are but ten, even if you've convinced the grown folk you are two years older. Might as well let that work in our favor as well."

Van skewed his face looking between his sister and his cousin. "So, we're now the same age? How will that pass?"

"Well," Thomas said, "the way I figure it, grown folks only see what they want to see and somehow they haven't stopped to figure that out." He pointed to Van. "You might as well say you are another year or two older. It could work in your favor as well. Think on it!

We'd be the same age." He gestured an open hand between them, indicating he and Van, "We'd both be fourteen now." Toward Lucy he made a similar gesture. "Lucy says she's twelve. So that makes us two years apart. See? We're now close in age."

"But that's a lie," Tommy blurted out.

"A lie started by Mr. Newhouse and mother, and we're told to obey our parents, aren't we?" Lucy smirked and dissolved into a full laugh. "It could work, but why would I need to make a handfast with you?"

"It would just make things a bit easier, is all," Thomas defended. "But if you'd rather take your chances with whomever they might choose next for you. No one else will want you if you've already been handfasted. That's what I've heard."

Lucy mulled this thought over. She tucked a stray lock of her short hair behind her ear. "You know this for sure? That's what Papa would want? Van what do you think?"

Van paused in swishing the paddle through the grass and looked between his sister and his cousin. "It might work. It sounds like Papa. If Uncle Joseph said so...then...," he screwed his mouth into a tight bow. "How would we go about this?"

"Simple." Cousin Thomas rose to his feet and brushed the dirt from his breeches. "All we need do is have Lucy and I hold hands and pledge to be married someday, and it has to be before witnesses."

"That's it?" Lucy felt a queasy tingle rise in her throat and a lurch to her insides. "But you're my cousin, more like a brother. It wouldn't seem proper, really."

Cousin Thomas shrugged and bent to retrieve the ball again, now lying idle in the grass. "Cousins marry all the time. It's perfectly legal and quite acceptable. Most well-bred folks in the county are matched up with their cousins for property reasons."

"Wouldn't it be better to choose and have the chance to fall in love someday?" Lucy mused over whom she might consider, other than Thomas, but just now she only wanted to be free to play trap ball and run in the warm sunshine of a spring afternoon. The only other image that came to mind was one she felt certain would not be remotely possible—a man working at a secretary in a library and her bringing him a tray of coffee and taking a respite to chat. She had rather liked that. Could that truly be her and Thomas someday? It wasn't exactly how she had pictured it, but there was time to consider it, wasn't there?

"You've been reading too many ladies' novels," Cousin Thomas wrinkled his nose. "The real world doesn't work that way. Practical marriages are what happen most, uniting families, securing fortunes, that sort of thing."

Van held the bat and swung as Thomas lobbed the ball in his direction. "It just might work, Lucy. We'd keep it all in the family that way. And no one could interfere in our business again."

"And just what cousin would you be planning to marry then, Andrew Van Swearingen?" Lucy watched Van swing a sound crack at the ball and traced its arc across the blue sky to bounce a good distance away.

He turned to his sister. "It's different for men, but if we had a girl cousin who lived near to us, and the opportunity was there..." He shrugged and knelt down on the grass. "And besides, it's not me that's being bartered off, now is it? I've got all the time in the world and will inherit my fortune outright."

"So, you think this would work?" Lucy shifted her gaze to Thomas.

"Well, if you'd rather take your chances with whomever your guardian sees fit to arrange a marriage with next..." Thomas motioned to Tommy to go fetch the ball back. "By all means, take your chances. I just thought it'd be a way out."

"So, you don't really want to be handfasted to me then?" Lucy questioned her cousin.

Thomas shrugged. "It mightn't be so dreadful now, would it? We are good friends and family. Who's to say how we'll feel in time? It won't be for years away anyhow. And it would avoid all that bother of courting. We'd know for sure, that in the event your Mr. Connell, or even your Mr. Stephenson, tries to arrange another match, we'd have a way out. It's just a precaution, in case something goes afoul."

"And if we change our minds?" Lucy twisted the corner of her apron around her finger. "If perchance, some other arrangement or opportunity is more to our liking? I mean, I hear courting can be rather pleasing."

"Spoken like a girl." Van lunged to catch the ball Tommy lobbed as he ran toward him and back to the circle. "It's always the females who are the fickle ones, don't ya know, and enjoy all that romantic poppycock."

Van and Thomas laughed. Tommy joined in, but Lucy wasn't laughing. "This is serious. We're talking about something that will change the rest of our lives. I just..." She bit the end of her thumb, thinking, and turned her attention down the hill toward the empty road. "I suppose if it would be in keeping with our family's interests, and I wouldn't mind so much honoring Papa's wishes." She thought about her father smiling on some distant shore but in some way being close to her at that very moment. He had organized a rescue mission when she was captured. She had never had the chance to even say goodbye to him a few years later when he was suddenly taken from her. This would be a way of knowing him, honoring him perhaps.

"Then, it shall be done." Thomas gave a curt nod to his head. "Honoring your father's wishes is the best reason of all, wouldn't you say?"

Lucy laid her hands flat against the cool grass and brushed her fingers across the tender blades. She squinted into the mid-afternoon sun. "So how shall we go about this?"

"It's simple." Thomas stepped toward Lucy and held out his hand to her. "Here, stand up and I'll show you."

From where she sat, Lucy squinted warily at her cousin's proffered hand. She surmised his curt nod and confident eyes, then placed her fingers lightly in his. In one swoop she was lifted to her feet.

"There now, you stand thus, and I'll take your hands like this. Van will be my witness and Tommy yours." Thomas reached to take hold of her other hand. "We face each other and—"

"Wait. You're certain this is legal?" Lucy gave a sidelong glance at her brothers. "I mean, to be here with just you and my brothers... shouldn't there be a minister or a magistrate?"

"No, it's perfectly legal. The law calls it verba de praesenti. It can be alone or before witnesses, but witnesses are the better way to go to ensure it's all done honestly. Congressman Stephenson loaned me a few of his law books to read before summer. It's all in there."

"But I would prefer to have at least another maid present." Lucy tensed her hands in Thomas's grasp. "I mean it's just you and my brothers here."

"Well, all right then." Thomas released her hands and looked to the other boys and then down the hill toward his home. "Here, you there, Tommy. Go fetch our slave Betsey. She can be Lucy's maid and witness."

A few minutes later Tommy returned up the hill not only with Betsey but also with Tobe following behind.

"Very well, all is ready now." Thomas turned to face Lucy once again and took her hands. "There, Tobe, you stand over by Van and be my witnesses whilst Betsey and Tommy stand over by Lucy and be hers."

Thomas stood very tall and looked down at Lucy with a resolute gleam in his eyes. "I, Thomas Swearingen, do solemnly swear to take you, Lucy Swearingen as my future wife." He paused during an interminable silence while Lucy just stared at her cousin. "There now, go on 'tis your turn."

Her hands felt clammy between Thomas's fingers. She stifled a giggle and took a deep swallow. "Er, I Lucy Swearingen do solemnly swear to take you, Thomas Swearingen as my future husband."

"There before God and these witnesses here now, so may it be done." Thomas swished their hands slightly from side to side, gave hers a quick squeeze, and then let them go.

"Shouldn't ya orta kiss?" Betsey prodded. "To make it legal and all. It's what black folks do at their broom jumpin' and such."

"Yea," Van chimed in, "I think you should." He glowered mischievously between them, daring them. "Unless you aren't really serious, of course."

"I suppose we should kiss to make it legal," Thomas said. "That isn't a bad idea."

Lucy made a face and recoiled. "Must we?"

"Just a little kiss to make it official, more a kiss of peace between cousins and all that."

"Well, all right then." Lucy leaned in a bit toward Thomas and closed her eyes. She was hardly aware of the slight warm pressure against her lips before it was all over. She opened her eyes to see Thomas bending down to pick up the trap ball.

"C'mon then, what say you to finishing our game of trap? With two new players, the game should be all that more enticing. Here, we'll take Tobe, and Betsey, you go with Lucy and Tommy."

Nothing much had changed and yet it had. Lucy took her position and readied herself for the next ball to lob her way, wondering in whose favor this next round would turn.

EPILOGUE

The September sky was a deep cloudless blue, perhaps a sign of better days to come and a promise for the future. Ben leaned against a barrel on the flatboat, puffing a clay pipe as the town of Wheeling dwindled in the distance. The year would soon draw to a close and the century as well. What changes the next one brought for him or for this new nation, he had no notion, but perhaps it was time to press onward. Eighteen hundred seemed a fair enough time to bring into fruition the plans he had spent nearly the past decade only dreaming about, wishing and wanting, and never getting anywhere.

It seemed a drastic plan still, even after all the legal paperwork was filed with the court and matters settled to all intents and purposes. The court case had gone well. Shepherd's claim was deemed invalid, and the judge ruled in favor of the Swearingen heirs. Their land rights were secure as the old captain had bequeathed in his will, and a more mindful watch would be placed on the unscrupulous caretaker of Swearingens Landing from hence forward. An annual accounting would be required of John Newhouse and Mr. Connell, lawyer to the estate. Ben had fulfilled his part, duly noted as he stood beside his brother, James, who pled the case with his fine legal air. The day was now a memory branded upon his mind and heart.

"You are the husband to one of the Swearingen heirs, as I take it?" Judge Harper remarked in his gravelly voice. "One, Lucy Swearingen, infant orphan."

"I am, your honor, here as family representative," he replied, standing there in his best suit, one fitted for him by the finest tailor in Harpers Ferry at James's insistence. Where he'd ever wear such a frockcoat, waistcoat, and trousers again, working along the river, he had no notion, but perhaps one day there'd be an occasion—perhaps once he had made his fortune and standing as a fine gentleman owner of a shipyard. The thought made him smile and gave him a boyish jolt that warmed his soul.

"She's as yet a minor child?" The arched eyebrow of the judge spoke of an unconvinced, doubting Thomas. "As are two other heirs, as I understand?"

"Yes, your honor." James outlined in a matter-of-fact tone the three youngest Swearingen children's plight, most in need of protection under the law, while the rest—one elder sister and two elder brothers—were all of legal age and had full rights to their land and property already. Also included in the suit was Zechariah's name, deceased now these six months, though the judge had not been informed.

Ben had not forgotten that crisp winter morning when he first met with Phoebe at Braucher's Ridge. Her eyes were as blue as this September sky, all at once aloof and calculating, sweet as berries in summer, and cold as the icy winter waters. Eyes so like another's had been—Ruth. He had fled Martinsburg seven years ago in hopes of forgetting the shame, the grief, and the degradation her death, among so many others, had left in its wake. A mere lad of twenty-two he was to her girlish eighteen, one among many camp followers to the militia and regulars serving under the command of General St. Clair. She had neither fortune, land, nor family name, but that had mattered little. Youthful lusts were at hand and war brought uncertainty whether tomorrow would even come to pass. Neither his father's stern disapproval, nor his brothers' scorn, could dissuade him then. She was all he thought he wanted. But the promise of marriage was not to be. Her mutilated body was found in the carnage along the Wabash River—that sight alone would have been enough to send a young man into madness or ruin. But the revelation of her duplicity, finding her entwined with the coward who had been her lover, and after he, the unsuspecting pawn, had doubly failed. Hundreds perished that day, but he survived as had James. Two brothers escaped death when so many did not. In the end, blame was all that grieving families had while he was denied everything.

Perhaps Ruth's death had been his fault, if not every last man, woman, and child who died that day at the hands of Chief Little Turtle and his thousands. Perhaps had he not left with the detachment to find the missing supply train, he could have saved her—or died with her that day. Might his father then have found his valor as impressive as Jamie's, the crack shooter in the elite rifleman's corps?

The Battle of a Thousand Slain. St. Clair's Defeat. Those were only a few of the names the men now called it. There remained an air of suspicion, shame, and guilt compounded by his father's last words, still echoing in his ears, harsh and bitter, at having a son who volunteered to flee the battle only to fail in bringing back salvation for a general's folly. And so Ben chose the only path opened to him—he fled again, this time...west. It was Colonel Joseph Swearingen's aid that led him to Wellsburg and to the Swearingen homestead where he found redemption in serving as one of Brady's rangers during some of the bloodiest battles of the Indian Wars' final days. His brother's glory may have been at Wabash, but Ben had proven himself along the Ohio, during the darkest and bloodies of times.

He had survived them all and owed more than his life to the captain, the Indian Fighter, who had kept him level-headed, taught him the ways of the wilderness, and became more than a father, more than a mentor. The captain's tragic death the following December left another casualty on his conscience. Why did it seem those he loved most, those he trusted most, were destined to leave him in cruel and senseless ways?

Zack's death had been equally tragic and cast more suspicion upon him. No one would ever know the truth, perhaps not even little Lucy. How could he tell any of them of Zach's murder at the hands of the chief that nearly stole everything from her? But ironically, Blue Jacket had saved Ben's life that day in more ways than one. Staring down the wrong end of Zack's gun that was poised with crazed intent and fueled by the fevers that tormented his mind, could Ben have mustered the courage to shoot his own friend if it meant saving his own life? This was one situation he couldn't talk his way out of, couldn't run from, but he knew then he wanted to live, perhaps at any cost.

"This is how it's got to be, Ben." Zack sat on the rock by the creek, rifle aimed at his friend's head. "I see how you look at her, how you wormed your way into my pa's good graces. Trying to replace me again, are ye?"

He hadn't meant it; the fever addled a man's brain to say all sorts of things and imagine things that weren't there.

"You brought your Injun friends with you too, have you? Always knew you were in with them, should've shot the bastard when I had the chance. Maybe should've kilt them all, including my bewitched little sister."

He hadn't meant that either, but the man wouldn't listen to reason. One shot over Ben's head came all too close before he reloaded with the precision of a militiaman, even with his fevers. In the ticking moments, Ben aimed his pistol, trying to regain his nerve, hoping to still reason with his friend. The whizz of an arrow, a split second before the gunshot, a slice of time and an eternity. One. Two. The pain, shock, and perhaps relief settled over Zack's face, streaming now with blood. Off in the trees across the unstill waters of the creek, bow in hand, stood Blue Jacket. These were images also seared in Ben's memory. He now owed his life to a savage, perhaps the debt was settled. Is that what the man meant as he nodded with raised hand, gestured between them, and then slashed through the air? Ben returned the same gesture, before tending to his friend. One arrow pierced the back of his head, the other speared through his chest, killing him instantly, ending his pain. He cleaned him up best he could, removed the arrows, bound up the wounds, and returned him to Phoebe, when he arranged for her to be alone with Zach. It took little convincing to agree to the ruse, make it seem as if her husband lingered long enough for one last hour together, after which she and a trusted servant prepared the body, washed and sutured the wounds, and sewed him into a shroud. No telltale marks would ever be seen. There was a price to be paid for her silence. A will was hastily drawn up, signed, and witnessed by Ben and Phoebe, giving her title to all lands and property bequeathed by her husband.

A miracle, madness, or science yet to be discovered. A savage savior. A child with a gift of tongues. A warrior chief's honor repaying a life for a life. Who was he to explain any of this? He was not a superstitious sort, but he vowed to find firm footing, to endure beyond this, and to find some peace and a place of his own. He had done his part for the little girl, the sister of a friend, who in the end would have seen to his demise, had an enemy he was spared, now turned to his aid. He had, indeed, done his part for little Lucy, long ago in the forest glen, when he had unwittingly spared her captor. Perhaps, in the end, that was penance and absolution enough.

This first trip downriver promised much, and he would ensure it fulfilled the dreams he and Gibson had for a flourishing business. Then it was the possibility of heading farther beyond the Ohio and the Mississippi. He had to see it just once and then return, perhaps with prospects for trade with Indians tribes, French, or Spanish. Word was conditions were looking favorable for future prospects within the new nation. The new century promised much in the way of trade, expansion of the nation, and new ways of order. Revolutions in America and France had changed a great deal of the social structure and ways people viewed government. In conversations with James during and after the court case, he had learned a bit more about how this new congress worked, and it intrigued him more than he would have imagined. His brother's jest at someday being a lawyer or even a politician himself, still rang in his ears.

The day they worked out the details of Lucy's future in James's office, it had seemed a drastic plan of action, but one he was willing to take—more than willing. At least now he had more reason than ever to make a go of his business. She could prove a burden, but all he kept thinking was now he had someone of his own to look after, to strive for, a reason to succeed beyond himself. Lucy was safe at school after spending the summer with her uncle and cousin. In June, Ben had returned the younger boys to Wellsburg where they preferred to attend school and live with their mother for the time being. It had been three weeks since he escorted Lucy along with one of the local girls and her mother, to the New Haven Academy for Gentle Ladies in Philadelphia. The Quakers were known for excellence in education, and the school came highly recommended by the Lane family, friends of the Colonel, who had a daughter about Lucy's age. From what he could tell, the two had the hopes of becoming fast friends.

And Lucy would be safe and well cared for. All was righted, yet why did he feel this strange emptiness since leaving her there? It should have been a weight lifted, a burden relieved, and yet his heart ached in ways he had not expected.

He had given his heart away once before and then sworn never to again. Ruth had stolen more than his heart, and then there was Phoebe, a conniving siren whose blue eyes were as cold and icy as Ruth's had been. Perhaps it was those blue eyes that caught his fancy once and nearly did again. That day in the woods, at Zane's Ridge. Phoebe had proposed a plan, one diabolical and debauched. He could have given her a child, a son, perhaps. The irony that he'd have found himself in precisely the situation he left in Martinsburg stayed in his thoughts since leaving her in the woods that evening. Raising a child he had not fathered or fathering a child he would not raise held no appeal for him. No, should he ever have children, a wife, a home, it would be at his bidding and in the proper order of things.

Instead he had wound up chasing an innocent little girl halfway across a state, a child to whom he was now legally bound and perhaps could be for some time to come. He had settled matters well with Newhouse. His debts were paid, now that Ben managed to wrangle a win at the card table—the stakes being the rogue's past debts for his silence. With Lucy away at a school of which neither parent had knowledge, his deception was secure. Ben closed his eyes and listened to the sounds of the river lapping against the side of the boat. At the bow, sitting cross-legged, a young Kentuckian coaxed chords from a concertina in time to the cadence of the river. Next to him a Negro bowed a haunting accompaniment on his fiddle to a familiar soldier's tune.

In hurried words her name I blest
I breathed the vows that bind me
And to my heart in anguish pressed
The girl I left behind me.

Those last moments at the school when he was getting ready to depart, she stood as staunch and brave as she had the morning they found her alone in that wretched cabin, tending her fevered little brother. He hadn't realized how hard it would be to leave her there in Philadelphia. He bid her a final goodbye in the entranceway of the school, a rather stark brick building, made even more brooding by the dismal day. How could he leave her in such a place, alone and on her own? But he had seen something in her face that reminded him of her father, her brother, and perhaps a wee bit of the little girl he had found defying her captors and speaking her mind in words only they understood and heeded.

For a time there was silence between them, the dour faces of past Quaker officials gazing down upon them.

"Lucy, I want you to pay mind to a few things before I must go," he said, dividing his view between assessing the suitability of this school and trying to memorize her every line and mannerism. He must believe this to be her place of refuge and seat of learning until he returned for her. And when he returned...what then?

"I shall strive to do my best in all things here. Will you be gone long?" Lucy looked at him with tender, trusting eyes and with wisdom and resolve far beyond her years. Twelve. That's what they told them. How could she actually be that age already? "I'll miss you." Her voice was soft, and her eyes flitted down while she ran a fold of her gown between two slender fingers.

It was then he knew all he wanted was to keep her safe and protected from any harm, shielding her from the harsh realities of this life and from those that would seek to mistreat her. She would never ache, as he had, never know the pain or sorrow of a false love. He would ensure that. Someday, she would find happiness, security, and a home of her own. If it were not to be with him, then some other more worthy man, someone who would love and esteem her properly.

"This first boat trip will last a few months," he said, more cheerfully than he felt, "but you'll be here at school. Holidays and summer will be back at your uncle's, or perhaps you'll take up Miss Lane's offer to spend some time with them." Judge Hardage Lane was a prominent figure in Montgomery, Maryland, a half-day's ride from Big Springs. He had a large family and several daughters. She would be welcomed there and soon forget this terrible year. "All will be well, you'll see." That is what he had said to her that day in the library and then again that day in Philadelphia.

Her mouth twitched at the corners. She drew in a breath and arranged her face in placid lines. "You'll write?"

"I'll certainly try, though the mail is not always so reliable from out west, as you know."

"But, you're my guardian now. You must write." She looked down and twisted her fingers through the strings of her bonnet. "I still don't quite understand it all. I don't mean to be a burden to you, Mr. Stephenson. I do appreciate all you've done, truly. I mean..." She hesitated, caught his eye, then looked away.

Ben could not tell her more. He was essentially a married man, or so the court had thought. Yet ironically he was unable to taste the fruits of that marriage for some time to come, not that this was any sort of marriage to bank on. He assured himself of that—for her, for him. He couldn't really say. It was wrong to deceive her, just as it was wrong for Phoebe to have attempted her own deception those many months ago. He could hardly blame her now, though. She had indeed gotten a child to bank on, one she claimed to be Zack's and would present to the Swearingens come fall. Who was he to dispute her? Perhaps in many ways, it was. Perhaps she had found a suitable replacement in Elzey and would indeed share the Swearingen bloodlines—rather than a passing stranger or lustful neighbor willing to offer a widow comfort. For Zack's sake, he still hoped it was indeed his friend's heir by some miracle or last feat of a dying man's will. All he knew was that it wasn't nor would ever be, his child. That was a bitter fruit he had once tasted and hoped never to again.

"You will return?" Lucy said with a renewed gaze. "I will do my best and enjoy the holidays with the Lanes and at Uncle Joseph's, if I know you'll return, if I know you'll write, now and again...as a good friend as well as a guardian."

"You can expect to hear from me," Ben heartily responded. It was then he acted on impulse and reached into his waistcoat pocket. "And I will expect letters in kind.

"I have something I want to give you, Lucy," Taking her small hand in his he placed one piece of a halved dollar firmly on her palm.

The other half he held between his thumb and forefinger. "This coin is my pledge that I will return, that we shall and forever be friends and if you should ever need anything, ever, I will always be there to help, so long as it is in my power to do so. You have but to ask and I'll move heaven and hell."

She fought bubbling laughter behind mischievous eyes. "I don't think we're allowed to speak that way here."

The river slapped a steady rhythm against the flatboat as he puffed his clay pipe, and whiffs of smoke curled into the fresh morning air. The wooden planks bobbed gently beneath his feet. The duo of musicians finished their lively tune and broke into a more somber one.

"Oh Shenandoah, I love your daughter, away you rolling river..."

What did a little girl know of love, of life? Of heartache? Of betrayal and the pain of this world? Yet this little girl, his Lucy, had indeed seen far too much of the world's pain, suffering, and savagery for one so young.

True, she stood to make him a very rich man, should he avail himself of her dowery and trust, were he the sort to press his advantage, in that regard. Yet he was far above the notion of molesting wealth and power from the helpless and innocent. That was why he needed to travel the river. The opportunities to learn the business of trade and see the ports of St. Louis, New Orleans, and Natchez, gather in the sugar, cotton, and tobacco so highly prized by those back East and the boon of traders in the West. It would all prove invaluable to making his fortune and providing a life both for himself and, God willing, a family of his own in the due course of time. Yes, he did see himself someday, with perhaps a wife, children, and maybe a fine home. But for now there was the lure of the West calling.

"...Away, away, I'm bound away, cross the wide Missouri."

The Kentuckian and fiddler drolled out the song of the river. The boat floated southward along the Ohio toward the Great River and beyond. Months, perhaps a year or more, would pass before he would sail up this way again and back to Philadelphia or even to Shepherds Town. In that time Lucy would grow, change, and be nigh on to full womanhood. He tried to conjure an image of her full-grown and in the bloom of youthful beauty—her mossy hazel eyes, soft honeyed curls, the pert little nose. He could only see a little girl for now and then another, an image cold and dead beneath the streams of the river. He swore under his breath. Impatiently he dismissed this latter image with a puff of his pipe and focused on a low-hanging branch tracing swirls in water near the shoreline. A sleek otter skittered past swimming against the tide beneath the trees. And the river flowed onward. Onward. Ever onward.

AUTHOR'S NOTE

Gore Vidal, the great historical novelist and historian once wrote:

"Why a historical novel and not a history? To me, the attraction of the historical novel is that one can be as meticulous (or as careless) as the historian and yet reserve the right not only to rearrange events but, most important, to attribute motive—something the conscientious historian or biographer ought never do."

Subconsciously, this was my goal in bringing the story of Benjamin Stephenson and Lucy Swearingen to life in the pages of fiction. Although rather obscure in American history, these people did in fact exist, and my development of these real people into fictional characters is far from unique. Countless novels through the course of literary history have gleaned characters and plot devices from the annals of obscure facts and folklore. As I conducted research for my story, I was surprised to discover that more than one American author, one rather well known, had already drawn upon one of my backstory individuals as the inspiration for a famed American character. In 1826, James Fennimore Cooper gave the world the Leatherstocking Tales, known today as *The Last of the Mohicans.* Cooper's iconic frontiersman, Hawkeye, is believed to have been inspired by none other than Lucy's brother-in-law, Captain Samuel Brady, who factors peripherally into my plot and has also been the subject of pioneer adventure novels by Allen Eckert.

Thus begins a laundry list of well-known figures who littered Lucy Swearingen's early upbringing. It was never my intention to make her early years into a full novel on its own. I had originally thought to write one comprehensive epic novel with either Lucy or Ben as the protagonist in a survey of their eyewitness roles in early America. Then it morphed into a possible young adult novel which proved not as interesting to young adults as it was to historically minded adults. Although my original aspirations for writing centered on children's literature and YA novels, I found myself faced with the prospect of expanding my real-life "American Girl" novel into an epic family series based on Lucy's entire life and her eventual marriage to Benjamin Stephenson, who makes his own contributions to the annals of American history. Still, it seemed too daunting a task, and many times I thought to forgo the entire project. However, research has a way of leading the writer down a rabbit hole of clues and surprising facts that entice the imagination, and my original idea for a single epic novel soon merged into a potential three-book series beginning with Lucy's tumultuous childhood as the daughter of a renowned "first" family of the early American West.

Lucy's father, Captain "Indian" Van Swearingen earned his handle for being a fierce opponent of the native tribes in the Ohio Valley. At one time his fame and exploits were as notable as Daniel Boone's. In Brooke County, West Virginia, his legend is still active in stories and plays depicting his part in the Indian Wars along the Ohio and especially his confrontation with Shawnee Chief Weywapiersenwah, also known as "Blue Jacket," a nickname he gained when he repurposed a soldier's coat claimed from the battlefield. The brief mention in the story, of a connection to Lucy's family in a distant relative captured by Blue Jacket's tribe, is true. For a long time, it was believed that this relative, Marmaduke Swearingen, adopted native life and rose to the ranks to become Blue Jacket himself. Recent DNA evidence between Swearingen descendants and the Shawnee chief's descendants proved no relationship between either family. While it was a tempting plot device to work with, I nevertheless chose the path of historic fact and found other opportunities to spin fictional adventures and intrigue, including aspects of magical realism in Lucy's uncanny ability to speak Shawnee as the result of some miraculous encounter following a horrific early childhood abduction. All this is fiction but based on the facts that Lucy's father had been a fierce "Indian fighter" pitted against an equally fierce native chief, and that horrific atrocities happened on both sides before the Treaty of Greenville settled matters for a time. It's believed by some that Lucy feared Indian attacks for most of her life, possibly due to early childhood experiences during perilous times. Given that her early years are a complete blank slate, prior to the document mentioned in the novel that ties her in "marriage" to Ben, it proved to be the perfect vehicle with just enough titillating evidence to weave in a true early American adventure tale.

In writing this novel, these were only a few fragmented pieces of history's puzzle I had to piece together to fit into a picture that would both give an accurate portrayal of events and still spin a worthy story. These were the two pillars I kept in mind with each plot decision and characterization. Ironically, I ignored the Blue Jacket connection for some time, thinking it a non-event, until it became evident this obscure fact provided just the right character motivation for an even stranger fact that is indisputable—the unorthodox "marriage" between Benjamin Stephenson, age 29, and Lucy Swearingen, not yet 11. The reasons still aren't clear and many beta readers and editors have encouraged me to increase Lucy's age to appease modern sensibilities. On this point I decided not to compromise, as the documentation pointed to nothing other than a very young girl likely betrothed to an adult man. Precisely when the arrangement was made and why remains a mystery. A lawsuit filed in April of 1799 lists all of Lucy's half-brothers, one half-sister and her three full brothers on behalf of her father's estate. The defendant in the suit was Abraham Shepherd. Why he had a claim to Captain Swearingen's estate is not known, but land disputes were common along the frontier, when claims were not always well documented. Curiously, also listed among Lucy's siblings is Benjamin Stephenson as an "orator" or litigant in the dispute. Even more curiously, Lucy's name is tacked on as "his wife." These two words are what have sparked the controversy at the historic site and fueled my imagination to tell Lucy's story. Could this arrangement have been made much earlier while Lucy's father still lived? There is no evidence Ben lived anywhere near Wellsburg during these years, but clearly some connection existed between the families, as evidence shows in other interactions that will be revealed in later books in the series.

Contrary to what we sometimes think of arranged marriages of the past, and despite the premises of modern historical romance novels, Ben's and Lucy's situation was an unusual case. Arranged marriages were less common than we think after the American Revolution, and brides were rarely younger than 18, unless extenuating circumstances necessitated some protection for a minor female, as is presumed to be the case with Lucy. Perhaps her mother's remarriage sparked the need to find her a permanent "protector." There is some evidence that points to John Newhouse or Eleanor, pilfering funds from the children's estate through charging rent and other sundry fees that would not be expected of a minor child. The strange nature of Eleanor's marriage to John Newhouse and Zechariah Swearingen's untimely death at age 24 became the perfect inciting incidents to begin my novel. Where Ben fit into all of this or if he was even living in Wellsburg is not clear. But in the absence of detail, the historical novelist's imagination can take over.

When I interviewed as a docent at the 1820 Colonel Benjamin Stephenson House, the first thing the director made clear was this "scandalous controversy" that haunted the historic site and how we were to deal with it on tours in our modern, "child-advocating," America. I think it was that first conversation that got my wheels of fiction spinning. It's said that the best books often come from writers who write what they want to read but just hasn't been written yet. If that is the case here, I can attest that at least for me, it has been worth the long journey to bring this tale to publication. My original goal was merely to have the story in hand that no one would write for me. Perhaps one day to see it sitting on my shelf, even if that meant a desktop-printed copy in a spiral-bound edition. Over the decade it has taken to get to this point, I have had quite the adventure down that twisting historical path, most especially in becoming an experienced docent at the Stephenson's House and meeting some truly incredible friends in the staff and volunteers not to mention the countless guests and children I've been privileged to lead in educational tours. As a bonus to all of this, I happened into a couple of writing groups that have been a great inspiration in helping me navigate this uncharted territory of writing, editing and publication. I think back on it all and wonder how one little early American girl's life on the Ohio, so long forgotten, could have affected so much change some 200 years later in my hectic modern life. For Lucy Swearingen's story, so long forgotten, and the house that continues to remain a beacon for her legacy, I am ever grateful.

ABOUT THE AUTHOR

D.L. Andersen has been spinning stories in her head since she can remember, but only recently took the plunge to write them down. After visiting a historic site in her neighborhood and enduring many sleepless nights, she finally heeded the "voices" of her characters and gave them their own place to come alive again. She holds a BA in education from Concordia University, Chicago, with a minor in church history and music. Her writing credits include a few short stories with Walrus Press and the Agorist Writer's Workshop and two novellas about the Stephenson family. She lives in Southern Illinois with her husband, two dogs and a cat.

Made in the USA
Lexington, KY
27 September 2018